Never Too Late

NEVER TOO LATE

For the collection of
the San Leandro Public Library
June 11, 2016
Julie Blair

by

Julie Blair

2014

NEVER TOO LATE

ISBN 13: 978-1-62639-213-7

THIS TRADE PAPERBACK ORIGINAL IS PUBLISHED BY
BOLD STROKES BOOKS, INC.
P.O. BOX 249
VALLEY FALLS, NY 12185

FIRST EDITION: NOVEMBER 2014

CREDITS
EDITOR: SHELLEY THRASHER
PRODUCTION DESIGN: SUSAN RAMUNDO
COVER DESIGN BY GABRIELLE PENDERGRAST

Acknowledgments

I can't describe the feeling when Radclyffe offered me the chance to become part of her extraordinary publishing company, Bold Strokes Books. My deepest gratitude to her for this chance of a lifetime.

My pursuit of making every sentence, chapter, and story better has been gracefully and expertly guided by my writing coach, Deb Norton. Thanks for her unwavering belief that writing matters and that I can do it. Her story wisdom shows in every part of this book.

I was terrified of my first editing experience, and Dr. Shelley Thrasher made it the perfect combination of teaching and encouragement. Thank you for showing me how to sort, lighten, and tighten my story.

Thank you to Sandy Lowe for her ultra professionalism and infinite patience.

Thanks to Cindy, Toni, Gabrielle, and the rest of the talented and dedicated staff at BSB who helped my story become a polished, published book with a beautiful cover. Thanks to my fellow BSB authors who have been so welcoming.

For me, writing is a roller coaster of ecstasy and agony, confidence and doubt, taking risks and battling fear. I'm grateful for friends and family who provide support, encouragement, and common sense when I need it. Dena and Susan, Ginny, Patricia, Cliona, Devon, Val, my aunt Lila, and my niece Summer—thanks for believing in me.

I've loved Melissa Etheridge's music since hearing her thirty years ago under a starry sky at the West Coast Women's Music Festival. Her song "The Wanting of You" was the inspiration for this book.

Thanks to all the readers of lesbian fiction. I've been a huge fan of the genre since discovering it in the late seventies and I'm honored by this chance to make a contribution to our growing body of work. I hope you like it.

Dedication

To Dena Mason—from softball diamonds to fly-fishing streams, thanks for a lifetime of friendship.

Prologue

September 1991

Jamie scooted her duffel with her foot and hiked her backpack up on her shoulder as she took a step closer to the Delta Airlines counter. It was Labor Day, and Atlanta's International Airport was a madhouse as people hurried for flights. The nearer she got to the counter, the more the anxiety that had left her alone over the weekend returned. The four days at the Southern Women's Music and Comedy Festival was worth the argument with her father about being away from the practice. She'd never forget all those tents spread out among the pine trees, the lake and tennis court she'd made good use of, the covered pavilion for the nightly concerts and dances. Or the women who'd redefined her idea of hospitality. Boarding that plane meant saying good-bye to her last hurrah of fun and freedom before settling down to a responsibility she wasn't sure she wanted.

A rowdy group of teenaged girls walked to a nearby gate with bat bags over their shoulders, led by a woman about her age with Coach written across her cap. That might have been her life, but it was too late now.

Tomorrow morning she'd walk back into Hammond Chiropractic Clinic, not as a child visiting her father, not as a part-time receptionist during summer vacations, but as the newly licensed chiropractor in her father's highly successful practice. He made being a doctor look easy. She tightened her grip on the strap of her backpack. It wasn't. By the end of the day she was so exhausted she barely managed to microwave a bag of popcorn before collapsing on the couch to watch mindless adventure movies. She'd tried to talk to him, but he'd brushed her off, saying, "Just focus on the patient and everything will be fine." Had he ever been afraid?

Jamie studied the woman in front of her. About her age, she wore navy slacks and a scoop-neck white T-shirt, a white sweater draped over her arm. What was she going home to? Or maybe she was flying to San Francisco for vacation. As the woman moved up to the counter Jamie stepped into a whiff of perfume, richly sweet, almost tropical. It seemed at odds with her stiff posture, conservative dress, and tight ponytail.

"The flight's been cancelled," the attendant told the woman. "We can get you on a flight tomorrow afternoon, and you'll get a voucher for the Best Western across the street."

Cancelled? Had she heard right?

"Please, I really need to get home today." The woman's voice was soft and most definitely Southern. "Isn't there any other flight?"

Jamie's shoulders relaxed. Yes. A reprieve.

"That's the best we can do."

The woman took the ticket and picked up a suitcase, looked around as if confused, and then slumped onto one of the gray metal seats in the boarding area. She dropped her head into her hands.

Jamie smiled at the attendant—Marge, according to her nametag—who asked for her ticket. "I'm not in a hurry."

"I appreciate that, Dr. Hammond."

Dr. Hammond. Would she ever get used to being called that? As Marge's fingers flew over the keyboard, Jamie noted the short hair and lack of makeup and decided to take a chance.

"Maybe you could join me for dinner."

A smile tugged at the corners of Marge's mouth. "I'm just starting my shift, but I can recommend some places if you don't mind going back into Atlanta." Marge handed Jamie her ticket and a folded piece of paper. "And a place you might enjoy if you like to dance. Enjoy your evening, Dr. Hammond."

Jamie hefted her duffel on her shoulder and stepped away from the counter, thrilled at her good luck. She was going to make this night count. She tucked the piece of paper into the back pocket of her favorite jeans, a new rip over her right kneecap, the result of tripping over a tree root while staring at a brunette with the kind of delts that made her mouth water. The woman laughed as she helped her up, and they'd spent a pleasurable afternoon in her tent. Southern women sure understood hospitality.

As she passed the woman from the line, she scooted around several people and sat next to her. The woman's head was down, her hands folded in her lap. Jamie wanted to fix whatever was upsetting her. Southern women had captivated her, and she wanted to make this one smile.

"Can I help?" Jamie asked gently, resisting the urge to wrap the woman in her arms until she stopped crying.

The woman looked up, seeming startled. The most beautiful eyes Jamie had ever seen captured her—amber, edged with delicate golden lashes. Even glistening with tears, they were kind eyes, eyes you could trust. "No, thank you," the woman said in that delicious Southern accent. The tight smile seemed more polite than genuine, but it was a start.

"What's wrong?" Jamie rummaged in her backpack and handed the woman a Kleenex.

"I was looking forward to sleeping in my own bed tonight." The woman dabbed her eyes. "And I only have a few dollars on me and can't find my credit card. I must have left it at my mom's." She clutched her purse to her stomach.

Jamie rested her hand on the neatly pressed slacks. "It's okay. I'll cover you. Come on. Let's get out of here."

"That's kind of you, but I couldn't." The woman dabbed her eyes again.

"Don't be silly. You can send me the money when you get home, if that makes you feel better." Jamie settled her backpack squarely on both shoulders and swung the strap of her carryon over her head. She put her hand under the woman's elbow and guided her up, steadying her as she swayed for a moment.

"Let me take that." Jamie picked up the small suitcase and cut a path for them through the crowd. "I'm Jamie, by the way."

"Carly."

Finally Jamie was rewarded with a genuine smile. She almost reached to wipe off a smudge of pale-pink lipstick at the corner of

Carly's mouth. "I need to make a call," she said, as they passed a bank of phones.

"Oh, my goodness," Carly said, pressing her palm to her chest. "So do I."

Jamie handed Carly a quarter and then dialed her father's office, hoping he wouldn't answer. She wondered who the "him" was Carly was leaving a message for, entranced by the way she drew out syllables as if in no hurry to speak. If only her own life were in no hurry.

"Mary, it's Jamie. Tell Dad my flight got cancelled and I can't get another one until tomorrow…Yes, I know it's hard for you to reschedule my patients but…All right, add them to Wednesday's schedule." Jamie hung up and tried to calm her racing heart. Reprieve. One more night of freedom.

"Let's go have some fun," Jamie said, picking up their luggage.

Jamie studied Carly as they stood under the sign for the Best Western shuttle. She usually went for athletic types, the more muscular the better, but something soft and inviting about this woman made her want to cuddle up against her. Noting the absence of a ring on her left hand, she wondered if she had a chance. She assumed Carly was straight, but if the opportunity presented itself she wouldn't turn it down.

"Are you feeling all right?" Carly looked pale in spite of the heat.

"Just tired and kind of hungry."

Jamie unzipped an outer pocket on her backpack and held up two items. "Power Bar or apple?" Carly hesitated. "Go on. Can't have you fainting. Then I'd have to carry you."

"Thank you." Carly took the apple, wiped it off on her sweater, and took a bite.

"Do you really want to spend the night out here in the middle of nowhere? How about if we grab a cab into Atlanta and get a room somewhere downtown? We can go out to dinner, have some fun." When Carly hesitated, Jamie added, "You'd be doing me a favor. I'd rather not go out alone." It wasn't true, but she really wanted to go out with this woman.

"Are you sure, Jamie? I can't pay—"

"I'm positive. Come on. We'll have a blast." Jamie picked up their bags and hustled toward a waiting cab before Carly changed her mind.

❖

Carly rested against the cab door as they drove through downtown Atlanta, answering Jamie's questions about the city she'd lived in until a few months ago. Her mother's penetrating voice invaded her thoughts, as though she was second-guessing her judgment, warning her that she was too trusting and knew nothing about this woman. She folded her arms and straightened her shoulders. Doing something a little reckless after the week of stony silence from her father and angry stares from her mother gave her a rebellious feeling she liked.

"Check that out." Jamie pointed to the marquee in front of the arena on their left. "Melissa Etheridge is playing tonight. Wow! Hey, stop."

"No place to pull over, lady," the cabbie said as he continued past the arena. Several blocks later he pulled into a Holiday Inn.

"Okay if we share a room?" Jamie took a wallet from her back pocket when they got to the registration desk.

"Um, sure," Carly said. She'd never stayed in a hotel room with anyone, not even her boyfriend Mike, but it would be rude to object when Jamie was paying.

Inside the sixth-floor room, Jamie tossed their bags on one of the queen-sized beds and opened the curtains. "What a view."

Carly collapsed on the other bed, yawning, cupping her hands behind her head. This was definitely better than spending the night in the airport or, worse yet, calling her parents for help. It would be fun, like the slumber parties she used to go to.

"Let's go see if we can get tickets to the concert and then get you something to eat."

"What concert?" Carly closed her eyes, ready to fall asleep.

"Melissa Etheridge."

"Who's that?"

"Oh, my God. She's the hottest woman rocker around!"

Carly opened her eyes when Jamie landed on the bed next to her and giggled when Jamie dramatically draped her arm over her eyes. Jamie pulled her arm away, and warm brown eyes captured her.

"And even better, she's a lesbian."

Carly's breath caught in her throat. Did that mean Jamie was? Maybe sharing a room with her wasn't a good idea. She sat up against the headboard and tugged her T-shirt down over her waist.

Jamie scooted up next to her, and their shoulders touched. "I saw her about five years ago at the West Coast Women's Music Festival," Jamie said, tapping her feet together as if to music. "God, she was hot. You just knew she was going to make it big. I heard her again last year at this club in San Francisco. That rock beat and all those women. I still remember—"

Carly realized she was staring when Jamie stopped in mid-sentence.

"Sorry. Guess I got a little carried away. You're okay with it, aren't you? My being gay, I mean?"

Carly knew what she should say, but nothing about Jamie seemed dangerous. Her warm smile clinched it. Carly didn't want to be like her mother. "Sure."

"Great!" Jamie hopped off the bed and unzipped her duffel, pawing through it. She held up a white T-shirt with Southern Women's Music and Comedy Festival across the front.

Carly didn't realize until it was too late that Jamie was going to change right in front of her. She followed the path of Jamie's T-shirt as it revealed her flat stomach, the flare of her rib cage, and breasts straining against the tight white tank top. Carly had never seen a woman with chest and arm muscles like this. Jamie scrubbed her hands briskly through the loosely permed dark curls that framed her face, then stretched her arms over her head and arched her back. When Jamie reached for her zipper, Carly stood and faced the window, feeling light-headed. "I think I need to eat."

"Do you want to change? Like into jeans?"

"Um, I don't have any jeans." Carly looked down at her slacks and low heels and then back at Jamie. "Maybe you should just go without me." All of a sudden she didn't feel up to going to a rock concert, especially with someone as sexy as Jamie. Carly looked back at the street below, afraid she was blushing. She'd never thought that about a woman.

"No way. You look terrific. I feel kind of shabby next to you."

Carly laughed at Jamie's obvious attempt to make her feel better. Her enthusiasm was infectious and such a relief after her mother's negativity. "Not if my frumpiness doesn't embarrass you."

"Carly, there's nothing frumpy about you." Jamie's eyes drifted slowly up her body, displaying nothing but kindness and appreciation.

Carly liked how Jamie treated her. Coming into Atlanta had been a good choice. Her life would resume its course tomorrow, but tonight she wanted to be confident and adventurous like Jamie. What could be the harm?

❖

Jamie looked up at the tall buildings surrounding them and found the bank the front desk clerk had directed her to. "I need some more cash. Scalpers won't take a credit card."

"Scalpers?"

"Yeah. They sell tickets to people like us who show up at the last minute." Jamie pocketed ten twenty-dollar bills and fingered the piece of paper the flight attendant had given her with the name of the lesbian bar. What would it feel like to dance with Carly?

"Wait here while I get us tickets," Jamie said when they got to the arena. "Then we'll eat."

"I want to go with you."

Jamie headed them toward a black guy wearing tight jeans and a Braves cap. "Got some good seats for a visiting A's fan?" Jamie flashed the guy her best smile. Carly stood next to her, arms folded.

"Wow, I should give you tickets, seeing's how you're stuck in the land of the losers," the guy teased her back.

"Okay. I can live with that."

"What's a California girl doing all the way out here?"

"Enjoying Southern hospitality," Jamie said in her best imitation of the Southern drawls she'd been absorbing. Out of the corner of her eye she saw Carly smile. She sure was cute.

"Are you really an A's fan?"

"Been going to the games since I was five. Even won a contest to be bat girl for a day."

"Okay, I believe you. So, how close you wanna be?"

"Close enough to see her eyelashes." Jamie glanced at Carly, whose eyes widened.

The guy reached into a small pack fastened around his waist and leafed through some tickets. "How about three rows back on the left?"

"How much?"

"For you, two large," the guy said with a wink. "Seeing's how we're cousins and all that."

"Ouch," Jamie said, holding her fist over her heart. "That doesn't leave me anything to take my girl out to dinner." Jamie pulled Carly close with an arm around her waist.

"Okay, okay. How about one fifty, and I tell you where you can get a hundred-dollar meal for fifty?" The guy grinned at them. "Gotta love you out-and-proud girls from the West Coast."

"Deal." Jamie folded the tickets into her pocket.

"Jamie, that's a lot of money." Carly gripped her forearm.

"Concert and dinner are my treat, Carly." Jamie headed them in the direction the guy had pointed.

"Why did he call you cousin?" Carly's shoulder brushed against hers as they walked.

"He's gay. He was acknowledging he knows I am, too."

"Oh. How did you know he was…gay?" Carly whispered the last word.

"You just kind of know. We call it gaydar." Jamie duplicated Carly's whisper.

"Gaydar," Carly repeated, not whispering this time. "Can I ask you something else?"

"Sure." Jamie stopped in front of a diner and opened the door for Carly. The place was full, which Jamie took as a good sign.

"What did he mean by out-and-proud girls from the West Coast?"

Jamie caught a whiff of the perfume she really liked as Carly stepped past her. So far Carly was being a good sport. Was there a chance they'd share a bed tonight? "He was referring to the fact that gay people are a lot more publicly visible in California than in most of the country."

Carly frowned, appearing to think about it. "What's the opposite of out and proud?"

"In the closet."

"Out and proud seems a lot better than in the closet," Carly said decisively in her unhurried accent, the sincerity showing in her amber eyes.

"No argument there." A waitress motioned them to a booth, and Jamie resisted the urge to sit next to Carly.

"What does your T-shirt mean?" Carly asked as they walked out of the restaurant. The heat and humidity hit them immediately.

"I just spent the weekend at a music festival for lesbians."

"I didn't know there were festivals for…um, lesbians."

"We're everywhere," Jamie whispered. Carly blushed but didn't move away as they passed a couple with three little kids in tow.

When they got to the arena, Jamie pulled Carly off to the side. "Have you ever been to a rock concert?"

"No." Carly looked scared as she eyed the crowd, and Jamie hoped she wasn't going to change her mind. "But I love rock music."

"Great." Carly's eyes settled on Jamie. God, they were beautiful. "Any concerts?"

"A few Christian concerts."

"You mean like Amy Grant?"

"Yeah!"

"She's got a great voice." Carly's smile was radiant, and Jamie wanted to kiss along her bottom lip. "This will be rowdier. If you get uncomfortable, tell me. I want this to be fun for you."

"Let's do this."

Jamie took Carly's hand and led them into the crowd moving toward the entrance. When Carly didn't pull away, Jamie's hopes rose. She was a lot more adventurous than Jamie had expected. Maybe they'd use only one of those beds tonight.

Jamie draped her arm across Carly's shoulder as they shuffled along in the crowd exiting the arena. She'd gotten bolder about touching Carly during the concert, and so far Carly hadn't objected. The more she touched her the more she wanted to. Carly's softness and curves made her decide she'd have to revamp her ideas about what kind of women made her hot. "Didn't I tell you she was the hottest woman rocker around?" Jamie looked back at the marquee. She was going to remember this night for a long time.

"That was the most exciting thing I've ever done," Carly said.

"Whew, does it ever cool off around here?" Jamie asked when they were finally standing in the open air. Her nipples tingled as the breeze cooled her sweat-soaked tank top.

"Oh, about three in the morning." Carly fanned her T-shirt away from her chest.

"That's a long time to wait." Jamie was vibrating with restless energy. She didn't want the night to end. "Wanna go dancing?" She was afraid she'd pushed too hard when Carly tensed.

"I'm not a good dancer," Carly said, ducking her head.

"You said you liked rock music. We can just listen." When Carly hesitated she said, "I don't know about you but I'm too wired to sleep."

"I guess it would be all right."

"I promise we'll have fun." Jamie reached into her pocket. She couldn't read the damp piece of paper with the name of the bar on it. "Hey, all you local girls, where do we go to dance?"

A chorus of voices answered.

"Guess we're going to Faces." Jamie flagged down a cab and held the door open for Carly. Two other women piled in with them, and Jamie smiled the whole fifteen-minute drive with Carly practically on her lap.

❖

Carly's heart pounded as she gripped Jamie's waistband and peeked around her back through the door, women behind her pushing to get in the bar. The music was deafening. She'd never been in a bar. It was dim, huge, and packed with women. The tiredness she'd felt before the concert was gone, replaced by an energy that made Carly feel hot and tingly all over. She couldn't believe she was doing this.

"You okay with this?" Jamie paid the cover charge for both of them.

"Yes," Carly said as a woman stamped her hand. Two more steps and she was hit by a sensory assault unlike anything she'd ever experienced. She gripped Jamie's waist tighter as the crowd swallowed her and the smells of perfume and sweat and smoke engulfed her. Everywhere she looked women were dancing, touching each other in ways she'd never even seen between men and women. She felt the sexual tension in the air as clearly as the heat. If not for the romance novels she devoured, she wouldn't have words for it.

"Water," Carly yelled over the noise when she realized Jamie was asking what she wanted to drink. Her mouth went dry as she stared at two women kissing, their hands drifting from hips to breasts as they caressed each other. Carly's knees buckled a second before Jamie picked her up and lifted her onto a bar stool, settling an arm around her.

"We don't have to stay," Jamie said into Carly's ear.

Carly was conscious of Jamie's hot breath on her cheek. "I'm fine." Her heart was racing and her skin tingled. She started to tuck a strand of hair behind Jamie's ear, but Jamie was staring down the bar.

A tall woman with dark hair and muscles to match Jamie's wiggled her way around bodies and stepped in front of Jamie. Breaking into a grin, she wrapped her arms around Jamie's neck and kissed her. Now Carly knew what her romance novels meant when they said the man assaulted the woman's mouth. She felt a burning sensation in her abdomen. Oh, God. Wrapping her arms around her belly she took deep, slow breaths. Jamie and the brunette were still kissing and she looked away, embarrassed and…angry.

"Trip over any tree roots lately?" the brunette asked Jamie.

"Can't say that I have, but I'll keep the fond memory of the last time I did."

"I'm going to find a bathroom," Carly said, sliding off her bar stool. Judging by the snippets of conversation, something was going on between them, and she didn't want to know what it was. She hadn't gone ten steps when Jamie took her hand.

"I'll go with you." Jamie shoved her way through the crowd, keeping Carly behind her.

"You don't need to babysit me, Jamie. Go back to your friend."

Jamie turned around. "You're my friend tonight, Carly."

Carly was pushed into Jamie as women jostled them on all sides. Seeing Jamie's breasts had been a curiosity. Feeling them against her own took her breath away. She reached out to steady herself, and her hand landed on Jamie's waist. Muscles tightened under her fingers. The music, the strobe lights, the press of bodies faded as Jamie's eyes locked onto hers and her lips parted. She'd never seen that look on Mike's face. It matched the description in her romance novels. Desire. Her nipples tightened inside her padded bra. Someone bumped Carly hard from the side, and Jamie clutched her around the waist to keep her from being knocked to the floor.

Carly startled as if waking from a dream and stepped back, embarrassed. Had she wanted Jamie to kiss her? She was shaking as she waited in line for the bathroom, confused by her reaction. Maybe coming here wasn't a good idea.

"Do you want to leave?" Jamie asked when Carly came out of the bathroom.

Carly looked around at all the women and shook her head. She'd meant to say, "yes, let's go," but her body felt alive in ways she'd never known. She should feel uncomfortable here but she didn't. This wasn't what she'd been taught about homosexuality.

"Are you sure?" Jamie's foot was tapping, and she kept glancing toward the dance floor.

Suddenly it hit her. "Oh my gosh, Jamie, I'm…what's the phrase…cramping your style? Why don't I take a cab back to the hotel so you can…mingle?"

Jamie held Carly's waist and put her mouth to Carly's ear. "I'm here with the cutest girl in the bar. Why would I want to mingle?"

Carly's heart pounded and blood rushed to her head. Was Jamie flirting with her? An instant later she knew exactly what she wanted. "Then why don't you ask me to dance?" She gave her best Southern-belle smile. Her knees went weak when Jamie's eyes darkened.

Jamie pulled her close and moved them in a tight circle. Carly felt self-conscious, but not for the reason she should. She felt wonder at dancing with Jamie, but no shame. She felt guilty for an instant, but the rightness of what she was feeling made it impossible to walk away. She had to know if this was the answer to her doubts. She loved Mike, but did she love him the right way?

Jamie's hands cupped her butt, and she was pulled into a rhythm she didn't know she had as rational thought left her. She rested her head on Jamie's shoulder, hot, bare skin against her cheek. Cocooned in strong arms, her hand held between another woman's breasts, she felt suspended outside herself, as if looking down on her body.

In the next breath she was slammed back into a body that felt changed, burning with new desires, strong desires, to touch and be touched, new sensations of heat and pressure deep in her core. Desire. Tears stung her eyes as she realized how little time she had to live out this fairy tale. As soon as she boarded that plane back to the out-and-proud West Coast, her life would revert to its ordained course. "Take me back to the hotel." When Jamie looked at her with uncertainty clouding her eyes, Carly said, "Please, I need to know what happens next."

Jamie tossed some bills at the cabbie and hustled them through the hotel lobby and into the elevator. She wanted to pull Carly against her, to press her hand where she needed it most. Carly's head was down, her cheeks flushed, her fingers fidgeting at the hem of her T-shirt. Protectiveness welled up in Jamie for the woman who'd been surprising her for the last eight hours. She took a deep breath, reorienting her priorities as the elevator door opened. This was about Carly.

Jamie closed the door to their room. "Are you sure you want to do this?"

Carly's eyes met Jamie's, tentative but tinted with desire. She swallowed twice and then nodded.

Jamie contained the need that was a tight ball in her groin as she undid Carly's ponytail and sifted her fingers through silky golden-blond hair that fell across Carly's shoulders. Carly's eyes were full of questions.

"I want to make love to you," Jamie whispered, as she wrapped her arms around Carly's waist. She kissed the side of Carly's neck and sucked her earlobe.

"Please." Carly's voice was low and she was breathing hard against Jamie's chest, her hands gripping Jamie's waist.

"I'll stop if you tell me to." Jamie slid her hands under the T-shirt and stroked up and down Carly's sides, just grazing her bra. "Don't do anything you don't want to do. I don't ever want you to regret this."

"I'll only regret it if I don't do it. Please. I…don't know how to ask for what I need." Carly trembled as she wrapped her arms around Jamie's neck.

Jamie circled Carly's lips with her tongue. "Let me inside." Carly parted her lips and Jamie slid her tongue between them. The kiss was soft and full of promise. Carly whimpered, and her arms tightened around Jamie's neck as she met Jamie's tongue stroke for stroke.

Jamie kissed her way to the pulse point in her throat and sucked on it. She pushed her center against Carly's thigh. When Jamie rubbed her fingers across her nipple, Carly groaned. "I don't know what to do," Carly said as she laid her cheek against Jamie's shoulder.

Jamie pulled her hand from Carly's breast and corralled the arousal that was making it hard to think. She'd wanted this all night, and her body was ready to back Carly up to the nearest bed, but her mind said to slow things down. "Do you like to take baths?"

"One of my favorite things." Carly's accent was thicker and heavier. It was the sexiest thing Jamie had ever heard.

"Mine, too." Jamie took her hand and led her to the bathroom, letting the lamp on the nightstand cast the only light into the small space. She turned the tap on and took a bottle of bubble bath from the sink and poured it in. Gripping the hem of Carly's T-shirt she asked, "Can I take it off?"

Carly hesitated for just a second and then lifted her arms. Jamie kissed along her shoulder, following the edge of her bra. When Jamie captured her nipple through the cotton, Carly sucked in her breath and grabbed at Jamie's T-shirt. "Take it off."

Stripping the T-shirt and tank top over her head, Jamie took Carly's hand and placed it on her breast. Her head fell back as Carly tentatively explored her. She moaned when Carly squeezed her nipple. She had her pants and briefs off in seconds and stood naked, nipples erect, letting Carly's eyes wander where they wanted before stepping close and helping her out of her clothes.

Jamie stepped into the tub and sat at the end, her legs stretched in front of her. Guiding Carly to lean back against her, she wrapped her arms around her and nuzzled her neck. "You're so beautiful." Carly stiffened.

"Do you really think—"

"God, yes. I want to touch you so much." Jamie moved her hands over Carly's belly and then up to cup her breasts, teasing and pinching the nipples until Carly groaned. She explored Carly's body with soapy hands and then let Carly explore her. They were both breathing heavily, kissing with abandon, when Jamie realized the water had cooled.

She stepped out and held up a towel for Carly, drying her before taking her hand and leading her to one of the beds. They lay on their sides, legs intertwined, kissing as they caressed each other's breasts. Nipples hardened and their kisses became more urgent, their moans more frequent.

"I want to make you come with my mouth." Jamie left a wet trail down Carly's neck as she licked her way to her breasts.

"Is that what women do with each other?" Her voice was breathy.

"It's one thing. Tell me if I do something you don't like." Jamie waited until Carly nodded, then fastened her mouth around Carly's breast and showed her what she wanted to do between her legs. When Carly squirmed beneath her, she traced circles slowly down Carly's abdomen with her fingers and paused just below the triangle of soft hair.

"Touch me. Please." Carly's fingers played erratically through Jamie's hair.

Jamie parted Carly's folds and stroked her clit. She pulled away from Carly's breast to watch her face, lips parted, those beautiful eyes half closed. Wetness coated Jamie's fingers, and when she pressed against her opening, Carly arched up to meet her fingers.

"Yes," Carly rasped. "God, yes." She moaned when Jamie slipped a finger into her and again when Jamie added a second finger. "Please, please, please," she kept repeating in long, slow syllables. Jamie matched her pleas with slow, deep thrusts. Carly tightened around her fingers. When Jamie stroked her tongue over Carly's clit she clasped the back of Jamie's head.

"It's never felt like this." Carly cried out and contracted around Jamie's fingers. Jamie sucked her clit into her mouth, and Carly bucked against her mouth as she came again. Jamie stayed inside as the spasms quieted. She kissed her way back up to Carly's mouth, letting her taste herself. "I could do that all night."

Jamie laid her palm against Carly's cheek. The look on Carly's face took her breath away. Her mouth was relaxed in a gentle smile, eyes full of wonder and softly focused on her, still glazed with desire, glistening with unshed tears. When Carly said, "Thank you," Jamie's heart skipped a beat. She rolled onto her back and tucked Carly against her. "I could stay like this forever." Carly's mouth kissing along her jaw pulled her from her thoughts.

"Show me what to do," Carly said after kissing her for a long time. "I want to touch you."

"You don't have to." She felt satisfied. Something about being with Carly was different and Jamie was content just to lie here.

"I want to. Please. You must…need it." Carly blushed but held Jamie's gaze.

"Give me your hand." She placed it against her center and pushed herself into her palm. Carly sucked in a breath, her eyes darting to her hand.

Carly's face changed from curiosity to something more serious as she explored, tentatively at first, then more boldly. "You're so soft and warm…and wet."

Jamie clenched her jaw, holding back as Carly played in her folds until she found Jamie's clit. When she stroked on either side of it, Jamie groaned.

"Will this make you orgasm?" Carly's eyes were on hers again, her breath hot on Jamie's cheek.

"Yes. Soon."

"I want you to." Carly's eyes turned fiery as her strokes became more confident.

"Suck my breasts." Jamie's breathing was ragged as her center heated up, ready to explode. Her nipple hardened the instant Carly's lips wrapped around it.

"I'm close. Don't stop." Jamie rocked against Carly's fingers and then convulsed on them as the full force of her orgasm ripped through her. "I'm coming. Don't stop…so good." Jamie opened her eyes. Carly's lips were parted, her eyes focused on her hand between

Jamie's legs, hair curtained around flushed cheeks. Jamie's heart skipped a beat. She was beautiful.

"Can you go inside me? I want to come again and I need you inside me," Jamie said, still panting from the first orgasm. She guided Carly to her opening and pressed down, drawing her inside. "Just like that. Now rub your thumb over my clit as you stroke inside me." Jamie spread her legs and rocked on Carly's fingers. "Yes…perfect." Jamie closed her eyes and arched her back, pressing her head into the pillow as she came, squeezing Carly's fingers. Finally unable to take any more, she gripped Carly's forearm to stop her as she floated on the release.

"Can I stay inside you?" Carly laid her cheek on Jamie's breast.

"For as long as you want. That was unbelievable." She meant it. Everything about Carly was a surprise. Jamie lifted Carly's chin with her finger and kissed her, intending to keep it sweet and soft. When Carly slid her tongue inside her mouth, she let Carly take the kiss where she needed it to go.

❖

Carly woke slowly, aware of an arm draped over her belly. Keeping her eyes closed, she breathed in these last precious moments of the best night of her life. Tears stung her eyes. How could she leave this woman, this bed, where so many questions had been answered? She traced her fingers over the back of the hand that not long ago had been buried deep inside her. Stroking over the muscled arm and up to the cheek that was turned toward her, she memorized the features of Jamie's face—the short nose, the full lips she'd kissed endlessly last night, the perfectly arched brows. She tucked curls behind Jamie's ear and let her hand rest in the softness for as long as she dared before sliding carefully from the bed. Jamie stirred and reached out toward Carly, but she didn't waken.

Carly brushed her teeth and washed her face but didn't dare take a shower for fear of waking Jamie. Pulling her hair into its customary ponytail, she checked her reflection in the mirror. No one would know by looking at her that she'd spent the night making wild love with another woman. She could walk out of this room and back into her life without a trace.

But she knew, as surely as she knew she was pregnant, that this night and this woman had forever marked her in the worst possible place—in her heart. She covered her mouth and choked back a sob. If things were different she'd fall back onto the rumpled sheets and wake Jamie with soft kisses across her back. They'd make love again and order room service and lounge around until they had to leave for the airport. They'd get seats next to each other and whisper secrets to occupy the time as the plane carried them back to the out-and-proud West Coast, where Carly would choose a different life.

She picked up the jeans from the floor and slipped two twenties from Jamie's pocket. She wrote a note on hotel stationery and set it on the nightstand. Staring at the tanned back with the broad shoulders and narrow waist, she moved her eyes down to the firm ass and muscular legs she'd run her hands over a few hours ago as Jamie straddled her face. Her cheeks warmed when she saw the marks her fingernails had left. Closing her eyes, she made sure she had this moment and this woman's body indelibly etched in her mind.

The flight home was a five-hour battle with tears and nausea. She smelled Jamie on her skin, and her eyes burned with images of their lovemaking. Songs from the concert floated through her mind, adding a soundtrack to her heartbreak. As she walked off the plane the exhaustion of the last twenty-four hours hit, and she fell into Mike's arms. They would be married soon and it was too late for any other choice. On the drive to their apartment it was easy to hide her real sorrow in the story about what had happened with her parents. She'd forget their cruelty, but she'd always remember Jamie's kindness.

Jamie sighed and stretched. Soreness brought memories of last night. And Carly. She rolled over, reaching for the warm, soft body. She was alone in the bed. The room was too quiet, and she knew before she pushed the bathroom door open. Towels lay where they'd tossed them last night, but the navy slacks and white T-shirt were gone. She trudged back to sit on the edge of the bed they'd demolished last night, pillows lying askew, sheets hanging to the floor. Holding her head in her hands she tried to calm her racing thoughts. She stood up.

If she hurried she could catch Carly at the airport. She sat back down hard. If Carly had left, it had been on purpose.

Jamie wasn't sure at what point she'd started to think of Carly as more than a one-night stand. Her eyes filled with tears, a rare occurrence. Reaching for the light switch, she saw the note on the bedside table, and read it without picking it up.

"I'll never forget you. Love, Carly."

Jamie showered quickly, desperate to get out of this room that smelled of sex, of Carly. She tucked the note carefully between two T-shirts in her backpack. Leaving her duffel with the bellhop, she walked out into the warm, humid air and wandered until it was time to leave for the airport. Feelings she'd never experienced bubbled up as she replayed the hours with Carly.

Jamie stopped at a pay phone on her way to the boarding gate. She needed to hear a friendly voice before she got on that flight. She stared at every girl that looked even remotely like Carly, but each time the hopeful beat of her heart skidded to a disappointing halt. "Hey, Penni."

"I thought you were getting back yesterday."

"Cancelled flight. I wish you'd come with me." Jamie stared at the faint outline of the purple stamp on the back of her hand. She hadn't tried to scrub it off.

"Me, too. I'm sure you had more fun than I did setting up my classroom. You sound tired. Bag too many babes?"

"Not exactly. I sort of got my heart broken." The explosion of laughter wasn't unexpected. The silence afterward was.

"Wow, you've never said that before. How 'bout if I come over for dinner tomorrow. We can gorge on Chinese takeout and Ben and Jerry's, and you can tell me about it."

"That would help a lot." Jamie watched a couple waiting by the boarding counter, their heads together in whispered conversation. That might have been she and Carly.

"That's what best friends are for."

"Will you still be my best friend after I tell you I saw Melissa Etheridge in concert last night?" Jamie burst out laughing at the shriek that made her jerk the phone away from her ear.

"You bitch."

"I assume you mean that in the nicest way." God, best friends meant everything.

Jamie slept on the flight home, her head on a scrunched-up sweatshirt against the cold window. She retrieved her truck from long-term parking and pulled into the first McDonald's she saw. She needed comfort food and this would have to do. An hour later she trudged up the steps to her apartment in San Jose and tossed her bags on the couch. Unpacking and laundry would have to wait until tomorrow. Picking up the phone, she took a deep breath and punched in the number.

"I just got home, Dad." Jamie cradled her forehead in her hand and yawned.

"I would have insisted they get me a flight on another airline. Patients depend on us, Jamie. We can't let our problems interfere with their care."

"I'm sorry. I did my best."

"You need to be in early tomorrow. Mary rescheduled some of your patients starting at eight o'clock, and I left files on your desk for you to look over."

"All right. I love you."

Jamie ironed a shirt and pants to wear tomorrow, almost too tired to stand. She collapsed on her bed, wondering where Carly was in this sprawling metropolis and whose bed she was in. Her eyes filled with tears, the lost opportunity pulling at other lost opportunities. Carly had touched her heart in a way it had never been touched before. Was this what her mom meant when she described what being in love felt like? "Your heart beats differently around them, like you've found a rhythm you didn't know you needed." She wanted more than one night and for the first time in her life felt the pain of a lover's rejection. She fell into an exhausted sleep and woke in the dark, reaching for the soft body in her dream.

CHAPTER ONE

September 2011

Jamie walked up Ocean Street toward the Pine Inn, balancing two cups of coffee and a bag of goodies from the bakery that had been there since her childhood. Best bear claws in the world. She'd been lucky to get a room on short notice at the romantic inn, and over Labor Day weekend no less. They hadn't been away for a weekend in too long, and Jamie felt guilty that she'd been neglecting Sheryl.

Anger bit at her when she thought about the reason. The discovery that her long-time office manager had been embezzling from her was still raw. She breathed in the cool, foggy sea air that she loved, and her good mood drifted back. "Nice morning for a run," she said to a man about her age, his face flushed and his T-shirt sweaty. She should have brought her running shoes.

Sheryl was propped against the headboard, her shoulder-length hair neatly arranged, wearing the new chocolate-brown silk pajamas Jamie had bought her yesterday. They matched Sheryl's eyes perfectly, and Jamie had visions of slowly addressing each of those buttons, then sliding her hands inside to caress Sheryl's breasts. It had been weeks since they'd made love, and Sheryl had been too tired last night. Jamie needed that connection. She needed them to be all right. She stared at the computer on Sheryl's lap. Work.

"Presents." Sitting down next to Sheryl, Jamie opened the bag and waited for her to dip her nose into it and inhale, a gesture Jamie had always loved.

Sheryl frowned at something on the computer screen. "I don't want—"

"They're fat-free blueberry muffins. And skim milk in your coffee. Come on." Jamie rattled the bag. "You don't have to diet every minute. You look great. Those jeans you had on yesterday made me want to peel them off you."

Sheryl kept typing. "With single-minded determination you can accomplish anything. Now, if I can get that promotion everything will be perfect."

"How 'bout if I feed you?" Jamie waited for Sheryl to open her mouth for the bite, a long-time game they'd played since Jamie had teased her about how they'd eat cake at their wedding. It hadn't happened and the disappointment was still there.

Sheryl pulled off a tiny piece of the muffin, sniffed it, and popped it in her mouth. "Not bad."

"I love Carmel." Jamie took a big bite of the bear claw. "Mmm."

"How can you eat all that sugar and fat?"

Jamie smiled at Sheryl's pinched expression and tucked strands of her blond hair behind her ear. The new highlights were pretty. "They were my mom's favorite. We'd walk down and get them every morning and—"

"I know. Every time we come here you talk about the summer vacations here with your mom when you were a kid." Sheryl frowned. "We couldn't afford to go anywhere but to see our grandparents in Atlanta for vacation."

"But you've had some nice vacations with me, haven't you?" Jamie chased the bear claw with a long sip of coffee.

"You've always taken good care of me." Sheryl kissed her on the cheek. "And yes, I love the Lexus. It makes me feel important." She kissed Jamie's cheek again.

"I wanted you to have something nice for your birthday." Jamie took Sheryl's hand. "Nothing's going to change, I promise. I'll get this business problem worked out. I've been going through patient files every spare minute and finally got a break. I've found some files where the EOBs—"

"I have no idea what that means. You just need to fix it so it doesn't become a scandal and get in the newspapers or something."

"I can't imagine it would."

"I can't take the chance. You saw what happened last year when that problem with those girls turned into such a big deal. I should have had that promotion." Sheryl's voice took on the venomous tone it always did when she discussed that subject. "I don't want to be a principal forever. I want to get to the district level, and I'm perfect for that new curriculum-development position." Sheryl's eyes sparkled as if she were looking at a diamond bracelet. Maybe that's what Jamie would buy her for their anniversary.

"I still wish there'd been another way to handle it." Jamie felt uncomfortable. She trusted Sheryl's judgment but didn't like the hard line she'd taken with the two high-school seniors. Sheryl had always been conservative about public displays of affection and Jamie respected her feelings, but being out and proud still mattered to her.

"School districts are a lot more conservative and political than you think. It's not just about how hard you work. It's about making allies out of the right people. You have your dream, Jamie. I want mine."

Jamie wasn't sure it was exactly her dream, but maybe she was just feeling old and tired. "I want you to be happy. You know I'll support you any way I can."

Sheryl patted her hand, nails perfectly manicured. The red polish looked sexy. "Get your business problem fixed. That's all I need from you."

"That's all?" Jamie moved her hand up Sheryl's leg. "Let's spend the morning in bed and then go for a walk on the beach."

"I'd rather go shopping in town this morning, then drive up to Pacific Grove and look around the shops there before dinner. I can't believe you got reservations at Pebble Beach." Sheryl's smile made all the last-minute work to plan this trip worth it.

"Maybe a walk on the beach tomorrow? Or a drive along Seventeen Mile Drive…take a picnic?" Jamie rested her cheek against Sheryl's shoulder as she typed. "You work too much, babe."

"And you don't? I like that we're a career-minded couple."

"Tomorrow maybe we could be less career-minded." Jamie kissed along Sheryl's throat.

"I have to be back by noon for the district back-to-school barbecue. I told you about it."

Jamie didn't remember, but with her preoccupation with her business problems she wasn't surprised. "Can't you be late?"

"It's all about making allies, Jamie. What if the district superintendent leaves early and I miss a chance to talk to him?"

Jamie cupped the back of Sheryl's head and pulled her into a kiss. Her disappointment was lost to the heat of Sheryl's mouth. Did it matter what they did as long as they were solid as a couple? Jamie slid her hand up Sheryl's tummy. "I love you," she murmured, and then kissed Sheryl deeper. She circled Sheryl's nipple with her finger until it hardened. "Maybe we could…"

"Come on." Sheryl closed the laptop and popped out of bed. "Take a shower with me. Then let's go have some fun."

CHAPTER TWO

Carla held the newly framed picture of her daughter to her chest as she stared out at her backyard. This morning they'd been having breakfast with the girls, and now she was standing in Lissa's bedroom, wondering how her daughter had gone from a child playing in that playhouse to a freshman in college.

"Penny for your thoughts." Mike wrapped his arms around her.

Carla absorbed the solidness she'd always trusted. "I miss Lissa already and I'm going to miss you."

"I'm moving out of the house, honey, not out of your life." He kissed the top of Carla's head.

"Look at them." She held up the picture of Lissa and her girlfriend, Steph, cuddled together on the new couch they'd bought for them. "They don't look grown up enough to be off living in an apartment on their own."

"They're only in San Diego."

"Might as well be another planet." Carla set the picture on the dresser with the other pictures that chronicled her daughter's life. Lissa's favorite brown teddy bear sat on her pillow. Carla hugged it to her chest. "What am I going to do? I'm not ready to be an empty-nester."

"Maybe you should consider going back to work."

"Maybe." Carla sat on the edge of the bed and rubbed the bedspread. "I hate this bed made." After a heartbeat of silence they both burst out laughing. "Maybe I should turn this into a sewing room."

Mike pulled her to her feet and kissed her cheek. "You don't sew."

"I know, but isn't that what middle-aged women without daughters or husbands do? Take up a hobby?" Carla rearranged the pictures on the dresser.

"Give yourself time. You can't decide the rest of your life in a day."

"I know we're doing the right thing, but I'm scared. What if Lissa doesn't take our divorce well? What if she hates us for it?"

"She won't. We'll pull each other through it," he said, taking her hand.

"Everything I thought was my life is ending. I don't know how to start over."

"It's kind of funny, though, isn't it?" Mike tried to keep a straight face. "If we'd been more…I don't know…self-aware or honest with each other, we might have figured out sooner that we're both gay."

"Better late than never, I guess."

"Are you going to start dating?"

"Oh, good heavens, no. I can't imagine falling in love at my age."

"You're a hopeless romantic, honey. Someone will sweep you off your feet."

Carla laughed when Mike took her in his arms and danced her around the room. They were a perfect fit in all ways but one. Sex had always been loving and gentle between them, but never passionate in the way Carla yearned for. She hadn't told him the specifics of how she knew she was a lesbian at heart. One night, but it had profoundly changed her, and she'd never forgotten it.

"Come on," he said. "Let's not sit around and sulk. You go for a run and I'll get the barbecue ready."

"Come with me."

It was after eleven when they blew out the candles on the patio table, set the coffeemaker for the next morning, and said good night with a long hug outside Carla's bedroom.

Mike had been sleeping in the guest room for most of the last year under the guise that his snoring kept Carla awake. Both had wanted some private space to begin the transition to their new lives.

After a long bath, Carla crawled into bed. She didn't like sleeping alone and wondered if she'd ever share this bed again. Picking up the romance novel from the nightstand, she settled back against the pillows and let herself be carried away.

CHAPTER THREE

Dr. Hammond, what do you want me to do about the new patient? She insists on seeing you." Her receptionist's long brown hair framed a face that looked frazzled. The phone rang and then went to voice mail because another call was on hold. "There just aren't any openings."

"We'll work it out." Jamie had two excellent associate doctors in the practice, but having new patients insist on being treated by her was all too common. Handing the patient file across the front counter to her receptionist, Jamie said to her patient, "Remember to do your exercises. We have to get some strength in your lower back or this will keep happening." She'd have a lot fewer problems if she lost thirty pounds and did her exercises, but Jamie had learned that people had to make their own decisions. She did her best to encourage them.

"Is she acute?" Jamie walked behind the counter and looked at the appointment book. The schedule was even busier than usual because of the holiday weekend. Nothing about her practice was easy these days.

"Says she can barely walk."

"She's not exaggerating."

Jamie looked up. Renee Rapp was standing at the counter, all five foot two of her. "We had dinner last night. You need to see her today, Jamie."

"Far be it from me to argue with you," Jamie said. When Renee's eyes held hers she knew there was more.

"Fund-raiser next month for the Women Mentoring Women Foundation. Second Saturday. I want you there."

"Renee—"

"No argument. I'll give you a reprieve for a while considering what you're dealing with, but then I'm pairing you up with someone." Renee held up her hand when Jamie started to protest. "You're a smart businesswoman, Jamie."

Not so smart, but Renee wasn't one to argue with. "Can I see her during my lunch?" Jamie asked her receptionist.

"No," Betty piped in, popping her head out of her office. "You have an interview." Short gray hair framed a grandmotherly face and the unusually stern gaze brooked no argument. Betty had been her father's patient and filled in over the years if Jamie needed office help. She'd gamely agreed to act as office manager until Jamie found a replacement.

"How optimistic are you about this one?"

"I don't know," Betty said, shaking her head. "We're getting plenty of applications, but doesn't anyone have a brain any more? Or common sense? Or phone sense?"

"Schedule the new patient for the second half of my lunch break," Jamie said to her receptionist. "It sounds like it'll be a short interview."

"I'm sorry, Jamie, but I can't do this forever." Betty took off her glasses and rubbed the bridge of her nose. "Frank packed the motor home over the weekend. He's getting cranky about delaying our trip. And you know I don't have the right skills. Every time I touch this darn computer I'm terrified it'll explode because I hit the wrong key. You need a real office manager."

"I'm scared of the same thing," Jamie said to Betty. Buffering her staff from her business problems was getting harder the longer this mess went on. But none of this was their fault, and Jamie wasn't going to pass any of the stress on to them.

"You'll get through this," Renee said, as they walked down the hallway to a treatment room.

Renee was one of the few patients who knew what was going on. They talked as Jamie adjusted her, and then she hustled on to her next patient. Getting behind schedule this early in the day would be a disaster.

"You got my shoulder working good again, Doc," the elderly man with stubble on his cheeks said as he hoisted his arm over his head.

"Now don't go letting your new puppy pull on it," Jamie said after adjusting him. Half of her patients could prevent their problems with a little common sense, but as her father always said, "It's our job to make sure they don't suffer for their lapses in judgment." He'd be tremendously disappointed in her lapse in good judgment that now jeopardized the practice he'd built.

Marci, her chiropractic assistant, met her as she was leaving the treatment room. "Your next patient is in treatment room three. I put heat on her neck and did some passive range-of-motion stretching."

"Perfect."

"I talked to my sister, Dr. Hammond. She's got time to help you out part-time with the bookkeeping."

"It's not your problem," Jamie said, more sharply than she'd intended. She reached up and squeezed Marci's shoulder. She'd been a patient and basketball star at Santa Clara University and was her right hand with patient treatment. "I'll work it out."

She had to, for the sake of her relationship, and the patients who depended on her for care, and the staff who depended on her for jobs. "I'm trying, Dad," she whispered to herself.

Alone in her office as her staff headed off to lunch, Jamie turned on the iPod on the credenza behind her desk. She was still in one of what Penni called her "Melissa moods," brought on by the concert last month at The Mountain Winery. It had been a magical night with Penni, her wife Lori, and a group of friends—one thing they still made time for in the midst of careers and kids. It was fun to pretend they were still young, screaming for their favorite rock star. If Sheryl had come it would have been a perfect evening.

"Got a minute?" Don Walker, one of Jamie's associate doctors, was standing in the doorway.

"Sure."

Don lowered his beanpole frame into the chair across the desk from Jamie. "Do you think I'm a good doctor?"

"Of course."

"I don't know, Jamie…I thought I did a good job with several patients last week, but they're not any better today. Maybe I'm not cut out for this." Don fidgeted with the pen in the pocket of his white clinic coat. "Maybe I should have gone into computers like my dad wanted."

"Nonsense," Jamie said. "Never doubt yourself. Patients place their trust in us, and we have to inspire confidence—" She stopped. That was her father's answer whenever she voiced any doubts. His dismissive attitude had hurt. She rubbed her forehead and took a deep breath. "You're one of the best associates I've had, Don. It took me… oh, about ten years to gain enough confidence to not panic every time a patient didn't get well right away."

"I find that hard to believe. You make it look easy."

"Trust me. I came out of chiropractic school as unsure of myself as you. Confidence takes time and experience. Be patient with yourself."

Don looked relieved as he stood. "Thanks, Jamie. I needed that. Sorry I bothered you."

"I want you to come to me with your concerns. Give this a fair try. If you're not happy in a few years, go do something else."

Jamie rested her elbows on the desk and ran her hands through her hair. Sheryl wanted her to color it, but Jamie liked the gray that was showing at her temples. She was forty-five and wasn't going to apologize for her age. She'd look for tickets to a concert Sheryl would like. Or maybe a pair of earrings like the ones she liked in Carmel. She needed to make sure Sheryl knew how much she loved her.

Betty opened the door. "The applicant's here."

"Show her back." Jamie rolled down the sleeves on her pink Oxford shirt and buttoned the cuffs.

"I'll bring you a sandwich. Do you want your usual?"

"Sure. And—"

"Iced tea. I know." Betty held up her hand, fingers crossed.

Jamie stood, ready to greet the woman she hoped would be her new office manager. Fifteen minutes later she was all too willing to tell the woman who chattered like a parakeet that she had another appointment. The choices must be dismal if Betty brought this one in for an interview.

She rubbed over her face, forcing back the fear and frustration. Shoving out of the chair that creaked its age, she steeled her resolve.

She'd gotten herself into this mess; she'd have to get herself out. Her father always said you reap what you sow. When had she sown the seeds of this disaster?

❖

Jamie set the stack of patient files on the coffee table and sat down on the brown leather couch in her office, tired and hungry after a long day. Her father had brought it with him from his old office, and right now she felt about as old and worn as it looked. Had it really been almost twenty years since his death? Sitting where he'd sat gave her a sense of comfort, but she actually needed his wisdom.

She clenched her jaw. Everything he'd worked for was in jeopardy. Why had Marjorie embezzled from her? Hadn't she treated her with the same regard her father had shown his office manager, Mary? What would Mary think of her daughter's behavior? It just didn't make sense.

She should be home having dinner with Sheryl instead of trying to figure out how a trusted employee committed insurance fraud and stole from her for God knew how long. She grabbed the top file. The only way to reconstruct what Marjorie had done was to match the treatments she'd billed for against what treatments had actually been done. She'd need to go through the files for every insurance patient as far back as she still had them.

The insurance companies were acting as if she'd approved of the fraud, and their lack of cooperation was making it harder. Too many files she'd looked at didn't have EOBs in them, and without copies she had nothing to compare the treatments against.

She checked her watch. Seven o'clock. One more hour. Then she'd go home and curl up on the couch with Sheryl and watch the worst adventure movie they could find.

CHAPTER FOUR

Breakfast in bed." Jamie frowned as she walked into the bedroom carrying the tray with cappuccinos, fat-free yogurt, and fruit. Sheryl had been asleep ten minutes ago. Now the shower was on, and she was booming out one of the country songs she loved. Jamie set the tray on the bed.

Opening the shower door she let her eyes wander over Sheryl's body. She felt guilty for missing those extra curves, but she had to admit Sheryl looked great. "I thought we'd have breakfast in bed and pick up where we left off last night." Jamie had surprised Sheryl with tickets to a sold-out George Strait concert. Thank-you kisses had led to making love.

"Cold air." Sheryl closed the shower door. "I'm meeting people for brunch. I told you. Did you make cappuccinos?"

Was her memory that bad? "Um, yeah." Jamie scooted Sheryl's makeup jars to the side and perched on the edge of the gray marble vanity with double sinks, last year's remodel.

"You make the best cappuccinos."

"You could, too. You wanted the Gaggia because it was easy to use."

"It's more fun if you make them." Sheryl stepped out of the shower and wrapped herself in a towel. Jamie wanted to peel it off her and carry her back to bed, but once Sheryl showered it was impossible to get her back in the mood. Shouldn't have fixed those blasted cappuccinos.

She followed Sheryl to the bedroom and handed her a cup. "How about a movie this afternoon, and then I'll take you to that new restaurant you've been talking about." Sheryl dropped the towel on a chair and disappeared into the walk-in closet, also part of last year's remodel. If Sheryl's new interest in clothes kept up they'd have to expand it again.

"I'm going shopping this afternoon, and that restaurant's in Los Gatos."

There went her great day. Jamie sat on the bed and downed half of her cappuccino. "It's dinner, not making out in the park."

Sheryl peeked out of the closet and glared at her.

"I'm sorry. I didn't mean it like that."

"It's a small community, and I just don't need people knowing about my personal life. You said you understood."

"I've always respected your feelings, but it just seems like…I don't know…that we've stopped doing some of the things that used to be a big part of our social life." Jamie listened to Sheryl pulling drawers open in the closet. She'd always been more conservative than Jamie when it came to being out as a lesbian. They'd talked about it a lot their first year of dating and worked out compromises that satisfied them both. "You won't go to concerts with me any more, and we can't do anything in Los Gatos, and we've stopped going out with a lot of our friends—"

"I don't want to go to Melissa Etheridge concerts, and there are a million restaurants we can go to that aren't in Los Gatos. Our friends were always your friends, and I want my own." Sheryl appeared in the doorway to the closet, her serious expression at odds with her lacy panties and bra. "You were handed your business in your twenties, Jamie. I'm thirty-five and I deserve this promotion. I'm not taking any chances this time."

"I know and I want you to be happy." Sheryl held up two blouses and Jamie pointed to the gold sleeveless one. It picked up the highlights in her hair. Sheryl tossed the other one on top of the towel on the chair. "How about if I grill halibut for dinner?"

"And make the papaya salsa you did last time?"

"Yep. And I'll get that Chardonnay you like." Jamie walked over and wrapped her arms around Sheryl. Her body was warm and smelled like the lotion that matched her new perfume. The one she'd worn for years was sweet and tropical, and Jamie loved it. This one was sharp and tangy and not her favorite. When Sheryl went to the bathroom and started what Jamie called her makeup process, she carried the breakfast tray back to the kitchen.

Jamie fixed herself another cappuccino and took it to the glass-topped table on the patio. Might as well get a caffeine buzz. The patio around the rectangular pool was cluttered with the furniture Sheryl had seen in a magazine and ordered before they moved in so they could entertain in style. She could count on one hand the number of parties they'd had.

Putting on her sunglasses, she stared at the pool, thinking back to the hot June day when the realtor had shown them the house. Sheryl had slipped off her shoes, rolled up her pants, and sat on the edge dangling her feet in the water in a childlike gesture that melted Jamie's heart. "I always wanted a house with a pool," she'd said. "Our rich cousins had one, and they made fun of us because we didn't."

That's the moment Jamie decided she could live with moving out of the house her parents had left her if it made Sheryl happy. Leaving behind so many memories had been harder than she'd thought, especially the memories of all the good times with her mom. She'd comforted herself with the certainty she was doing the right thing. After all, hadn't her father made sacrifices to ensure her mom's happiness?

"I'll see you later," Sheryl said from the doorway, looking good enough to eat in the blouse and yellow capris. "What are you doing today?"

"I'll probably go in to the office." Jamie looked longingly at the pool. Running and swimming had both been sacrificed since finding out about the embezzling.

"I appreciate how hard you're working to get your problem fixed."

"Do you remember when we first saw this house? You said you always wanted a pool?"

"I did? I don't remember, but it adds value to the house."

"Value? Yeah, I guess. But are you happy here?"

"For now. If I get that promotion we can look for something bigger."

How much bigger did two people need, Jamie wondered as she watched Sheryl walk back to the house in heels that were way too high.

❖

"Thanks for letting us crash your pool. This heat wave is crazy." Penni handed Jamie an iced tea and sat on the chaise next to her. "God, she's beautiful. Am I lucky or what?"

"You got everything you wanted," Jamie said watching Penni's wife, Lori, frolicking in the pool with their two kids. Jamie drank greedily. Penni made perfect iced tea—just the right mix of lemon and sugar.

"Speaking of beloveds…dare I ask where yours is?"

"Shopping."

"Again?" Penni's eyebrows went up. "You're under financial stress and she's out spending your money? Jamie—"

"Our money, and it's her way of having fun." Jamie laughed at Lori and Travis, their ten-year-old, splashing each other.

"She should be helping you."

"She's never been involved in my business."

"And you've never had a problem like this. When the going gets tough, some people roll up their sleeves and pitch in, and some go shopping."

"I love her the way she is."

"Do you have to?"

"Not listening," Jamie said as she went over to the table and turned on the iPod. "Requests?"

"Like there's any choice. It'll be another month before you're out of your 'Melissa mood.' If there's a more loyal fan, I haven't met her. How many concerts?"

"Forty-two."

"What's the farthest you've gone?"

"Atlanta." Jamie flopped onto the chaise. Was anything better than lying in the sun? It had always been her instant ticket to relaxation.

"How long's it been since that concert?"

"Twenty years."

"Do you ever think about that girl?"

"Nope." Her last image of Carly was looking down the length of her body—her breasts, the soft roundness of her belly, the triangle of blond hair—as she lay snuggled in Jamie's arms. Jamie sat up, and sweat rolled down her chest.

"But don't you ever wonder what your life would be like now if—"

"It was one night a long time ago. Fun. Meaningless." Penni was so ridiculous sometimes. "My contribution to a straight woman's education."

"I forget her—"

"Carly."

"Oh, yeah. I always remember her as the Southern girl who broke your heart."

"She did not break my heart." Jamie tossed her sunglasses on her towel and walked to the pool. She dove in and surfaced near Lori. "Your wife's being a pain."

"You mean stubborn? Pushy?"

Jamie picked up Travis and catapulted him into the air. "Exactly."

"She loves you. It's her only defense and it's a good one."

Jamie threw Travis until her arms ached and then returned to the chaise. She was just dozing off when something cold touched her shoulder.

"You drink this stuff like water," Penni said as she handed Jamie another iced tea, shoving Jamie's leg over with her hip as she sat facing her. "Any luck hiring a new office manager?"

"Interviewed three more this week. I wouldn't trust any of them to wash my car. Betty's husband is going to kill me if I don't get her replaced soon." Jamie's attempted laugh came out strangled. "Maybe my standards are too high."

"Or maybe you're just scared to trust anyone. How's the rest of it going?"

"Dismal. I can't even count how many hours I've spent going through patient files or how many phone calls I've made to the insurance companies. And having to get together the documentation for the DA and IRS…" Jamie felt her good mood disappearing.

"One day at a time." Penni patted her thigh. "Aren't your accountant and attorney helping?"

"My attorney's trying to keep the DA happy. My accountant's working with the IRS. But neither of them can go through the patient files, and that's the root of the problem. They wouldn't know what to look for. And I got into this mess because I trusted someone else to run my business. I'm not making that mistake again."

"Why not hire a forensic accountant?"

"No." Jamie wiped sweat off her throat. "I'm not letting anyone go through my books until I've figured out what Marjorie did. I'm going to know everything there is to know about it so I'm not dependent on my next office manager."

"Has the DA decided to press charges against her?"

"I don't know." Jamie rubbed the back of her neck, trying to loosen the knots that hadn't been there two months ago. "I'm scared, Penni. I thought I'd resolve this quickly, but it keeps getting to be a bigger mess. What if I lose the business? My father would be so disappointed in me."

"You don't know this wasn't happening under his nose, too. Like mother, like daughter."

"I doubt it," Jamie said with a snort. "You knew him. He was the most diligent, hard-working, responsible person imaginable."

"Scoot forward," Penni said, sliding behind Jamie and digging her fingers into Jamie's shoulders. "Lot of weight on these shoulders."

Penni's hands froze, and Jamie opened her eyes. Sheryl was bearing down on them. "Don't make a scene. Please?"

"Jamie? You didn't tell me they were coming over." Sheryl smiled, but her eyes were like daggers.

"I didn't—"

"We must have called after you left to go shopping," Penni said. "How are you, Sheryl? Nice outfit." When Sheryl stormed off into the house, she said, "Oops. Did I offend the wicked witch?"

"I asked you not to call her that. This is her home. And her pool," Jamie tossed over her shoulder as she hurried after Sheryl.

"Can't you get along with her for an hour?"

"She hates me. I don't want her here. I've told you that." Sheryl banged a glass on the kitchen counter.

"She doesn't hate you. She's my best friend, and she used to be your—"

"Not since we bought this house." Sheryl popped the top on a Diet Coke and filled the glass. "What business was it of hers—"

"Please try?" Jamie put her hands on Sheryl's waist.

"I'll be in my office until they leave." Sheryl's voice was as cold as the ice in the glass.

"You deserve better." Penni's voice was gentle, and she put her arm around Jamie's shoulders.

"Can't you try to get along?"

"I tried for years, but when she made you sell your childhood home because of some ridiculous idea that being a lesbian is hurting her career…I can't forgive that."

Jamie jerked away. "It's not that simple. The house was old and drafty—"

"And a block from her school." Penni's jaw muscles tightened. "If she gets this next promotion, are you going to have to buy another house for some other reason?"

"Relationships are about compromise." Jamie crossed her arms.

"And where is she compromising?"

"I need to go talk to her."

"And we need to be going. Thanks for the swim."

Jamie headed for Sheryl's office. The day hadn't gone the way she'd planned, but she intended to salvage the evening.

Chapter Five

Jamie let herself in the back door of the clinic. It was quiet as she turned on lights, started coffee, and checked her schedule for the day. She'd woken up restless and gone for a run, the first one in weeks. The only trace of Sheryl when she got back was the steamy bathroom, towels strewn across the vanity, and the new perfume Jamie tried to like. No note saying, "I love you" or "Have a great day." It had been a while since she'd gotten one of those, and she missed them. So many ways they used to connect. She'd pick up flowers and a card on her way home. She felt bad about yesterday. Sheryl was right; she should have called to tell her Penni was there.

She had an hour before her first patient and a stack of patient files to go through. Why couldn't her week begin with great coffee and a hologram of Marjorie sitting across the desk answering questions about what she'd done and why? Instead, her father's face stared at her from the picture on the corner of the desk. He was smiling that movie-star smile that added to his charm, but Jamie always thought of him as stern and serious. He always had an answer, a certainty about what to do and the right way to do it, whether it was treating patients, tying the red ties that were his trademark, or building this clinic. *What would be the right way, Dad, to solve this problem?* She startled when a voice said, "Good morning."

Sara Michaels, her other associate doctor, stood shoulder to shoulder with Don in her doorway. He was lanky and blond, Sara almost his comedy-duo opposite, short and dark-haired and solidly built from years of weight lifting.

"We wanted to catch you before you got busy," Sara said as they approached Jamie's desk.

"What's up?" Both had their hands in their pockets, like nervous kids approaching the principal.

"We want to help," Sara said. "You're coming in early, staying late, interviewing during your lunch."

"It's not—"

"Our problem. We know," Don said, his deep voice at odds with his build. "We worked with Marjorie, too. We should have noticed something was off."

"We can go through files," Sara said. "Or let us take some of your patient load."

"I appreciate the offer." Jamie stood and cupped Sara's elbow, walking her to the door. "But it's easier for me to deal with this myself."

"At least let one of us adjust you every week. You're tired and stressed, two causes for subluxations and tight muscles."

"You sound like a textbook, Don. I'll make sure I stay healthy."

Sara stepped into the hallway and then turned back toward Jamie. "Sometimes we can't solve our own problems. Isn't that what we do for our patients?"

"It's not the same thing." It was her job to take care of her staff, not the other way around.

"Remember when I strained my rotator cuff but I kept working out, and it just got worse until it hurt to adjust patients? And you worked on my shoulder but also chewed me out for ignoring the pain? Please let us help."

"I'll think about it," Jamie said. Returning to her desk she took a sip of coffee. It was terrible, but she hadn't had time to go by Peet's for more Kona. One of the songs from the concert was playing, and her eyes fell on Penni's picture. She'd brought it in one day and plunked it down next to the one of her father "He's gone, but I'll always be here for you." Jamie stared at the blue eyes full of mischief. Penni's arm was draped over her shoulder, their hair blown back, the ocean in the background. They'd escaped for a day of goofing around at the Santa Cruz Boardwalk. "Yeah, I know. You agree with them," she murmured.

"Don't schedule anyone during your lunch," Betty said when Jamie popped her head in her office to say good morning. "You have an interview." Her eyes sparkled as she smiled. "I didn't want to get your hopes up on Friday when I got her resume. I talked to her Saturday on the phone, and I like her. She ran a dentist's office and has a great phone voice."

"Sounds promising."

"I don't know how much longer I can hold Frank off. He threatened to pick me up after work on Friday and hold me hostage until we get to Oregon."

"Tell Frank one way or the other he'll have you back in two weeks," Jamie said. She needed to be realistic and lower her standards. If this woman was even moderately qualified she was going to get the job.

"Renee Rapp referred her," Betty whispered, as if afraid to jinx it.

Jamie perked up. "Then I'll risk being optimistic."

By the time Jamie settled down to the sandwich and iced tea Betty left for her, she was almost giddy that one of her problems might be solved before her lunch hour was up. She read the resume. It looked impressive, and Renee's judgment was impeccable.

Hearing a knock at her door, Jamie set the sandwich aside and rolled down the cuffs on her blue Oxford shirt, then moved to greet the woman she hoped would be her new office manager. Betty ushered in a well-dressed woman in an ivory linen suit with shoulder-length golden-blond hair. Jamie's mouth went dry, and her skin felt as hot as if she were back in the heat of Atlanta. She stared into amber eyes she still recognized after all these years. She hesitated, then extended her hand as questions swarmed.

"Dr. Hammond, this is Carla Grant. Can I get you anything to drink, Carla?"

"I'm fine. Thank you, Betty," Carla said.

"Please, sit down." Jamie motioned toward the chair across from her desk. Carly's—no, Carla's—voice still had the barest hint of Southern accent, and Jamie's cheeks burned as random memories circled her. She searched for recognition in the eyes that had once looked at her with desire. Nothing. Just a polite smile. Carla didn't recognize her. Why would she? It was one night—a straight girl's experiment. But what was Carla doing here? Did Renee have any idea they'd once known each other? Of course not.

Jamie picked up the resume and studied it, buying herself some time. There was no tactful way to end the interview. She could get through fifteen minutes. But explaining to Betty and Renee that she hadn't hired Carla would be a problem. Realizing she'd left her iPod on, she reached behind her to turn it off. The song was one Melissa had played that night in Atlanta. When she looked back at Carla, there was no sign the song meant anything to her.

"You ran a dentist's office." Jamie's eyes drifted to Carla's hands folded in her lap. The ring was right where it should be. She clenched her jaw. Yep, a straight girl's experiment.

"Yes, for thirteen years." Carla uncrossed her legs and then crossed them again, settling her hands back in her lap.

"Why did you leave?" Jamie's voice came out sharper than she meant.

"Dr. Rose died last spring of cancer."

"And since then?" Just ask a few questions and get this over with.

"I got my daughter settled at college and decided the best antidote to empty-nest syndrome was to go back to work. I like being useful and I'm good at what I do."

This woman radiated poise and confidence. Was she really that innocent, shy woman in Atlanta? "Why aren't you looking for a dentist's office to run?" Did she already have a family when they met?

"Renee Rapp said this job would be a perfect fit for me."

"How do you know Renee?" If they were just casual friends it would be easier to explain to Renee why she didn't hire Carla.

"We've been good friends since our daughters played soccer together. I've even been rooked into helping with a fundraiser or two. I'm sure you know how pointless it is to argue with her."

Jamie laughed in spite of her self-consciousness. "She's about as subtle as a steam roller." An argument was exactly what she'd get if she tried to explain to Renee why Carla wasn't perfect for the job. Hadn't she said she'd hire the next even moderately qualified applicant? No, this was crazy. Looking at the picture of her father she knew what he'd say—do what was in the best interest of the clinic. And Penni? She didn't even want to think about that.

"Our billing system is different from what you're used to." Maybe she wouldn't want the job.

Carla looked surprised before she said, "I had no trouble learning Dr. Rose's. I'm sure I could learn yours."

Jamie tapped her pen on the desk. She didn't really have a choice. This wasn't personal. It was business. And what difference did it make if they had a past? Just one night and they'd both moved on. She was being ridiculous. With a competent office manager she'd get this mess cleaned up that much quicker.

She cleared her throat. "Before you consider whether this is the right job for you, I need to tell you something. I fired my office manager last month. She'd been embezzling and committing insurance fraud. I'm under investigation. It's not a pretty picture, and you may not want to get involved."

Carla's eyes held hers and Jamie thought she saw anger. Then she looked over Jamie's shoulder, as if lost in thought. When their eyes met again, there was only kindness. "I'd like to help."

"When can you start?" There, it was done. Jamie looked at her father's picture, pretending his smile signaled his approval.

Carla hesitated. "Tomorrow morning?"

"All right. Betty will show you the ropes." She held the door open as Carla walked out, leaving a trail of perfume—a rich, sweet, flowery scent. Jamie closed the door. Her legs felt like jelly. Had she really just hired the woman who had—

Betty burst through the door, her face one big smile. She squeezed Jamie's shoulders as she kissed her cheek. "She'll be perfect for you." Betty wiped at the corners of her eyes as they filled with tears. "I'll feel better leaving if I know you're in capable hands."

"Tell Frank to plan for your departure." Another reason she'd done the right thing.

Rubbing the back of her neck, she sat and dialed Sheryl. "How's your day, babe?"

"Terrible. I can't believe it. Those…those girls? The ones that paraded their relationship around campus last year? They apparently set a precedent because we have two gay couples this year that are demanding the same privilege."

"The district doesn't think it's a problem," Jamie said carefully.

"It's not that simple. I'm going to get complaints from parents again, including the head of the PTA. He's conservative and powerful and expects to get his way. Oh, why am I trying to explain this to you? You don't understand the politics of having to make hard choices to get what you want."

"Sheryl—"

"I'm going to get screwed again."

"I'm sorry." Why were all of their conversations about work problems? "Look, I was calling to tell you I'm not working late tonight. How about if I pick up Chinese and we cuddle up and watch a movie?"

"I'm meeting another principal for dinner to strategize how I should handle this. I can't lose out on another promotion."

"You can strategize with me. We need to support each other. I hired a new office manager today. She ran a dentist's office for thirteen years. Betty likes her and she's a friend of Renee and I—"

"I don't need to hear her resume. Is she going to help you get your business problem sorted out?"

"No. She'll manage my office while I resolve my business problem." What was the point of explaining to Sheryl that she'd met her before? All that mattered was having a competent office manager. Jamie rubbed her temple. The headache was spreading.

"We're so close to getting it all, Jamie."

"We have each other. Isn't that all we need?"

"You're such a romantic." Sheryl made her sound childish.

"You won't be late, will you?"

"I don't know. Better not wait up for me."

"But…" Jamie heard a woman's voice in the background. Was it her secretary? She didn't know any of Sheryl's staff.

"Gotta go. Another crisis."

"Love you." Jamie turned on the iPod and "That Voice" filled the room. She ignored the sandwich, her appetite gone. For twenty years she'd done the right things, according to her father's standards. Why wasn't she reaping the rewards of all her hard work the way he had? She grabbed the file from the top of the stack and opened it. She'd solved one of her problems by hiring an office manager. Now she had to figure out what Marjorie had done.

She tried to focus, but her mind kept drifting to Carly. She shook her head, irritated with herself. No, Carla. What were the odds of their paths crossing again? She mouthed the lyrics to one of her favorite songs as the present conceded to the past. So long ago, but she'd never forgotten that weekend—the music festival, the unexpected Melissa concert… Maybe those memories were a good thing, reminding her how far she'd come from that scared new doctor. Ten minutes later a knock on her door brought her back to reality. Time to face an afternoon of patients. She shoved out of her chair. *I'm doing my best, Dad.*

Carla clutched the steering wheel tight to stop the trembling in her hands. Had she just agreed to work for the woman who'd been on her mind lately? Sadness replaced the shock. Jamie hadn't recognized her. She fingered her hair. It wasn't much different. That night just hadn't mattered to Jamie the way it had to her. Her heart sank as twenty years worth of fantasies crumbled and left her feeling exposed, and silly. Could she say she'd made a mistake and turn down the job?

Curiosity wiggled its way into her thoughts. What was Jamie like now? Certainly any lingering feelings would fade in the light of current reality. She'd get this crush out of her system or…if Jamie was single, maybe something would spark between them.

Two blocks from the office she realized she was going in the wrong direction. She pulled into a parking lot and sat, engine running, air conditioner blowing cold air on her, as she tried to calm her racing thoughts. How was it possible the woman who'd changed her life was now back in her life? Was it fate? Stranger things than this happened in the romantic comedies she loved. She smiled as she pulled back onto the street. Jamie might not recognize her, but anything was possible.

Chapter Six

Carla pulled into her driveway. She gripped the steering wheel and let the car idle, her thoughts a muddled mess, her body hot in spite of the air conditioning. She wasn't tired from her first full day of work in months but…angry. She hadn't been this angry since her battle last year with the principal who accused Lissa and Steph of flaunting their relationship.

Why had she thought she could be in close proximity to Jamie for eight hours and survive it? She felt like a hormonal teenager—elated by being close to the woman of her fantasies, then close to tears when she searched Jamie's face for any inkling of recognition and found only polite professionalism. It had to be fate to have that night and its importance brought up so clearly at this moment in her life, but what kind of fate? Was Jamie single? She still didn't know. She didn't wear a ring and she'd heard nothing about a partner. Carla shivered. Jamie single scared her more than Jamie with a partner. Then she'd have to act instead of staying safely tucked in fantasies.

On the surface it had been an uneventful day. She'd worked the front desk, setting appointments, taking phone calls, and talking with patients; then with Betty on the insurance billing. After she got up to speed on the billing codes specific to chiropractic, this would be a replica of what she'd done for Dr. Rose. Except for the volume, which was mind-boggling. Jamie saw more patients in a day than Dr. Rose had in a week.

By lunch she'd been ready to jump in her car and not return, sure she couldn't contain the volcano threatening to erupt and incinerate her manners. Feelings fenced inside the boundaries of memory for twenty years were now free to roam. She'd never reacted this way to any of her female friends, not one of Lissa's teachers, not a grocery clerk, not the cute woman who walked dogs in her neighborhood. But a day around Jamie and her body had taken off at a full gallop. Being a lesbian in her mind was one thing. The full force of desire ruling her body was another. It took her a minute to realize Mike was tapping his knuckles on the window. She turned off the ignition and stepped out.

"Are you all right, honey?"

He seemed surprised when she wrapped her arms around his waist. "What are you doing home? I thought you and Rob were going to a Giants game."

"I cancelled. I want to celebrate your new job. Champagne on the patio, and then I'm taking you out to that new Italian restaurant. Hey, why are you crying?"

"Just…everything," Carla said wiping away tears. "Don't mind me. I'm just being silly." Mike took her hand, and they walked up the flagstone path to the front door like two teenagers on a date.

"You're never emotional without a reason. Bad day at work? Boss yell at you? Spilled coffee all over her desk?"

Carla smiled at his attempt to cheer her up. "Something like that."

"Maybe it's not the right job for you."

"Maybe." Mike led her to the patio, where he'd set two glasses and a bottle of her favorite champagne.

"This was so sweet. I can't believe you gave up a date." Carla sat and kicked off her low-heeled shoes, propping her feet in Mike's lap. She groaned as he dug his thumbs in.

"It's fine."

"Can I ask you something personal?"

Mike poured the champagne. "Is there anything you don't know about me?"

Carla took a long sip. The bubbles tickled her throat and the alcohol hit her stomach with a calming thud. "It's different with Rob. In bed, I mean."

Mike choked on his champagne. "How do you mean?"

"It feels right, doesn't it? Like in a movie? The music swells and stars paste themselves to the inside of your eyelids?" Carla brushed hair away from his forehead. Who was she without him? Without their marriage?

"You're a hopeless romantic. I love Rob differently than I love you, but not more."

"I'm not asking for reassurance." Well, maybe she was—the reassurance it felt right to be in the arms of someone who ignited passion in you.

"Yes, it feels right sexually. Can I ask you something?"

"Turnaround?"

"You think you're gay because you've been attracted to a few women over the years."

Carla looked away. Should she tell him about Jamie? He'd understand, but her feelings were so jumbled she couldn't talk about it right now. And if she quit it would be irrelevant.

"But how do you know? I mean, don't you want to have a one-night stand or something? To see what sex with a woman is like?"

Now it was Carla's turn to choke on the champagne. "No. I can't imagine—"

"I know it's scary, but you can't be a lesbian without a girlfriend."

"Yes, I can."

"You won't want to be. You're beautiful and smart and the most loving person I know. You need to find someone who gives you all the passion you deserve."

"Romance novels make it sound easy." Carla's laugh came out choked and she reached for Mike's hand. "I wouldn't know where to begin."

"You can find gay-oriented groups and activities online. Maybe a book club?"

"I never thought past getting Lissa off to college and helping you move out."

"You've always taken care of us. Now you need to focus on you. We have a chance to follow new dreams, honey." Mike squeezed her hand. "Honest dreams. Not what our parents and upbringing told us we should want. Don't make me set you up on blind dates."

Carla smiled. Would she ever find someone as loving and caring as Mike? Passion had been a small sacrifice over the years.

Mike's cell phone rang. "Hi, Lis. Yep, right here."

"Hi, sweetie," Carla said, taking the phone. Her mood lifted at the sound of her daughter's energetic voice.

"Steph has a craving for your spaghetti sauce. How do I make it?"

Carla's world circled around her as she recited the recipe, reminding Lissa to use fresh marjoram and oregano. "Give Steph a hug for us." She handed the phone back to Mike. "I hope the reasons for our divorce don't throw her into a tailspin. For all the books out there on coming out, I've never seen one that explains how to come out to your teenaged daughter."

"She'll be fine. We'll all get through this and be stronger for it. Promise me you'll think about dating?"

"Think. That's all."

Mike kissed her on the cheek. "I made reservations for eight. Plenty of time for a hot bath. I'm sure you need one."

Carla groaned. The last thing she needed was a bath.

CHAPTER SEVEN

One day at a time. Carla repeated Mike's advice as she pulled into the parking lot, the end of her first week eight hours away. Jamie's Highlander was in its usual place. No matter how early she got here with thoughts of making coffee for Jamie, she was always here first, shut in her office going through patient files.

She sighed as she got out of her Subaru. Part of her wanted to go home, crawl back into bed, and waste the day on a romance novel. Fictional love was less heartbreaking—the girl you'd never forgotten scooped you up and carried you off to a future in her arms.

Smoothing the skirt that was one of her favorites and feeling silly for hoping Jamie would like it, she took a deep breath and stepped into the clinic. It was quiet except for Melissa's voice coming from the office to the right, Jamie's office. She hesitated at the closed door. She couldn't lie to herself that she'd hoped to see Jamie, maybe even talk to her alone. Chickening out, she went to the break room and poured coffee into one of the chipped brown mugs. They could use a whole new set of dishes.

Betty's office was behind the front counter, secluded from patients' view but close enough that she could keep an ear on the goings-on. Her office. *If I stay.* Turning on the Mac, she took a sip of coffee and held the cup away as if it'd bitten her. She was a coffee snob, but this wasn't even tolerable. She could remedy that. *If I stay.*

A week and she still wasn't sure. The job was interesting and a good fit for her skills. But to be teased every day with the future she couldn't have kept her off balance in a way she didn't like.

Jamie not remembering her was part of the dilemma, but so was her own cowardice. She'd listened for the staff to mention a partner or any call from one. The thought of Jamie single sent her heart into excited cartwheels, but it would be unprofessional to approach her in a personal way. Ten minutes later she knocked lightly on Jamie's door, her heart pounding. She hadn't been alone with Jamie since the interview.

❖

Jamie had just found something interesting in the patient file when she heard a knock at her door. She was making some progress now that she wasn't struggling to find a new office manager. She expected Don or Sara when she opened the door, but instead Carla stood there, wearing a pretty peach-colored floral-print skirt and matching knit top. Carla in her office took some getting used to. "Good morning."

"Do you have a minute?"

Jamie pulled her eyes from the white sweater draped over Carla's shoulders. "Sure." She closed her eyes for a moment as Carla walked by. She liked that perfume.

"I was entering yesterday's billings and had a question." Carla clasped the patient file in both hands. "I'm sorry to bother you, but Betty's not coming in until after lunch."

Jamie sat down behind her desk. "No bother."

"I've been reading your chart notes so I can get used to your handwriting, and the terminology you use. If I'm reading this file correctly," Carla said, setting it on the desk, "you adjusted this patient and put heat on her neck and did ultrasound on her shoulder. But you checked only the boxes on the billing page for the adjustment and the ultrasound. Did you mean to not bill for the heat pack, or was it an oversight? I want to make sure I'm doing everything right with the billing."

Jamie put her forearms on the desk. Carla's eyes held hers, subtly shaded with eye shadow that brought out the gold tones, and still as kind as they'd been the first time she'd seen them. She was beautiful, an older version of the woman she'd known for a night. She shook off the memories. "Legally I can bill for any physical therapy, but I don't.

I bill for only one. I don't run my clinic like a hospital where they nickel-and-dime insurance companies for every syringe and Band-Aid. At the heart of it, we're charging the patient."

"I'd say that's honorable of you, Dr. Hammond." Carla crossed her legs. "What about the exercise program you noted in the chart? You don't bill for that either?"

"Not usually."

"So you're under-charging the insurance companies."

"I don't look at it like that." Jamie tried to keep the defensiveness out of her voice. This was one area she and her father had been in complete agreement. "I'm a big believer in getting patients to do even a little exercise because it gets them involved in their healing process. I consider it part of the treatment package I provide."

"It's a lot different than the dentist's office." Carla looked at the stack of files on Jamie's desk.

"I'm sure the billing system is very different."

"Yes, that, but I meant what you do. I've never been to a chiropractor so it's all a little mysterious. Several of your patients tried to describe how it works, but each one had a different explanation."

Jamie leaned back in the chair. She always expected it to gently cradle her, but it felt stiff and unyielding. "Some people want me to pin down an exact scientific explanation of how chiropractic works. But you can't pin down healing. So I give them the basics of what a subluxation is, how it affects their health, and how adjusting joints helps relieve their pain."

"Sounds like Greek to me."

"Why don't you shadow me this morning since Betty won't be in. You need to be able to answer patients' questions about what we do." She wasn't thrilled by the idea of having Carla in close proximity all morning, but it was true Carla needed to know what she did.

"I'd love to," Carla said. "I mean, it's probably a good idea for me to know what goes on in the treatment rooms. I'll be in my office if you need me."

Jamie rubbed her face. There was always some awkwardness with a new employee, but the employee wasn't usually someone she'd slept with, and memories cropped up unexpectedly. Like when Carla had pulled her sweater around her shoulders. She was competent and catching on quickly, according to Betty. Patients liked Carla. Her staff liked Carla. If she was honest with herself, she liked Carla. But it was hard to have a past she'd so thoroughly left behind invade her present. And she still nurtured that pang of anger at being used and left.

❖

Carla stood stiffly in the corner of the treatment room, unsure what to do with her arms. Folding them across her stomach seemed unfriendly, yet letting them hang at her sides felt awkward. She clasped them behind her back, but that didn't dissipate the uneasy intimacy of the small room. Three steps and she could be in Jamie's arms.

Carla cringed when the middle-aged woman yelped in pain as Jamie helped her lie facedown on the dark-brown adjusting table. The woman had needed help walking to the treatment room. Carla grimaced, hoping she was never in the same position.

"I know it hurts, Priscilla, but I promise the pain isn't permanent." Everything about Jamie's movements spoke of confidence. The white Oxford shirt was snug over shoulders that were still broad. She laid her hands on the woman's back, and Carla wondered what they would feel like on her body now. A shiver went through her and she crossed her arms.

"But I saw the doctor yesterday and he gave me pills and said it would be a couple weeks before the pain went away."

"I have a different approach than your medical doctor," Jamie said, her hands still moving over the woman's back.

"We're supposed to leave on a cruise next week." Priscilla's voice broke. "I haven't had a vacation in two years."

"Let's see how you do in the next few days. Now I know you've never been to a chiropractor—"

"Is it going to hurt? My husband swears by you, but I'm afraid of that cracking sound."

"It might hurt a little when I do the adjustment."

Priscilla's head popped up from the headpiece.

"It won't hurt more than it already does. I'm going to adjust you using a drop table. You won't hear a cracking sound." Jamie wrote something in the file on the small counter against the wall. "You'll feel me press on your back, and part of the table will drop away under you. Now take a breath and let it out slowly."

Jamie adjusted something on the table and then settled her hands on the woman's back. The movement was so fast Carla almost missed it. A quick thrust and the sound of the table as the section below the woman's abdomen dropped. Jamie's hands never left Priscilla's back, and she continued to work her fingers over the muscles.

"Okay?"

"That wasn't so bad." Priscilla sounded less frightened.

Jamie knelt by the woman's head, her hand on her upper back. "I'm going to send my assistant in. Her name is Marci, and she's going to put an ice pack on your back for half an hour. Then I'll come back and we'll see how you feel. And just between you and me, your husband's a bit of a baby about getting adjusted."

Priscilla laughed. "It doesn't hurt." She lifted her head. "Last night I thought I was going to die when I laughed."

"That's a good sign," Jamie said, before she left the treatment room.

"Interesting table," Carla said as she tried to keep pace with Jamie. It was a silly thing to say, but she felt tongue-tied being in Jamie's presence. Renee swore by her, but would Priscilla really feel better just from that?

"There are a lot of ways to adjust patients," Jamie said as she opened the door to the next treatment room. "I vary my technique based on what I think will be most effective for the patient's problem."

Carla shook hands with a middle-aged man in a business suit as Jamie introduced her as her new office manager. Did she want to be that?

Jamie opened the man's file. "Did you get your HR department to have someone look at the ergonomics of your work station?"

"I haven't had time, Dr. Hammond. I'm working sixty-hour weeks on this new project." The man rubbed the back of his head. "I've been waking up with headaches the last couple weeks."

"You were supposed to come in once a month so the problem I fixed six months ago wouldn't come back."

"I know, I know."

"Your health matters." The man lay on his back on the table without any prompting from Jamie, and she put her hands under his neck.

Carla stood in the corner again, listening as she surveyed the room. It was exactly like the last one, right down to stark-white walls, dark-brown adjusting table, anatomical charts on the walls, and plastic model of a spine sitting on a small cabinet that housed a variety of medical-looking instruments. Carla visualized a soft green on the walls, some art prints, maybe an orchid on the cabinet. *If I stay.* This time Carla heard a popping sound as Jamie adjusted the man's neck.

"Marci will bring in a heat pack."

"I need to get back to—"

"You need to lie here for twenty minutes. Are you doing your exercises?"

"I don't have—"

"Time. I know," Jamie said. "How 'bout if you show your son the exercises and you do them together at night while you're watching the ball game?"

"That might work."

"Don't wait two weeks if the headaches come back. Call your HR department. Today. And set an appointment for next month."

Carla hustled to keep up with Jamie as she went to the next treatment room. "Feel like a babysitter?" Her heart galloped for a minute when Jamie laughed. She wanted to hear more of that. The fun-loving woman she'd known for a night was much too somber, not that she didn't have reason.

"Sometimes," Jamie said. "I get that people are busy, but their well-being is my concern so I advocate for them to pay attention to it."

Carla thought someone should advocate for Jamie to take better care of herself. She watched Jamie treat four more patients and then go back to check on Priscilla.

Jamie put her hands on Priscilla's back and Carla wanted to know what she was feeling. This was nothing like watching a dentist work.

"I want you to wiggle around and lower your knees to the floor." Priscilla's head jerked up again. "Trust me. It'll be easier than twisting to sit up."

Priscilla gingerly did as Jamie instructed. "It's not too bad," she said as Jamie helped her stand. "Wow. It hurts but it's a dull ache." She took a tentative step, and a smile replaced the grimace she'd come in with. "It's not stabbing me."

"Let's not test it too much. Here are the rules, Priscilla. Don't lift anything heavier than your purse. Ice your back for thirty minutes every two hours. Lie down with a pillow under your knees as much as you can today. Sleep that way or put a pillow between your legs if you sleep on your side. Make an appointment for tomorrow. I'll have Marci walk with you to your car. I think you'll be on that cruise."

"I don't know how to thank you, Dr. Hammond," Priscilla said, as she walked down the hall with them.

Carla trailed behind, staring from Jamie to Priscilla. How had that happened? If Jamie lost her clinic because of what Marjorie had done, how many people like Priscilla would have to live with pain? There was more at stake here than her own conflicted feelings. She had to find a way to help Jamie.

Carla sat deep in thought in an uncomfortable chair in the waiting area, quiet now that it wasn't full of patients. Sara had invited her to join the staff for their Friday lunch, but she needed to collect herself before they went out. She was emotionally worn out from so many people in pain, mentally fatigued from listening to the stories patients brought in with them about their families, their jobs, their personal problems. And she didn't bear the burden of responsibility for relieving their pain. How did Jamie do this day after day?

Light filtered in through the blinds on the large windows, casting shadows over the brown carpet and white walls that were the same throughout the clinic. The boring colors fought the warmth and friendliness that both staff and patients contributed. The half-dozen chairs around the coffee table looked like leftovers from an old dining set. And the magazines in the rack mounted to the wall—

Sports Illustrated, *Architectural Digest*, and the like. Some fashion or cooking or gardening magazines would appeal more to women patients. *If I stay.*

Sara sat down next to her. "You look kind of shell-shocked."

"I shadowed Dr. Hammond this morning," Carla said, grateful to have someone to talk to about it. "I like to think of myself as intelligent and open-minded about health care. I get a massage once a month, I do yoga occasionally, and I went to an acupuncturist a couple of years ago for allergies. But…I can't believe what I saw this morning. The first patient who limped in, barely able to stand, and then walked out…that was impressive…but the fifth? Not to mention the patients whose headaches were gone by the time they left…" Carla shook her head.

"Kind of miraculous, isn't it?"

"Yeah." It was hard to match the woman who'd taken her to that concert with this doctor who got people out of pain with her hands.

"My parents took me to a chiropractor from the time I was a kid. I can imagine how strange it seems to someone who's never been adjusted. Come on. I'll adjust you before we go to lunch."

Carla followed Sara to one of the treatment rooms on the east side of the clinic. Sara and Don shared four treatment rooms on this side, and the three treatment rooms on the west side were all Jamie's. The middle of the large space contained the front office, a physical-therapy room, and the break room. The layout had been well thought out and allowed for easy movement of patients and staff. Everything about the office suggested professionalism and efficiency. But the décor annoyed Carla. She had both a flare and love for interior decorating, and ideas were already forming. *If I stay.*

"Dr. Hammond isn't joining us?" Carla asked when they were all seated. She loved the food at Mama Mia and to think Jamie's clinic was just down the street. How had they never run into each other?

"Probably not," Sara said.

Carla tried to set aside her disappointment. She'd wanted to see Jamie outside the clinic.

"She used to come with us but not in a while. A lot of things have changed since…you know, don't you?" Sara asked.

"Yes." Carla detected both concern and uncertainty in Sara's voice.

"She holes up in her office poring over patient files. Don and I offered to help, but she says it's not our problem."

"I have great respect for Jamie," Don added. "I'll be a better doctor because of her mentoring. But she's doing what we tell patients not to do—she's trying to diagnose herself and fix the problem with home remedies. I want to strangle her." He laughed nervously and Sara put her arm around his shoulder, a sight that made them all laugh because of the height difference.

"What was she like before all this?" Carla couldn't help trying to sneak a peek at a different Jamie, a Jamie without those dark circles under her eyes, a Jamie who smiled more.

"Serious, but funny and energetic," Marci said. "It's hard to explain. She takes patient treatment seriously, always demands the best of herself and all of us, but we had this, I don't know, camaraderie in the clinic."

Carla soaked up every tidbit of information about Jamie that came out during the lunch where conversation bounced easily from chiropractic to their personal lives. She liked Jamie's staff and could see herself fitting into the fabric of the clinic. *If I stay.*

"I'm going to order something to take back for Dr. Hammond," Carla said as they were finishing their meal. "Any suggestions?"

"She usually ordered pasta," Don said.

"I'll skip dessert and head back so Dr. Hammond has time to eat," Carla said when the take-out order arrived. Someone needed to make sure Jamie ate lunch. She needed to get her full lunch hour, too. Anyone who wanted to come in got added to Jamie's schedule. Putting a stop to that was another in the list of changes she'd make. *If I stay.*

Jamie answered the knock on her door and stepped back as Carla brushed past her holding a white Styrofoam box. Carla's perfume matched her personality—sweet but not too, subtle, easy to like.

"I took a chance on rigatoni with meat sauce."

"Thank you." Jamie's stomach growled its appreciation. "What do I owe you?"

"Don't be ridiculous. You have fifteen minutes before your next patient." Carla closed the door behind her.

Jamie opened the box and inhaled. Betty often brought her lunch, but Carla doing it surprised her. When was the last time Sheryl came by to have lunch with her? Last year? Jamie tried to remember as she ate the delicious pasta. They were drifting apart and she didn't like it. She needed to get this business mess sorted out so she could pay more attention to her relationship.

Fifteen minutes later she took a deep breath, forcing her focus into the zone she entered when treating patients. It would be eight again before she finished because of the patients added to her schedule. Success came with a price. Her father had never turned anyone away and neither would she.

She started to turn off the iPod but stopped when she heard the opening lines of one of the songs from Melissa's first album. She'd played it that night. Jamie had written down every song she remembered from the concert on the plane ride home. She still had that list and Carla's note. Surely the memories would stop once she got used to seeing Carla every day.

Carla stared at the stack of insurance forms that needed Jamie's signature. Betty must have forgotten to deliver them to Jamie's office on her way out. Everyone had gone home except Jamie, who still had another hour of patients. Maybe she should stay until Jamie finished for the day. She could take payments, work on the billing. Maybe afterward they could go out to dinner.

She heard Jamie's voice from the treatment room as she walked past. Just dinner, she told herself. No expectations. Stepping into Jamie's office, she tried to fit Jamie into the somberness of the room—a heavy Mission-style desk, an old brown leather couch and chairs, dark paneling on the walls, and a hideous Oriental rug.

She set the forms in a neat pile on Jamie's desk next to a stack of patient files. Fingering through them she noticed the most recent was five years ago. Marjorie. How did Jamie manage her patient load and find time to piece together what Marjorie had done?

Carla couldn't resist sitting in Jamie's chair. She closed her eyes as she rubbed her palms over the arms. Jamie might not let Sara or Don help, but she wouldn't be able to turn Carla down. In fact… she wouldn't even have to know what Carla was doing. She could surprise Jamie with…what…the solution to her business problem all neatly tied up in a bow? Silly. But possible.

She opened her eyes and looked at the two pictures on the corner of Jamie's desk. Her heart stopped for a beat and the excitement drained away. The older man was Jamie's father, the facial features unmistakable. The woman in the other picture had to be Jamie's partner, the smiles and arms around each other marking them as a happy couple. Jealousy drove her out of the room, and tears wet her cheeks by the time she reached her car. Whatever hope she'd had of ever being part of Jamie's life tumbled to ruins, leaving her with a terrible emptiness inside.

❖

Jamie was bone tired by the time she pulled into her driveway. Lights were on and the yawn became a smile. She wouldn't be eating alone. Steaks, wine, hot tub…

She set her keys and the grocery bag on the kitchen counter and went to the liquor cabinet. Her father had always ended his day with a Scotch—to ease away the day's tension, he'd say. The voice of some country singer Jamie didn't recognize blasted through the house. Turning down the volume she called out, "How about steaks for dinner?"

"Just a minute," Sheryl said from the bedroom. Jamie hummed along with the lyrics about lovers reunited. Maybe Sheryl would come out in that new silk robe, the one that clung to her body in delicious ways. Maybe give Jamie one of those long, slow kisses, then pull the tie at her throat and slide the robe suggestively off her shoulders and tell her how much she loved her.

"I already ate. Sorry. You're always so late on Fridays." Sheryl walked into the kitchen and spun in a slow circle, her legs bare. A taupe-colored suit jacket covered a gold silk blouse. "Colors good together? On sale at Macy's."

"Very nice." Jamie slipped her hands inside the jacket. Not that robe but… "How about if I help you out of it?"

"I have two more outfits to try on," Sheryl said, a frown settling on her face. "Please don't be mad at me, Jamie, but I'm going up to the city for a leadership seminar tomorrow."

Jamie stepped back. "You'll be home in time for the concert, won't you?"

"Um, that's the thing. It's a two-day seminar—"

"Sheryl." Jamie's disappointment changed to anger. "I bought those tickets for you."

"I know, but I just found out about it this morning. The speaker's a leader in the field."

"It was supposed to be a date, Sheryl, where we focus on each other and not on business problems or promotions. I'm scared we're drifting apart." Jamie waited for Sheryl to come to her, wrap her arms around her and say, "Of course I'll go to the concert with you."

"We're not drifting apart. We're pursuing our goals."

"You've been going to seminars for years. How does one more make any difference?" Her question came out harsher than she intended.

"Nice support." Sheryl's voice was clipped. She folded her arms across her stomach, and Jamie almost laughed at Sheryl's attempt to look officious with no pants on. "After I get the promotion I won't have to work so hard and we can do more things together. You're the one who just got home."

Jamie stared at Sheryl's feet, at the nail polish that was a different color than it had been last week. How often did she get pedicures?

"We're so close to getting—"

"Everything we want. I know." Fatigue engulfed Jamie. Was she overreacting? Maybe the knowledge that her business wasn't as solid as she'd thought was making her look for problems in her relationship that weren't there.

"I'll be home Sunday afternoon. Doing things separately lets us miss each other." Sheryl kissed her cheek and took a sip from her glass.

Jamie nodded. They'd had too many opportunities to miss each other lately, but it wasn't all Sheryl's fault. "We'll do a concert another time."

"Come keep me company while I pack."

Jamie stepped away from Sheryl, away from the irritating perfume. "I'm going to barbecue." She unwrapped the steaks. "Come join me if you want."

"You know I don't like being out there at night. Too many bugs."

Jamie watched Sheryl walk away, resisting the urge to follow her. Don was right, and tonight she was going to take care of herself.

CHAPTER EIGHT

Carla sat in the boarding area waiting to see if she'd get a seat on the eight o'clock flight to San Diego. Her carry-on was on the seat next to her, a buffer against the middle-aged man in jeans and cowboy boots who looked like he wanted to engage her in conversation. He better not ask her if she was all right. If she hadn't let Jamie into her life in another airport she wouldn't be sitting in this one, an emotional wreck because she'd seen a picture of Jamie's partner. The tousled, sun-bleached blond hair, those piercing blue eyes, the smiles on their faces. Of course Jamie would have a partner. Some start to her new life. Right back where she'd been twenty years ago—wanting someone she couldn't have.

By the time she'd driven home she was crying one minute, then laughing at the ridiculousness of the situation the next. Thinking of Lissa was the only thing that calmed her. She'd changed into her favorite white blouse and new jeans, tossed some things in a bag, and scribbled a note to Mike: "Gone to visit the girls. Will call tomorrow."

Could she find love again? Not unless she looked for it. The thought shriveled her. Any doubts she'd harbored over the years that she'd fallen in love with Jamie in a single night had been put to rest this week. That part of romantic comedies was true. But the picture of Jamie and her partner squelched any fantasies Carla had to admit she'd been encouraging. She wouldn't have a second chance. She checked her watch and tucked the book into her purse, too keyed up to read. When her name was called she practically sprinted to the counter. She let out her breath when the woman handed her a boarding pass.

❖

Carla stood in front of the apartment door for several minutes, clutching the bag over one shoulder and her purse over the other. Now that she was here she felt embarrassed.

"Mom! Oh, my gosh, what are you doing here? Nothing's wrong—"

"No." Carla stroked Lissa's cheek. She had her father's thick, dark hair, loose from its customary ponytail. Her eyes were Carla's. The smile was all Lissa's. "I'm sorry. I should have called—"

"Don't be silly, Carla," Steph said, stepping past Lissa and hugging her before pulling her through the door. "You don't need a reservation."

Lissa stepped into her arms and Carla's heart settled. This was her life. "You've lost weight. Are you two cooking? You can't let soccer and school work interfere with taking care of yourselves."

Steph held up a container. She was taller than Lissa, with hair as dark but bright-blue eyes. "Spaghetti," she said. "Lissa's been experimenting with the recipe you gave her. Don't worry about us. We know what's important." She came around the counter and wrapped her arm around Lissa.

"You two look…" Carla frowned. "All dressed up. New blouse?" Carla straightened Lissa's collar. "Orange is a great color on you."

Lissa looked at Steph. "Um…we were going out tonight."

"To a movie? Isn't it kind of late?"

"To a bar, Mom. A couple of girls I met in my English class invited us to meet them."

"We'd like to make some friends to hang out with," Steph said.

"I'll call 'em and tell them we can't make it."

"I'll go with you," Carla said. Her cheeks felt hot as she walked to the kitchen.

"Mom! It's a lesbian bar. Noisy. Crowded. Dancing. I'll bet you can't remember the last time you were in a straight bar."

"Oh, for heaven's sake, Lissa." Carla glared at her over the counter that divided the kitchen from the living room. "Do you think I'd be uncomfortable, or are you embarrassed to have your mom along?"

"It's just…" Lissa looked at Steph, who shrugged.

"We'd love to take you out on the town," Steph said.

"Good." Stephanie's crooked grin was infectious, and Carla relaxed. "I could use a glass of wine. Wait a minute. How are you two getting into a bar? Don't tell me you have fake ID's."

"No, Mom." Lissa rolled her eyes. "The bar's inside a pizza place."

"Great. I'm starving." A lesbian bar. Excitement replaced the disappointment of finding out Jamie had a partner.

❖

"How's work?" Lissa asked as they stood in line outside a brick building with a red neon OPEN sign in the window.

"I'm not sure it's right for me." Carla clamped down on the hundreds of emotions attached to that statement. The air was crisp, and she tugged her sweater around her shoulders as she realized she was in a line of women, lesbians, waiting to get into a bar. She tried not to think about what Jamie and that woman were doing tonight. Her stomach felt jittery, and she tapped her foot to the beat of the music coming from the open door. How would she react to women dancing with each other? She tingled with nervous anticipation.

"Sure you're all right, Mom?" Lissa asked, as the two women in front of them kissed.

"It'll be fun," Carla said, mostly to reassure herself.

Lissa and Steph entwined their hands, and Lissa's eyes softened when Steph whispered something to her. Love. Carla was glad her daughter had found it.

"Wow," she said, when they stepped through the door. Pictures of actresses covered every inch of the walls, many autographed. She looked for Meg Ryan's picture as she followed Lissa and Steph past booths where people sat eating delicious-looking pizzas.

As they stepped through a burgundy curtain at the back of the restaurant a flush crawled up her throat, and she wrapped both hands around her purse strap. She couldn't scan the room fast enough. Women. Everywhere. A gorgeous black woman stood nearby wearing a T-shirt with FEARLESS LOVE in gold letters across the front. A Melissa fan. Carla returned her smile.

"Are you okay with this, Mom?"

"I'm fine, sweetie. Let's find your friends, and then I'll get a glass of wine and order pizza." Carla took a deep breath, and the smell of body heat and perfume poured into her. She relaxed like a cat that had found its spot in the sun as she followed the girls to a table just off the dance floor. Two dark-haired women, one with half-a-dozen silver studs in one ear and the other wearing a tight black tank top, jumped up and greeted them with hugs for the girls and a "Wow, how cool," for Carla.

Carla sipped her wine and nibbled on the tomato-and-pesto pizza that was a big hit as she kept her eyes on the crowded dance floor. She had no idea who the singer was, but the beat was perfect for dancing, and she couldn't keep her feet from bouncing as she watched Lissa and Steph. This was the first time she'd seen Lissa dance, and she added it to the other firsts—haircut, kindergarten, soccer game. The song ended and most of the floor emptied when a slow song began. Lissa moved into Steph's arms and tears stung Carla's eyes. They were a striking couple, and Carla hoped with all her heart they stayed together for the rest of their lives.

"Would you like to dance?" The woman in front of her sported a wide smile and inviting brown eyes, topped by dark bangs. And looked about twelve. "I'm Kristen." She slid onto the chair next to Carla. Okay, maybe twenty.

"I'm Carla, and I'm here with my daughter and her girlfriend."

"Cool," Kristen said. "I like older women. I'm thirty."

Carla didn't know whether to be flattered or embarrassed. No one but Jamie had ever flirted with her. It was strange but nice, she decided, as Kristen amused her with stories of her job as a dog trainer.

"So…" Kristen said as the music changed. "Dance?" She stood, flashing a smile and holding out her hand.

Carla broke into a smile of her own and decided to do something daring. She loved to dance. Standing, she took Kristen's hand. The feel of it—warm, soft, small—sent heat up her arm. It felt right. Not perfect. That would have taken Jamie's hand. She wiggled her fingers at Lissa, whose mouth dropped open as she stared at her. "I'm fine," she mouthed. Kristen stopped and Carla bumped into her back. Her breasts touched strong muscles that contracted beneath the tight blue tank top. Her nipples responded and Carla drew a deep breath. Yes. This was where she belonged. Even without Jamie.

Kristen took the lead and they moved to the music, a boisterous song with a definite dance beat. Carla couldn't understand the words, didn't know the band, and hadn't danced anything but ballroom in twenty years. Kristen held Carla's hips and, much as Jamie had that night, guided her. She felt Lissa's eyes on her as she tried to relax into Kristen's hands. She put her hands on Kristen's shoulders and melted into the sensations of soft skin and strong muscles, perfume, and women's voices all around her. Her body hummed with excitement, a sexual excitement she didn't know she was still capable of feeling. The disappointment and resentment she'd boarded the plane with faded a little.

"That was fun, Carla," Kristen said when they returned to the table. "I don't want to monopolize your time, but if you want to dance again I'm over there with some friends." She pointed to a table across the room.

"Thank you."

Lissa's eyes widened. Carla held up her hand. "I'm a grown-up. It's harmless and I'm having fun."

"Okay, Mom, but remember, I have my phone. If you get too crazy I'm going to take pictures of you and blackmail you into letting me get a motorcycle."

Carla kissed Lissa on her cheek, then wiped a bit of cheese off her lip. The other two girls were funny and kept them all laughing. They'd been together about as long as Lissa and Steph, high-school sweethearts also, and Carla hoped the four of them ended up friends. Her ears stayed on the conversation flying around the table, but her eyes stayed on the dance floor.

Questions bombarded her. Could she find someone she was attracted to? Not the way she was to Jamie but...She stopped at that thought. Hadn't she spent twenty years in a relationship with someone she loved with all her heart but didn't love passionately? She couldn't do that again. Musky perfume hit her a moment before a voice said near her face, "Would you like to dance?"

A woman about her age with spiky blond hair, slate-blue eyes, and a little too much makeup stood next to her. A sleeveless blue blouse and tight jeans showed off a nice figure. The smile was as warm as the hand on her shoulder.

"All right," Carla said, ignoring Lissa's raised eyebrows. She'd have a lot of explaining to do after she and Mike talked to her about the divorce, but it would be a challenging discussion even without this night, and Carla desperately needed this.

The music shifted from a rock beat to a slow dance tune as she and the blonde found a spot in the crowd. "My luck," the woman said, holding up her arms. "I'm Vanessa."

"Carla." She stepped into the woman's toned arms, and as the long song evolved, the space between them disappeared until they were cheek to cheek. Conflicting emotions roiled inside Carla. Her body responded to the woman's gentle touch, her confident lead, her perfume, the softness of her body. She absorbed the pleasure of being in this woman's arms. If only they were the right arms. The song ended and Vanessa kissed her on the cheek. "Another?"

Carla smiled back and nodded. They danced three more fast dances. Carla was hot and sweat trickled down her front as Vanessa walked her to her table. "I'll be right back," Vanessa said. Five minutes later she placed a glass of water and a fresh glass of wine in front of Carla. "Do you live in San Diego?" she asked, squatting next to Carla.

"San Jose. I'm visiting my daughter." She nodded toward Lissa. A slow smile and a mischievously raised eyebrow took Vanessa's face from attractive to seriously attractive. Carla gulped.

"Looks like we're neighbors. I live in Los Altos. I'd love to get together with you."

Carla gulped again as Vanessa rubbed up and down her lower back, discreetly out of sight of Lissa.

"My daughter's in college back in Boston. I envy you having yours so close. Here's my card. Call me. Soon."

Carla stared at her hips as she walked away. Heat rushed to her cheeks when Vanessa turned around and winked at her. She looked at the card—attorney. As a child, when Carla was upset about a fracture with a best girlfriend, her mother would say there were plenty more fish in the sea. Maybe for once her mother was right. She fingered the card as she replayed the feel of Vanessa's hands on her.

"Ready to go, Mom?"

Carla closed her hand around the card. "Sure." Her second chance with Jamie wasn't going to happen, but maybe another chance at passion was waiting for her. Determination shoved aside her disappointment. She wasn't waiting the rest of her life for what she wanted.

CHAPTER NINE

Carla stood at the kitchen counter, nursing her second cup of coffee. It was lukewarm, but at least it was Kona.

Mike set aside the morning paper. "I'm sorry the job isn't what you wanted."

"I am, too." Carla wiped off the counter for the third time. "I'll stay until Dr. Hammond can hire a replacement."

"You won't have any problem finding the right job, honey."

Carla squeezed the sponge and fought back tears. She'd never see Jamie again. Was she being unfair? Childish? Maybe, but she couldn't be around Jamie knowing they wouldn't have a second chance. "Don't forget to pick up more boxes." Carla poured the coffee down the drain. "I want to pack stuff you don't use all the time. Eighteen years in this house. Where did the time go?"

Mike kissed her cheek. "Eighteen great years. I'm glad you're keeping it. Can I have visiting privileges?"

"Are you kidding? You're still my plumber, lawn mower—"

"I'm not listening."

Carla swatted at him as he grabbed his briefcase. She was going to miss his playfulness. Less than a month and he'd be gone. Then what would she do?

Carla rehearsed what to say as she made the fifteen-minute drive to the office. "It's not the right job for me." "My skills aren't what you need." "I'm not a good fit with your staff." She laughed at that one. "I've decided to spend more time with my daughter." Plausible. Did it matter what excuse she gave? "I can't work for you because I'm in love with you and you don't remember me and you have a partner." Her throat tightened.

The driver behind her tapped his horn. She'd missed the light change. In the bar she'd decided to find the life she wanted, but that determination had slipped away on the flight home. She wanted love and passion and all the trimmings, but could she make room in her heart for someone else when Jamie filled up all the space? Out of sight, out of mind was the saying, right? She needed to be away from what she couldn't have.

Carla put her purse in her office and walked to Jamie's office. The door was closed. She was about to knock when she heard Jamie speaking in a loud, angry-sounding voice.

"I have talked to your legal department. That's my point. How can I prove I didn't commit fraud when you won't provide me with the EOBs so I can compare what was billed with what should have been billed? I've called six times this month alone, and each time I have to talk to a different person and—I know I have a time limit to prove I didn't—No, don't put me on hold again. Damn it!"

Carla flinched when the phone slammed down and backed away from the door when Jamie uttered another expletive. She retreated to her office, her thoughts in tatters. She wrapped her sweater tighter around her shoulders and was deep in thought when a voice startled her.

"You don't have to come in early." Jamie's voice was tight and she looked tired.

Carla gripped the edge of the desk to keep from wrapping her in a hug. That was someone else's job. "I like the quiet before everyone comes in." Maybe tomorrow would be a better day to tell her she was leaving. "Gives me a chance to get a jump on the billing before I have to put out fires." She could at least get the billings caught up before she told her.

"Never a dull moment. Betty's last day is Friday. Will you be all right on your own?"

The perfect opening. Carla hesitated.

"If not…" Jamie's face tightened, and her brown eyes were full of worry.

"I'll be fine, Dr. Hammond." Jamie's face relaxed, and Carla created a smile she hoped looked genuine. The smile faded as the truth she'd been avoiding poked through. Deep down she wanted to help Jamie. Deep down she wanted a little more time with her. She trembled. She wanted so much to tell Jamie they'd met once. She wanted her to say, "Oh, my gosh. I didn't recognize you. Of course I remember that night." If she laughed and said, "We had some fun, didn't we?" that would be enough.

❖

Sitting in her chair, Jamie stared at her father's picture. *One problem solved, Dad.* Now, how did she solve her relationship problem?

All weekend she'd been plagued by loneliness—not just short-term, Sheryl's-gone-for-the-weekend loneliness, but a deep sense of aloneness she realized had been there for a while. She fingered the blue mug with What's Up, Doc? hand-lettered on the side in Penni's curly script and took a sip of the lukewarm coffee. It would be terrible even if it were hot. Would the end of the embezzlement problem breathe new life into her relationship? It had to. She couldn't shake the feeling they were in trouble.

Sheryl had come home jazzed by her seminar, but instead of sharing what happened with Jamie over dinner and a glass of wine, she'd given her a quick kiss on the cheek and said she needed to work while it was all fresh in her mind. She'd still been typing away in the office when Jamie went to bed. How had they ended up living their lives in separate rooms of their home?

Jamie looked at the stack of patient files on her desk. It seemed taller every day this mess went on. She was tired of arguing with insurance companies. She was tired of losing precious time with Sheryl. Wasn't she supposed to be reaping the rewards of middle age instead of struggling everywhere in her life? Fighting to hang on to what she'd worked for? What mattered? She turned up the volume on the iPod and didn't care if it boomed through the clinic. Her first patient was still an hour away.

CHAPTER TEN

Jamie heard someone come in the back door as she stood in Carla's office, searching through patient files, pulling out ones she wanted to examine. She tossed another one on the pile. Without the EOBs, she was looking for a needle in a haystack, and she was tired of making calls to the insurance companies that left her feeling like she'd already been tried and convicted. How could she not have noticed EOBs were missing from patient files? Or had Marjorie known she was about to get caught and tried to cover her tracks by destroying them? She clenched her jaw, barely containing the urge to punch the file cabinet. She could lose everything she'd worked for. Why had Marjorie done this to her?

She took a sip of coffee and grimaced. It was an insult to drink, but the caffeine kept her going. Maybe she should turn over more of the burden to her accountant. She slammed the file cabinet shut. No. She'd allowed this mess to happen right under her nose, and she was going to clean it up. The room smelled faintly of Carla's perfume and she paused for a moment, resting her hand on the sweater draped over her chair.

"Good morning."

Jamie startled. Carla was standing in the doorway in the same suit and peach blouse she'd worn to the interview. Not even two weeks, but it seemed like she'd always been here.

"What? Do I have lipstick on my blouse?"

Jamie realized she'd been staring. "No." She picked up her coffee and the files and backed out of the office, trying not to brush against Carla. "You really don't have to come in early."

"I brought Kona coffee and thought I'd get a pot made before you got here. Have you ever tried it?"

"It's my favorite."

"Good." Carla set her purse on her desk. "I brought back ten pounds from Hawaii. I don't know what I was thinking. Why don't we dump that out and I'll bring you a fresh cup?"

"Um, okay." Jamie handed her the mug and took the files to her office.

A few minutes later Carla set a mug of coffee on Jamie's desk, holding another one. "Try this."

Jamie took a long sip. "God, that's good. So, you were in Hawaii recently?" It seemed polite to ask.

"I don't want to take up your time."

"It'll give me an excuse to enjoy the coffee." And maybe she wanted a peek inside Carla's life.

Carla sat across from Jamie and crossed her legs. "I took Lissa and Steph over for a month. Graduation present."

"Is Steph your other daughter?" Jamie had always wanted to go to Hawaii.

"Lissa is my only daughter. Steph is her girlfriend."

"Um…good for them." Jamie looked away. She'd assumed the conversation would be about vacation destinations. What were the odds Carla's daughter was a lesbian?

"I agree. They met freshman year on a soccer team. Started out rivals and ended up best friends."

"I remember quite a few friendly rivalries that turned into friendships when I played softball at that age."

"The summer before their senior year they realized their feelings were more than friendship. It was an interesting summer—teenage angst coupled with coming-out issues—but they were clearly falling in love, and I encouraged them to follow their hearts."

"Commendable," Jamie said, unsure what else to say. Had someone told Carla she was a lesbian? Should she tell her?

"Coming out was harder on her than it was on me. I've always supported gay rights." Carla's gaze was uncomfortably fixed on her. "It was also an interesting year. I had my first experience of being called to the principal's office."

Jamie's heart skipped a beat and she swallowed the coffee wrong. She knew who that principal was. She coughed, wishing she hadn't invited this conversation.

"Are you all right?"

"The caffeine just hit me wrong." Jamie sank back into the chair. She cringed, remembering some of the things Sheryl had said about the girl's mother. "Go on," she said cautiously, unable to deny she was curious to hear the other side of the story.

"Their principal demanded they stop showing affection in public because she'd received complaints from parents that their behavior was offending other students. The girls are conservative with PDAs so that didn't make sense. And her unwillingness to support their rights outraged me. We threatened legal action against the school district, and she finally backed down."

"And now your daughter is in college?" If Jamie was doing the math right, Carla already had a family when they met. She stared at Carla's hands. *Why hadn't she been wearing that ring? If I'd known...*

"They both are. At San Diego State. I miss them so much." Tears filled her eyes. "Aghh. Ignore me." She pulled a Kleenex out of her pocket and dabbed her eyes. "This empty-nest stuff is hard to get used to." Carla stood. "I'll get to work on the insurance stuff." She turned back at the door. "I'm glad you like the coffee."

Jamie nodded, but her thoughts were on the disaster this would become when Sheryl found out who her new office manager was. The relief she'd felt at having her office-manager problem solved flew out the window. The thought of replacing Carla without Betty's help was too overwhelming to consider. Sheryl never came by the office. Could she make this work until she got the embezzlement problem under control?

Jamie slammed a file down on her desk and opened it. *When do I get a break?*

❖

Marci was standing in her doorway and Carla signaled that she'd be off the phone in a minute. "Thank you so much, darlin'. Southern gals gotta stick together. You get me those billing records, and I'll keep you in See's candy for the rest of your life."

Carla set the phone back in its cradle and crossed her fingers. She'd been calling insurance companies every spare minute, often from home before she came in, trying to find someone who would help her get copies of what Marjorie had submitted. Most times she got the run-around, but when she heard Pearl's accent, she'd played the Southern card to the max.

"We're all taking Betty out to dinner tomorrow to celebrate her retirement. You'll come, won't you?"

"Sure."

"Seven at Maggiano's. Spouses included."

"Oh, gosh, I can't. I forgot. We have tickets to a play." Carla looked back at her computer screen. Her ears always burned when she lied, but she couldn't face meeting Jamie's partner.

"That's too bad. We'll miss you." Marci squeezed her shoulder. "We're all glad you're here, Carla. The office is running smoother than it has in a long time, and Jamie seems less stressed."

"Thanks." Carla sighed. Maybe she should call Vanessa. She could use another dose of dancing. If only she could banish her attraction to Jamie. Shaking her head she entered the data for the next patient. Might as well finish up today's billings.

An hour later Carla locked the file cabinets. It had been a productive day. She was caught up on current billings and had made progress in her plan to help Jamie. As soon as those EOBs got here she could match what was billed against what should have been billed. She had a pretty good idea how Marjorie had been embezzling. Jamie probably had the same suspicions, but Carla wanted facts to present to her.

She pulled her sweater from the back of the chair and picked up the insurance forms Jamie needed to sign. Everyone else had left, and Jamie had retired to her office after her last patient twenty minutes ago. She knocked and, when she didn't get an answer, went in. She was lying on the couch, eyes closed, hands clasped over her stomach. Carla watched her for several minutes before clearing her throat. Jamie didn't stir.

Standing over her, she studied the woman whose face held a slight frown even in sleep. She wanted to sit and cradle her head in her lap, run her fingers through her hair. Was it as soft as she remembered?

Lifting the file off Jamie's chest and not seeing a blanket, she laid her sweater over her. Her heart filled with the same regret she'd felt that morning watching a younger Jamie sleep. Her mouth went dry and her pulse pounded in her throat. She wanted to touch Jamie again with a ferocity that scared her.

Carla rushed out of the building breathing hard, aching with need, aroused in a way she hadn't been in twenty years. Why had she thought she could set Jamie aside and move on with her life?

She drove home in a fury of desire, barged through the front door, and threw her purse on the dining table. Kicking off her shoes, she strode down the hall to her bedroom, pawing at the buttons on her blouse. The bra confining her breasts was unbearable, and she bit back a curse of frustration as she ripped it off over her head, then discarded her pants in a heap. She rummaged through the CDs on the dresser and put one in the CD player. Melissa. It didn't matter which one; they all connected her to Jamie.

She turned on the faucet to the Jacuzzi tub, pacing, surrounded by memories of another tub, another anxious wait for it to fill. She cupped her breast, massaged it, and pinched her nipple, groaning with frustration. It wasn't her hand she wanted on her aching flesh. She slipped her other hand inside her panties and dove between her lips. Spreading her wetness over her clit, she started the stroking that would release her from the need burning through her.

Tossing her panties aside she slid into the steaming hot water. She wanted to feel scalded. As the jets pounded her back she stroked herself to a hard, fast orgasm, devoid of any pleasure other than release. Tears fell into the water surging against her. She wanted all the passion she'd missed out on. She wanted Jamie. Ten minutes later she stepped out of the tub, angry. No more memories.

Bundled in her favorite pink chenille robe, she marched to the kitchen. Wine first. She opened the refrigerator. Not going to mope over what she couldn't have. Pasta. She set out eggs and flour. Going to get on with her life. Pesto. She went to her backyard for the last of the basil. There were other women besides Jamie.

At midnight she sat down, exhausted, and stared at the kitchen. Cookies covered the counters. More cookies were bagged and in the freezer. What was she going to do with enough spaghetti sauce to feed ten people? She turned out the lights, set the coffeemaker, and walked to her bedroom, wishing Mike wasn't out of town. She didn't want to be alone in the house, alone with memories of laughter and good times.

She slid beneath soft yellow sheets. Maybe she'd get a smaller bed so it didn't feel so empty. She hadn't thought about redecorating the bedroom, but that would give her something to do. She reached for the romance novel on the nightstand. After a few pages she set it aside. She was tired of reading about passion instead of living it, and she was tired of reading about heterosexual romance. She'd seen a paperback on the counter in the girls' apartment, surprised the cover showed two women embracing, even more surprised when Steph explained about lesbian fiction.

What else didn't she know about? She needed to look at that website and order some lesbian romance novels. That was something she could do for her future. Sadness engulfed her. Did she want a future that consisted of reading about women falling in love? She wanted to feel love—her lips raw from kissing, her skin flushed from orgasms, her fingers wet from…She turned off the light, hugged her pillow to her chest, and cried for the uncertainties of her future.

Jamie woke with a start. What was that fragrance? Carla. Sitting up, she looked around the room. The sweater fell to her lap. She fingered it and then held it to her face. Was it the same perfume she'd worn that night? It was close enough to bring a flood of memories. Tossing it on the coffee table, she fled the office.

She pulled into her driveway expecting to see lights on. Sheryl didn't have a meeting tonight. There was a note on the kitchen counter: "Went to a movie with a friend." She crumpled it. This had to stop. She needed to get out of the office at a decent hour. They needed to spend time together. Her stomach growled. She should have picked up takeout, but she'd assumed Sheryl had gotten dinner for them. She poured a generous amount of Glenlivet into a tumbler and took a long sip. It landed hard in her stomach.

Her loafers made a hollow tapping sound on the hardwood floor as she walked to the bedroom. She flopped on the bed and lay on her back. Loneliness crept over her like a malevolent shadow as she rubbed her palms over the bedspread. It was satiny and soft, and she liked the deep blue and burgundy. It was the only thing she'd picked out in the room Sheryl had decorated—pale-blue walls, light-colored furniture too modern for Jamie's tastes. Jamie remembered pulling the bedspread from the shopping bag, tossing it over the bed, and the two of them jumping on top of it and making out.

There used to be lots of moments like that. Would they have them again when her business problems were resolved and Sheryl got her promotion? Could they wait that long? She ran her hand over her abdomen. It was still flat but not as defined as it had been in her youth. Did Sheryl still find her attractive? She fingered the hair at her temples. She'd do something about the gray. She was starting to doze when her eyes snapped open. Sheryl's car. Vaulting off the bed she hurried to open the door for her.

"Wow, you look terrific." Jamie followed Sheryl to the kitchen, taking in the tight jeans and apple-green scoop-neck T-shirt. "God, I'm happy to see you." She wrapped her arms around Sheryl, lifted her off the ground, and kissed her. "How was the movie?"

"Good. A romance. You wouldn't have liked it."

"I like romance." She kissed her way up Sheryl's neck.

"Tickles." Sheryl pulled away and filled a glass with ice from the refrigerator door. "I have some good news about the promotion."

"You got it? Why didn't you call me?" When Sheryl smiled, Jamie saw the happy woman she'd fallen love with.

"I didn't get it," Sheryl said, "but I got ten minutes alone with the superintendent when I went by the district office today, and he said he liked my preliminary plan for revamping the advanced-placement curriculum. And…" A smirk replaced the smile. "He said that just between the two of us he supported how I handled that situation last year."

Jamie's stomach dropped. She didn't like the way those girls had been treated. She didn't like that Carla's version differed from Sheryl's. "Are you sure—"

"He said I'm the kind of person he wants on his team." Sheryl pulled her shoulders back. "I'm the front-runner for the new position."

"That's great, babe." Shouldn't she just share this moment of victory with Sheryl?

"Do you know what that means?"

Jamie hoped it meant spending more time together. She looked away from Sheryl's hungry expression. How had the determination she'd once admired turned into this obsession that made her feel irrelevant? "Do you really want his backing if he doesn't support who you are?" Sheryl's mouth tightened. "Isn't there someone at the district office, maybe someone gay, who could…I don't know, mentor you or advocate for you?"

"I thought you supported me."

"I do." Jamie stepped toward her. "I have a patient, a retired high-school principal, who's a lesbian. I could talk to her. Maybe she knows someone at the district who—"

Sheryl eyes softened. "Oh, Jamie. Always trying to help. I appreciate it, but honestly, his backing is all that matters. If he wants me on his team, I'm in."

Jamie closed her eyes when Sheryl kissed her. She wrapped her arms around Sheryl's waist and held her tight. Isn't this what mattered? Being connected? Sheryl was right. She deserved to have her dreams fulfilled, and it was her job to support that. She burrowed her face against Sheryl's neck. *I wish she'd change perfumes.*

"I'm so close to having what I want. By the time I'm your age I'll be as successful as you." Sheryl stepped away from her and poured Diet Coke into the glass.

"Middle age isn't all it's cracked up to be," Jamie said, yawning. Had she ever been this tired?

"Are you making progress with your business problem? I don't want anything to go wrong this time."

"I won't let it interfere with your promotion." Sheryl's smile softened the hard knot in her stomach.

"Will you take me on a celebration trip after it's official? Maybe New York? Now there's a city for shopping." Sheryl's eyes sparkled.

Jamie's hopes rose. "Sure." They'd get back to how they used to be. Soon. She pulled Sheryl into a hug. Their bodies still fit well together. "And in the meantime we need to talk about where to go for our anniversary."

"That's next year."

"I guess technically that kiss was just after the stroke of midnight." Jamie stroked Sheryl's back. "Ten years. Now that's something to celebrate. How about Hawaii for two weeks over your Christmas break?" Sheryl stepped out of her arms.

"Two weeks is a long time."

"Haven't you been complaining that I work too much? Come on, babe. Sun, beaches, just the two of us—"

"The timing's not good. I don't want to be gone and miss an opportunity that could seal the promotion for me."

Jamie watched Sheryl walk away, her optimism sliding away with each step. What could she say to get Sheryl to put their relationship first? Worry settled in the pit of her stomach as she followed Sheryl to the bedroom.

Chapter Eleven

Jamie smiled at the laughter coming from the break room. Sara and Don were teasing Betty about abandoning them for silly things like vacations. This is how her office used to be. Poking her head in the doorway, she asked, "Has anyone seen Carla?"

"She had errands to do," Betty said, her words garbled by the bite of sandwich in her mouth.

"Join us," Sara said.

"I was going to—"

"Come on." Sara pulled out the chair next to her. "We'll loan you a sandwich."

"How can I refuse an offer like that?" Jamie sat down between Sara and Betty. "So, last chance to change your mind," she said to Betty.

"I love you, Jamie, but not as much as my marriage." She handed Jamie a sandwich. "No iced tea. You'll have to settle for coffee."

"Speaking of which," Don said, "who upgraded our coffee? This is great." He set a cup in front of Jamie and sat across from her.

"You can thank Carla for that," Jamie said.

"And I guess we can thank her for the beautiful bouquet on the front counter," Sara said. "Just about every patient has commented on it."

"She brought the flowers in from her own garden," Betty said.

Half an hour later Jamie pushed back from the table, full from the sandwich and revived by the conversation.

❖

Carla came back late from lunch. She'd made up a nonexistent errand as an excuse to get out of the office. Away from Jamie. She ignored the patients in the reception area. She usually made it a point to talk to them, but she just couldn't today. She reached for the Kleenex in her sweater pocket as she ducked into her office. It was the sweater she'd put over Jamie last night, neatly folded on her desk this morning.

This wasn't going to work. She'd planned to tell Jamie first thing this morning, but Betty kept hugging her and telling her how glad she was that Jamie was in such good hands. Monday. She'd tell her Monday and offer to stay until she found someone else. The phone rang, and she blew her nose before picking it up.

"Carla, it's Pearl. We spoke the other day about your insurance billing problem."

"Yes, I remember."

"I have good news for you. I'm going to get you those EOBs."

"How long?"

"A couple of weeks."

Carla clenched the receiver. "That's great." She forced cheerfulness into her voice. Yesterday she would have been thrilled. After last night all she wanted was to be far away from Jamie and her problems.

Jamie let the hot water sluice over her back as she bent her head forward to rinse the shampoo from her hair. She indulged in a few more minutes of the gloriously hot water, moving her shoulders around to loosen the knots in her traps. Maybe Sheryl would come home before her meeting. She tried to remember the last time they'd showered together.

"Are you almost done? I need to freshen my makeup and the mirror's all fogged."

Jamie opened the shower door. "I was just thinking about you. I'll be out in a minute. Unless you want to join me?"

"No." Sheryl pulled makeup jars from the drawers.

Jamie shut the door and turned the faucet to cold, bracing herself for the shock. She was shivering when she stepped onto the bath mat and wrapped a towel around her. Sheryl put a dab of one of her hair products on her palms and stroked it through her hair. "You look good with short hair." She did, but Jamie missed the shoulder-length waves she loved to sift through.

"Thanks."

Jamie dried off as she watched Sheryl apply blush to cheeks that already looked rosy. For all the job stress, Sheryl always looked fresh. She hung the towel on the bar and wrapped her arms around Sheryl's waist. Sheryl outlined a lid with eyeliner. It was a mystery to Jamie how she drew such a perfect line. "I love watching you put on makeup." She rubbed Sheryl's belly in a slow circle and then undid the button under her fingers.

"You'll make me smudge."

"I'd like to do more than that." Jamie slid her hand inside the silk blouse. Sheryl's skin was soft and warm. Jamie's pulse quickened. "Ten years and I'm still attracted to you," she whispered in Sheryl's ear.

"I don't have time, Jamie."

"Not even for a kiss?"

"I'm running late." Sheryl twisted a lipstick tube and puckered her lips as she applied the dark-red lipstick.

"Just a kiss." The edge of pleading in Jamie's voice matched the panic that reared up from the back of her mind. She was owned by the notion that there was a magic moment when they would reconnect, that the right gesture or the right thing she said would undo their growing separation. What was that right thing? What if this were the moment?

Sheryl turned, and Jamie slid her arms around her shoulders and kissed her. Hadn't it been a kiss that shifted them from friends to lovers on that long-ago New Year's Eve? Sheryl's lips were cool from the lipstick. Jamie tried to draw her into the kiss, like opening a door and hoping Sheryl would walk through it. When she ran her fingers through Sheryl's hair she stiffened. She could hear the unspoken words, "Don't mess my hair." She covered Sheryl's hands that were braced on the vanity. Not that long ago Sheryl would have lifted herself onto the vanity and wrapped her legs around her. Desperate to ignite a spark between them, Jamie slid her tongue into Sheryl's mouth. It was warm and tasted of the cinnamon gum she chewed. "Mmm," Jamie said in her throat. She waited for Sheryl to deepen the kiss.

"I've gotta go." She turned back to the mirror, reapplied lipstick, then sprayed perfume toward her throat.

Jamie stepped back from the stinging scent, another missed opportunity drenching her with disappointment. "Why don't you come by after your meeting? We're having dinner at Maggiano's. They have a nice bar. We could have a drink, talk." Maybe that would be the moment they looked in each other's eyes and time stopped and…Sheryl kissed her cheek, and was gone, only the bite of her perfume left.

Jamie stared at the jars and tubes of makeup spread across the counter. She picked up a round tub and read the label. Face cream. She'd always loved Sheryl's femininity. Opening it, she rubbed some into her cheek, cool and slippery on her skin.

Jamie pulled dove-gray linen pants from a hanger and chose a dark-blue sweater, not her usual business attire. Her staff teased her about her preppy style of dress—pleated pants and Oxford shirts. She'd heard a practice-management guru comment once that doctors should wear long sleeves so their patients couldn't see their tan arms and assume they were leading lives of luxury and leisure at their expense. Jamie had laughed, but it made her think about the image she wanted to portray. She never wore a white clinic coat like her father because it hindered her mobility when adjusting and she didn't have a stethoscope draped around her neck that signified "doctor." Wearing tailored pants and long-sleeved shirts that looked professional in a slightly masculine style was her way of establishing a "doctor" look.

Standing in front of the full-length mirror, she adjusted the V-neck sweater over her shoulders. She fingered the pendant she never took off, a diamond set in a gold star, a gift from her mom on her eighteenth birthday just months before she died. "You'll always be my star," the card read. *Am I still your star, Mom?* Tears stung her eyes. Her mom had been gone longer than she'd been a chiropractor.

All the talks that last summer about dreams and following your heart. She'd known she wouldn't be around. Jamie shook off the sadness. Tonight was about Betty.

❖

Jamie rested her forearms on the rounded edge of the bar and wrapped her fingers around the tumbler of Glenlivet, listening to nearby conversations—the dramas of boyfriend problems, a forgotten anniversary, money wasted on a bad concert.

Dinner was great fun, and Jamie had made a point of being upbeat because she knew her staff was worried about her. Betty had cried over Jamie's parting gift—a gold charm bracelet with charms she'd chosen to remind Betty of her days in the clinic. Sara and Don had joined her at the bar for one drink, but she'd been on her own for the last hour. She felt guilty for being relieved Carla hadn't come. She didn't want to meet her husband.

She'd known Sheryl wouldn't show up. How many meetings would it take for her to get that promotion? She found morose satisfaction in sitting here, playing the jilted lover. It was melodramatic and Jamie was never melodramatic. She was the strive to be better, stay after practice to throw just a few more pitches type; the work hard six days a week for twenty years type; the never leave dirty dishes in the sink type. Responsible and hardworking all her life, but what had it gotten her? She left the last of the Scotch she'd been nursing. She was the responsible type who didn't drive drunk; the loyal type who went home to a partner who seemed more distant each day.

Sheryl was already in bed. Jamie put on her favorite plaid boxers, the waistband comfortably stretched out. She lay on her back, willing Sheryl to reach out and pull her close. Sheryl stirred but didn't wake. She was inches from the woman she loved. It might as well be a mile.

CHAPTER TWELVE

Thank you," Carla said to the plumber, who'd agreed to come as soon as he could and unclog the sink in the break room. She set the phone down and checked the time. Two more hours and she could go home. She'd go look at new bedroom furniture this weekend. Monday morning she'd tell Jamie she couldn't keep the job. She heard someone walk behind the front counter.

"Hey, Betty." It wasn't a voice she recognized.

"Be nice to me. It's my last day," Betty said.

"So I heard. Who's taking over?"

Carla stepped out of her office. "That would be me." She froze, staring at the blonde with the tousled hair, cut shorter, but unmistakably the woman in the picture—Jamie's partner. Her pulse went into overtime as she said, "Carla Grant. New office manager." The blue eyes took her measure in a gaze that was piercing, almost edgy. Possessive.

"Penni Morgan. Best friend."

"Excuse me?" Was that some lesbian term for a partner?

"Which part? Penni Morgan or best friend?"

"Carla, this is Jamie's best friend." Betty wrapped her arm around Penni's waist.

Carla gripped the doorframe as the pieces fell into place. Best friend. That meant…Jamie didn't have a partner or she would have a picture of her on the desk. "A pleasure to meet you," Carla said, shaking Penni's hand as her heart leapt into her throat. She was sure a silly grin was plastered to her face, but she didn't care.

Jamie set a file on the front counter. “Aren’t you a little early?” she asked the older couple sitting in the waiting room.

“We finished at the store sooner than we thought,” the man said. “We’re happy to sit here and read. We love your new magazines.” He held up *Bon Appetit* and his wife held up *Sunset*.

“When did we—”

“I brought them in,” Carla said, all thoughts of quitting gone.

“Um, good idea. Thanks.”

“What’s up, Doc?” Penni wrapped her arm around Jamie’s shoulder and kissed her on the cheek. “Time for a haircut,” she said, ruffling Jamie’s hair. “And time to lose the gray. I’m not ready to give in to middle age yet, and I don’t want to be outed by association.”

Carla watched this exchange with amusement. Anyone who treated Jamie that way and got her to smile was someone she wanted to know. A little boy who looked too much like Penni to be anyone but her son ran up and wrapped his arms around Jamie’s waist.

“Aunt Jamie, Tommy said I was lying when I said I get my back cracked.”

“Well, we can’t have that,” Jamie said, placing her hand on the boy’s shoulder. “I’ll bet if we ask real nice, Carla could print out a certificate that says you survived getting your back cracked. Would that work?”

Carla’s heart fluttered in triple time when Jamie looked at her and winked.

“Yeah. Cool,” Travis said.

“Don’t pay attention to anything Penni tells you,” Jamie said over her shoulder to Carla. “She pushes the limits of her best-friend status.”

Carla couldn’t stop smiling as she watched Jamie and Penni disappear around the corner. She had to delete the layout for Travis’s certificate twice before she got it right. Jamie didn’t have a partner. Her pulse was tripping all over itself with excitement. She frowned. How did one go about…what…asking her boss out? Trying to get her attention so she’d do the asking? God, she was so not prepared for dating. Carla looked up from her desk. Penni was studying her from the doorway.

"You're gonna take good care of the doc, right?" Fierce blue eyes pinned her.

"You have my word."

"Right answer. Got plans this weekend, new office manager?"

"Why?"

"We're having a birthday party tomorrow for my wife, Lori. The big four oh. This is your official invitation."

"Sounds like fun." Carla hoped she wasn't blushing. Jamie would be there. "When and where?"

"Saratoga Springs. On Highway 9."

"I know where it is."

"Any time after noon and no presents"

"I'll be there." Carla flew through the rest of the afternoon. Her weekend had just got a whole lot better than shopping for bedroom furniture.

Chapter Thirteen

That tingly feeling erupted in her belly, like little sparks, as Carla walked from the parking lot to the entrance of Saratoga Springs, a private park nestled in the forest in the Santa Cruz Mountains. She'd been here several times for Mike's company picnics. She followed two women holding hands, and a fresh flurry of sparks erupted. Would she be walking out hand in hand with Jamie? Could it be that easy? It'd worked out for Meg Ryan and Tom Hanks after he admitted who he was, she reminded herself. Too excited to sleep and hopelessly addicted to romantic comedies and happy endings, she'd stayed up late watching *You've Got Mail*, one of her favorites. If she told Jamie about that night, would she remember?

Inside the entrance, she searched the map on the board for Redwood Grove picnic area. The sounds of people having fun drifted up in waves from areas she couldn't see. She tucked her hair behind her ears, wishing it hadn't been three weeks since her last cut and highlight, and tugged on the topaz earrings she'd picked to go with her sleeveless yellow blouse. It was a good color on her. Khaki shorts would show off her legs, toned from running. She was pretty sure Jamie liked athletic-looking women.

She inhaled the scent of sun and dirt and redwood trees as she followed several teenagers across a bridge over the stream that wound through the canopy of redwoods and oaks. The girl pushed both her male companions into the ankle-high water and raced off, laughing, the boys in close pursuit. Fingering the Kleenex in her pocket she wondered if the day would end with her crying after Jamie took her in her arms and kissed her. A jolt of desire shot from her center like fireworks and flowed lazily down her limbs. Happy endings.

Carla crossed her fingers for luck as she reached the end of the path. Standing in a patch of sun breaking through the trees, she searched for Jamie among the fifty or so women mingling around picnic tables. Her body hummed with excitement. The rest of her life she'd have the freedom to be around lesbians. Maybe she'd meet some women she could be friends with. If she was going to build a new life, she wanted more than a girlfriend. Her breath caught in her throat. Girlfriend. Only one woman fit that bill, and she didn't see her anywhere.

Jamie checked the map of the park on the board by the entrance. She'd never been here, but it was beautiful, with a swimming pool, volleyball court, playground, and half-a-dozen private picnic areas. The atmosphere reminded her of an amusement park—crowded and noisy but everyone having fun. A couple stopped to check the map, while holding the hands of little girls that looked to be twins. Tired from work and staying up late, she was glad Penni had told her about the pool. A quick swim would relax her before socializing.

Jamie took the path to the pool on the opposite side of the park from the picnic areas. It ended at a large rectangular pool surrounded by grass and ringed with redwoods and oaks that reached up to a sapphire-blue sky. Kicking off her tennis shoes and stripping down to her suit, she tossed her shorts and Polo shirt on the grass and flopped onto a chaise. Kids played in the pool and women sat along the edge, talking as they kept their eyes on them. Work stress slipped away as the sun relaxed her. Her phone rang and she pulled it out of the pocket of her shorts. "Are you coming?"

"No," Sheryl said. "I got busy reading a new study on curriculum development that just came out. Have you seen my diamond earrings?"

"On the counter in the bathroom behind your makeup jars." Jamie's excitement faded. Don't push too hard, she cautioned herself. She'd talked Sheryl into staying home last night, and their easy conversation over a romantic dinner reminded Jamie of how they used to be. A movie in bed and a lot of kissing and snuggling had loosened some of the worry. "Lori would love it if you came."

"The invitation was addressed to you."

Jamie's jaw tightened but she kept her voice calm. "You know it was for both of us."

"I've got errands to run later. Besides, you'll have more fun without me."

Shopping. "That's not true."

Penni waved and knelt to talk to Travis before he walked to the edge of the pool and dove in. Patience, Jamie reminded herself. "I'll be home for dinner." She tucked the phone back in her shorts.

"I figured I'd find you here." Penni took the chaise next to Jamie. "I'd point out that the wicked witch boycotted in spite of the fact I called her, but my wife made me promise I wouldn't pick on you today."

Sheryl had left out that part, but there was no point letting it upset her. "Lucky me." Jamie stretched her arms over her head and then behind her, interlocking her fingers. "Remember the pool at the West Coast Women's Music Festival?"

"What made you think of that?"

"The setting. All the trees."

"Except that pool was filled with naked women." Penni waggled her eyebrows and rubbed her palms together.

"You're such a lesbian."

"Remember hanging out up in the Castro on Sunday afternoons—"

"Dancing our asses off, picking up babes." Life had been easy and fun back then. Now it was just a lot of work. "Do you realize we've known each other over half our lives?" Jamie waved to two women who were part of the group she and Sheryl used to go out with. One was a massage therapist whom she referred patients to. She should make an appointment. "Lori like her present?"

"Oh, my God. I should have videoed it and put it on YouTube. She actually did a back flip…always the gymnast." Penni's grin devoured her cheeks. "She's wanted to go on one of those Olivia cruises for years."

"Me, too."

"So, why don't you?"

"Maybe some day. I'm trying to get Sheryl to go to Hawaii for our anniversary."

Penni snorted. "Not enough malls there."

"Be nice or I'll tell Lori you broke your promise. Back in a sec." Jamie walked to the pool, dove in, and did several laps across the pool and back, winding her way around kids. She surfaced and shook the water from her face before swimming over to Travis. She sent him up in the air to an ear-piercing war whoop and then swam to the edge where Penni was sitting with her feet dangling in the water. She splashed water on the concrete edge to cool it and then hoisted herself up next to her.

"Your new office manager seems nice."

"She's great with insurance billing." Jamie kept her tone nonchalant. She didn't need Penni finding out who Carla was. The sun was glorious; the water was a perfect temperature; she and Sheryl were going to be fine. Nothing could ruin this day.

"I'm going to go find my wife. Keep an eye on Travis?"

Jamie shielded her eyes with her hand and looked at Penni. She had a strange look on her face. "Sure."

"And by the way, your office manager is over there."

"You invited her?" Jamie scanned the area. Carla was standing where the path ended at the grass, sunglasses holding her hair back from her face. Shapely legs disappeared into shorts. Toned arms extended from the blouse that dipped down in a V. She was barely used to having Carla in her office. She didn't want to be around her outside the office. Penni should have checked with her before inviting Carla.

"Of course. I haven't interviewed her yet. I'll send her over to keep you company."

"Um…sure." Jamie hurried to the chaise, pulled her shirt over her head, and reached for her shorts.

Penni said something to Carla that caused her to laugh and look at Jamie. Jamie reached for her sunglasses, mirrored Oakleys, as Carla sat down in the chaise next to her.

"You don't want me to know where you're looking?"

Jamie wasn't sure how to respond to Carla's flirty tone. She looked away from the gold pendant that hung in the V of Carla's blouse. She'd have to talk to Penni about boundaries with her employees.

"Penni told me to keep an eye on you. Something about a rafting trip…She left you lying on some rocks to go flirt with a girl and you fell asleep in the sun and burned your butt?" Carla's eyes were full of amusement and something more personal.

Great. Penni had just outed her. She made her sexual preference clear up front to new employees. Why hadn't she with Carla? Resentment bubbled up. She knew why she hadn't. A straight girl's experiment.

"Thanks for the files." Keep it about business. There'd been a stack of them on her desk this morning with pink sticky notes in them. In her graceful handwriting Carla pointed out discrepancies between what Marjorie had billed and what she should have billed. She'd noticed the same things, but the fact that Carla had caught them surprised her.

Carla looked away from Jamie. She seemed disappointed. "I found them stuffed in the bottom drawer of the file cabinet. I have a pretty good idea how she was embezzling."

Jamie lifted her sunglasses and looked at Carla.

"I'm not a rookie." Carla sounded amused. "It looks like she billed for multiple PT on the same visit in some cases. That isn't illegal, just—"

"Not my policy."

"If you claimed that money on your taxes there isn't a problem. If you didn't…"

"Then it's a tax problem," Jamie mumbled. Definitely not a rookie. Carla had grasped the magnitude of the problem.

"In some files it looks like she added PT or extremity adjusting that isn't noted in the chart, which is illegal. I lucked out finding those files because they have her billing records and the EOBs to compare them against. It's none of my business, Dr. Hammond, but—"

"Call me Jamie."

"All right. Is the IRS investigating you, too?"

Jamie nodded, her good mood fading as her business problems invaded her life again. When she looked up she almost choked at the kindness in Carla's eyes, and something else. Jamie pulled the sunglasses down over her eyes. They wandered to Carla's bare feet, then her ankles and up her legs to the hem of her shorts.

"I have time to help you go through files, Jamie."

Jamie looked back to the pool. Travis was having a splash fight with another little boy. Not far away were two women, one floating on her back supported by the other's arms. What would it be like to have that kind of support? "I'd appreciate it."

"Where's Jamie?" Penni sat down on the end of Carla's chaise.

Carla nodded at the pool. "Travis kidnapped her."

"We're gonna play volleyball. You two are on my team."

"Sounds like fun." Carla had never played, but the chance to be near Jamie was worth looking foolish. She could imagine high-fiving Jamie after a good play. What would her hands feel like now? That tingly feeling flared up. She needed to get Jamie alone to talk to her before she lost her nerve.

"I'm going to do laps," Jamie called from the pool. Carla could barely pull her eyes from all that exposed skin.

"Mom, I'm hungry." Travis skidded to a halt in front of Penni.

"You had lunch an hour ago. Where does it go?" Penni squeezed Travis around the waist. He wiggled away from her. "Can you find your way back to the picnic area?"

"Yes," Travis said, as if insulted.

"Get a snack but not too much. Birthday cake in an hour."

"K," Travis said as he scampered off.

"Do you mind if I ask you something?" Penni's expression was much too serious.

"Would it stop you if I said yes?" She liked Penni. She was funny, an attentive mom, and obviously devoted to Jamie.

"No." Penni paused. "Are you that girl? The one Jamie met in Atlanta when her flight was cancelled?"

Carla's heart did a slow roll in her chest and then beat furiously. She put her hand over it. Jamie had recognized her. Why didn't she say so? She kept her eyes glued to Jamie. "Yes, I am."

"That's appropriate, given the concert you went to. Jesus." Penni shook her head.

"How did you figure it out?"

"Earlier, at the pool, you were looking at Jamie like…" Penni shrugged. "Then the name and accent clicked."

"Ah. I wasn't so subtle." The sight of Jamie in that two-piece suit had made her want to run her hands over the body she'd never forgotten.

"No." Penni rubbed her face briskly. "Jesus."

"Say what you have to say, Penni."

Penni looked toward Jamie, seeming to gather her thoughts. "That night with you changed her. She moped for months in a way I'd never seen before."

"Go on," Carla said, swarmed by emotion that made her feel hot and cold at the same time. Jamie not only remembered that night, but it had affected her. Her heart leapt, but why hadn't she said anything? Could this be just a silly misunderstanding? She resisted the urge to jump in the pool and pull Jamie into her arms and tell her she remembered, too.

"She'd never talked about a girl the way she talked about you."

Carla flinched. It had been so personal, so private.

"No, she didn't give me details." Penni met her eyes and smiled. "I understood better when I fell in love with Lori, but that was several years in the future," Penni said, a wistful quality to her voice. "She kept talking about what might have been if you hadn't left. She was never the same after that weekend, Carla. Partly because of you, partly because of her difficulties being a doctor."

Carla frowned. "I don't understand."

"No, you wouldn't. Jamie makes it look easy now, but she had a hard time finding her way in the beginning. She was joining her father's practice and those were big shoes to fill. Nothing short of perfect was ever good enough for him. Or for her."

"That hasn't changed," Carla said. "Do you hate me?"

"Of course not. Why would you think that?"

"Because I walked out on her." The sorrow of that decision had been absorbed into the joys of her life, but she'd never imagined it had hurt Jamie. Was that why Jamie hadn't acknowledged her? Would she give her a second chance?

"You can't change the past. What matters to me is whether you're going to walk out on her again."

"That night affected me, too, and she still matters to me. I don't know what I mean to her."

"You're the one she can't forget."

"Ditto for me."

"You're married. Jamie would never—"

"Not in the way you think. It's…complicated."

"If you still have feelings for her I suggest you do something about it."

A woman walked up and put a hand on Penni's shoulder. "There you are. I thought we were going to play volleyball."

"Carla, this is Lori, my wife and the birthday girl."

"Happy birthday." Carla stood and extended her hand but was pulled into a hug by the short woman with hair as blond and a smile as bright as Penni's.

"Congratulations on the job. You'll love working for Jamie."

"Hey, birthday girl," Jamie said, picking Lori up off the ground and planting a kiss on her cheek.

Jamie's suit was plastered to her, and water dripped off all the curves Jamie covered up too quickly with a towel. Carla caught Penni grinning at her.

❖

"Come on, Jamie," Penni said. "We're playing volleyball, and you're on my team."

Jamie pulled on her shorts and then her shirt. Carla was staring at her when she poked her head through the collar, something too friendly about the look in her eyes. Did Carla think they were going to be friends outside of the office? Penni really shouldn't have invited her. "I'm going to savor a few more minutes in the sun and then go mingle. It's been a while since I saw a lot of these people."

"No argument. You know how I hate to lose."

"Volleyball's not my sport."

"I know it's not softball, but you can suffer through." Penni hooked one arm through Jamie's and the other through Carla's as they all followed Lori along the path away from the pool.

"You're a softball player?" Carla asked.

"Star pitcher," Penni said. "We played together at San Jose State. That's how we met. Shall I tell Carla the story?"

"Carla doesn't need to hear about that." She didn't need Penni telling more stories about her.

"Now I'm curious," Carla said.

"I was walking across campus and saw a group of football players sitting on a picnic table by the cafeteria. You know, how they sit on the table part and put their feet on the seat and spread their legs like we cared to see their equipment?"

"I remember that pose," Carla said, her voice too bright.

"Those bozos were rating every girl who walked by, actually calling out numbers. So I trotted over and sat down and gave my own ratings—all tens. They asked what the hell I thought I was doing. I said I liked to look at women, too, and thought I was better qualified to rate them since I'd probably slept with more than any of them had."

"Good for you," Carla said.

"So my friend here, whom I hadn't met yet came over and said she was qualified to judge, too. We both called out tens to the next dozen girls."

Jamie clenched her jaw. Sometimes Penni's boundaries left a lot to be desired.

"Bet that went over well," Carla said.

"Predictably, we got called *dyke*, *bitch*, and several other single-syllable names."

"I'll bet you two were trouble," Carla said.

"You have no idea. Remember that time we were playing in Reno? And we snuck out of the hotel and went to that lesbian bar?"

"Don't," Jamie said, now furious with Penni. When Penni winked at her a sick feeling curled up from her stomach. Penni had been talking to Carla while she was in the pool. "I haven't interviewed her yet," she'd said. What if—Shit. Carla didn't remember her and that was just fine, but she didn't need Penni needling her about an irrelevant past.

"Remember that chick who wanted to come back to our room for a—"

"Stop." Jamie yanked her arm free. Was Penni leading up to asking Carla if—

"You think I'm shocking Carla?" Penni turned to Carla. "Are you shocked?"

"Not at all," Carla said. "I've succumbed, willingly, to a night of unexpected passion."

"My, my, new office manager has secrets. Do tell."

"I forgot my phone in my car," Jamie lied, as she walked back the way she'd come. What the hell was Penni doing?

"Get it after the game," Penni called after her.

"Patient might call." Jamie ran down the path. Shit. Penni was having fun at her expense.

Carla stared after Jamie's fleeing figure, embarrassed.

"Go after her," Penni urged her.

"That wasn't fair, Penni. We put her in an awkward position."

"So, fix it. Tell her you remember her. She'll want to know."

Carla hurried to catch up to Jamie. This wasn't how she'd envisioned their reunion.

CHAPTER FOURTEEN

Take a walk with me?" Carla wrapped her fingers around Jamie's wrist and guided her along a dirt path shaded by overhanging branches of oaks and redwoods.

"I need to get my—"

"Let's walk down by the water." Carla led them to a small sandy area alongside the creek. It was churchlike, with redwood trees enclosing the area like columns and a large boulder in the middle, almost like an altar. A heart was drawn in black on the boulder, SANDY AND LEON FOREVER written inside. She took a deep breath but couldn't calm her racing heart. "Are we going to talk about that night?"

Jamie's breath rushed out as if she'd been punched. She crossed her arms. "It was a long time ago." Their shoulders touched. Jamie inched away.

"So you do remember." Carla's heart was beating as fast as a hummingbird's wings. She could think of a dozen movies where this was the moment the lovers turned toward each and…

Jamie was looking down at the ground. "Yes," she finally said.

Carla stared at the water drifting past them, little more than a trickle this time of year. Why weren't they embracing? Why did Jamie seem angry? Was Penni wrong? "I never forgot that night, Jamie. Never," she said, her voice shaky.

Jamie squeezed her fingers into her arms, still looking at a spot on the ground in front of her. "You left," she said, her voice tight.

"I think you know why." Tears filled Carla's eyes. Jamie was as stiff as a tree next to her. This wasn't going the way she'd imagined.

"You had a family."

Was that what Jamie thought? Carla shook her head.

Jamie was quiet, then looked at her, head cocked. "You were pregnant."

"Yes." Carla made no attempt to stop the flow of tears.

"Why didn't you tell me?" It was more an accusation than a question.

Did it matter now? Wouldn't one kiss be better than a dozen explanations? "Walking out of that hotel room was the hardest thing I've ever done. I stood there for a long time praying for things to be different so I could wake you up, so we could make—"

"It doesn't matter." Jamie walked to the edge of the creek and crossed her arms.

"It matters to me." Carla stepped next to her, so close she could hear her breathing. "That night marked me." Why was Jamie angry?

"I thought I was just an experiment. Sex with the lesbian and then back to your straight life."

The harsh tone felt like a slap. "Oh, Jamie, that wasn't it at all." Carla met Jamie's eyes and the pain there made her heart stop. No wonder she hadn't said anything. Her heart fluttered as she envisioned that happy ending again. She took Jamie's hand and held tight when she tried to pull away. I'm not leaving this time, she wanted to say. "I never meant to hurt you. My life was no longer my own, and I'd made a commitment that I couldn't betray."

Jamie said nothing, her gaze back on the ground in front of her. At least she hadn't pulled her hand away.

"I'd gone home to tell my parents I was pregnant. By the time I got to the airport I was an emotional wreck, and having the flight cancelled was the last straw. I'd probably have sat in that seat all night if you hadn't come by and rescued me. A total stranger, and you asked me if I was all right. In the week that I was home, neither of my parents bothered to ask me that. You can't imagine how that affected me." Carla waited. "Please say something."

"That answers some questions." Jamie looked at their linked hands. "You could have stayed. You could have told me this. The loneliness of—" Jamie shoved both hands into her pockets.

"I was shown a magical night by a kind stranger. I didn't know what it meant to you, but I assumed it was just a one-night stand. I got the impression you were kind of a lesbian Casanova." Carla nudged Jamie with her shoulder, trying to lighten the mood. "That girl at the bar?"

"What girl?"

"The brunette who came over and said something about a tree root and kissed you?"

"Oh, that girl. I felt bad about that." Jamie looked at her, the hint of a smile on her face. "Why didn't you say anything in the interview?"

"You acted like you didn't recognize me, and I was so shocked I didn't know what to do. I didn't want to embarrass either of us. I hoped you wouldn't offer me the job. Why did you?"

Jamie kicked at a rock. "I didn't think you recognized me either…and your ring. There's sort of this stigma about straight girls satisfying their curiosity."

"Oh, Jamie, it wasn't curiosity." To finally be having this conversation was both a gift and a painful reminder of loss. She ached to feel Jamie's arms around her. But Jamie had stiffened again. What did she have to say to get them past this and into the present? "I don't know why fate has brought us together again, but I'd give anything to have a second chance with you." Carla held her breath as her heart beat nearly out of her chest.

Jamie shook her head vehemently as she backed away. "It really doesn't matter, does it? You have a husband and I have a partner."

Carla watched Jamie's retreating back, too stunned to speak as her fantasy reunion shattered and fell like leaves at her feet. Telling Jamie about Mike wouldn't have made any difference. Oh, God, what had she done? The look of torment in Jamie's eyes just before she left…Her heart dropped to her stomach. She stared at her surroundings. They'd looked magical. Now they were just trees and sand. She wouldn't be writing their names in a heart on the boulder. She sat down against it and cried for a long time.

The noise increased but Carla barely heard it as she walked back along the path. Where was her future now? She startled when a hand grabbed her arm.

"Did you talk to her?" Penni asked.

"Why didn't you tell me she has a partner?" Carla let her anger into her voice.

"Travis," Penni hollered across the playground, "go find Aunt Jamie, okay? Tell her I want to talk to her." Penni turned to her. "If I had, you wouldn't have talked to her. Carla, please. Her personal life is rocky. You said your marriage was complicated. You don't impress me as the type to cheat, so I assume you're either separated or about to be."

Carla nodded and crossed her arms, not at all sure she wanted to hear this.

"Then you understand how hard it is to come to terms with a longtime relationship that's not working. She's fighting to save her business. She's overwhelmed and afraid. Please don't walk out on her."

"I'll do my best as her office manager. If she doesn't fire me," she added bitterly. "That's all I can do." Carla walked away, dabbing at her eyes as she took the path toward the entrance, the future she'd wanted now impossible. The sun was hot on her skin but she felt cold inside.

"Don't give up on her," Penni called after her.

Jamie gripped her car keys inside her pocket as she trailed behind Travis. She'd said good-bye to Lori. She needed to be as far away from here, from Carla, as possible.

"I found her, Mom."

"Thanks, Trav." Penni kissed his head and smoothed an errant curl of hair.

"Is it time for cake yet?"

"Just about. Go find your other mom and tell her I'll be right there."

"I'm going to take off." Jamie pulled her keys from her pocket.

"Did you talk to Carla?"

"Why?"

"I know she's the girl from Atlanta."

Jamie was silent. She didn't want to talk about this, even with Penni. Especially not with Penni.

"Jamie, the woman who affected you more than any other suddenly shows up in your life again. You can't ignore this. I know you're overwhelmed and struggling, but—"

"Don't." Jamie held up her hands as if she could repel whatever Penni was about to say. "What happened twenty years ago is over. She has a husband and I have a partner, and she's my employee." Was that last part still true? Her mind reeled.

"Maybe she has a husband like you have a partner, and we both know what I'm talking about. Damn it, Jamie, you deserve to be happy. Don't suffer out of some misplaced sense of responsibility."

"Don't fucking tell me what to do, Penni." Jamie stormed off, plowing through a group of older men in black Harley Davidson T-shirts, banging her knee against a motorcycle helmet. She was fed up with Penni's campaign against Sheryl. Where the hell was the entrance? A real friend would support her relationship, not undermine it. Damn it. How'd she end up back at the pool? Backtracking, she found a sign that read Exit and ran down the path.

And Carla…Her breath caught in her throat. *She remembers me. That night mattered.* Jamie's thoughts took off in all directions as she tried to amend twenty years' worth of assumptions.

She bolted across the parking lot to her car. Biology. Carla leaving hadn't been about feelings. A laugh bubbled up, but she swallowed it. The resentment, the neat little box called "straight girl's experiment," now had a huge hole blown through it. Did knowing the truth make it easier?

The leather seat was hot under her legs as she jammed the key in the ignition. Turning the air conditioning on full blast, she yanked the seat belt across her chest. She cranked up the volume on Melissa, the only rebellious act she could think to commit. Backing out of the space, she cursed the driver who'd parked inches from her.

"I never forgot it." The words bounced in her head and dropped to her heart with a thud. She squeezed the steering wheel. She'd kept that note. How silly was that?

At the exit to Highway 9, the Harley in front of her turned right and she looked in that direction. In an hour she could be in Santa Cruz. The beach. Her toes scrunched inside her Nikes. She looked to the left. In fifteen minutes she could be home. She could take care of that squeaky door and have dinner ready for Sheryl. She rolled her shoulders and followed the Harley. She'd go over to the wharf and surprise Sheryl with fresh crab for dinner.

The forest engulfed her, and memories of that weekend collected around her, stray images and feelings forming a collage. The Harley zipped around a car going ten miles under the speed limit. Usually a patient driver, she swore as the idiot passed another turnout. She rolled her shoulders again, trying to relieve the pain racing up the back of her neck. People didn't fall in love in one night. You don't go back for second chances. Tears stung her eyes.

She swerved into a turnout. That damn weekend. So what if she still remembered everything about it? She'd called it her last hurrah, not thinking it really would be. It had become a dividing line between hope that she could still pursue her dreams and the reality of the responsibilities she'd agreed to. Many choices had disappeared that weekend. She hadn't known many more would disappear with the new clinic and her father's death. Lowering the window, she sucked in the scent of warm soil and redwoods and turned down the music.

A sporty white convertible sped by. She loved sports cars. She'd had one once—a 280 ZX the blue of her shirt, T-tops, racing mags. She'd bought it a few months after starting in her dad's practice. He'd criticized the purchase as frivolous. She'd needed to reward herself with something fun to combat the growing fear that she'd made a mistake by becoming a chiropractor. Of course she hadn't, but back then she'd chafed at finding herself locked into his expectations. Now she drove a SUV, a solid, responsible car he'd approve of. She tried to think of a single frivolous thing she'd done lately as she pulled back onto the road.

Chapter Fifteen

Opening the refrigerator, Carla realized she should have stopped at the store. Sure she'd be spending the evening with Jamie, she hadn't planned anything for dinner. Tears filled her eyes again—for today, for the past, for the future she wouldn't have. Tears for the lack of anything she needed to make lasagna. It was comfort food, and she could justify drinking wine, maybe a lot of it, while she cooked. She dialed Mike's number.

"Could you stop at the store on your way home?" She gave him the list of things she needed. Little pebbles in her shoes infuriated her, and she kicked them off as she sloshed wine into a glass. She marched to the patio and sat at the table, lost in thoughts about the vagaries of fate and timing. When she heard Mike come in she brushed away tears.

Mike settled on the chair next to hers, rubbing a bottle of beer across his forehead. "Jeez, it's hot." He continued with a description of his dismal round of golf until he seemed to realize she wasn't paying attention.

"Honey? What's wrong? You haven't heard a word I've said. Is it about the move?"

Carla's throat tightened and she shook her head.

"Then what?"

"Oh, Mike, I've made such a mess of everything."

"We'll get through—"

"No. Work, Jamie." The heartbreak of the lost opportunity twenty years ago and the lost opportunity today welled up in her. When Mike said, "Tell me," she decided it was time.

"I met Jamie once before," she said, praying he'd understand.

When she'd finished the story, leaving nothing out but personal details, Mike was silent, his brow creased. "That's a lot to digest," he finally said.

"I should have told you." Carla reached for his hand. "Are you upset with me?"

"Of course not." He kissed the back of her hand.

"I never meant to cheat on you." Carla rubbed her thumb over his wedding band. "It just sort of happened."

"I understand." He gave a wry smile. "I had the same shock when I realized I was attracted to the guy I worked with on that project last year. It's just…you knew before we got married that you were attracted to women, that you were gay. Twenty years is a long time to be in the wrong relationship."

"It wasn't the wrong relationship. You've been my best friend since kindergarten and I've always loved you." The gangly boy had grown into a handsome man, and just as kind. "I wouldn't trade a minute of what we've had. It's just…where do I go from here?"

"Can you talk to Dr.—to Jamie about it?"

Carla laughed harshly. "I'll be lucky if she doesn't fire me for coming on to her."

"Maybe it would be best if you—"

"I can't walk out on her again. I can help her, and as hard as it is to be around her—"

"It's harder not to. I remember." Mike scooted his chair closer and put his arm around her. "I wanted that project to be over so I wouldn't have to be around him, but then I'd find a reason to go to his office to talk about anything."

"What am I going to do?" Carla sobbed into his shirt. It was sweaty but she didn't care.

"Shh. You're going to make lasagna, we're going to have dinner by candlelight, and tomorrow we're going to get you on Match.com."

Carla's sobs turned to laughter and then hiccups. No one would ever understand her the way Mike did. Why couldn't they both be straight?

An hour later she tucked two pans of lasagna into the oven. It was more than she could eat in a week, but she could take some to work. If she had a job.

"Call Lissa." Mike handed her the phone. "Talking to her always makes you feel better. Then you can take a bath while the lasagna cooks."

Waiting for Lissa to answer, she noticed the business card from the attorney she'd met at the bar. She picked it up and rubbed her fingers over the heavy card stock. If she wanted a future other than the emptiness of this house she'd have to tuck her sorrow in her apron, as her mother often said, and go on with life.

The smells of tomato sauce and garlic comforted her as she listened to Lissa complain about Steph leaving dirty clothes all over the bedroom and hair in the bathroom sink. They didn't know how lucky they were to have those problems.

CHAPTER SIXTEEN

Lost in thought, Jamie realized she was at the junction of Highway 1 in Santa Cruz. She took River Street to Laurel and wound her way with all the tourists toward the wharf. At the entrance she veered right instead. It was too pretty of a day not to cruise up West Cliff Drive. She'd still make it back with dinner. Crawling along in the line of cars, windows down, the ocean a carpet of gray-blue in front of her, she let the sound and smell calm her.

At the last parking area she lucked out and pulled into a spot vacated by an old VW van covered in bumper stickers. Only in Santa Cruz. Surfers off Lighthouse Point bobbed in the ocean. Kelp beds swayed in giant surges, left then right. A woman ambled along the asphalt path that ran the length of West Cliff, an exuberant Labrador puppy tugging on the leash. She sat for a long time watching people doing nothing more than having fun. The conversation with Carla replayed itself like a loop in her head. She remembered. It had mattered.

Shoving the car door open she walked to the lighthouse and back and then settled on a bench overlooking the ocean. Her phone signaled another text from Penni. "Sorry. Call me. Love you." She texted back, "Not forgiven."

She gazed out at the ocean, mere yards away but not accessible from the steep cliffs clearly marked as hazardous. She had a wild urge to shimmy down one of the foot trails that rule breakers had forged. She checked her watch. She should get the crab and head back.

Standing in line at Stagnaro's fish counter, she watched the Ferris wheel on the boardwalk adjacent to the wharf. How many times had she made that loop sitting next to her mom? She could spare the time. Tying her laces together, she draped her shoes over her shoulder and stepped onto the beach that fronted the boardwalk. The sand was soft and warm, the breeze cool against her skin. She still had her swimsuit on under her clothes. Maybe she'd go in the water. A football landed at her feet, and instead of handing it back to the guy, she threw it down the beach to his buddy, smiling at his "Nice arm, lady."

She stepped around a sand castle under construction as two little girls packed sand into turrets. Jamie still had Kodak pictures of castles she and her mom had built. She looked up at the boardwalk, at the rides she'd loved as a kid. What the heck? Sheryl was probably still shopping.

Jamie took advantage of the short line to the Giant Dipper roller coaster, feeling childishly pleased when she got the front car along with a teenaged girl. She raised her arms as they were transported through the dark tunnel and then ratcheted up the steep first climb. The view from the top was as breathtaking as she remembered. Time stopped for that split-second view of the Pacific Ocean spread out to the horizon. Jamie screamed with everyone else as they plummeted down, the girl's long hair flying around her face. She couldn't stop smiling as she hurried down the exit ramp, tempted to vault the railing and hurry back in line like she had as a kid.

Jamie dashed over to the Ferris wheel. A kid wearing a wide leather bracelet closed the safety bar across her. She'd wanted to work here the summer after her sophomore year in high school. Her mom was concerned about her driving Highway 17 but willing to let her do it. Her father shut the idea down decisively. She'd worked in his office that summer and every summer after.

She wished her mom were next to her, holding her hand, as they made the slow rise. Her mom's fear of heights had never stopped her from having fun. Jamie let her eyes wander over the boardwalk, the beach, the wharf. "It's a lot like life," her mom would say. "You go up, you go down, but you keep moving." What words of wisdom would she have about Carla?

She saved her mom's favorite ride for last—the merry-go-round. Jamie climbed onto one of the big horses on the outside—a white one with blue and yellow adornments. She pulled a brass ring from the metal arm as she passed it and aimed for the picture of the clown face on the wall, remembering how her mom would cheer every time she got it in the clown's mouth, causing bells to go off. So many fun times.

She checked her watch again. Wasn't Sheryl the one promoting more separate time? Coming to Santa Cruz was the first spontaneous thing Jamie had done in longer than she could remember, and she suddenly craved that feeling of not knowing what would happen next, of being directed by no agenda other than fun. Shoving her hands in her pockets, she strolled the boardwalk soaking up the sun, the sounds of the rides and people having fun, the smells from the food stands. When she reached the end, she stopped in front of Marianne's ice cream. She loved ice cream, and usually had several pints of Ben and Jerry's in the freezer. Since starting her diet, Sheryl didn't want her to bring any home. She ordered a double-scoop butter pecan, her mom's favorite flavor. Settling on a bench next to a guy drawing in a sketchbook, she watched kids frolic in the gentle waves and let her mind wander back to a time before business problems and responsibilities.

The air was cool and the fog bank was rolling in as she laced her shoes and stepped up onto the wharf. Her gaze kept drifting to the Dream Inn, the boutique hotel that fronted the ocean just beyond the wharf. She sat on a bench and stared at the tall white building with balconies facing the ocean. She'd always wanted to stay there. Why not? She called Sheryl.

"Hey, babe, you're not gonna believe—"

"Where have you been?"

"I'm in Santa Cruz looking at the Dream Inn. Come over and we'll spend the night."

"I can't. That car you bought me won't start."

"That doesn't make any sense." Jamie watched the fishermen lined up along the railing. An older man wearing an A's cap pulled up his line and checked the bait.

"I was with friends. It was so embarrassing. One of them had to drive me home."

"You left the car?"

"I called you to come get me, but I guess you had better things to do."

Jamie rubbed the back of her neck. "That's why we have Triple A. You call them, they come—"

"I couldn't find the card. What are you doing in Santa Cruz?"

"I decided to take a drive and ended up here. Come join me."

"I. Don't. Have. A. Car."

Jamie walked to the wooden railing. The smell of fish wafted up from a bucket next to the man in the A's cap. He dropped his line back into the ocean, and Jamie had a wild urge to fling her phone after it.

"Are you with Penni?"

The icy tone made Jamie clench her jaw. "No."

"How soon will you be home?"

"I already paid for the room," Jamie lied.

"You can't be serious."

"You're right, I'm not." Jamie laughed and the tightness in her chest loosened. "It's purely spontaneous, no good reason, no plan, fun."

"How am I going to get around tomorrow? I have things to do."

Shopping. She watched a surfer wobble for balance before toppling from the board.

"Jamie—"

"Gotta go." Jamie stood for a long time staring down into the churning water. Sea lions congregated near the pilings, their barks echoing under the wharf. They probably wouldn't have a room.

She flashed her best smile at the cute young woman behind the counter before realizing she was a graying middle-aged woman about to flirt with a woman who couldn't be a day over twenty. She'd once been bold, cocky even, when it came to flirting. Where had the time gone?

"Ocean view?" the woman asked.

"Um, sure." Tucking the keycard in her back pocket, Jamie did a double take when a woman about her age with long tan legs and a disarming smile gave her the once-over. Was she cruising her? A slow smile relaxed the tension in Jamie's face. It was nice to be appreciated.

When Jamie's stomach growled she considered her dinner options. Passing on the hotel restaurant, she headed back to the wharf.

It was cold, and she ducked into one of the tourist stores. She put on the navy-blue hooded sweatshirt with the Santa Cruz Beach Boardwalk emblem in white across the front, complete with exaggerated curls of waves beneath the words.

She took one of the quarters the clerk gave her back in change and flipped it. Heads she'd go to her father's favorite restaurant, tails, her mom's. She walked into Gilda's, her mom's favorite, and headed for an open seat at the counter. She didn't want to sit at a table by herself.

As a kid, she'd always ordered the fried prawns that came with fries her mom would steal off her plate. As an adult, she favored the Louie salad piled high with crabmeat. At least she and Sheryl agreed on that. Maybe she should go get Sheryl. The thought of listening to her bitch about the car settled Jamie back onto her seat at the counter. She lathered a piece of French bread with butter. She wasn't on a diet.

After dinner she retrieved a travel toothbrush from her glove compartment and rode the elevator up to the fifth-floor room. It was decorated in predictable blues and greens, the furnishings a retro nod to the hotel's origins in the sixties. Smiling when she saw the docking station, she inserted her iPod and lunged for the volume control when Melissa blared into the room.

She moved her hips in time to the music. She hadn't danced in years. Why not? She might as well make the night count. She looked down at her shorts. By Santa Cruz standards she was almost dressed up.

"I'm looking for somewhere to go dancing…a lesbian bar or dance club?" Jamie asked the woman at the front desk with bright-blue eyes and a customer-service smile to be proud of. She'd make a great receptionist but she didn't need a new receptionist, just a new office manager. She shoved the sour thought aside.

"The main one closed but…" The woman pulled out her cell phone. "There are often meet-ups for dance parties. Yep, there's one at a bar in Capitola."

Fifteen minutes later Jamie was standing outside what looked like a neighborhood bar. No line, no bouncer, no purple stamp of a face like the bar in Atlanta. She'd left it on until it wore off. How silly she'd been then.

Opening the door, she stepped into more noise than she expected. It wasn't big, but there was a nice-sized dance floor at one end. A woman DJ stood shuffling through a stack of CDs in a booth next to it. Jamie ordered a beer and sat at the bar, lost in wondering where the last twenty years had gone until an elbow settled next to her arm.

"Would you like to dance?" The woman had hair shorter and grayer than hers and a turquoise blouse snugged across ample breasts.

"Sure." *Sheryl doesn't like to dance and I'm not doing anything wrong.* Jamie hadn't danced in forever, but by the end of the song she was loose and in her rhythm, and when the woman suggested another, Jamie obliged. Three dances later, she shed the sweatshirt. The woman kissed her on the cheek and said to come join her if she wanted to. Jamie returned to the barstool, guzzling most of the beer. She'd just cooled down when a woman with a blond ponytail and dolphin earrings took the stool next to her.

"You're a good dancer."

"Thanks."

"I sort of dragged my mom out here. She'll kill me for asking, but would you dance with her?" She pointed to a table toward the back where a woman about Jamie's age sat alone, looking at the dance floor. "Please?"

"Sure."

"Great," the woman said, breaking into a smile.

Jamie approached the woman sitting on the edge of her seat gripping her beer in both hands. Her face was identical to her daughter's, but her hair was light brown and short with wisps of bangs above brown eyes.

"I'm Jamie. Would you like to dance?" The words came out easily, as if she were still that bold, out dyke she'd once been. She tucked her thumbs into her waistband and added a broad smile.

"Um…" The woman looked toward the bar and scowled at her daughter.

"Come on," Jamie said, holding out her hand.

"Okay." A shy smile replaced the scowl. "I'm Becky."

Jamie laid the sweatshirt on the chair and led Becky to the dance floor. She'd missed the transition from Madonna to Lady Gaga over the years. Becky shuffled her feet, staring at Jamie's hips as if looking for directions.

"Here," Jamie said, placing her hands on Becky's hips and moving her. "Bigger steps...that's it...now more wiggle." Becky's laugh blended with the music, and she lifted her arms and gradually found her own rhythm. "That's great," Jamie said.

"This is a lot different than the ballroom lessons I took last year. My husband refused, but I always wanted to learn to dance." She shrugged. "I got partnered with a woman who was a great dancer, and that's when I realized...well." She blushed.

"Better late than never," Jamie said as a young woman in a cut-off white T-shirt bumped her into Becky.

"I guess. Have you always been a lesbian?"

"Yep." God, it felt good to be in a bar full of music and lesbians. An awkward moment ensued when the music shifted to a slow song. What the heck? Jamie held out her arms and Becky stepped toward her.

"I'm a better follower than a leader," Becky said, her cheek close to Jamie's.

Jamie hadn't held a woman on a dance floor in years. Becky was soft with plenty of curves and smelled like lavender. Jamie took a deep breath when Becky moved a little closer and then closer still. *It's just a dance.* Jamie closed her eyes and shut out everything but the music.

When the dance ended, Becky took Jamie's hand and led her back to the table. Jamie nursed a beer and listened as Becky regaled her with funny stories about her three cats, two lovebirds, and recently rescued dachshund.

"It's hard to go from living with someone for twenty years to being alone," Becky said. "I decided sharing my home with animals would be good for them and keep me from coming home to an empty house."

Jamie twirled the bottle on the table. How often was her house empty when she got home?

"My husband didn't like animals. Should have been a clue," Becky said.

Jamie shifted in her seat. She'd once had a lot in common with Sheryl. Did they still? She rubbed the back of her neck.

"I don't know how this is done but would you like to...um... come meet my menagerie?"

It took Jamie a minute to realize the anticipatory look in Becky's eyes was meant for her. "Um…I'm sorry, Becky. I have a…I have to leave early tomorrow to get home. I'm from out of town."

"Oh." Becky's eyes telegraphed her disappointment.

"It's been fun." She kissed Becky on the cheek. "You'll find what you want."

By the time Jamie opened the door to her room her good mood was gone. She didn't like coming back to an empty hotel room any more than she liked coming home to an empty house. How was she going to get Sheryl to see that they'd drifted apart? Would success matter if they lost each other?

She tugged the sliding door open and went to the railing. The boardwalk was dark and quiet. So was the wharf. The only sign of life was the occasional bark of a sea lion. She'd enjoyed holding a woman who stepped into her arms instead of away from her, being around women who openly expressed their affection for one another.

Jamie stomped back into the room and snatched up the binder from the desk, rifling through it until she found the room-service menu. She ran her finger down the list of scotches. Glenlivet wasn't on it. She dialed room service and ordered a bottle of Wild Turkey. She liked the name. While she waited she turned on her iPod. Did Carla still like Melissa? Did she still dance? Would they ever have that conversation?

She tipped the young man and poured a generous amount of the amber liquid into a glass. Not cut crystal. She couldn't stop the laughter that overtook her at the absurdity of drinking cheap whiskey out of a generic glass, alone in a hotel room. The laughter gave way to anger as the whiskey burned its way down her throat. Why couldn't Sheryl give her this one night? Jamie took another sip of the whiskey, not smooth but with a bite she was starting to like. Once, Sheryl would have jumped at the offer. When had fun been usurped by career paths?

Pulling the sweatshirt hood over her head against the cold, she stood at the railing on the balcony, inhaling the ocean smell she loved. And who wouldn't go on a ten-year-anniversary vacation because she might miss a minute with some conservative, homophobic jerk? She took another, longer sip as she stared out at the dark ocean, the sound of waves crashing against the cliffs a counterpoint to Melissa's voice. She'd loved that voice since the first time she heard it blasting from the speakers at Amelia's bar in San Francisco on a sunny fall afternoon. Penni had convinced her to blow off studying and go up to the city and "cruise babes." She let the happy memory take her back to days when fun was easy.

"You can't subsist on studying. Your clit needs attention, too," Penni said, pulling Jamie out of her chair and tossing jeans, a white T-shirt, and her brown leather bomber jacket at her. "Bus leaves in ten. Dress or go naked."

They'd cruised the Castro, gorged on burritos, and ended up at Amelia's, where they melted into a surprisingly large crowd for a Sunday. They were sitting with their backs against the bar, sipping Coronas, laughing at the dance-floor antics of one particularly large but graceful woman, when "That Voice" filled the bar. The crowd of women rose as one and flooded the dance floor, whooping and hollering and gyrating to the hard rock beat. She and Penni looked at each other, shrugged, and joined the sea of dancers. They were sweating by the time they found their stools and beers again.

"Who the hell is that?" Penni asked.

"No idea."

A gorgeous redhead with C cups conveniently pressed against Jamie's shoulder put her lips near Jamie's ear and said, "M.E."

"Me?"

The redhead laughed, her breasts bouncing against Jamie's arm. "Melissa Etheridge. Some voice, huh? Clarissa, by the way." She slid between Jamie's thighs and draped an arm across Jamie's shoulders. "New album just came out. She didn't, but we all know she is."

"Is what?" Jamie asked, her brain slowed by the rush of blood heading south.

"One of us." Clarissa cocked her head to give Jamie an appraising look. "Where have you been? She's the hottest thing around right now. Saw her in some clubs in L.A. over the summer. Cute as hell, and that voice could almost make me come. Wanna help?" Clarissa gave Jamie a flirtatious smile and lowered her eyelids to cover part of her liquid hazel eyes.

Penni tossed her the car keys and said over her shoulder, "Have fun, sport. I'll find a ride home."

Jamie's protests were captured in a soft, lush kiss followed by a thorough exploration of her mouth by an insistent but gentle tongue. When Clarissa tugged her shirt from her jeans and grazed her fingers over her abdomen, Jamie groaned and slipped her arm around the lean waist that fit perfectly into her pelvis. Twenty minutes later they were ensconced in Clarissa's small bedroom in one of the Victorians in Noe Valley. Jamie did a double take at the law books scattered across the corner table.

"Law school. USF," Clarissa said before unbuttoning her blouse and tossing it over a chair, revealing those luscious breasts straining their way out of the maroon bra. Clarissa yanked Jamie's T-shirt out of her waistband and over her head in one swift motion and pulled her down onto the twin bed that made anything but full body contact impossible. Jamie slid one thigh against Clarissa's center, and they found a rhythm that had them both breathing heavy. Jamie licked her way down the soft skin of a long neck and along the edges of the breasts begging to be released. After biting Clarissa's nipples into stiff peaks, she gave in to whimpers of need and flicked the front opening clasp, cradling one beautifully full breast in her hand and wrapping her mouth around the other. Sucking caused Clarissa to pump harder on her thigh.

"Come on, baby," Jamie whispered against an erect nipple. "Let it go." Clarissa did, screaming and groaning as she came against Jamie's leg. Jamie's clit was pulsing so hard she knew she wouldn't last, and when Clarissa pushed her hand inside Jamie's jeans and entered her, Jamie exploded. They stared at each other with glazed eyes before bursting into laughter.

"That went well." Clarissa nibbled across Jamie's collarbone before running her tongue along Jamie's lower lip. They spent a long time kissing, deep probing mixed with gentle licks and small bites, just the mix of insistence and softness Jamie loved. The rest of the afternoon and well into the evening entailed one of the most delicious sessions of sex Jamie could remember, coming so many times she finally had to admit that she couldn't come one more time, although Clarissa could, and did.

Jamie shivered, from either the chilled air, now heavy with fog, or from the memory of how free and easy her life had been. She'd studied hard and played hard, but now she just worked hard. Sinking into the hard chair, she picked up the glass and took a long sip. She let the whiskey warm her as she searched for the source of the ache settling in her stomach. Was it sadness for a youth that had ended too soon? She hadn't wanted to build the new clinic. It had been her father's dream, and unbeknownst to her, he'd bought the property the day she graduated from chiropractic school. She'd argued with him for weeks—she wanted more time to get used to being a doctor, she wasn't ready to take on the financial burden, the clinic was too big—but the deed was done and he'd brushed aside her concerns with "It's time to grow up."

She fell into another memory as Melissa's voice sang the opening of "Ain't It Heavy" from her *Never Enough* album. Jamie knew exactly where she'd been the first time she heard that album. She'd wanted to market to the gay community, to build a practice that felt more like "hers" and less like an offshoot of her father's. They argued, and she accused him of pretending to accept her lifestyle but only if he didn't have to see it. She remembered storming out of the office and racing home in her Z, the new album blasting from the cassette player. She'd persuaded Penni to drive up to the city with her.

They'd hooked up with a couple of women they met in line at a taqueria, and Penni had teased her when she draped her arm across the curvy blonde with the Southern accent. They'd gone back to their apartment, surprised to find their new friends were big Melissa fans. Over beers they traded Melissa facts and fantasies and ended the night dancing around the small living room.

Memories surged around her like the ocean as she sat in the dark and tried to chart the course from her college years playing softball and goofing around with Penni to the owner of a business in trouble. Graduation from chiropractic school. State boards. New doctor in his practice. Partner in the clinic. That one weekend at the music festival stood out like a shooting star amidst all of it.

Jamie woke to a dark room and, still half asleep, reached for the warm body she'd been dreaming about. She jerked upright, heart racing. Alone. Sadness spread through her like a gray fog, and she couldn't stop the tears that turned to angry sobs for everything she'd left behind—freedom to make choices, softball, fun. And everything that had been taken from her—her father's business expertise, her mom's wisdom and support. She hugged a pillow and cried herself into a restless sleep.

When she woke again she saw the ocean through the sliding door, a dull gray under the overcast sky. Her phone rang as she pulled the covers up and rolled over to go back to sleep.

"Are you on your way back? I have my brunch at eleven."

"Can't one of your friends—"

"No. I want to go shopping afterward."

Jamie closed her eyes and took a deep breath. "I'll be there in time."

"Thank you."

Jamie ended the call and pulled the covers over her head. Why was everything her responsibility?

The problem with running away was having to go back. Maybe she should run away for good. She pressed harder on the accelerator as if forcing herself to keep going against the gravity of not wanting to. She had responsibilities and running away wasn't an option.

She rubbed the back of her neck. What was she going to do about Carla? She almost wished she didn't know that Carla remembered her. It complicated things just when it was apparent Carla could help with the embezzlement investigation.

When she walked into the kitchen, Sheryl was staring at the Gaggia, the grinder and a bag of coffee next to it.

"Hi, babe." Jamie kissed her cheek. *I don't like that perfume.*

"I figured out how to make the espresso, but how do you use the steamer?"

"This symbol." Jamie rotated the knob.

"Can you do it?"

"Sure. About yesterday—"

"It's no big deal. You got home in time."

Jamie held the container under the frothing wand as the milk sputtered into peaks of foam.

"I'll just be a few hours, and then you can go take care of the Lexus." Sheryl took a sip of the coffee Jamie handed her. "Thanks."

She draped her arm over Jamie's shoulder and kissed her. It was over too quick. "I missed you last night."

Jamie tucked her hands inside her new sweatshirt as she followed her to their bedroom. "I was thinking," she said, watching Sheryl spread her makeup containers over the counter. "What if we just went for a week? To Hawaii."

"I'll have to see." Sheryl opened a tube and rubbed beige foundation over her face.

"This is important to me, babe. We need a vacation, some time alone together."

"We're fine." Sheryl brushed a rosy powder across her cheeks with a black-handled brush.

"It doesn't feel that way to me." Jamie stared at the towels tossed on the floor.

"You get this way every time you're around Penni." Sheryl pawed through several containers, opened one, and brushed a dark-brown eye shadow onto her eyelids.

"Do I?" She could rattle off the moves that led to a pretty face. "They've been together longer than we have and they still seem—"

"Joined at the hip?" Sheryl looked up, her expression in the mirror mocking.

New lovers and best friends, Jamie was going to say. Now came the mascara.

"I know you idolize their relationship, but really, Jamie, don't you find it silly they're clinging to some childish infatuation? I like that we've gotten past all that. At our age we should be focusing on careers that will get us where we want to be." Sheryl opened a lipstick.

Need surged through Jamie, and she turned Sheryl her toward her. "Before you put that on, how about a real kiss?"

Where was the spark she used to see in Sheryl's eyes just before she kissed her? Jamie wasn't sure where to put her hands. A total stranger had stepped eagerly into her arms last night. She felt the tension in Sheryl's shoulders and heard the unspoken words—don't wrinkle my blouse, don't muss my hair, don't smudge my makeup.

She entwined their fingers. "I love you," she whispered as she tried to show Sheryl how much.

❖

Jamie was hoisting herself out of the pool when her phone rang. "What's up, Don?"

"I hate to bother you, Jamie, but Charlotte Burns threw her back out again. I went in last night, but she says it's worse today and insists you're the only one who can get it right."

Jamie wanted to throttle the woman who thought her VP job title gave her the right to be demanding. She was overweight, didn't exercise, sat too many hours at a desk, and then wondered why her lower back was a disaster.

"I didn't guarantee her I could get ahold of you, but I thought you should make that decision."

"Give me her number." Jamie gouged the number onto a sticky note.

"I'm sorry."

"It's not your fault. And Don…Charlotte's difficult even for me."

"Thanks."

Jamie stared at her phone for a long time before making the call. Her reprieve from responsibility was over. She rubbed the knots in her neck as another text came through from Penni. "Forgiven yet?"

She sighed and texted back, "Yes. Gonna cost you. Will call later." Half her life. Nothing could break a friendship like that.

Chapter Seventeen

Jamie's SUV was the only car in the parking lot when Carla pulled in. She marched to the back door before her resolve failed. In a weekend of roller-coaster emotions, she kept coming back to one truth—she refused to walk out on Jamie again. She intended to fight for her job.

A burst of longing shot through her as she clasped the doorknob to Jamie's office. Her friends would be shocked if they knew that behind her reputed emotional calm and level-headedness was a woman who wanted to storm into her boss's office, pull her into her arms, and kiss her senseless. When Jamie didn't answer the knock she peeked in.

Jamie was standing in front of the window, her back to Carla, the phone against her ear, and a sheet of paper crumpled in her fist. "You can't just cut off my preferred-provider status." The tone was part anger, part fear. "I never got the first notice. I know I can appeal, but I was only recently made aware of the problem. I'm trying to find out what…Fine, you'll be hearing from my attorney." Jamie's arms fell to her sides. She stood rigidly still.

"I couldn't help but overhear. How can I help?" When Jamie turned around, her eyes were flat with anger. Carla ached to rub away the frown that hooded them.

Jamie dropped heavily into her chair. "I can take care—"

"I'm your office manager."

Jamie smoothed out the paper and slid it across the desk.

Carla read it. "What's this about a previous notice?"

"Must have come when Marjorie was still here. If they revoke my preferred-provider status—"

"Patients will have a higher co-pay," Carla said. "It's one of the smaller companies we bill. Not as many patients will be affected."

"I'll have to explain why." Defeat replaced the anger in Jamie's voice.

"Let me see what I can do."

"I should call my attorney." Jamie's gaze went to the pictures on the corner of her desk.

"Give me a day." Carla closed the door behind her and marched to her office. If she ever got her hands on Marjorie she'd strangle that woman. She tossed her purse and sweater on the desk and picked up the phone. She wasn't leaving this office until she fixed this problem.

Jamie leaned back in her chair and rubbed the back of her neck. An army of hands couldn't loosen the knots. Carla evidently wasn't going to quit and she hadn't brought up Saturday. Good. Maybe they could just pretend it hadn't happened.

Now on to the next problem. She called Sheryl. "The dealership says it's an electrical problem. They'll have it fixed tomorrow. If you can get someone to drive you over there, they'll give you a loaner."

"Why can't you take me?"

"I'm dealing with a serious problem. I got a letter from an insurance company threatening to revoke my preferred-provider status." She wanted Sheryl to ask if she could do anything to help. Support went both ways. "It's a big deal, Sheryl."

"Well, I hope it works out." Sheryl said something to someone about arranging a parent conference. "Can you pick me up after work and take me? I don't have a meeting tonight. Maybe we could get dinner."

"I won't be done till after six."

"But—"

"I gotta go. See you tonight." As Jamie got out of the chair, her elbow bumped a stack of patient files and they toppled to the floor. What was she thinking? She hadn't gone through files since Friday.

She needed to deal with her business problems. Hadn't the letter made that clear? She forced back anger as she restacked the files. Gripping the doorknob she took deep breaths until everything faded but the responsibility in front of her. She was a chiropractor. She took care of people.

❖

Carla hung up the phone and jumped from her chair, anxious to share the good news with Jamie as soon as she finished with her last patient. Was it her imagination or had Jamie been avoiding her all day? She hadn't been fired, but Jamie hadn't said anything about Saturday. Should she bring it up?

Jamie's voice captured her attention as she walked her patient to the front. Just her voice… Carla sighed as she endured another rebellion from her body.

Jamie looked tired, but this morning's tightness was gone from her face as she set the file on the front counter. "I'll see you next month, Renee. Thanks for referring the two new patients."

"I'm happy to refer people, Jamie, because I know you'll take care of them. I'm glad to see your office in such good hands," she said to Carla. "I knew you two would be a good fit."

Jamie's cheeks reddened and she wouldn't meet Carla's eyes. She disappeared into Carla's office.

"How would you like some good news?" Carla asked after locking the front door behind Renee.

"It would make my day." Jamie looked up from pulling files and rubbed the back of her neck. "Maybe my month."

"I got the insurance company to postpone further action against you for thirty days. By then we should have it sorted out."

"How did you manage that?" Jamie looked confused.

"A little Southern charm," Carla said, adding a thick accent. She gulped when Jamie's eyes sparked. "A little letting them think I was your attorney and we were serious about legal action."

"You impersonated my attorney?" The confusion changed to a look of surprise.

Carla shrugged. "I didn't discourage the assumption."

"I don't know what to say, Carla."

"It was my pleasure." Carla's throat tightened with everything she couldn't say.

"About Saturday," Jamie said, shifting her weight. "We should probably talk about it. Get it out in the open…" She cleared her throat.

"I'm sorry if I gave you the wrong impression." Carla looked away from Jamie. She couldn't say this next part if she had to look at everything she wanted and couldn't have. "I meant I want a second chance at a friendship with you." Carla blinked back tears and set a smile on her face. Jamie's expression changed but she couldn't read it. Relief?

"Um, that sounds good…friendship. I'm sorry I left so abruptly…before you could explain. Well, I'll see you tomorrow." Jamie gathered the files and squeezed past Carla in the doorway. Their eyes met for an instant and the gratitude in them was unmistakable.

Carla clasped her hands behind her back to keep from reaching for Jamie. Would a quick hug be wrong? A sharp pain went through her heart as Jamie walked away. She'd done the right thing, the only thing. Fatigue from the long sleepless weekend washed over her. A hot bath, leftover lasagna, and a glass of wine would help. She'd have to settle for being part of Jamie's work life. How could fate be so cruel?

❖

Jamie set her keys on the kitchen counter and opened the refrigerator. "Hey, Sheryl?" she hollered toward the back of the house. "Didn't you pick up something for dinner?"

"Sorry," Sheryl said, walking into the kitchen. "My secretary took me over to the dealer so I could get the loaner, and I took her to dinner as a thank you. She's single, and works hard for me. Never hurts to build loyalty in your employees."

Jamie bent over, hands on her thighs as the refrigerator door slowly closed. She took her secretary out to dinner and didn't bring anything home for her. "I'm going out." She picked up her keys and stormed from the kitchen. When had Sheryl become so clueless? Or was it careless?

❖

Jamie nursed a beer as she watched the A's get trounced on the big screen on the wall of the sports bar. The pepperoni pizza had soothed the hunger but now sat heavily in her stomach. So did her mood. How could she get Sheryl to put their relationship first?

At least she hadn't given Carla her "I don't cheat" speech. She'd misunderstood, and how embarrassing would that have been? She wouldn't have to find a new office manager, and Carla had solved the problem with the insurance company in one day. It was about time she got a break.

Televisions filled the walls, and any direction she looked someone was winning and someone was losing. Which side was she on? In softball it was easy to make that call. Where was the scoreboard that told her where she was in life right now? It felt like she was losing, but she had no idea what skills she lacked.

Watching baseball always made her want to be on a diamond, grass under her feet, the sound of bats connecting with balls. She pulled out her cell phone and called Penni.

"What's up, girlfriend?" Penni asked.

"When's your Bobby Sox practice this weekend?"

"Who is this, and what have you done with Jamie?"

"Funny." Jamie finally had to smile.

"Saturday. Ten o'clock."

"Damn." If she went in an hour earlier, moved those scheduled between ten and twelve to later, she could sneak out for practice and then go back. It could work. "I'll be there," she said as the restaurant broke into cheers. The A's had just hit a home run.

"Where are you?"

"Sports bar. Felt like pizza."

"More like you got home and no dinner was waiting for you. Why do you—"

"Don't start." She raised her arm in salute as the batter crossed home plate.

"Oh, all right. I'm too happy to argue with you. See you Saturday."

Jamie stayed until the game was over. The A's rallied to win. Never give up hope. She packed the leftover slices in a box for lunch tomorrow. Couldn't she have a business and still have time for fun? There had to be some middle ground.

CHAPTER EIGHTEEN

Mike held the door for Carla as they walked into La Foret, the elegant French restaurant they loved. They were going to start their last weekend together with a celebration of their marriage. Mike looked handsome, as always, in his gray suit with the royal-blue shirt. She took his arm as they were led through the dimly lit restaurant to a table set with white dishes on a white tablecloth.

They hadn't talked much during the fifteen-minute drive to the restaurant. Carla didn't know what Mike was thinking about, but she was remembering the day last fall that had led them to this dinner. She'd come home to find Mike crying on their bed. Afraid he'd been diagnosed with a serious illness, she'd held him. He finally composed himself and admitted he was attracted to a manager of another department.

Carla's shock had been diffused when he said the manager was a guy, and she'd felt oddly relieved when he confessed he was afraid he was gay. Their mutual homosexuality explained so much about their relationship—as close as two people could be but lacking the sexual spark Carla had assumed only she missed. They'd talked late into the night, and his honesty had prompted her to confess her doubts about her own sexual preference. They'd fallen asleep early in the morning after tears turned to peals of laughter at the irony of their situation. Many more conversations led them to agree that honesty and self-respect were more important than appearances. In three months their divorce would be final.

Mike took Carla's hand as the waiter poured champagne. "To the love of my life." He slid a small black box across the table.

"Are you celebrating your anniversary?" the young man asked brightly.

"No, our divorce," Mike said. Their eyes met a second before they burst out laughing.

Carla opened the box. "Oh, Mike, it's beautiful."

He fastened the gold watch around her wrist. "For all the good times." He leaned over and kissed her.

They chatted and shared memories as they worked their way through one wonderful course after another. While waiting for dessert, Carla noticed the couple being seated in the far corner of the small room. "I can't believe it," she whispered. A blond, slightly pudgy thirty-something man was pulling a chair out for the principal she'd done battle with last year.

"Don't let her spoil the evening."

"I feel sorry for that poor guy." When Sheryl glanced her way, the look of surprise that turned sour made Carla laugh. The poor schmuck, her husband, she assumed, was undoubtedly about to get an earful from the sharp-tongued principal.

Friday night's celebration gave way to the thankless grunt work of moving. Rob, the guy Mike had met during a 10k a few months ago and was now dating, had gamely agreed to help. As the day wore on she was both grateful for his help and increasingly fond of the man who might replace her in Mike's life. Would she find someone who put that look on her face? She still hadn't worked up the courage to call Vanessa. In spite of Mike's encouragement, dating scared her. But she'd joined a book club and a running club. Meeting lesbians she might become friends with seemed like the place to start.

By the time they called it quits for the day, Carla was tired and her back hurt. Declining Mike's offer to join them for pizza, she opted for a glass of wine and a hot bath. She woke stiff and tried to soothe her back into cooperating with another long soak in her Jacuzzi tub.

She might have gotten away with just soreness if it hadn't been for the fifty-inch plasma TV she and Mike moved at the end of the day. Mike lost his grip going up the steps to the front door, and Carla lurched sideways to keep it from falling against the doorframe. Something popped in her lower back, and she gritted her teeth against the pain until the TV was safely in place. Then she slumped to her knees and clutched her back.

"Carla? What's wrong?"

Carla tried to stand but couldn't as muscle spasms grabbed her with a ferocity she couldn't have imagined. "My back. Ow. God, that hurts. I can't get up." Mike put his arm around her waist and helped her to the couch.

"I'm sorry, honey." Mike rubbed her lower back. "I knew we should have waited for Rob. Do you want some Advil?"

Carla tried to stand, but biting pain dropped her to the couch again. "You won't find it in all these boxes. I'll take some at home." Mike supported most of her weight as she shuffled out to the truck he'd borrowed for the move.

"Maybe we should take you to emergency," Mike said after they'd repeated the maneuver to get Carla into the house.

She gripped the kitchen counter for support but kept her voice light. "I'm sure it'll be fine with some Advil and a night's sleep." She'd never had more than a minor backache from too much gardening and was scared, but she didn't want Mike to know. He'd offer to stay.

"Why don't we call Jamie?"

"I'm not bothering her on a Sunday."

"But—"

"I'll be fine. You have a date. Don't forget the bag of peanut-butter cookies."

"With crunchy peanut butter?"

Carla laughed at the little-kid face he always made over cookies and regretted it as her back seized up. What did Jamie tell patients to do? "Can you get the ice pack for me?"

"Promise you'll call if it gets worse," Mike said after he helped her to the couch. "It feels weird saying good night and then leaving."

"We're still the best friends we were always meant to be." Now that the moment was here, letting go was so much harder than she'd expected. He knelt in front of her and they held each other for a long time.

An hour later she was able to get up, albeit slowly. She stood at her kitchen counter and ate salami and cheese and French bread for dinner. A hot bath sounded heavenly but she didn't think she could get in the tub, so she settled for another dose of Advil. She got into bed, stuffed pillows behind her, and opened one of the lesbian fiction books that arrived yesterday. She smiled at the cover—two women holding hands, looking longingly into each other's eyes. She wanted that.

Her eyes filled with tears, and she reached for a Kleenex on the nightstand as her back protested. Her first night in her new life and she was alone with a book. Would one night be all she ever knew of passion?

Carla woke up at two A.M. needing to pee. It took her ten minutes to roll onto the floor and crawl to the bathroom. Getting onto the toilet was agony. Getting off was almost impossible. After swallowing more Advil she made it back to bed by grabbing onto every piece of furniture along the way. Tears ran down her cheeks as she tried to find a comfortable position. This wasn't the new life she'd envisioned.

CHAPTER NINETEEN

Jamie closed the patient file she'd been halfheartedly looking through and checked her watch again. It was almost nine, and Carla wasn't here for their morning meeting. It had become a ritual—coffee in her office while they reviewed the status of the insurance investigation and any clinic issues that needed attention. Every day she was aware of what an asset Carla was. Thank God they'd gotten past that awkwardness at Lori's party. Sure, her pulse occasionally jumped, but didn't everyone have an ex-lover they sometimes reacted to? There was still the problem of Sheryl finding out, but for now she'd have to ignore that. She smiled at her father's picture. Everything was going to be fine with the clinic.

Rubbing her neck, she thought back over the weekend. She still didn't know how to feel about it. Sheryl had been in high spirits because of a lunch with the superintendent whom she described as her "winning ticket." Their conversation had included the importance of family values for teenagers. Jamie's questions about what constituted family values weren't well received. Sheryl's "does it matter as long as I get my promotion" left her queasy.

Jamie hated that Sheryl's happiness depended on a homophobic jerk, but Sheryl happy improved their relationship. They hadn't made love like that in months. They were spending more time together, and things often felt like they used to. Maybe after Sheryl got the promotion she wouldn't have to suck up to him. She took a long sip of coffee. It was so good she moaned. That alone was worth hiring Carla.

She rolled down the sleeves on the red silk shirt she'd bought shopping with Sheryl yesterday and walked to the front counter. "Has anyone talked to Carla this morning?" No one had. Maybe she'd just overslept.

Fifteen minutes later Jamie was coming out of a treatment room when she saw Carla in the hallway—shuffling steps, tilted to the right, bracing against the wall. She dropped the file and rushed to her.

"Easy." Jamie wrapped her arm around Carla's waist. "Let's get you into the treatment room." She put Carla's arm across her shoulder and inched her toward the treatment room. "Marci," she hollered, "I need help here."

"I'm scared," Carla said, gripping Jamie's shoulder.

"It's okay," Jamie said as she and Marci helped Carla sit on the adjusting table. Kneeling in front of Carla, she rubbed her hands over Carla's knees and met eyes clouded with pain and tears. "I promise you'll be fine." Jamie gripped Carla's knees tighter to keep from brushing the tears away. "How did it happen?"

Carla explained the incident with the TV. "I've never hurt my back before. It really hurts. Can you fix it?"

"Yes. I promise you'll be standing straight by the end of the day and able to tie your shoes by Friday." Jamie would do whatever it took to keep that promise. "Let's get you facedown." Marci moved to the other side of the table and they helped Carla lie down. "Tell me if the pain gets worse." Jamie laid her hands on Carla's back and did what was second nature to her.

"My back's always been so strong."

"The lifting you did Saturday fatigued your back muscles, and when you tried to catch the TV they weren't up to the stress."

"I should have called in sick. I'm sorry to take you away from your patients because I did something stupid." Carla's voice broke.

"You did the right thing by coming in, but you should have called. I would have picked you up. I want you here where I can take care of you." There was heat and tension in the paraspinal muscles, and restrictions at L3, L4, and L5, bilaterally but worse on the left. This was bad. "You jerked to the left when the TV fell, and this is the most tender spot," she said, pressing a little harder just to the left of the L4/L5 joint.

"How did you know?"

"It's what I do." Jamie was never sure how to explain it, but the minute she touched a patient she knew where their pain was. She massaged the muscles until she felt the telltale softening she was waiting for.

Carla sighed. "That feels good. Your hands are so warm."

"I'm going to adjust you now. You might feel a little jolt of pain but I promise it won't last. Okay?"

"I trust you." Carla gripped the armrest.

Jamie did a quick downward thrust on Carla's back and the table dropped away beneath her. She did two more adjustments, satisfied that the vertebrae had moved back into alignment. It would take a series of treatments to resolve the problem, but she was sure Carla would feel better immediately. "Okay?"

"Fine."

"Get an ice pack for her," Jamie told Marci. Resting her hand between Carla's shoulder blades she said, "I'll check on you in a few minutes."

"I don't want to interrupt your schedule."

"You're my first priority."

Several hours later, Carla felt like she was spending a day at a spa as she lay on her back on Jamie's couch, a pillow under her knees, a cup of coffee at hand. She'd been shocked when she stood up in the treatment room and felt a dull pain but no bite. Relieved, she'd hugged Jamie without thinking. Since then she hadn't had ten minutes to herself, with everyone checking on her. Jamie had set her docking station within arm's length with instructions to do nothing but lie there and listen to music. When Carla protested that she could at least read through patient files, Jamie staunchly refused.

Carla hadn't meant to snoop when she scrolled through Jamie's iPod. All of Melissa's albums were on it, which wasn't a surprise. But she found forty-two playlists, listed by year and city, beginning in 1991and ending this year. She realized what she was looking at—concerts. Jamie had gone to even more than she had. Carla clasped the iPod to her chest as tears filled her eyes. The impossibility that they'd never bumped into each other was almost more than she could bear.

"How are you feeling?" Jamie asked when she bounded into her office.

Carla had to clear her throat before she answered. "Much better. I don't know what I'd do without you." She held up the iPod. "You went to all those concerts?" Jamie took a step back from the couch and put her hands in her pockets. "I'm sorry, Jamie. I wasn't prying." Carla tried to sit up. "Ouch."

"Easy. Slow movements." Jamie helped her sit. "It's a miracle we didn't run into each other, isn't it?"

"Maybe we can go sometime." Carla wanted to take Jamie's hand and pull her down next to her. She wanted to talk about those concerts, and share memories. She'd thought about Jamie at every one. Melissa's music had been a slender but cherished thread linking her to that night. She'd been listening to her first two albums for hours during those difficult months following her return from Atlanta when responsibility pulled her in the only direction she could go while her heart looked back at the other path. They hadn't mentioned that night since Lori's party, and it suddenly wasn't all right. "Jamie—"

"Let's get you up for a short stroll. I sent Marci for lunch. If you can do ten lengths of the hall you can have your choice of sandwiches."

Carla reined in her sadness. Jamie obviously didn't want to talk about it. She let Jamie help her up, although she could have done it herself. She wasn't about to forego a chance to feel that arm around her waist or the sinfully good sensation of Jamie's breast against her side. They enjoyed a companionable lunch in Jamie's office, but all too soon Jamie gathered up wrappers and cups.

"I want to adjust your back again."

"I didn't know you did more than one adjustment in a day." She wasn't complaining. Jamie's hands on her again would be more than welcome. Jamie's touch was different than Sara's. Something indescribable came through her hands. Carla felt the power even if she couldn't find words to describe it.

"I don't usually because it's intense. When it works it can drastically speed up the healing time for acute injuries like yours." She sat back down in the chair. "That same intensity can be too much for some people and make them really sore, but I think it will work for you."

Carla sensed that Jamie wanted to say more. "Go on."

"There's definitely a science to chiropractic, but I've learned to respect and value the art of it more than the science. Healing is a funny thing, Carla. Not as predictable as people want, or expect, it to be. I've come to trust that even though I can't always control it, I know when it's happening and when it isn't. When it is, I do more of what I've been doing and encourage people to be patient. When it's not, I try a different approach or refer them out."

Carla remembered Penni's comments from the party and tried to imagine Jamie as anything less than the confident doctor sitting across from her. "It's important to me to understand what you do, and how you make treatment choices, so I'm better able to answer patients' questions." Carla wanted to say so much more, but a line separated them. They were polite and friendly with each other, but with an edge of awkwardness Carla regretted. She was afraid to spook Jamie again by bringing up anything about that night, but this repressed quality to their interactions frustrated her.

"Let's take you on another stroll." Jamie reached for Carla's arm and helped her up. For now she was happy to settle for Jamie's arm around her waist, but she hoped she would have an opportunity some day to talk about that night and get it out in the open.

CHAPTER TWENTY

I'm driving you home or you're calling your husband to come get you." Jamie folded her arms across her chest as Carla got to her feet. Her movements were guarded, but she got up by herself, which was a good sign.

"Really, Jamie, I feel much better. I'll go home and ice it."

"Not negotiable." She picked up Carla's purse and sweater from the desk. "Driving involves two things—sitting and lifting your legs to work the pedals—that are hard for your back right now."

"All right." The pain was gone from Carla's face but she looked tired.

Jamie cupped her elbow as they walked to her SUV. Carla caught her toe on a crack in the asphalt, and Jamie put her arm around her waist. "You have to consciously pick up your feet. They still want to shuffle." She didn't let go of Carla's waist until she helped her into the car.

Jamie pulled into the driveway of the front-gabled bungalow on a tree-lined street in Los Gatos. Sheryl's school was nearby. The sage-green paint and burgundy trim looked tasteful with a bit of flare, two adjectives Jamie had come to associate with Carla. "I lived on the other side of Los Gatos until a few years ago. It's crazy we never ran into each other."

"You'd think we would have crossed paths at the market or dry cleaner or something." Carla's hands were folded in her lap, and she was tapping her fingers to the Melissa song.

The front yard justified the gardening advice Carla gave patients. A small lawn was bisected by a flagstone path and surrounded with flowers. She wished her front yard looked that inviting. The song ended and Jamie got out of the car. She cupped her elbow as she helped her out. "What's that smell?" she asked when they were almost to the front door. It wasn't Carla's perfume, but it was just as sweet.

Carla pointed to a rosebush covered in ivory blossoms with dark-pink edges. Jamie took one of the stems and pulled the rose to her face. The scent was intoxicating.

"Secret," Carla said. A bee landed on the rose and crawled around the stamens. "The name of the rose. Do you like to garden?"

"I don't know." Jamie let go of Carla's arm and stepped to the next rose, a yellow one. It smelled a little like apricots. "I've never had time. My mom loved to—roses, especially. I wish I'd paid more attention." She took in the exuberant flowerbeds and the birdbath nestled among tall pink and white flowers. Two little birds splashed around in it before flying off. The yard was obviously a labor of love. Intimate was the word that came to mind. "She would love this."

Carla disappeared around the side of the house and returned with pruners. She handed Jamie roses as she cut them. "Hold these."

A rainbow of roses grew in her hand. "Careful," Jamie said when Carla knelt down to cut some pink flowers close to the ground. Jamie helped her up and her hand ended up sandwiched between Carla's arm and her breast. Her cheeks felt warm when she let go. Touching Carla again, even therapeutically, brought back their past in a way Jamie didn't like. She'd get Carla in the house and go home—a swim to relax, then she'd fix dinner for Sheryl.

"Put these in water as soon as you get home."

"I'll help you get settled with an ice pack."

"Jamie, I can—"

"An ice pack is heavier than you should lift."

"The house is a bit messy." Carla hesitated before unlocking her front door.

"I won't look." Jamie followed Carla across the tiled entryway into the living room. "Looks like you're the one moving." Empty boxes were stacked haphazardly in a corner, and rolls of packing tape littered the coffee table. "You aren't, are you?"

"No."

"Good." The room had all the warmth and casualness she'd come to associate with Carla—pale-peach walls, floral-print fabrics in pastel shades covering the rolled-arm couches, extra pillows. A house where people spent time together.

"I'll put these in a vase for you." Carla lifted the flowers from Jamie's hand, their fingers touching as she did.

Jamie followed Carla through a dining room to the kitchen. Yellow-tiled counters and an orangey-red on the walls gave the room a cheerful feeling. A KitchenAid mixer stood next to an array of glass bowls and baking sheets. A copper pot sat on the stove, a plate of cookies next to an espresso machine. A cook's kitchen.

Carla reached for a vase on the top shelf of a cabinet. "Ouch." She set the vase down hastily, bracing herself on the kitchen counter.

Jamie hurried to support her around her waist. "That's my point. Something you wouldn't have thought twice about doing yesterday is likely to cause you pain for a while." When Carla seemed stable she lowered her arm and backed away, shoving her hands in her pockets. "If you do too many of those things you risk a relapse."

"Point taken." Carla straightened, rubbing her back.

"Keep icing it tonight. You're likely to be stiff again in the morning so don't panic."

Carla snipped the ends off the roses, pulled off some of the outer petals, arranged them in the vase, and then arranged them again. "Can I take a hot bath?"

"Not tonight." Jamie's pulse hitched as she remembered that tiny tub in the hotel. Why did her mind keep going places it shouldn't? She crossed her arms and watched a hummingbird land on the feeder outside the window over the sink and drink greedily.

"The heat will relax your muscles, but that's not necessarily a good thing right now. They're supporting the injured joints. Go ahead and take one in the morning if you're stiff when you wake up."

Carla set the vase of flowers next to Jamie and pulled the Secret blossom above the others.

"How 'bout if we get you settled on the couch with that ice pack?" Jamie opened the freezer and pulled an ice pack from between neatly labeled plastic containers and packages of frozen meat. Her freezer was filled with Sheryl's store-bought diet meals. "Will your husband be home soon?"

"Umm…I'm not sure. I want to get out of these clothes before I lie down."

Jamie watched Carla's hips and back as she headed through the living room toward a hallway on the far side. Her gait was stiff, her steps careful, but overall Jamie was pleased at the progress. The cold from the ice pack penetrated her awareness, and she set it on the counter. She went and stood at the French doors that led to the backyard. Just like the front yard, it was well tended. Trees lined the back, a small lawn filled the middle of the space, and flowerbeds curved around a flagstone patio. Intimate and cared for. A table was off to one side of the patio, two place mats and a candle on it. Romantic dinners. A hand on her shoulder startled her from her reverie.

"I could barely get into a skirt this morning," Carla said. "Now I can bend over enough to put pants on. I'm more grateful than I can say, Jamie."

"A back injury is scary if you don't know it can be fixed." Jamie watched a squirrel shimmy up an oak tree in a neighbor's yard, a second squirrel in hot pursuit, but her focus was on the warmth of Carla's hand. She smelled Carla's rose-scented lotion. "You'll be fine in a few days. I'll have Marci work with you next week on strengthening your back so this will be less likely to happen again."

Jamie stepped to the side and Carla's hand fell away. "I should—" Her usually well-put-together office manager was wearing black leggings and a yellow V-neck sweater. Jamie's eyes went where they shouldn't. An uncomfortable silence descended.

Carla stepped closer and lifted Jamie's hands from her side. "Can we do something to make things less awkward between us?" Carla's eyes were soft, and radiating kindness. "That night mattered to me, and I don't want to have to pretend it didn't happen. Can't we talk about it like two old friends reminiscing?"

Jamie felt glued to this spot by Carla's eyes, soft and inviting. "I don't like the awkwardness either. I don't know what to do about it."

"How about if we agree it was special and—"

"Important," Jamie said in a whisper as she looked down at their clasped hands. Two old friends…She couldn't hold back the words.

"I wasn't fair when we talked at the party. I let you admit how much it mattered without telling you how much it meant to me." She'd been trying so hard not to mention anything about that night, and right now she didn't know why. They'd both gone on with their lives, but wasn't a night that special important?

"That whole weekend…" Jamie shook her head, thoughts falling into place. "I remember everything about it—the heat, the music festival, the incredibly friendly women I met. And you—how brave you were to go to the concert and the bar, dancing…I never forgot it." Jamie's heart loosened with the relief of saying what she'd always wanted to say to the woman who'd shared it with her. She let her eyes travel from their hands to the V between Carla's legs, then up her stomach to breasts that filled out the sweater, to her mouth and the hint of a smile, and last, the eyes that pleaded with her to keep going. She owed Carla the truth. Then she could let it go.

Jamie's heart was pounding and she looked back at their hands. "As the night went on you brought out feelings in me I hadn't felt before." Did she dare say the rest of it? "I think I fell in love with you." She laughed but it sounded wrong. "Silly, huh?" Jamie stroked her thumbs over the backs of Carla's hands, her awareness narrowed to exclude anything but the softness. Tomorrow they'd be on the other side of this moment. They'd be past the awkwardness.

Carla remained quiet with everything but her eyes that were filling with tears. They spoke volumes. Jamie soaked up the kindness. Just two old friends reliving the past, putting it to rest.

The words escaped. "I wish it had ended differently. That room was so lonely when I woke up…realized you'd left. I thought about trying to find you, but I didn't know your last name." Sadness engulfed her. "I still have your note."

"Oh, Jamie, I wish it had ended differently, too."

"The shock of seeing you again…" Jamie frowned as she reached for words that fell into place as she spoke them. "It's made me look back at my life. I don't know where the last twenty years have gone. I don't think I've felt that carefree since that weekend." She tightened her grip on Carla's hands. "I wish we could have a second chance."

Jamie realized what she'd said, and she started to add, "at friendship," but Carla wrapped her arms around her waist and pulled her close. Jamie slid her hands up Carla's back and rested her cheek against Carla's. She sighed with the familiarity of it as the moment swallowed them. Their bodies shifted until they were pressed against each other, their breath warm on each other's cheeks. The sound of the front door opening pierced Jamie's awareness. She flinched and pulled away.

"I brought takeout," a man said as he walked toward them carrying a plastic bag.

Jamie backed up, almost tripping over the coffee table. Carla's husband.

Carla lunged for her and caught her arm but let go as her knees buckled. "Shit. Ow, that hurts." The man rushed to catch Carla with an arm around her waist. "Jamie, wait," Carla cried out as she clutched her back.

Jamie stopped her exit when she heard Carla's cry. She knew what it meant. She'd never felt so embarrassed in her life as she faced Carla and the tall, good-looking man. She didn't know how much he'd seen, but she knew guilt and shame were written all over her face. She stood frozen in place, waiting for his reaction.

"Jamie, please." Carla's face was pinched with pain and tears rolled down her cheeks.

She would probably be tossed out in a few minutes, but she had to make sure Carla was all right. She supported Carla's other side as they helped her to the couch. "Lie down." She put one of the pillows under Carla's knees. "I'll get the ice pack. Take deep breaths. It'll be okay, Carla." She heard them talking but couldn't hear what they said as she went to the kitchen. When she slid the ice pack under Carla's back, Carla grabbed her hand with both of hers.

"I have to explain." Her eyes were as pleading as her voice.

Jamie couldn't think straight, but she knew her hand didn't belong in Carla's. She backed away. The man cleared his throat behind her. Jamie hoped her cheeks weren't as red as they felt as she turned to face him.

"I'm Mike. You must be Dr. Hammond."

"Jamie, please." She took his outstretched hand but couldn't meet his eyes. Why was he smiling?

"Mike's the friend I helped move this weekend," Carla blurted out.

"I don't understand." Jamie looked between the two of them.

"We're getting divorced. Mike moved out." Carla's voice sounded defeated and her face was tight with pain.

"That's my cue to leave." Mike kissed her on the cheek. "I'll put the sushi in the refrigerator. Sorry I interrupted."

"Don't go."

Jamie tried to make sense of this exchange. Divorce? Had Carla said they were getting a divorce? That meant…a tingle of dread spread over her body. Her confession. The hug. Second chances. "I need to get home."

"Please stay. We need to talk." Carla struggled to a sitting position with a groan. "We can't keep running from that night."

Is that what they'd been doing? What she'd been doing? Maybe they did need to get it all out in the open, and then it would fade away. Jamie relaxed a little until she realized Mike looked like he understood this conversation perfectly. *Oh, God, he knows.*

"Wine or Scotch?" Mike asked, squeezing her shoulder. "Sorry, those are the only two choices."

"Scotch," Jamie said. "Make it a double." This didn't make sense. They didn't act like two people getting divorced. Jamie dropped into a chair across from the couch and gratefully took a large swallow of the drink Mike handed her.

Carla held Mike's hand when he sat next to her, but her attention was on Jamie. "To make a long story short, Mike realized he's gay. And since that night with you I knew the truth about myself, too."

Jamie's thoughts whirled. Carla wasn't straight? Or married? Jamie gulped more Scotch. She coughed as the burn hit her stomach. It growled menacingly.

"How about if I set dinner out and you two finish this discussion," Mike said.

Jamie was too confused to do anything but listen as Carla went on.

"I can't say I wish we'd figured out we're both gay before we got married because we wouldn't have Lissa, but it explains a lot about our relationship over the years."

Jamie listened to the sounds of plates being set on the counter and water turned on. Did she want to hear this?

"We were best friends, and if life in a small Southern town hadn't forced us to be more, things might have been different. I worried something was missing between us. I didn't know what it was until that night with you."

Heat crawled up Jamie's throat. Surely Mike could hear them.

"I want to keep working for you, Jamie. And I could really use a friend. I'm kind of in transition." Carla smiled, but it was a sad smile. Her voice broke as she said, "We have to find a way to get past this."

Was there a way past it? How did one night carry more than its fair share of importance in her life? She took a deep breath. Sure, they were ex-lovers, but weren't they just sealing that door and moving on to the next phase in their relationship?

"Dinner," Mike announced.

"I should be getting home." Her stomach growled again.

"You need some food to go with that Scotch or I'll have to drive you home," Mike teased her. "And I always order way too much."

Jamie was a little unsteady as she stood. She did need to eat. "I have to make a call. Excuse me for a minute."

"Hurry," Mike said. "We're pretty cutthroat when it comes to sushi."

❖

Carla clung to Mike's hand as he helped her off the couch. Her emotions were on overload from Jamie touching her all day. And the hug…she'd been ready to kiss her before Mike's untimely entrance.

"Sorry if I screwed things up for you."

"Not your fault." Just bad timing again.

"She's cute." Mike kissed the side of her head as he lowered her into the dining chair.

Carla tried to get comfortable as her back muscles spasmed. Jamie was standing in front of the French doors talking to someone. She had to figure out how to get them past this awkwardness.

"We love sushi," Mike said, when Jamie joined them at the table.

"I do, too." Jamie added wasabi to the soy sauce in the tray on her plate. She picked up a piece with the jade chopsticks, dipped it, and put the whole piece in her mouth.

"Try a piece of Red Dragon," Mike said, pointing at a roll with bright-red tuna on top.

"How about if I get it for our Friday staff lunch?" Carla asked, as if this were a perfectly normal conversation.

"Um, sure." Jamie reached for another piece.

"Jamie's an ex-softball star," Carla said.

"Wow, a real athlete. I'm a huge baseball fan, but I was never good enough to play. Did you play college ball?"

"San Jose State." Jamie's eyes watered as the wasabi hit her. "Had a scholarship to UCLA," she added in a voice garbled by the bite in her mouth.

"I'm impressed. Why didn't you go?"

Carla watched this back-and-forth between her soon-to-be ex-husband and the woman she'd been in love with for twenty years. It made her giggle, but no one noticed.

"My mother died the summer after I graduated and I decided to stay close to home."

"That's tough," Mike said. "How long have you been a chiropractor?"

Carla reached under the table and squeezed Mike's leg. "Thank you," she mouthed, grateful for his leading the conversation.

"Twenty years in August." Jamie reached for a piece of unagi at the same time as Carla, and their chopsticks clinked.

"Shall we sword fight?" Carla held up her chopsticks.

"No, I'll just beat you to it," Jamie said as she stuffed the whole piece into her mouth.

"I can't thank you enough for taking care of Carla today. I feel terrible she got hurt helping me move. I told you we should have waited for Rob." Mike waved a chopstick in Carla's direction.

"Mike's boyfriend," Carla said, and Jamie choked. She resisted the urge to slap Jamie on the back. She liked the unflappable Dr. Hammond a little ruffled.

"I don't quite…" Jamie looked down at her plate, shaking her head.

"Ask whatever you want, Jamie."

Jamie set her chopsticks across her plate. "You two just…agreed to divorce? And you're friends with his boyfriend?"

Carla's heart broke for the confusion on Jamie's face. This wasn't how she'd wanted to tell her about the divorce. "We can't continue a marriage just for the sake of appearances. We know truths about ourselves that dictate a different lifestyle."

"Didn't you tell me you found a lesbian bar in San Diego a few weeks ago? And met an attorney who lives up here?" Mike smiled sweetly at the daggers Carla sent him. "I'll clean up. Why don't you tell Jamie about it? Maybe she can give you tips on dating." He took their plates to the kitchen.

Jamie folded the napkin into a square and set it in the middle of the place mat. "Wow. Dating." She gulped some water.

"Yeah." Carla shrugged. "Seems like the next thing for me to do if I want a new life. I can't exactly ask Lissa for advice, and since you're my only lesbian friend..." Jamie shifted in her chair. "Like, should I call her at home or her office? And should I suggest we go to dinner or let her make a suggestion? The whole dating thing...I never did it." Carla tried not to smile as she watched Jamie digest this. Her puzzled expression was adorable.

"It's been a long time for me, too."

"I vote for the bold approach," Mike offered from the kitchen. "Call her up at home and invite her to dinner Friday night. Doesn't she live in Los Altos? There's that great Mediterranean restaurant up there we liked. If it goes well I'll give you my tickets to that new play in San Francisco for Sunday. Anybody want ice cream? Macadamia nut or green tea."

"I should go." Jamie scooted her chair back.

"Jamie loves ice cream. Bring her a little of both." Just a few more minutes and she'd let her go. "How 'bout I make us cappuccinos?"

"Um...sure." Jamie sprang to her feet and helped Carla up. "How's it feel?"

"Stiff, but I'll be fine." She missed Jamie's arm around her waist the instant she let go.

"Guest of honor," Mike said, as he set a bowl piled high with ice cream in front of Jamie, and Carla set a cup next to it with a "J" drizzled in the middle of the foam. Conversation drifted to sports and then to books.

"I joined a book club for lesbian fiction," Carla said.

"Okay, that's my cue to leave," Mike said. "I'll check on you in the morning." He kissed Carla on the cheek. "And you better take good care of my best girl." Jamie blushed when he kissed her on the cheek, too.

"You two should go running as soon as Carla's back is up to it," he tossed over his shoulder. The front door closed, encasing them in silence.

"I should get going, too." Jamie carried dishes to the kitchen.

"Thank you for staying for dinner." Carla followed her, sadness settling over her. She didn't want Jamie to leave yet. "Are we going to be friends, Jamie?"

Conflicting emotions passed over Jamie's face and she put her hands in her pockets. "I'd like to."

"I'm sorry you found out about the divorce this way. I was going to tell you but then with my back…"

"Speaking of which, let's get you on ice." She opened the freezer and grabbed the ice pack before helping Carla to the couch.

"Do you need anything before I leave?" Jamie tucked the blanket around Carla.

"No," Carla said, aching to pull Jamie to her for another hug. "Thank you for taking care of me today." She tried not to think about the woman Jamie was going home to.

"I'm glad I could help." Jamie looked tired. "Do you need a ride in the morning?"

Carla wanted to say yes. "Mike will take me." She reached toward Jamie's chest and saw her breath catch.

"I've wanted to ask you about this." She fingered the pendant at Jamie's throat, a diamond set in a gold star that Jamie always wore. "It's lovely."

"A gift from my mother."

"Both my parents are gone too, Jamie. We have a lot in common."

"Sleep well," Jamie said. She left without looking back.

Sobs broke through the minute the door closed. Carla held her arms across her stomach as her back rebelled. Both her past and her future were gone. She struggled to her feet and went to the stereo, bringing Melissa's voice into the room. She wasn't going to be alone.

❖

Jamie let Melissa's music envelop her as she headed home, her mind processing the strange turn of events. She liked Mike, and their closeness reminded her of Penni and Lori. She respected their willingness to make such a big change in their lives at this age. Could she and Carla be friends? Should they, given how Sheryl felt about her? Her phone rang. "Hey, Penni."

"Where are you?"

"Headed home from Carla's. I had dinner with her and her gay husband." Jamie smiled as the silence stretched. It took a lot to silence Penni.

"Carla's husband is gay and you had dinner with them?"

"Yep. They're getting divorced. It was weird but fun. Carla wants us to be friends."

"Maybe you could be more than—"

"Stop. She's my employee and I'm happily married." Jamie rubbed her chest. Must be a little heartburn.

"Sheryl has separate friends. So should you."

"Maybe if I have someone to pal around with I won't feel like such a nag." Should she tell Penni about Sheryl's run-in with Carla? No, she didn't need any more drama tonight.

"I agree. Let's have dinner after my appointment tomorrow and get caught up."

"Sounds good."

Jamie pulled into her driveway and let the song end as she stared at the dark house. She hated the sterile lawn and shrubs. Maybe Carla could help her—No, of course not. Should she be friends with her? Wasn't it dishonest to Sheryl?

Tossing her keys on the counter she went to the living room and poured a tumbler of Wild Turkey, her new drink of choice, not bothering to turn on lights. The house felt less lonely if she couldn't see the emptiness. She smelled Carla's perfume on her shirt as she unbuttoned it and realized she'd forgotten the flowers. Sadness stopped her fingers. She wanted those roses. She undressed and got a towel from the bathroom.

Setting the tumbler on the edge of the hot tub she lowered herself into the water and put the jets on high. She took a long swallow. The whiskey burned down her throat but landed softly in her stomach. Why shouldn't she and Carla be friends? Sheryl had friends Jamie had never met.

Jamie climbed out of the hot tub, irritated at Sheryl's absence. She marched to the pool and dove to the bottom. The cold took her breath away, and she surfaced sputtering. Breaking into freestyle strokes, she swam until her arms felt like lead sticks.

Jamie showered and put on sweats and a light-blue sweater Sheryl always said looked good on her. She cupped her breasts through the soft chenille fabric and pinched her nipples. She wanted Sheryl's mouth on her. Sitting against the headboard she tried to focus on the book. Every time she heard a car she willed it to be Sheryl. She yawned and turned another page. Maybe she and Carla could trade books.

Jamie stirred from sleep and then closed her eyes against the glare of the bedside light. Checking the clock, she was surprised it was after midnight. She was alone. Wasn't Sheryl home yet? She went to the kitchen and found her purse on the counter. The guest room again. Anger gripped her as she marched down the hall, the hardwood floor cold under her feet.

"Sheryl." Jamie sat on the edge of the bed and gently shook Sheryl. She lifted the book from her chest—*Ten Tips for Getting the Promotion You Deserve*. Sheryl opened her eyes. "Come to bed."

Sheryl tugged the sheets up to her chin. "You were asleep. I didn't want to wake you."

"No more guest room." She pulled the covers back. "I want to be close to you."

"Jamie..." Sheryl yawned.

Jamie pulled Sheryl to her feet, wrapped her arms around her, and kissed her. She found Sheryl's breast and rubbed her palm against it. They needed this. Sheryl's nipple responded and she deepened the kiss. They needed to stay close.

"Jamie—"

"I want to make love to you." She explored Sheryl's mouth as she caressed her breast. Pulling her mouth from Sheryl's she took her hand and led Sheryl back to their bedroom in silence. Lowering her to the bed she began to unbutton the chocolate-brown pajamas, kissing along the exposed skin.

"Jamie, slow down—"

"No. Everything about us is too slow."

"Have you been talking to—"

"I haven't been talking to anyone." Jamie lifted her head and looked into Sheryl's eyes. She wanted to see in them the same desire that was heating up her center. "I want you." She took Sheryl's mouth before she could protest, slid her tongue in, coaxing, waiting. Finally Sheryl moaned and explored her mouth. *Yes, more.* Sheryl was warm, and tasted minty, and smelled of the perfume Jamie loved at the moment, and Jamie wanted to devour all of her.

She slid her hand inside the pajamas, down Sheryl's side and then up her stomach to her breast. She squeezed it in rhythm with Sheryl's tongue. Sheryl wrapped her arms around Jamie's shoulder, and that's all the encouragement Jamie needed. She straddled Sheryl's thigh to give her clit the pressure it needed as she deepened the kiss and teased around the edge of Sheryl's nipple.

Sheryl spread her legs, and Jamie slid her hand inside the pajamas. She wanted Sheryl to press against her fingers, to coat them with wetness. "Come for me," she whispered, as she buried her fingers in Sheryl, stroking deep as she rubbed her clit against Sheryl's thigh, holding back, waiting for Sheryl. Sheryl moaned against her cheek and clenched around her fingers, and Jamie let herself come with a long moan. She lay on top of Sheryl, spent, breathing heavy, kissing her neck. Sheryl shifted under her.

"I have to be in early." Sheryl kissed her cheek. "I love you. Let's get some sleep."

Jamie rolled onto her back and a shiver ran through her. She clutched Sheryl's hand. She was with Sheryl in their bed. They'd made love. It would be all right. She closed her eyes but sleep wouldn't come.

CHAPTER TWENTY-ONE

Jamie sat at the dining table and sipped her coffee, trying to focus on the newspaper. Her thoughts kept drifting back to the dinner with Carla and Mike. They seemed so committed to each other. She and Sheryl had once been like that—a team, rooting for each other, planning and dreaming about their future. Now it felt like they were on parallel paths that seldom touched. She had to get this business mess sorted out.

"Thanks for the coffee."

Jamie lifted her face for a kiss. When Sheryl pecked her cheek, Jamie pulled her onto her lap, and before Sheryl complained about wrinkling her suit or messing up her hair, Jamie cupped the back of her head and kissed her slow and deep. She could get used to the new perfume. She broke the kiss and cleaned a smudge of lipstick from Sheryl's cheek with her thumb. "You look nice."

"Like I belong in the district office?" Sheryl's eyes gleamed. Jamie wanted to think it was from making love last night.

"Like a kick-ass director of curriculum."

"I'm so close." Sheryl stood and straightened her navy-blue suit. "The superintendent called yesterday to ask my advice on a situation at another high school. I hope I said the right thing."

"Is kissing up to him really what you want to do?"

"You do what you have to to get what you want."

"Isn't it kind of dishonest?"

Sheryl patted her shoulder. "No. It's what grown-ups do. You're in such a bubble with your business—no politics, no compromising, everything the way you want it."

"I wouldn't say that."

"You're going to have your business problem solved soon, right?" Sheryl rubbed her hands over Jamie's shoulders.

"Yes." Thanks to the office manager she couldn't tell Sheryl about. Was this one of those compromises? "Let's make reservations for our anniversary vacation." Sheryl's hands left her shoulders.

"Let's wait."

"Can't you compromise with us like you do at work?"

"What do you think last night was? I wanted to sleep. You wanted to make love."

A cold shiver spread through Jamie, and she shoved her hands in the pouch pocket of her sweatshirt and clasped them. That was a compromise? "I needed us to be close." Jamie looked up at Sheryl, searching her face for a sign she felt the same.

"And we were." Sheryl kissed her cheek. "Now I need to go get that promotion. I'll be late tonight."

Jamie watched her walk away. "Those heels aren't the best for your back."

"Always the chiropractor, aren't you? Shoes are about fashion." Sheryl wiggled her fingers as she closed the door.

Jamie's office chair creaked as she leaned back in it and stared at the picture of her father. He would never have done something like hide the identity of his office manager from her mom. But he'd also tell Jamie to do what was best for the business. Compromises. She heard the back door open and was on her feet before Carla appeared in the doorway. Her pulse jumped with nervousness and she laughed at her silliness. This wasn't the morning after.

"You forgot these last night." Carla set the vase of flowers on Jamie's desk.

"Thanks." Jamie's throat tightened with emotion that made no sense. Why were these flowers so important? She stood and stuck her nose in the bouquet. Just as fragrant as she remembered. Yesterday rushed back—telling Carla the truth about that night, Carla in her arms. She pulled her head from the bouquet. Today they were on the other side of it. Friends. “You look like your garden.” Yellow sweater and pink blouse, and a necklace of colorful beads.

“I hope you mean colorful rather than in need of pruning.”

“Thank you for reading my mind.”

“It’s not hard.” Carla closed her eyes and touched her temple. “You’re thinking you need a fresh cup of coffee.”

Jamie handed her the mug, and for a second they both held it. “You’re not wearing your ring.”

Carla looked at her hand and lifted her finger from the mug. The skin was lighter where it had been. Her nails had the same tasteful French manicure they always did. “I was going to keep wearing it until we talk to Lissa, but…”

“If I can help…” Carla looked like she needed a hug but it probably wasn’t a good idea. “How’s your back?”

“Stiff when I got up, but I didn’t have to crawl to the bathroom. You have no idea how grateful I am.”

“I’m glad I could take care of you. And thank you for dinner. It was…”

“Strange?” Carla’s eyes sparkled with humor.

“Yeah. But fun. I like your hus…um, Mike.” Carla smiled and Jamie let it lift her spirits. “I’m glad we’re going to be friends.”

“Me, too. I’ll get us coffee and then we can go over some things.”

“I want to adjust you first.” Jamie followed Carla out the door. She liked the subtle sweetness of her perfume.

❖

“Thanks, Dr. Hammond. I can already move my neck better.”

“Easy. Don’t undo what I just fixed,” Jamie said to the energetic young contractor she’d been treating for several years. She handed his file over the front counter to Carla.

“We’ll see all of you in a couple weeks for your family tune-up,” Carla said. “Tell your wife I have that cheesecake recipe she wanted.”

Jamie stared at Carla. This was one of those moments she couldn’t believe the shy woman she’d met twenty years ago had matured into someone with Carla’s confidence and ease with people.

She'll have no trouble finding a girlfriend. No trouble at all. "What?" Jamie realized Carla was talking to her.

"Your next appointment called to say he's running late."

"Looks like I've got a minute. Let's put it to good use and let me check your back again. Is it my imagination," Jamie asked as they walked down the hall, "or are my lunch hours getting longer?"

"They're just not getting interrupted."

"And what's happening to all those patients that aren't interrupting my lunch?" Jamie held the door to the treatment room open.

"They're filling Sara and Don's schedules," Carla said as if it were obvious.

"And when were you going to run this past me?" Jamie tried to sound stern, but it was hard with Carla standing so close, trying to look tough with her arms folded and her lips pursed. Those eyes gave her away—they couldn't look hard if she tried.

"Today. See, I'm right on schedule."

"On the table," Jamie said, shaking her head.

"If you insist on going through patient files during your lunch, you need the whole hour, and you need to eat, too."

Carla's back was cool. She'd iced it recently. Carla was following her instructions. Maybe she should follow hers. "Okay."

"And it's ridiculous that you work such long hours. Dr. Rose worked four days a week when I started and was down to three before he got sick."

"I said okay."

"You did?" Carla lifted her head, a surprised expression on her face. "Well, good."

Jamie set the drop table and did an adjustment. "You'll be fine by the weekend." Jamie watched Carla get off the table unassisted, pleased she was better. Opening the door she noticed her receptionist hurrying towards her.

"Dr. Hammond, it's Lucy Marsh. She was just in a car accident. There aren't any openings this morning. Should I schedule her during your lunch?"

Jamie held Carla's gaze as she said, "No."

"How about if I talk to her and see what we can work out?" Carla smiled and squeezed Jamie's arm before heading to the front.

Her father had always taken Mary's advice and they'd been a seamless team. Maybe she could have that with Carla.

❖

Carla signed the form for the driver and kissed the white FedEx envelopes as she hurried to Jamie's office. "I have a surprise for—" Jamie was sitting at her desk with tears in her eyes. "What's wrong?" Carla set the envelopes on the desk and touched Jamie's shoulder.

"Sylvia has breast cancer. I've treated her since…in fact, my father treated her. I feel so helpless."

"I'm so sorry, Jamie." Stepping behind her, Carla massaged her shoulders. The freedom to touch her was a guilty pleasure. "How about if I have flowers sent to her home tomorrow?"

"Why didn't I think of that?" Finally Jamie opened her eyes. "What's this?" She picked up one of the FedEx envelopes.

"Open it."

Jamie worked the flap open, pulled out a large stack of EOBs, and leafed through them. She looked up at Carla, a frown on her face. "How did you get these?"

Carla gave Jamie's shoulder one last squeeze. "Persistence and a little Southern charm." She infused a bit of that charm into her voice. Jamie looked up at her, and her eyes sparked for an instant with something more than gratitude. Carla's pulse responded as if they were alone in a bedroom, not Jamie's office. She stepped away and sat in the chair across from her, crossing her legs.

"I don't know how to thank you." A collage of emotions passed over Jamie's face. "Do you know how hard I've been trying to get these?"

"It's my job." Jamie's smile was so full of gratitude Carla had to look away or her heart would hijack common sense again. It's just business, she reminded herself. "I assume you want to start comparing these with our records, and I thought I'd stay and help. I can pull files while you relax for a few minutes."

"You don't have to." Jamie was opening one of the other envelopes.

"Hmm…staying here and helping you or going home to a messy house. Unless you need to leave." She wasn't ready to ask about Jamie's partner. She never mentioned her, and that made it easy to ignore.

"No. These are my first priority." Jamie held up the EOBs.

"I thought I'd get dinner for us." Carla stood and fiddled with the bouquet on the desk.

"That's not—"

"Eating leftovers alone at home or—"

"I get the picture." Jamie shook her head but was smiling.

"Good. It's a date. I mean—"

"Speaking of which…did you call that attorney?"

"Um, no."

"The first rule of dating is don't wait until Thursday to ask for a date on Friday night." Jamie flipped to another EOB.

"I knew I could count on your expertise."

"And the second rule is don't go home with her on the first date."

"Oh, like you demonstrated on my one other—" Carla gulped when Jamie looked at her, an instant of heat in her eyes before they were all business again. "Don't start without me."

It took Carla the whole five-minute drive to the restaurant to calm her heart into not jumping out of her chest. She'd call that woman as soon as she got home. She definitely needed to start dating or she was going to combust. She fanned her blouse away from her breasts.

Jamie hopped out of the Highlander, anxious to share the good news with Sheryl. They'd made real progress. Maybe Sheryl's promotion had come through and they could celebrate.

"Where have you been?" Sheryl's voice sounded accusing.

"Working," Jamie said, walking into the bedroom. "I thought you were going to be late." Sheryl was sitting up in bed, a magazine across her lap. "I finally got the EOBs from one of the insurance companies and I have to compare them to—"

"I needed you," Sheryl said, icily.

Jamie sat on the edge of the bed. "What's wrong, babe?" Tears and anger filled Sheryl's eyes.

"The promotion," Sheryl choked out, shaking her head.

"What happened?" Jamie took her hands.

"It's like déjà vu. The president of the PTA called me to complain that his daughter was upset about seeing two boys making out in the hallway. He demanded I put a stop to it. I tried to explain that I couldn't do anything, and he said I better not forget everything he'd done for me."

"I don't understand."

"He goes to the same church as the superintendent." Sheryl's voice had an edge of impatience. "He put in a good word for me last year and made sure the PTA raised enough funds for some of my on-campus projects."

"You traded favors with a—"

"Don't look at me like that, Jamie. You have no idea…" Sheryl started to cry.

"You're right. Shh, it's okay." She pulled Sheryl to her and held her.

"I just can't win, Jamie. If that bitch last year hadn't put up such a fuss, we would have a precedent I could uphold and everyone would be happy."

Not the kids, Jamie thought, as she fought the urge to defend Carla. How had she ended up having to keep secrets from Sheryl in order to keep her business from costing Sheryl the promotion she wanted? She was in a no win situation, too.

"I've worked so hard." Sheryl wiped her eyes with her pajama sleeve.

"Sheryl, you can't please everyone."

"They're not everyone." Sheryl's eyes went cold. "The superintendent can make my career, and the president of the PTA can make my life miserable."

"Don't you want to set a precedent by standing up for what you believe is right?" Jamie hoped deep down inside that Sheryl believed in gay rights.

Sheryl's face crumpled. "I want that promotion, Jamie. I don't want to be stuck babysitting rich, bratty teenagers for the rest of my life. For once in my life I want to feel good enough."

"Shh. You're good enough with me."

"I can always count on you." Sheryl nuzzled her face into Jamie's neck.

Jamie held Sheryl and rubbed her back as she cried. Her heart broke for Sheryl's disappointment. Were Sheryl's compromises any worse than hers? She was the one not telling her partner that her new office manager was the woman Sheryl blamed for her problems. Jamie hugged Sheryl tighter. They'd get through this.

CHAPTER TWENTY-TWO

Lunch is ready," Carla said, walking into Jamie's office.

"Just one more." Jamie didn't look up from the patient file.

"No one will eat without you, and they're all drooling over the sushi." Carla closed the file and lifted the pen from Jamie's hand.

"That's blackmail." Jamie's eyes followed the hand up the sleeve of the green blouse that made Carla look like a spring day and then up to the smile she knew would be there. She needed that smile. She needed the kindness in her eyes.

"We've made it through half those EOBs. I'll come in tomorrow and work on them."

"Don't you have a date tonight?"

"Yes."

Jamie waggled her eyebrows, amused by the hint of a blush Carla tried to hide as she rearranged the bouquet of roses on her desk. They'd been sitting there this morning along with her cup of coffee and the stack of patient files with the sticky notes. She had help, an office manager who made her job easier, and she wasn't quite sure what to do with it.

"As I was saying, I'm expecting my other angel to come through with EOBs next week."

"You don't have to come in." Jamie shoved herself out of her chair. There was a new crack in the leather arm. It really was time to get a new one.

"Penni made me promise I'd boot you out the door on time for practice. You know, Jamie…"

"I know where you're headed, and I can't, Carla."

"Change is hard." Carla crossed her arms. "We could start with every other Saturday."

"I'll think about it." Jamie knocked over her father's picture as she set the file back on the stack. The wood frame looked its age. He'd worked six days a week for almost forty years and made it look easy. "We do what we have to for our patients," he'd always say. She followed Carla down the hall, enjoying the faint whiff of her perfume. Maybe she could get Sheryl to go back to the perfume she liked.

Jamie's staff gave a standing ovation when she stepped into the break room. She took a bow and slid into the chair next to Marci. "Chopsticks ready," she said, lifting hers in the air. "Set, go." Six pairs of chopsticks dove for the sushi at once. Conversation circled around the table punctuated by groans when too much wasabi hit someone. The camaraderie that used to be in her office was back, and she had Carla to thank.

"Oh, my gosh, look at the time." Marci gathered plates, and they all pitched in to help while Carla made a fresh pot of coffee. Teamwork.

"Thank you for the extra patients," Sara said. "I'm glad you aren't giving up your lunch any more."

"Team effort." Jamie squeezed her shoulder. "You've got more muscle."

"I'm training for a fitness competition." Sara raised her arms in a mock bodybuilder pose.

Jamie mimicked the motion. "I used to be pretty buff, too."

Everyone looked toward the sound of glass banging against the sink. "Not broken," Carla said, holding up the glass, a funny look on her face.

"Carla was going to run with me this weekend, but now that she's out of commission maybe you'd run with me like we used to."

"What's this about being replaced?" Carla asked, joining the conversation.

"Well, if Jamie gives you the go-ahead, why don't we all go?"

"What's safer than running with two chiropractors?" Carla looked from Sara to Jamie.

Jamie hesitated. Was it a good idea to do things with Carla outside the office? Sheryl often did things without Jamie, and she did have her weekly brunch. "Sunday?"

"Great," Carla said, rubbing her hands together.

❖

Carla studied Jamie from the doorway of her office. She looked tired, but the dark circles under her eyes weren't as pronounced as they had been, and who wouldn't be tired with the kind of hours she worked? She'd been in a good mood all day, and Carla wanted to take advantage of it to press her newest plan for the office. "I can't stand it any more." Jamie looked up from her desk. "I don't want to insult you, but your clinic could use a face-lift."

"Don't scare me like that." Jamie patted her chest.

"What did you think I was going to say?"

"That you don't like working here."

"Sorry, you're stuck with me. But this office—"

"You're just trying to bury your empty-nest woes."

Carla rubbed the back of one of the chairs, her enthusiasm slumping. Maybe she was trying too hard to make a difference. "You're right. Bad idea."

"You know what, it's a great idea," Jamie said. "I'm embarrassed to say it looks pretty much the way it did the day we opened it."

"We could start with your office and have the whole clinic redone by the end of the year. I'm sure the embezzlement will be resolved by then, in your favor, of course. You could begin the year on a whole new note."

"I'm all yours…I mean." Jamie cleared her throat. "You can do whatever you want. And yes, please start in here. In fact, start with this chair." Jamie stepped behind it and shook it with mock viciousness. "I hate it. It doesn't fit me, and I feel about five years old in it."

"Well, we can't have Dr. Hammond feeling five years old, now can we?" Carla used her best Southern accent. Jamie's eyes darkened and her pulse responded. Penni wasn't kidding about Jamie and Southern accents. She was thrilled to have the awkwardness gone, but the absence of barriers and the new…well, friendliness, between them was encouraging Carla's unrealistic fantasy to be more than friends.

The chair creaked when Jamie sat back down. "Could you find me something…I don't know…comfortable and not dark brown?"

Ideas formed as Carla surveyed the room. She could scout new furniture and then take Jamie shopping for the final approval. Personal time with her. “New chair. First on my list.” Carla walked to the desk and ran her palm over the scratched surface. “And a new desk.”

“This was my father’s desk.” Jamie placed her fingers on the edge.

“If you don’t want to replace it—”

“I do,” Jamie said. “I’ve never liked it, either.”

“What was he like?” Carla sat across from Jamie. She was curious. Several patients had spoken about Jamie’s father like he was a legend. She was nervous about her date tonight and grateful for the excuse to have a few minutes with Jamie.

“Great with patients—gregarious and charming. Ex-navy. Very active in chiropractic organizations—president of the local and state associations several times. Smart—graduated at the top of his class. Excellent adjuster. He taught me a lot.” Jamie’s description sounded more like a résumé than a daughter’s recollection of her father.

“If you think I work long hours…” Jamie smiled when Carla nodded vigorously. “We didn’t always see eye to eye, but I have tremendous respect for him. He was devoted to my mother and dedicated to his patients.

“When did he die?”

“About six months after the clinic opened. Pancreatic cancer.” Jamie looked at the pictures on the desk. “It was so hard to watch him dwindle to a shadow of who he’d been.” She seemed far away for a minute. “Thank God for Mary. When he couldn’t work anymore she took care of him. With my mom gone and the demands of the clinic…I don’t know what I’d have done without her.”

“What was she like?” Carla had also heard comments about Mary.

Jamie steepled her fingers under her chin and looked at her father’s picture. “Officious is the word that always comes to mind. I wouldn’t say she was warm, but she was efficient and loyal to my father. She’d been running his office since before I was born. In fact, she decorated the clinic.”

“And where does Marjorie come into the picture?” She knew Marjorie was Mary’s daughter but she wanted to understand the history Jamie was dealing with.

"She'd worked in the office off and on." Jamie's voice was tight. "After my father died, Mary brought her in full time. She retired about a year later, and there was never any question that Marjorie would take over."

"What was she like?"

"Cranky. Like nothing I did for her was ever good enough. My father and Mary were a seamless team. I thought I'd have that with Marjorie." Jamie made no attempt to hide the bitterness in her voice.

"How did you discover the embezzlement?" Carla had gotten some of the story from Betty, but she wanted Jamie's version.

Jamie's hands closed into fists before she answered. "I didn't. I discovered the insurance fraud. By accident."

"It might help if I knew the whole story."

Anger and guilt settled on Jamie's face, and she didn't say anything for a while. "I was going through the mail because Marjorie called in sick. There was a notice from Blue Cross that payment on my claims was being suspended pending their investigation. It was a second notice and I was furious, but I assumed it was just a case of wanting more documentation. The next day I got a notice from United Healthcare. It was a final notice threatening legal action against me for fraud. That's when I knew I had a problem." Jamie looked up. "It was a nightmare," she said, her voice collapsing to a whisper.

"I've found a lot of files where pages were ripped out—treatment notes and I think EOBs. Looks like she knew the jig was up and was trying to cover her trail. How did you figure out she'd been embezzling?"

"I didn't." Jamie clenched her jaw. "My accountant got a notice from the IRS. Income on my return didn't match what the insurance companies reported paying me."

"She was doctoring the 1099s." The woman's boldness bothered Carla.

Jamie nodded.

"I wish I'd been running your office," Carla said, before she could stop herself.

Jamie was silent, her expression guarded. "You should get going. You don't want to be late for a first date." Jamie stood and shooed Carla out of the office.

"Any last words of advice?" Carla asked as they walked to her car. "That blouse looks great on you, by the way." The red silk gave Jamie a softer look than her usual starched Oxford shirts.

"Lots of compliments is always a good idea." Jamie laid her hand on Carla's arm as she reached for the car door. "And remember, it's about having fun."

Carla's pulse quickened. "I remember." Jamie nodded, and her eyes said she remembered, too. "Enjoy your dinner and tell Penni hi for me."

Carla hadn't gone a block before angry tears filled her eyes. Why couldn't she have the woman she wanted? By the time she got home it took a glass of wine and a stern lecture to herself not to call and cancel. The phone rang and she smiled. Of course he'd call.

"Just called to make sure you weren't backing out." He knew her so well. "Wear that burgundy sweater that you fill out so nicely. And the heart pendant I gave you the day Lissa was born. For luck."

"I need it." Carla twirled the glass of wine.

"Your problem's going to be that everyone will fall in love with you."

"Not the right everyone." Carla looked out at the patio, at the garden she'd nurtured over the years. Would anyone share this home with her again?

"I saw the way Jamie looked at you the other night."

"Mike—"

"Go have some fun. Call me when you get home."

"What if I don't come home?" With all the pent-up desire stuffed in every corner of her body, anything was possible.

"Then be safe and call me in the morning. I love you."

Carla finished the wine and closed her eyes, waiting for it to take the edge of longing away. She needed to get over her feelings for Jamie. Walking to her bedroom she replayed how it had felt to dance with Vanessa. Maybe they'd go dancing tonight. Maybe they'd do more than dance.

Chapter Twenty-three

The back door opened and Jamie looked up from the patient file on her desk as Penni bounded into her office in shorts and a yellow T-shirt with the name of her softball team across the front. "I thought we were going to dinner." Penni set tennis shoes, shorts, and a T-shirt on the corner of the desk. Jamie held up the faded green A's T-shirt. "These look like my—"

"Stole them from your house. Just because I never use my key doesn't mean I don't still have it. Does Sheryl ever hang up her clothes? Like in the closet?"

Jamie ignored the comment. Sheryl's messiness irritated her, but weren't relationships about compromise? "Practice isn't until tomorrow."

"I have a surprise for you." Penni's smile couldn't have been bigger as she pulled a softball glove from behind her back and tossed it to Jamie. "You're our left fielder tonight."

"What are you talking about?"

"Practice game." Penni mimed swinging a bat. "Every year you say you'll play with us. League starts in a few weeks."

Jamie picked up a file and waved it but she couldn't keep her eyes off the glove.

Penni took the file. "Come on. It's Friday night."

Jamie almost laughed at Penni's smug expression. It conveyed her enthusiastic don't-take-no-for-an-answer attitude that Jamie had always loved. Would one night off hurt? She stared at the stack of files that didn't look so tall when Carla was going through them with her. She wanted to throw them against the wall. "God, I'm sick of this mess."

"Which is why I'm kidnapping you." Penni poked at the stack of files, and they fanned out across the desk. "You need something in your life besides these. One night. We need you."

"What you mean is half your team mutinied at having a game on a Friday night and you've resorted to kidnapping your friends."

"Well, if you insist on being particular." Penni put her hands on her hips. "You know you want to," she said, in a singsong voice.

Jamie slipped the glove on and pounded her fist into the web. "Left field, huh?" When she wasn't pitching she'd loved to play the outfield.

"Where's Carla? I was going to talk her into coming with us."

"She left."

"Call her and have her meet us at—"

"She's on a date," Jamie said, taking off the glove and restacking the files.

Penni was silent and the smile was gone. "Wow. That must have thrown you."

"Why would it?"

"Cut the crap." There was too much sympathy in Penni's expression.

"It's no big deal, Penni. I even gave her dating advice." Jamie shrugged and rubbed her neck. It was stiff, even though she'd let Sara work on her this afternoon.

"I'll bet that was some conversation."

"Why are you making a big deal out of this?"

"Because I remember what you were like when you got back from Atlanta, what you said about—"

"We're friends. That's it. Don't make something out of this that isn't there."

"You don't have to yell." Penni handed the clothes to her. "Go change."

Jamie marched to the bathroom with the clothes. She needed a night of fun. After changing, she walked through the clinic, checking that file cabinets were locked, computers and lights turned off. When she reached Carla's office she saw the white sweater over the back of the chair. Forgotten again. Apparently she didn't need it for her date. She jabbed at the light switch and the room went dark.

❖

Jamie eyed the batter walking from the on-deck area, swinging two bats before tossing one to the ground. Clean-up hitter. She'd smacked one deep to left center last time up, and it had cost them two runs. Now it was the top of the seventh and they were tied. Jamie backed up even before Penni lifted the catcher's mask from her face and waved the outfield back. Better to let her get a cheap single than a game-winning home run.

Jamie wiped sweat off her face with the hem of her T-shirt. The front was streaked with dirt from her headfirst slide into second. She hadn't hesitated, and not until she'd crossed the plate with the tying run had it occurred to her someone could have stepped on her hands. The instincts for the game were still there if the skills were a little rusty, but she hadn't dropped a fly yet.

She banged her fist into her glove and danced on the balls of her feet to stay loose as the batter stepped up to the plate. On the third pitch the woman tagged one to left. Jamie sprinted toward the foul line, gaining on the hard-hit ball as she neared the line. If she let it go it would be a foul ball. Jamie reached for a last burst of acceleration from her screaming quads and launched her body at the sinking ball. It landed in her glove and she squeezed it into the pocket as she hit the grass hard. She rolled and slammed into the chain-link fence.

She was already on her feet, holding her glove up as her teammates crowded around her, a dozen versions of "Great catch" and "Are you all right?" tossed at her.

Penni picked her up in a bear hug and planted a sloppy kiss on her cheek. "Awesome."

"Eww. Sweaty," Jamie said, but she couldn't stop smiling.

"Scared the shit out of me," Penni said, as they jogged back to the dugout. "You don't have to risk getting hurt."

"Didn't even think," Jamie said, trying to catch her breath. "God that felt great." Teammates slapped her on the back and someone handed her a bottle of water.

"I told you it would be fun." Penni nudged her shoulder. "Have I ever steered you wrong?"

Jamie looked at her and cocked her head. "Do you want me to—" The first batter beat out an infield hit, and Jamie cheered with the rest of the team.

"Where softball's concerned," Penni said. "Remember our final college game? I called for a change-up and you kept shaking me off?"

Jamie would never forget that last game. "It was a full count and it's not my most reliable pitch, and walking her would have brought the tying run home."

"But I promised to get you a date with the cute center fielder on the other team you'd been drooling over, if you'd trust me and throw that pitch?" Penni pumped her fist in the air as she said, "Strike-out, league champions, and one of the best dates of your life." Penni bumped her hip. "You just need to trust me. Don't I always know what's best?"

"You're up, Jamie," Lori called, from her spot coaching third base. "Winning run's on second." She pointed to the woman standing on the bag.

"Show 'em your stuff," Penni said.

Jamie picked up the bat and wrung her hands around the taped handle. The woman on second was fast. A hit between the outfielders and she'd probably score. A part of herself she'd lost track of joined her as she walked to the plate. She was breathing hard and sweat trickled down her back, and she was happier than she'd been in a long time.

The second pitch was a waist-high dream pitch, and she sent a line drive over the shortstop's head. As she sprinted to first base she watched it slice between the outfielders and roll toward the fence. Rounding first she pumped her legs hard for second. The outfielder picked it up and pegged a hard throw to home, but her teammate crossed the plate a step before the ball landed in the catcher's glove. Jamie jumped up and down as her teammates ran out and huddled around her, congratulating her on the game-winning hit. It was just a practice slow-pitch game, but Jamie was elated.

After shaking hands with the other team, they collected their gear and tossed themselves on the grass under the shade of a tree, guzzling waters, unlacing shoes, talking in that post-game chatter Jamie loved.

"Don't take your shoes off, yet," Penni said, pulling her to her feet. "I want to see if you can still pitch."

"I've been pitching to the kids at practice."

"Real pitching to real batters."

"You're kidding."

"Nope. Come on. Let's see what you've got."

"I haven't pitched in—" Jamie stopped. She did want to know if she could still do it. "All right," she said, catching the ball Penni tossed to her as they trotted back to the field. Penni squatted behind home plate and held up her glove.

Jamie spun the ball until she had her grip right on the seams. Fastball. She pumped her arms over her head and then whipped her right arm around her body as she pushed off the mound. The ball hit Penni's glove with a satisfying crack. Her teammates clapped, and Lori picked up a bat and headed toward home plate. Penni gave her their old signal for a rise. Jamie adjusted her fingers along the seams and went into her windup. Lori swung and missed, and Penni bounced up from behind the plate.

"Wow." Jamie looked at her hand. "Did that rise a bit?"

"Yep. You've still got it." Penni threw the ball back to her.

Lori dug her feet in and pointed her bat at Jamie. "Do that again."

Jamie tried not to smile when Penni gave the signal for the changeup. She dug her fingertips into the seams, palmed the ball, and went into her windup again. The trick to throwing an effective change was keeping your motion the same so they expected a fastball. By the time the ball floated lazily into Penni's glove, Lori had already finished her swing.

"Yes!" Penni danced around home plate in a victory dance, and Lori laughed, shaking her head as she handed the bat to someone else.

Everyone wanted a turn, and Jamie kept throwing pitches as they all shared softball stories. Was there anything better than the camaraderie of a team?

"Maybe I will play with you," Jamie said, as she caught the bottle of water Penni tossed to her, guzzling half, then dumping the rest down her back. "Time flies when I'm playing softball. Sorry I was a little grumpy earlier."

"Grumpy is allowed. I know you've got a lot on your plate. I just don't want it to drag you under." Penni tossed her glove near a bat bag and pulled out a sheet of paper. "Team roster for fall league. Sign," she said, handing Jamie a pen.

Jamie couldn't stop smiling as they walked back to Penni's truck. Her stomach growled, her shoulder hurt, and both her knees were grass-stained.

"Hey," she said, as Penni unlocked the car door for her.

"What?"

"I'm still a pitcher."

Penni ruffled her hair, and Jamie thanked the fates that had brought them together all those years ago. Maybe Penni was right—it's never too late to get back to the things you love. Jamie looked back at the diamond, now mostly in shadow. Some of the best times of her life had taken place on a softball diamond. Yeah, she could get out early one night a week to play on Penni's team.

❖

"So, our usual place?" Penni asked as she drove away from the park.

"Do you even have to ask? Is Lori gonna meet us there?"

"Nope. She's going out for Indian food with her sister."

"Do you want to go there instead?"

"Nah." Penni pulled the visor down. "We need a little breathing space."

"You guys are okay, aren't you?"

"Of course. We're just having one of those weeks where we're on each other's nerves about stupid stuff like who empties the dishwasher and who stops at the store on the way home. I'll do some bitching to you and she'll complain to Janet. Whoever gets home first will light candles and put on romantic music, and we'll laugh and talk and make love."

"You have the best relationship I've seen, other than my parents'."

"You could have one, too." Penni's voice had its usual sarcasm.

Jamie ignored the comment as she watched a woman running with two little white dogs trying to keep pace with her, their legs pumping furiously. She wanted to laugh but then realized she knew how they felt—running as fast as she could and barely able to keep up. She moved her shoulders around to try to loosen the tension that was creeping back as she pictured that stack of files on her desk. "I can't play," she said. "I don't know what I was thinking. Not with—"

"Don't go there," Penni said, tapping Jamie on the side of her head. "Let it go for tonight. That clinic's going to be the death of you."

"I couldn't live with myself if I let my father down. The clinic meant everything to him."

"You'll get through this. Justice will prevail, as they say. But maybe it's time to decide what the clinic means to you. Hear me out," Penni said, when Jamie started to protest. "You never wanted a practice that big. You wanted time for softball and—"

"That was twenty years ago. We all have to grow up." Jamie lowered her window and rested her arm on the edge.

"I grew up, but I didn't give up everything that mattered to me."

"I have responsibilities I can't walk away from. It's too late to—"

"You don't have to walk away, and it's never too late for the things that make you happy. You have some funny ideas about responsibility. It isn't something you decide once and then stick to like you're chained to it. Take Carla, for example."

"How so?"

"She's not continuing in a marriage she chose twenty years ago out of a blind sense of responsibility. Now she's in a different place and choosing new directions for her life."

"Yeah, I guess," Jamie mumbled. She fiddled with the laces on her glove. She needed a new one but couldn't bear to part with all the nostalgia rubbed into this one. "Do you think hiring Carla was a good idea? I mean, with all our history?" She stroked her fingers over the well-worn leather. Joan Joyce's autograph was almost gone. Taking a pitching clinic with her was a day she'd never forget. She'd once thought softball would be her life.

"It was a great decision."

"Do you think it's okay for me to be friends with Carla?"

"It's more than okay."

"But we're ex-lovers."

"Oh, for heaven's sake," Penni said, poking Jamie's shoulder with her fist. "That's the lesbian way."

"I'm supposed to go running with her and Sara on Sunday." Would Carla still want to be friends if she and the attorney became a couple?

"Good. Sheryl does stuff all the time without you. You should have your own friends, too."

Jamie rubbed her face. Her hands smelled like grass and dirt and leather. "If I tell you something, will you promise not to be a smart-ass?" Penni nodded, and Jamie told her about Carla's run-ins with Sheryl. "I can't tell Sheryl. But I can't fire Carla. I don't know if I can get this embezzlement mess sorted out without her." Why wasn't life as clear-cut as softball?

"I wouldn't worry about it."

Jamie looked at her. Why wasn't she launching into her usual diatribe against Sheryl?

"Sheryl hasn't come to the office in what—"

"About a year."

"And Carla's daughter's out of high school. I don't see how the two would ever meet."

"You don't think it's wrong I'm not being honest with Sheryl?"

"Oh, please. Carla's good for your business, and like you've said, the faster you get your business problems worked out, the faster Sheryl won't have a reason to be mad at you."

Jamie stuffed a softball in the web of the glove and set it on the seat next to her. "And my father would say I was doing the right thing." Jamie's shoulders relaxed again. When all this business mess was over she'd decide what to do about Carla. Her heart skipped a beat when she tried to picture her office without Carla.

"Did Sheryl really hassle those girls?"

"Her version and Carla's are a little different." Jamie lowered her sunglasses from her head as sunlight blinded her.

"I'll take that as a yes. Jamie—"

"I don't know what it feels like to be in Sheryl's shoes, and neither do you. Maybe she's right. Maybe getting passed over for this promotion is political." Penni pulled into a parking space and braked hard. "What?" Penni's eyes pinned her in a hard stare.

"And maybe it's because Sheryl's bossy, egotistical, and not a team player. This isn't about her getting or not getting that promotion. It's about where her priorities are. Giving gay kids a hard time is just wrong."

"Supporting her is the right thing. Every relationship has challenges."

"Challenges are like chisels—they work on the cracks in a relationship. When Lori and I feel that fracture, we get tighter and mend it. When you and Sheryl have challenges—"

"We're just a little out of sync."

"Who are you trying to convince?" Penni was quiet for a minute and then added in a softer voice, "Aren't you tired of trying so hard and getting nothing back?"

"You don't throw away ten years because things are a little rocky."

"God, I wish I hadn't invited her to that Thanksgiving dinner. If I'd known she was going to pursue you—"

"It's a good thing she did," Jamie said. "It's been a great ten years."

"For Sheryl. You were a great catch for her. You support her financially."

"I can afford it."

"You take care of the house."

"I like to."

"You pay for the vacations."

"What's your point, Penni?"

"I'm just saying, don't you want a partner who supports you?"

Jamie shouldered the car door open and strode toward the restaurant. Why did Penni always pick on Sheryl?

Penni caught up and draped her arm over her shoulder. "I love you even if I don't like your partner."

Jamie put her arm around Penni's waist. Best friends meant everything and she knew Penni would always be there for her.

❖

Jamie's spirits lifted when she saw Sheryl's car in the garage. She was home early from her dinner. A shower, music, some candles.

"For you." Jamie handed Sheryl a bouquet of flowers as she sat down next to her on the bed. "I know how much you love lilies."

"Thanks. That was sweet."

Jamie straightened the collar on Sheryl's blouse and stroked the backs of her fingers along the exposed skin. She leaned forward for a kiss, but Sheryl pushed against her chest.

"You smell sweaty, Jamie, and why are you dressed like that?"

"I played softball." Jamie grinned. "I even pitched. You never saw me in my glory days, babe. I was good." Jamie stood and went through her windup, almost slipping on a sock as she strode forward. She rubbed her right shoulder—sore, but a good sore.

"I thought you were working late."

"I had dinner with Penni. She surprised me by asking me to play in a practice game."

"Do you really have time for all that?" Sheryl tucked a strand of hair behind her ear. New highlights.

"I took a night off. I'd have invited you to join us, but you don't like sports and don't eat pizza any more." Why couldn't Sheryl be happy for her?

"There's no need to be sarcastic." Sheryl's eyes filled with tears.

"What's wrong?"

"I'm scared about the promotion. I thought it was mine, and now I'm going to get screwed again because those boys want to flaunt their relationship. This gay-rights nonsense." Sheryl shook her head. "I have to find a way to appease—"

"Sheryl. You're gay. Can't you stand up for that?"

"I don't have that luxury. The district is a lot more conservative on the inside than it looks to the public. The president of my PTA is too powerful for me to go against, and the superintendent doesn't like controversy."

"You know I want you to get that promotion, but if you'd been my girlfriend in high school I'd have wanted to hold your hand and kiss you." Jamie rubbed her thumbs over the backs of Sheryl's hands. "And I'd have expected the principal to uphold my rights."

"I see." Sheryl yanked her hands away. "I thought you supported me."

"I do. You're smart and hardworking—"

"But out and proud is more important. I thought you'd outgrow that, Jamie."

"I don't want to outgrow standing up for who I am. This is who you fell in love with."

"And maybe I'd rather have my promotion than out and proud. What difference does it make? I can be a lesbian without waving the rainbow flag." Sheryl's cheeks were red with anger.

"But you sell yourself out, and you send the message to those kids that there's something wrong with them. And how am I supposed to interpret the fact that you're afraid to hold my hand or kiss me in public?" Jamie tried to control her anger. She wanted romance, not an argument.

"I've never believed in making out in public, and you said you were fine with it." Sheryl's voice was white fury, but tears ran down her cheeks. "You want a public display? Is that what love is to you? Fine. Why don't you come to my school and we'll parade around campus holding hands and making out and really show them what out and proud is. I'll stand up for gay rights and watch years of hard work go down the drain."

"I know you're in a tough spot—"

"You have no idea. I want this so much."

"And you'll get it. Look, when things get tough, we need to pull together." Penni's words came back to her—*we pull together in the face of challenges*.

Sheryl stiffened. "More time." Sheryl folded her arms. "You always complain about us when you've been around Penni."

"Can you leave her out of this? I don't want to argue. I want us to be close." Jamie took Sheryl's hands again and kissed her palms.

"I'm not in the mood."

Jamie dropped Sheryl's hands and stood up. When was the last time she'd been in the mood? "I'm gonna shower and then sit in the hot tub. Join me if you want." Jamie stalked to the closet. Stripping off her clothes, she tossed them in a pile on the floor. What was one more mess?

Loneliness trailed Jamie to the patio. She heard Sheryl in her office, typing. She lit several candles and set them on the edge of the hot tub. The water enveloped her and the jets pounded her back, vibrating her whole body. She thought of Penni and Lori, romancing their way back to connection. She started to get out of the tub. Maybe she could talk Sheryl into—She sat back down and closed her eyes. Not tonight.

Sheryl wasn't in bed when she walked into the bedroom. Wrapping the towel around her waist, Jamie checked the office. Not there but she'd left the desk light on as usual. Reaching across to turn it off, the desk jiggled and Sheryl's computer screen came on. She moved the mouse over the icon to close her e-mail. The short message puzzled her. "Me, too. Looking forward to spending the day with you. We have a lot to talk about." It was from a Dennis at a Yahoo address. Was that the principal she was working on the project with? She knew few of Sheryl's friends any more. How had they drifted apart?

The door to the guest room was closed and no light seeped under it. She gripped the doorknob and pressed her forehead against the door, willing Sheryl to open it, pull her inside, curl up with her, reconnect. She waited, then waited some more. Finally she went back to the bedroom and closed the door.

Chapter Twenty-four

Carla found a parking spot half a block from the restaurant that looked like it would be at home on a Greek hillside—bright white with large windows thrown open to the warm fall evening. Date. Her heart skipped a beat, and nervousness gathered in the pit of her stomach. What would they talk about? What if Vanessa tried to kiss her? What if she wanted to go back to her place? Her phone rang—Lissa's ring—and her tumbling thoughts stopped. Lowering the volume on one of her favorite Melissa songs, she said, "Hi, sweetie. What's up?"

"I aced my calculus exam and Steph won her game."

"That's worth celebrating. What are you guys doing tonight?" Vanessa strolled past her, talking on her phone. The light-gray suit hugged her body, accentuating the toned body Carla remembered from the dance floor. Her short blond hair was brushed back from her face, and she was smiling as she gestured with her free hand. *I'm really about to go on a date. With a woman.* Carla nervously rubbed her slacks. "What was that, sweetie?"

"I said, we're going to dinner and a movie with those girls you met. They can't stop talking about how cool it was for you to go to the bar with us."

"I had fun." Carla frowned. Would Lissa find it so amusing after they told her about the divorce?

"What are you doing tonight?"

"Meeting a friend for dinner." Vanessa leaned her hip against the railing that separated the outdoor patio from the sidewalk, still on her phone. Her shapely legs descended from the skirt to end in high heels. Jamie would say they were too high. "What? Oh, yeah. I'll give him a kiss for you. I love you."

Carla took deep breaths as she walked toward Vanessa. Her lips parted into a warm smile when she saw Carla, and she made a kissing sound to whomever she was talking before ending the call. Those lips covered in dark-red lipstick were the focal point of a beautiful face. Carla ran her tongue across her lips and smoothed her sweater.

"My daughter. Boyfriend troubles." Vanessa rolled her eyes.

"I was just talking to my daughter, too." So they had that in common. Carla relaxed a little.

"You look beautiful." Vanessa cupped her elbow. "Great sweater."

At the last second Carla redirected the intended kiss from her cheek to her mouth. Vanessa's lips were soft and tasted like strawberries. Carla's stomach fluttered as she pulled back. Had she really just kissed her?

"Nice greeting." Vanessa kept her hand on Carla's elbow as they stepped through the door held open by an older man. He gave them a hard look. It took Carla a moment to realize why. She met his stare without flinching. If she was going to be out, she was going to be proud.

"You said you've eaten here?"

"Yes, with my husband…um, ex-husband…oh, heck, I don't know what to call him," Carla said, as they were shown to a corner table on the patio that was nearly full. A few sprigs of lavender sat in a small vase in the center of the white tablecloth. A waiter set a basket of bread and menus in front of them.

"I know a great divorce attorney if you need one," Vanessa said, her expression unreadable. After Carla's explanation, her playful smile returned.

"For a minute there I was worried I was on a date with a married woman."

"Date." The word felt huge as Carla said it.

"Well, technically it's our second date." Vanessa winked and chased it with a smile as she passed Carla the wine list. "You choose," she said, in a voice both sultry and full of authority.

"Um, sure." Carla looked down the list, trying to gauge what Vanessa would like. Mike usually did this part. Vanessa's face was close enough for Carla to see the dark flecks in the slate-blue eyes.

"I was married, Carla, so I understand what you're going through. I take it you've just recently converted?" Vanessa brushed her hand through her hair. A ring with a large green stone gave weight to long, slender fingers.

Carla remembered what those fingers felt like against the nape of her neck. "I like that term. And yes, very recently." She signaled the waiter and gave her selection.

"I hated the phrase 'coming out.'" Vanessa snickered. "It made me feel like a Southern debutante…like I should be wearing a pink dress with too much taffeta."

"I did wear a dress like that to my prom."

"I thought I detected a bit of the South in your voice."

Carla nodded her approval when the waiter presented her with the bottle. He filled their glasses with the pale Prosecco, and bubbles raced each other to the top. Vanessa's throat lengthened as she tilted her head back and took a long sip. "Very nice."

Carla swallowed hard and reached for her glass—so many places to kiss along that throat. "So, how did you…"

"Convert?" Vanessa's eyes twinkled.

"Is it rude of me to ask?"

"Not at all. But it is a rather clichéd story. Christmas party. Champagne. Flirting from an attractive junior attorney. More champagne. More flirting. Kiss. Hotel room." Vanessa ticked off each point on her fingers. "Boy, was I surprised, but it explained a lot about my marriage."

Was her experience with Jamie not that unusual? She hoped Vanessa wouldn't ask how she'd gone from married to dating women. Sleeping with your boss, now that was clichéd.

Vanessa slipped off her jacket to reveal the tailored lavender blouse, every curve deliciously obvious. "Here's to happy endings and new beginnings." Vanessa lifted her glass to Carla's.

Carla took a generous sip of Prosecco and stole a glance at the revealed cleavage. She glanced up to see a knowing look on Vanessa's face. This new freedom to look at women might be dangerous. Heat crawled up her throat.

"I'm flattered by your appreciation." Vanessa's eyes held Carla's, soft and inviting. "It is appreciation, isn't it?"

"Yes." The flush crept up her cheeks and Carla looked away. She was confused at the attraction she felt to Vanessa. At the bar she'd assumed it was just the sensual assault of dancing with a woman. But in daylight her body was just as mutinous. Was she in love with Jamie or just hanging on to an old infatuation?

"Why don't you order for us? Any pasta for me. I'll just sit here and watch you." Vanessa closed the menu and draped her arm across the back of Carla's chair.

Carla's eyes followed the movement of Vanessa's blouse snugging across her breasts as if she had no control over them. She heard Vanessa's soft laugh as she studied the menu, trying to find the pasta dish at the nearby table that smelled so delicious. She was rescued when the waiter stopped at their table and recited the specials. "We'll both have the pasta special," Carla said, as Vanessa nodded her approval.

"Dating women takes some getting used to…in the mechanics of who does what, I mean. Relax, Carla." Vanessa caressed the back of her neck. "I already like you."

Carla took a deep breath, reminding herself she was reinventing her life and was entitled to stumble along the path to finding what she wanted. "So, I take it your conversion didn't last. Oh, gosh, that's not quite what I meant."

"Well, the conversion did but the woman didn't. We were a couple for about a year. Then she got offered her dream job and off to D.C. she went. It took a while but we're great friends now." Vanessa's fingers traced a circle on the tablecloth and her expression softened. "It's hard to know what to do with all those feelings. I guess it makes sense to recycle them into friendship that can be satisfying in its own way. That odd ex-lovers-as-best-friends thing that lesbians do."

"Mmm. I guess." Was that what she and Jamie were doing? Would it be satisfying? And what would she do with all those inconvenient feelings? "What?" she asked, when she realized Vanessa was talking.

"I was saying I've been dating off and on for the last year, but I'd like to find someone to settle down with." Her eyes became serious.

"So, your daughter's in Boston?" Carla asked, as the waiter set plates in front of them. She nodded when he held a block of Parmesan and grater over her plate.

"Nice diversion." Vanessa's eyes took on a teasing quality. "Don't worry. I won't get serious on you too soon. That's one lesbian cliché I can do without."

Carla wasn't sure what she meant. There was apparently a lot about lesbian culture she hadn't picked up from Lissa and Steph. Flavors of garlic and basil burst on her tongue with the first bite.

They spent the rest of the meal in amiable conversation. Vanessa's daughter had played lacrosse, which led to shared stories about being sports moms. Vanessa didn't like to cook but loved to eat if Carla was offering. She loved jazz and opera and hated rock. Carla covered her heart in shock when Vanessa said yes, even Melissa Etheridge. She was indifferent to coffee, Carla discovered, as they sipped espressos and shared chocolate mousse.

"I had a great time, Carla." Vanessa tucked her arm into the bend of Carla's elbow as they strolled down the sidewalk. "If I knew of somewhere for us to go dancing I'd suggest it."

"I had a good time, too." Carla's excitement lost some of its effervescence. Dancing would have been fun. Vanessa's body was warm against hers and she slipped her arm around Carla's waist. The feel of a woman's body against hers was still a novelty, and she let arousal surge up.

"Would I insult you if I invited you back to my place? I don't want to spook you away from another date, but I do have some great music. Not that noise we danced to in San Diego." Vanessa's hips moved in a sensual rhythm against hers. "Have you ever danced to Ella?"

"No." Carla's mouth was too dry to say more as heat erupted in her center. Was it a good idea to go to her home? They stopped at Carla's car, and the question slipped from her mind as Vanessa's arm slid over her shoulders. The gentle smile did nothing to stop the nervous tingle that devoured her. She was going to be kissed by a woman. She ignored the fact it wasn't Jamie as desire made her skin feel scorched. Vanessa's lips were soft and warm, her tongue more so when she slid past Carla's lips. She gripped Vanessa's waist as her legs went weak.

"Come home with me. Just dancing, I promise."

"I should go…" Vanessa's breasts were soft against hers. Carla's breath stuttered in her chest. "All right."

"Follow me. I promise I won't lose you."

Carla pulled in behind Vanessa in a gated community of upscale condos. Vanessa walked toward her car, and Carla couldn't pull her eyes from the sway of her hips. Before her mind caught up to her body she was out of her car and in Vanessa's arms, kissing her. Soft lips, probing tongue, warm mouth. The taste of Prosecco and strawberries and chocolate. The smell of her musky perfume. The feel of her stomach against Carla's, her breasts rising and falling with each breath. Carla broke the kiss and rested her forehead against Vanessa's, as sensations she hadn't felt in twenty years overwhelmed her. She wanted to rip her sweater off. A cool palm against her cheek steadied her.

"Let's take this upstairs." She slid her arm around Carla's waist and led them down a walkway.

"Are you a cognac drinker?" Vanessa tossed her jacket over the back of an expensive-looking chair upholstered in pale-green fabric. The whole room was tastefully decorated. Dim recessed lighting revealed an impressive number of paintings around the living room, most of them seascapes. There was the sound of a needle dropping onto a record, and then music filled the room.

"Ella," Vanessa said, as she reached around Carla's waist from behind, a tumbler in her hand.

Carla took the glass and a long swallow as Vanessa's pelvis nestled against her. Carla dropped her head back against Vanessa's shoulder and let her lead as they swayed to the romantic melody, her hand warm against Carla's stomach as she caressed in slow circles. Carla's body relaxed like melting butter. The glass was lifted from her, and then she was turned, and they were embracing. Softness and curves, warm breath on her cheek, Vanessa humming softly in her ear.

Carla needed more. She slid her mouth against Vanessa's cheek until she found her lips. She moaned when her tongue met no resistance. Fingering the hair at Vanessa's collar, Carla devoured her mouth, while Vanessa's hand slid up her side and stroked the outside of Carla's breast. They swayed and kissed and caressed until another song ended.

"You're beautiful, sexy, and easy to be with." Vanessa's words were quiet, her lips warm against Carla's ear. "I'd love to hear that Southern accent as a passionate whisper in my ear."

Carla tensed, and her fingers tightened on Vanessa's collar. Was that what she wanted?

"But I don't want to rush things with you."

Carla's mind collapsed around the words. She was ablaze with sensations—heat like a furnace in her center, breasts that felt heavy, skin flushed anywhere that could flush. She rested her forehead on Vanessa's shoulder, breathing fast, and fighting back tears.

Vanessa's hands returned to her back, warm and strong and reassuring as they rubbed up and down her spine. A shiver went through Carla's overheated body as she let Vanessa hold her, wrapped in softness and perfume.

Finally, Vanessa stepped back and held her hands. "Can I see you again?"

Carla nodded as she struggled for control.

Vanessa walked Carla to her car and kissed her softly. "Drive safely. I'll call you next week."

"I'd like that." Carla's heart was pounding, and she fumbled to get the key in the lock. By the time she reached the freeway she was shaking—not just her hands but her whole body. She lowered the window, letting the freeway noise numb her mind and the cold air cool her skin. She was aroused and confused. She'd wanted Vanessa. She wanted Jamie.

She put on Melissa the minute she walked into her home and paced in her kitchen, wanting coffee one minute, then opening the refrigerator deciding she really wanted wine and then leafing through a new cooking magazine on the counter, trying to make her mind focus on something. Her emotions fought for her attention like little kids. Relief she was in her own home, then disappointment she was in her own home.

Frustration for no good reason made her go back to grinding coffee beans, which made her childishly angry because it wasn't Kona. Confusion drove her into the chair Jamie had sat in just a few days ago. Dating was what she would have to do if she was going to have the life she wanted—a life of passion, taking care of someone and being taken care of, weaving all the little moments in a day into a lifetime of connection. But would she survive wrenching her heart away from Jamie so it could search for someone else?

Back at the refrigerator for wine, she felt more confused than ever. If this was what lesbians did—became friends with their ex-lovers and moved on to dating someone else—then she'd have to get used to the program.

Chapter Twenty-five

"Ouch." Jamie kicked the high-heeled shoe digging into her toe because she couldn't see it under Sheryl's clothes strewn all over the closet floor. She pulled on her favorite purple running shorts. Sitting on the chair by the closet, she laced up her shoes, cursing that she'd overslept and didn't have time for the hot tub. Muscles she hadn't used in years were complaining.

Bracing herself against the kitchen counter, Jamie stretched her quads while she waited for the bagel to toast. She looked longingly at the espresso machine, but coffee before a run wasn't a good idea.

"The bathroom sink isn't draining right. Can you take a look at it?"

"I will later. I'm late." The bagel popped up and Jamie spread butter and blueberry jam over it.

"But—"

"Lift the stopper out. There's probably hair clogging the drain. I'll see you later." Jamie kissed Sheryl on the cheek, grabbed her keys, and hurried to the door, the bagel wrapped in a napkin.

"Where are you going? I thought we could go to breakfast and then over to the mall."

Jamie stopped. "You're not going to brunch?"

"Boycotting today. I can't hang out with friends who aren't loyal. Last week at a meeting they actually talked to that bitch who's trying to steal my promotion."

"I'm sorry." Jamie rubbed the back of her neck. Should she cancel out on the run? They'd gotten past the argument Friday night, but Sheryl had spent yesterday with the principal she was working on the project with. They could use time together but she'd promised Sara and Carla.

"Why can't you just go later?"

"I'm meeting Sara and my office manager." Guilt flared that she wasn't telling Sheryl who she was.

"Aren't you the one who wanted us to spend more time together?"

"You've gone to brunch every Sunday morning for the last couple months." She looked at the clock above the sink.

"Can you at least make me a cappuccino before you go?" Sheryl brushed her hand over Jamie's back as she walked by.

Jamie gritted her teeth. Would they wait for her? "Sure." She set her stuff on the counter and turned the espresso machine on. A minute later the house was filled with the voice of a male country singer.

"Do you want to go shopping with me when you get back? I want to get a jump on my winter wardrobe." Sheryl sat at the dining table, leafing through a magazine.

"You're buying winter clothes when it's going to be eighty degrees today?" Jamie ground beans and packed the portafilter. She tightened it in place and drummed her fingers on the counter as she waited for the indicator light to come. The machine screeched as coffee filled the cup one slow drop at a time.

"Fashion is always a season ahead. If you shopped more often you'd know that."

Jamie held the stainless-steel container so the frothing wand forced steam into the nonfat milk. As soon as the thermometer read one hundred forty degrees she shut off the machine and spooned the frothed milk over the coffee. She handed Sheryl the coffee and kissed her.

"Call me when you're done."

"Okay." Jamie dashed out the door and then had to come back for the stuff on the counter. She could have her own friends and still spend time with Sheryl. This could work.

"We were wondering if you were standing us up." Carla's eyes strayed to Jamie's calves and worked their way up. She refused to let them go above her waist to the snug-fitting T-shirt. Sure she would blush if she stared one more minute at those bare legs, she went back to stretching her quads. This wasn't a date, but it was the first time she'd been with Jamie in public since the party, and pretending wasn't breaking any rules.

"What, are you two twins?" Sara pointed at their identical white T-shirts with Midtown Women's Center in red on the front.

"Renee," Jamie and Carla said at once.

"5k fundraiser a few years ago," Carla said.

"Oh, that Renee." Sara rolled her eyes.

"What are the odds we didn't run into each other?" Jamie braced against the tree and stretched her calves. "You sure your back's okay?"

Carla jumped in place and then bent forward, touching her toes. When she straightened she caught Jamie looking at her legs. The black running tights had been a good choice. "All good. Race you," she said, taking off.

Sara set a challenging pace, but by the end of the first mile Carla relaxed into the rhythmic pounding of her feet on the trail that wound through scattered oak trees and open grassy areas along the creek. Holding her shoulders back she matched her breathing to her gait and fell into that space where her mind relaxed and her attention was all on her body. Sara and Jamie were involved in a conversation about running shoes when a lizard darted across the trail and a dog on a leash lunged for it. Jamie and Sara sidestepped the dog, but Carla got tangled in the leash and started to go down. Jamie grabbed for her and caught a handful of her T-shirt. She let go as Carla righted herself.

"Are you okay?" Sara's hand on her back pulled Carla from her spell as the woman pulled the leash free of her legs, apologizing to Carla and scolding the dog.

"Fine." Carla tried to shake off the feel of Jamie's hand against her breast as they resumed the run, but it took her a while to find her rhythm again.

"Anyone up for breakfast?" Carla asked, as they walked around to cool down.

"I'm on a diet until the competition," Sara said.

"I'm sure you can get egg whites and cottage cheese," Carla said. This morning wasn't going to end here if she could help it.

Jamie checked her watch. “I’d like to but—”

“Great. Let’s walk.” Carla made sure she was next to Jamie as they crossed the bridge over Highway 17 and walked into downtown Los Gatos. Yes, her body had responded to Vanessa but there was nowhere she’d rather be than next to Jamie. If she was lucky she’d have the afternoon with her, too. Tomorrow she’d make friends with reality again.

“Do either of you come to the Farmer’s Market?” Carla asked, as they passed vendors lined up along the street. She missed Sunday mornings with Mike when they’d visit the farmers’ market and then go to breakfast.

“I do,” Sara said. “Chicken and vegetables, fish and vegetables.”

“Dedication,” Carla said. “My taste buds would rebel if I didn’t indulge them. Although it’s not as much fun cooking for one.”

“I thought you were married?”

“We’re getting divorced.”

“I’m sorry, Carla.”

“It’s mutual and amicable. How about here?” Carla stopped in front of a diner.

❖

Jamie looked at the people lined up outside and checked her watch again. “Um, okay.” If she went home now she’d still have to eat breakfast, and she was enjoying the camaraderie.

“I’ll go put my name in,” Carla said, walking away.

“I didn’t think you guys could keep up with me,” Sara said, looking smug.

“If I’m limping around tomorrow it’s all your fault. I’m already sore from playing softball Friday.” The practice slow-pitch game had kindled something in Jamie, like a forgotten favorite song that kept replaying. She was going to figure out a way to play on Penni’s team.

“Didn’t you play in college?”

“Yep. Pitcher.” Jamie went through her windup, almost bumping into a woman who walked in front of her.

“If you love a sport you never get over it, do you?””

“No. You don’t.” She needed softball back in her life.

Carla came back with coffees for all of them and Jamie almost groaned. She drank greedily as Carla and Sara talked recipes.

They were finally shown to a booth. Jamie slid onto one side and Sara the other. Carla hesitated before sliding in next to Sara. The waitress set menus on the table and said she'd be right back with coffee.

Jamie snapped the menu shut after barely looking at it. "Blueberry pancakes," she said, smacking her lips.

"A woman after my own heart." Carla closed her menu.

Sara groaned. "Can I have a teensy little bite?"

"Maybe." Jamie said, smiling at the hungry look on Sara's face. "So are you training seven days a week?"

"I was but I'm backing off. The competition's Saturday, and I'm ready to have a life outside the gym again. In fact," Sara said, with a laugh, "I went up to the Castro last night with some friends to a comedy club."

Jamie tensed. She knew what was coming. Should she have told Carla?

"It was lesbian comic night and we laughed our asses off."

Carla's eyes shifted from her to Sara with a puzzled expression. "Are you gay, Sara?"

"Yep. Thought you knew. You have a funny look on your face. It's not a problem, is it?"

"No, no problem at all. In fact…" Carla looked at Jamie, her face the picture of proud. "I'm a lesbian, too."

"You are?" Sara's eyes widened.

"Yes, I am."

"You're…wow…I don't know what to say, Carla."

"Congratulations?" Carla offered, smiling broadly.

"Coming out at your age…and you don't seem shy about it."

"I believe strongly in out and proud."

"Excuse me," Jamie said. She headed toward the back of the restaurant, irritated. How was it that her office manager came out with such ease to someone she barely knew and her partner was trying to pretend she wasn't a lesbian to get a promotion?

Standing outside the back door she stood against the stucco wall and propped her foot against it. The sun was warm on her face, and she tried to chase away the anger with deep, measured breaths. Was she irritated at Carla or Sheryl or herself? Why should she care whom Carla came out to? She clenched her jaw. Sara was a lot younger, but they were becoming friends. Would Sara ask Carla out? That's all she needed in her office…under her nose…right in front of her eyes. She walked back to the table, anxious to get this breakfast over with.

"I was just telling Sara a woman I went out with Friday night called it converting. She said coming out had too much of a Southern-debutante association to it."

"Dating already. You won't be single long," Sara said.

"I don't want to be single for a minute. I love being joined at the hip."

"I'll have the blueberry pancakes and bacon," Jamie blurted out when the waitress came to take their order. "Extra crispy." Was Sheryl the only one who didn't think being joined at the hip was good?

"I'll have the same," Carla said, smiling at Jamie.

"Next time we go up to that club do you want to come with us?" Sara asked, after she'd given her order.

"I'd love to."

"Great," Jamie muttered. *No, she won't be single long.*

"I ordered some lesbian fiction from a website my daughter's girlfriend told me about. Some yummy stuff. There's so much lesbian culture to explore." Carla rubbed her hands together.

Jamie choked on the coffee she was drinking. "Maybe you should slow down," she muttered, under her breath.

"Your daughter's a lesbian, too?" Sara asked.

"Oh, guess I forgot to include that part."

Jamie panicked when Carla started to tell the story. Sara knew Sheryl was principal of Los Gatos High. "So," Jamie blurted out, "maybe we could do this next week?"

"I'm in," Sara said.

"Me, too," Carla said.

"With Carla on board we're now fifty percent of the office. Have you ever marketed to the gay community, Jamie?" Sara draped her arms over the back of the bench. She was wearing a sleeveless T-shirt that showed off the defined muscles of her arms.

"A little bit before my father died," Jamie said. Carla was looking at Sara. Was she checking her out? She wouldn't really go out with her, would she? "Then things got crazy and it was all I could do to handle his patient load. I wasn't looking for more."

"I can't imagine what that must have been like for you. You'll get through this and the clinic will be okay. Especially now that Carla's running things." Sara patted Carla's shoulder.

Jamie looked at Carla. She'd become the lynchpin of her office. The waitress set plates in front of them and conversation drifted to lesbian culture. Carla asked questions with the same curiosity and eagerness she had that night in Atlanta. So much was different about her but so much was the same.

"I'll see you tomorrow," Sara said, when they got back to their cars.

"I should be getting home." Jamie lifted her sunglasses up on her head and fished the car key out of her pocket.

"I went furniture shopping yesterday," Carla said, as she bent over and untied a key from her shoes. Her T-shirt rode up to expose a bit of her back. "I found a desk and chair I think you'll like. I could show you."

"Um, lemme make a phone call," Jamie said, as she stepped away and dialed Sheryl's number. Carla had gone furniture shopping on her own time. The least she could do was go look at it.

"I got tired of waiting so I'm over at Valley Fair mall. Are you gonna meet me?"

Jamie kicked at a hole in the asphalt. "I can't."

"Why not?" Sheryl sounded more curious than irritated.

"I need to go look at some furniture. My office manager is redecorating the office. Finally," she added, with a laugh. "How about if I make that Chinese chicken salad for dinner that you like so much?"

"Okay. And can you fix that drain?"

"Sure. I'll see you later, then." They'd go their own ways for a few hours and then have a cozy dinner at home. Yeah, this could work. "I'm all yours," she said to Carla. "New chair. Yippee!"

"Shall I drive and bring you back here?"

"Where are we going?"

"Santana Row."

Jamie's good mood faltered. It was across the street from where Sheryl was shopping. "I'll meet you there." Surely Sheryl wouldn't wander over.

❖

"I like it," Jamie said, leaning back in the chair. "It fits me." She rubbed her palms over the arms. "And it's not dark brown."

"We can order it in any color you want." Carla crossed her arms and smiled. Outside the office Jamie reminded her of the adventurous woman who'd swept her off her feet. A couple nearby was debating the merits of a sectional couch. She envied them. She'd never be picking out new home furniture with Jamie. As close as they might be at the clinic or as friends, that piece would always be missing. "What?" she asked, when she realized Jamie was talking.

"I like the burgundy. Unless you think it's not okay. I'm not good at picking colors."

"Take cues from the clothes you like to wear. My living-room colors were from a print blouse."

"Would you believe I have a burgundy silk shirt with blousy sleeves and pearl buttons that I love?"

"There you go. The main color for your office is officially burgundy. We can do a lot with that…gold is great with it, or greens. Do you want to order it today?"

"You mean I can't take it with me?" Jamie stroked the arms of the chair.

"No. You have to leave this one here." The little-kid smile was adorable, and Carla's heart skipped a beat. How could Jamie in sweats and an old T-shirt make her heart throb? Right feeling, wrong woman.

"Can we look at the desk, too?"

"Over here," she said, leading Jamie down the aisle. She'd take what time she could get with her. She pointed out several desks, explaining the differences between them

"You know a lot about furniture," Jamie said, appreciation in her voice. "I like that one." She pointed at a medium-sized desk. "I like the color of the wood…cherry, I think you said…and I love that it doesn't have drawers on either side. I won't feel all boxed in." Jamie hunched her shoulders together and made a sour face.

"I like a woman who knows what she wants." She glanced up to see Jamie looking at her, and for an instant there was that spark in her eyes that undid all Carla's resolve about common sense. "Um, I take it you want to order it?" The look was gone and Jamie was smiling at an approaching sales clerk, who gave her an appraising look. Don't even think about it, lady, Carla wanted to say.

"There's a couch upstairs I think you'll like. If you have time." How much longer could she extend the afternoon? A chicken breast and broccoli and a glass of wine were all that waited for her at home.

"Lead on."

"Do you mind if we detour for a quick peek at a bedroom set? I saw one yesterday I liked, and I want to see if I still like it."

"Redecorating?"

"It seems like a good way to start my new life." Jamie was quiet as they walked past bedroom furniture. Carla stopped in front of a canopy bed, light oak with darker wood inset on the foot and headboards. "It's called a plantation bed. Is it silly for me to get something so old-fashioned?"

Jamie fingered the gauzy fabric fastened around one of the posts. "It's beautiful, Carla."

"You're not just saying that because the bedspread's burgundy, are you?"

"Some woman will be lucky to share this bed with you." Jamie's voice was soft, like a caress.

"Thank you." Carla's chest constricted with longing. Why couldn't it be Jamie?

"My parents had a canopy bed. I'm sure it was my mom's choice. I loved it. On days when she wasn't feeling well I'd sit next to her and read to her. With the side panels pulled together it was like being in our own little tent."

"What illness?" Carla knew she'd died young but not the details. Jamie was rubbing the bedspread in a slow back-and-forth motion. She wanted those strokes on her skin.

"Lupus. She was diagnosed before I was born."

"I'm sorry. It sounds like you were close. What was she like?"

Jamie's face softened in a way that surprised Carla. When she talked about her father she always looked so serious.

"You would have liked her—one of the kindest people I've known. She loved to garden, loved romantic comedies and historical romances. Wicked funny. It was impossible not to have fun around her. Would you believe she introduced me to rock music?"

"Did she teach you to dance, too?" She gulped when Jamie's eyes darkened. Was she remembering that bar in Atlanta, too?

"As a matter of fact she did. I'd do my homework while she cooked dinner, and when a song came on we liked we'd dance around the kitchen."

"What was her name?" Sadness clouded Jamie's face, and Carla had to move away or she'd wrap her arms around her.

"Mary Anne. My middle name is Anne."

"She sounds delightful, Jamie." She would probably have bought the set anyway, but Jamie's approval made it a definite.

"I've been thinking a lot about her lately. Maybe everyone does when they get close to the age when a parent died. I miss the talks we had about life, sports, my dreams. I think she knew she wouldn't be around." Jamie was quiet for several minutes. "You should buy this, Carla. It suits you."

Carla nodded. All that Jamie had lost…no matter what it took she refused to let Jamie lose her business. "Let's go look at the couch."

Fifteen minutes later they'd ordered the couch in a burgundy-and-gold fabric. The sales clerk assumed it was for their home and there'd been an awkward moment. Carla squeezed onto the same step with Jamie as they rode the escalator down, soaking up these final moments.

"I can't thank you enough for helping me make changes in my office." Jamie fiddled with her keys as they stood outside the store.

"Like you said, you're helping me through my empty-nest woes." Carla could already feel Jamie's absence. She was tempted to ask if she had time for a cup of coffee but there was no point in dragging it out. She was always going to lose Jamie to another woman. As they walked to the parking lot, they talked about their progress on the embezzlement—safe ground and the only part of Jamie's life Carla would ever be part of.

❖

Jamie set candles on the table on either side of the bouquet of flowers she'd bought on the way home. They'd make up for not spending the day together. It was quality not quantity, after all.

Jamie was fixing the salad dressing when Sheryl came in holding several shopping bags. "Looks like you had fun."

"Lots of sales." Sheryl's eyes were bright. "I don't know why you don't like shopping."

Maybe she just didn't like shopping for clothes. She'd enjoyed the afternoon looking at furniture. "What do you think about new bedroom furniture?"

"I like what we have. You're not going to believe the sweater I got. Yummy," Sheryl said, drawing out the word and pulling the sweater out of the bag.

Jamie stared. Burgundy. She started to laugh.

"What's so funny?"

"That's the color of my new office furniture."

"Good taste."

Jamie laughed harder at the ridiculousness of her situation. If Sheryl knew who'd picked out the furniture she'd be furious.

"Nothing like shopping to lift my spirits." Sheryl wrapped her arm around Jamie's waist and kissed her.

"Me, too." Jamie deepened the kiss. This would all work out. It had to.

CHAPTER TWENTY-SIX

Jamie hung her jacket in the break-room closet. They were fully into fall—her favorite time of year. Cool mornings perfect for running and warm afternoons that made her want to stretch out on a chaise by the pool and read. Coffee was still dripping into the pot, which meant Carla hadn't been here long. She liked the company. Maybe there was one bright spot in this mess. She'd found an office manager who was everything Mary had been for her father. Now if she could just figure out how to keep her after the embezzlement was sorted out.

"Good morning." Jamie set Carla's hummingbird mug on her desk.

Carla mouthed, "Just a minute." It sounded like she was talking to Lissa, and her voice was strained. "No, you're not bothering me. I want you to call me any time you need to talk. It's a change for all of us… Yes, your father and I still love each other."

Jamie stood at the front counter and studied the reception area, trying to visualize what it would look like with the new furniture they'd ordered. After twenty years the office needed the update, but a part of her felt funny about it, as if she were erasing her father's presence.

Looking through her appointment book she smiled at the gap in tomorrow's schedule marked "softball practice" in Carla's handwriting, as if it had as much importance as the patients before and after it. Now that it was part of her Saturday schedule, she wasn't giving it back. Even after joining her father's practice she'd been determined to play and coach. She didn't regret taking over the clinic.

She'd wanted her father to be proud of her. Maybe Penni was right that it wasn't too late to reconnect with the things she loved.

"Have fun with your dad this weekend…I love you, too."

"How's Lissa?"

"On our roller coaster of crying and laughing, she's on the crying end this morning." Carla pulled a Kleenex from her sweater pocket and dabbed at her eyes.

Jamie squeezed her shoulder. "I'd say she's doing remarkably well. Anything I can do for you?"

"No. But thanks for asking. It helps that you know. We still haven't told any of our friends." Carla looked up and smiled, but it was a sad smile. "It's one thing to talk about changing your life but another to do it."

"I admire your courage." Carla's eyes filled with pain Jamie rarely saw. Her fingers played over the rim of her mug and Jamie started to reach for her hand. The back door opened and she pulled back. Sara and Don walked toward their office, discussing a new treatment for frozen shoulder.

"Hand me my half?" Jamie pointed to the stack of patient files on the file cabinet.

"With the forensic accountant working on it you don't need to push so hard."

"I let it happen."

"Have you heard from your attorney about where things stand with the DA?"

"Nope. But when I talked to him last week he agreed with you that what we've found should get me out of trouble with the state board."

"Did you tell him my idea for leveraging the insurance companies into dropping the fraud charges?"

"He said he should have thought of it."

"Money will win, Jamie. They won't want to pay for all the services you didn't bill for but legally could have. You should be out from under this soon."

"I hope." It was hard not to believe in Carla's optimism.

Jamie smiled at the Ziploc bag full of cookies sitting in the middle of the new desk. Carla. Melissa's voice came from the iPod behind her. Carla. Yes, she could get used to being taken care of. As she slid into her new chair she noticed the pink envelope under the bag with her name written in distinctive left-handed script. Carla again. She slid her index finger under the flap and pulled out the card, laughing at the sepia-toned picture of two little girls holding hands on a swing. "I'm glad we're back in each other's lives. C." She set the card next to her father's picture and opened the Ziploc. Sticking her nose inside, she inhaled the buttery, sugary smell.

"Most people prefer to eat them, but if you have a cookie-sniffing fetish, be my guest."

Jamie pulled a cookie out of the bag. Stuffing the whole thing in her mouth she made exaggerated chewing motions, moaning the whole time. She held the bag out to Carla.

"I put some in the break room so those are all yours. I'll be up front if you need me."

Jamie snuck into her office for several more cookies throughout the morning. In fact the whole staff was wiping cookie crumbs off their faces. Carla had even set a plate on the front counter for patients. So many ways Carla took care of people.

Jamie looked up from her desk when Carla walked into her office and said, "Lunch is ready. We're having—"

"Lasagna. It was one of my favorite meals when I was a kid."

"You peeked. And your attorney's on the phone."

"Okay. I'll be there in a minute." Jamie picked up the phone. "Pete. Please give me some good news. Did you hear from the state board?"

"Not yet, but I'm sure the evidence we sent them will prove you didn't know what Marjorie was doing. The DA's office called this morning. They want to meet with us Monday." Jamie stared at Carla's card, trying to ignore the anxiety and fear that were combining in her gut.

"Do they want us to bring anything?"

"No. And don't worry, Jamie. I'm sure it's good news. I'll swing by your office and pick you up about noon. Have a good weekend."

Jamie twirled her pen and stared at her father's picture. The new pewter frame set off his silver-gray hair, and she tried to draw strength from his confident expression.

"Everything all right?" Carla asked from the doorway.

"The DA wants to see me Monday."

"I'm sure it's good news."

"You're probably right." Jamie got up from her chair and set a smile on her face. Her mom always said to expect the best and ignore the worst. "I love my new chair." Jamie sat back down and then stood up again. It felt great not to fight her way out of it. "I love the whole room, Carla." The dark paneling was gone, replaced with Sheetrock and a fresh coat of creamy yellow paint that lightened the room and blended well with the burgundies and golds. The ugly Oriental rug was gone.

"It suits you. I'm glad you brought these in." Carla straightened one of the botanical prints on the wall.

"Me, too. My mom loved collecting them, and I remember them on the walls of her bedroom." It felt good to look around her office and see reminders of her mom.

❖

"We'll see you next month. Good luck with the new job." Carla locked the front door behind the young man who was still in his white chef jacket. She straightened up the reception area and then finished entering the day's billings. Taking the bouquet to the break room she snipped off the stems and put them back in fresh water, pulling a few of the pink roses up higher in the center.

She was stalling and she knew it. Leaving at the end of the day always felt like pulling herself away from a favorite movie. Tonight the fantasy of music and being swept into Jamie's arms was painfully strong. Maybe it was her birthday bearing down on her—the first one in her new life. At least she'd spend part of it with Jamie. The Sunday-morning runs had become the cornerstone of her weekends.

Carla gathered her things and stopped at Jamie's office on her way out. She was leaning back in her chair, eyes closed, an open patient file on the desk. Maybe by this time next week this ordeal would be over. The knot she'd felt when Jamie told her about the meeting with the DA wound itself into her stomach again. She had a bad feeling about this whole mess. She'd spent so much time retracing Marjorie's tracks she felt she knew the woman. She'd been devious and incredibly daring to do so much right under Jamie's nose. It was also odd that she hadn't altered billings for any of the associate doctors. It felt personal against Jamie.

"I'll see you in the morning."

Jamie opened her eyes and motioned for Carla to come in. "Got your usual Friday-night date?"

"Dinner with Vanessa." One of Melissa's early songs was playing, and Carla wanted to pull Jamie out of her chair and dance with her.

"Seeing a lot of her," Jamie said, as she leafed through the file.

"She's fun to be with." Carla forced all the frustration of her feelings for Jamie behind a smile. For all that she valued their friendship, there were things she'd never be able to talk to her about. Like why she found herself physically attracted to Vanessa when she knew she was still in love with Jamie. She wanted to fall in love with Vanessa. She wanted to have her feelings for Jamie replaced, but her heart wasn't cooperating.

"Have you considered dating other women? You're kind of new to this and...well, you wouldn't want to get tied down until you're sure you've found the right person."

Carla ignored the stab of jealousy that made her feel childish. The right person wasn't available. "I had coffee with a woman from the book club I joined." The date with the college professor was intellectually enjoyable but lacked sparks. Carla sighed as disappointment settled around her. For all the dating and joining groups and meeting new people, her life wasn't moving forward. "Mike wants me to go on Internet dating sites."

"You'll find someone. It takes time."

"I guess." Carla stood and pulled the outer petals off some of the roses, freshening the bouquet. "I want more than I had with Mike. I want to fall in love." Carla's throat tightened in a rush of longing. "Heart pounding, body tingling, doodling her name in the margins, can't wait to kiss her..." She pulled herself back to reality, unable to look at Jamie for fear her expression would give away her feelings. "Enough dating talk. I should get going. Like the earrings, by the way."

Jamie fingered the diamond studs. "I hope so. You helped me pick them out. I always wanted my ears pierced."

"You should keep doing the things you always wanted to do."

"Careful what you encourage. I went through a phase in college when I wanted to buy a Harley and just take off." Jamie moved her hands as if revving the engine.

"That doesn't seem like you." Carla's mouth went dry when her mind created an image of Jamie in tight leather pants and one of those jackets with all the zippers. And a tight white tank top under it.

"I was lost for a long time after my mom died."

"She'd be proud of what you've done with your life."

"Would she?" Jamie looked sad. "Enjoy your evening."

Carla couldn't say what she wanted, couldn't comfort Jamie the way she wanted. She walked to her car, her body tingling in all the right places but for the wrong woman. Her mind was clear on the boundaries but her body had missed the memo. At this rate she'd be married to her vibrator for the rest of her life. She groaned in frustration.

Jamie was barely inside her front door when Sheryl shoved an envelope under her nose. "It says they're putting a lien on our house."

"You opened my mail?" Jamie snatched the envelope from her.

"How could you let this happen?" Red blotches on her cheeks marred Sheryl's usually flawless skin.

Jamie sat down hard at the dining-room table and read the letter from the IRS. "I knew I was being audited but—"

"You didn't tell me?" Sheryl's voice was close to a screech.

"I'm handling it, Sheryl." Jamie surged to her feet, furious with Marjorie and the IRS and Sheryl and anyone within two miles. "You don't want to know anything about my business problems." She stormed to the liquor cabinet.

"It's not just your business." Sheryl's angry voice followed her. "You've put our home at risk."

Jamie sloshed Glenlivet into the tumbler and drank half of it. She rubbed the back of her neck. The muscles were bunching into what would soon be a headache. Would she ever have her life back?

"What are you going to do about this?"

Jamie banged the glass down on the cabinet and marched to the bedroom, unbuttoning her shirt, Sheryl close behind. "Tonight? Not a goddamn thing. I'm going to sit in the hot tub and—" Jamie stopped. Overnight bags were on the bed. "What are those?" Her heart clenched. Was Sheryl leaving her?

"I told you I had a seminar this weekend."

"You did? I guess I—"

"You're forgetting a lot lately," Sheryl said, sarcasm topping the anger. She reached for the bags.

Jamie grabbed her hand. "Don't go tonight. Please." Tears filled her eyes. "I'll make it all right. I promise." Jamie flinched at the cold look in Sheryl's eyes. Not a speck of understanding warmed them.

"You've been saying that for months, Jamie. I trusted you," Sheryl hissed as she yanked her hand away. The bags banged against the doorframe as she stalked out.

"I always carry her bags," Jamie said to the empty room before collapsing onto the bed, tears rolling down her cheeks.

All the optimism she'd let Carla talk her into was gone. She was going to lose her house, and for all she knew, the DA would press charges against her. Clutching the bedspread she battled mounting anxiety with forced deep breaths that did nothing. Sheryl's car roared out of the driveway and an unwelcome silence filled the room. Everything she cared about was slipping away, and she was afraid it was too late to stop it.

CHAPTER TWENTY-SEVEN

Jamie watched the sprinkler spraying back and forth across Carla's lawn as she rolled the corner of the yellow place mat. Melissa's voice was coming through the open patio doors—a song from her first album. It seemed like a lifetime ago. Plates with sunflowers and a small white vase with two of the roses Carla had called Secret leant a festive air, but Jamie wasn't in a festive mood.

The energy from their run was wearing off and fatigue was replacing it. She'd barely slept Friday night after Sheryl left, and she'd stayed at her office until after midnight yesterday, matching the last of the patient files against the EOBs. She'd be ready with whatever the DA wanted. A preliminary total of the dollar amount of Marjorie's embezzling shocked her and sent her into another sleepless night.

She should have cancelled out on the run but just couldn't face a whole day in the empty house fighting the panic that Sheryl might not forgive her. If she'd known Sara wasn't joining them for breakfast she would have backed out. Holding up her end of the conversation would be hard and hiding that something was wrong, harder.

Carla had asked her too many times yesterday if she was all right. She couldn't exactly confide in her. Another thing she hadn't handled well. If Sheryl was this angry over the IRS problem, what would happen if she found out who her office manager was? Could this weekend get any worse?

The chime that meant she had a text startled her, and she snatched her phone from her pocket, praying it was Sheryl. Penni. Her heart plummeted, but she had to smile as she read the joke. She'd been sending them all weekend—her way of trying to boost Jamie's spirits.

"Something wrong?" Carla set plates on the table, one piled high with blueberry pancakes, the other with bacon.

Jamie put her phone back in her pocket. "No."

Sitting down across from Jamie, Carla stacked three pancakes and twice that many pieces of bacon on each of their plates. "Extra crispy," she said. "Just the way you like it."

"I can't eat all that," Jamie said, her stomach rebelling.

"You always eat this much after a run." Carla sounded hurt.

Jamie reached for the butter and syrup, feeling guilty for her bad mood. It wasn't Carla's fault her appetite was lost in anger at Marjorie and fear about the DA meeting and financial problems and worry about Sheryl. "You didn't have to fix breakfast just for me." The butter she slathered over the pancakes was soft and dripped down the sides as she added her usual liberal amount of maple syrup. The syrup was warm. Jamie stared at the plate. Was there any end to Carla's thoughtfulness?

"You know how much I love to cook, and it's hard to get used to cooking for one. You're doing me a favor."

"Sara will be sorry she missed this." Jamie finished the fresh-squeezed orange juice. "What's wrong?" Carla looked like she was about to cry.

"Sometimes I miss my old life."

"I'm sorry it's hard." For all Carla's competence and thoughtfulness, Jamie sometimes forgot that she had struggles, too. She squeezed Carla's hand. "How's Lissa?"

"Better. Last night she asked more questions about how I decided I was a lesbian. It's a little awkward to explain."

Jamie looked up from cutting the pancakes into little bites, hoping she could get them down. "You didn't—"

"Of course not, but that night affected her, too." Carla's eyes had a mischievous spark.

"Her name." Jamie had suspected it. Why had she thought that night hadn't mattered to Carla?

"If she'd been a boy she would have been Bruce. Springsteen is Mike's favorite rock star. I never had a favorite until that night. I love this song," Carla said, air tapping her fork to the beat. "I remember it was the last one she played that night."

"When did you start going by Carla?" Jamie asked, when the song was done. It was one of her favorites, too.

"Shortly after Lissa was born. Carla sounded more like the name of a woman with a baby." Carla hesitated, swirling a bite of pancakes in syrup, as she seemed to gather her thoughts. "That night…you gave me something to pass on to my daughter—a sense of what it felt like to find myself. I decided before she was born I'd make sure she had that chance, too." Carla's eyes held Jamie's. "I never forgot how out and proud you were. I want her to know she'll always be loved for who she is."

"She's a lucky girl," she said, because she didn't know what else to say. Jamie was so far from that person. They hadn't talked about that night since the day Carla hurt her back. It was the past and they'd moved on. Ex-lovers and new friends—wasn't that the lesbian way? "Tell me about your book club," Jamie said, looking for safe ground as emotions swirled through her.

"More coffee?" Carla asked, when their forks stopped for good.

"Half." Closing her eyes and stretching her legs out, Jamie tilted her face to the sun, seeking the relaxation it always gave her. She yawned. A nap in the sun sounded heavenly. By the time Sheryl got home she'd be rested and ready to fix her favorite dinner. She'd make this up to Sheryl. With luck, tomorrow she'd have good news and all this would be behind them. Jamie relaxed into the sound of Carla's voice as they sipped coffee and Carla talked about her garden. Finally, coffee cups empty, they gathered up the dishes and carried them to the kitchen.

"Did you have a birthday recently?" Jamie looked at the cards arranged across the sideboard.

"Would you believe it's today?"

"Wow…forty-two."

"How did you know?"

"I asked that night." A rush of memories captured her and she shook them off. That was the past. "I wish I'd known it was today. I would have—"

"Your company is present enough." Carla was standing next to her, drying her hands on a dishtowel.

Jamie fingered one of the cards, and her heart clenched with emotion she couldn't name.

"What's wrong, Jamie? Is it the meeting tomorrow?" Carla put her hand on Jamie's back.

Jamie shook her head. Her throat tightened, and she couldn't move away from the warmth and comfort. When Carla pulled her into a hug she didn't fight it. She held Carla's waist and counted the seconds. How long was too long for friendship, and how had this friendship come to mean so much to her? How badly she wanted to tell Carla everything. Stepping back she looked down at Carla's bare feet so close to her tennis shoes, the nails a tasteful pink. She put her hands in her pockets and took another step back.

"What are you doing for your birthday?" She'd get a present next week—something for her garden or her kitchen.

"Mike's taking me out to dinner. I was thinking of treating myself to an afternoon curled up on my couch with popcorn and my favorite movies. There's something decadent about watching movies in the middle of the day. Kind of like playing hooky."

"I could use a day of playing hooky."

"Join me."

"I should get going."

"It's my birthday."

It was a small thing to ask, and after all Carla had done for her how could she say no? Maybe doing something nice for Carla would cheer her up and she'd be in a better mood when Sheryl got home. Maybe she just didn't want to go home to an empty house. "If you're sure."

"Of course I am." Carla's face brightened and Jamie was glad she'd agreed.

"I should go home and clean up—"

"You can shower here. Come on, guest bath is this way. I'm sure I have a T-shirt that will fit you."

Carla tried not to think of a naked Jamie in her shower as she did the dishes. And then as she sipped a third cup of coffee she didn't

need, her hands trembling as she leafed through a cooking magazine, her mind wandering into versions of a shower fantasy. Maybe she was reading too much lesbian fiction, but her heart couldn't resist a hopeful flutter—Jamie, her couch, a bowl of popcorn between them, maybe the accidental brush of their fingers.

She shook her head, disgusted with herself. She'd made her uncomfortable with the hug. She'd pressured her into staying. Boundaries, always boundaries. She was sick of them. She looked out at the flats of purple pansies and yellow Iceland poppies she'd bought to cheer herself up. Was this her new life—gardening and book clubs, dating people she'd never fall in love with, cooking for people she couldn't keep?

"Thanks for the T-shirt."

Carla sprang out of her chair and the magazine fell to the floor. Sexy was the only word her mind would offer as she looked at Jamie. Her face was flushed, hair damp, strands curling over her ears and forehead. The V-necked blue T-shirt was too tight in all the right ways. Sure her face was beet red, she collected her cup and hurried to the kitchen. "Think I'll take a quick shower, too. Make yourself comfortable. There's more coffee if you want."

Carla took more care dressing than she knew was sensible, choosing a sleeveless peach blouse she always got compliments on, putting on her favorite gold bracelet and a touch of makeup and dab of perfume. This wasn't a date but she could pretend. It was just one afternoon and it was her birthday.

Jamie was sitting at the patio table, and Carla halted in the doorway as her heart clutched at the rightness of Jamie in her home. She checked her phone again as Carla approached. Something was bothering her, but she was afraid to ask again. Jamie looked up, her eyes sad and the smile strained as she put her phone back in her pocket.

"So what are your favorite movies?"

"I'm hopelessly addicted to romantic comedies." Carla sat and crossed her legs. It was safe for her thighs to touch now. She'd taken care of the ache between her legs in the shower, coming to an image of her wet body sliding against Jamie's. Fantasies weren't breaking any rules.

"Romantic comedies, huh." Jamie rolled her eyes.

"You can never have enough romance."

"I'm more of an adventure, thriller kind of gal."

"Ahh, you want a little action with your kissing." Carla's heart broke into a rhythmic thumping. She remembered those kisses. "If you humor me today, I'll humor you on your birthday." She gathered up the placemats and walked back inside. "When is it?"

"April sixth."

"That's Lissa's birthday."

"Wow. Easy for you to remember," Jamie said, as she followed Carla into the house.

Carla pulled a plastic box from under the TV stand and set it on the kitchen counter. "My favorite movies," she said, as she lifted the lid. "I usually just pick one at random. Why don't you do the honors while I fix popcorn."

Jamie groaned. "On top of blueberry pancakes?"

"You can't watch a movie without popcorn. Those are the rules." Carla put a bag of Orville Redenbacher in the microwave and butter in a pan on the stove.

"*You've Got Mail* is the winner."

"Don't look so horrified. Have you seen it?"

"Nope."

"You're probably the only person on the planet who hasn't."

The microwave dinged, and Carla poured the popcorn into a bowl and stirred in the butter. She put the movie in and claimed her usual end of the couch, tucking her feet under her and setting the popcorn next to her, shamelessly forcing Jamie to sit close to her.

"I confess to having a bit of a crush on Meg Ryan," Carla said, as the movie began. "Is that a lesbian thing?"

"I have no idea."

"Some expert you are." Carla threw a piece of popcorn at Jamie.

"How many times have you watched this movie?" Jamie asked, as Brinkley hovered around the kissing couple and the closing credits ran.

"Why?"

"You quoted half the dialogue with them."

"Oops. I usually only do that in private. Pick another," Carla said, as she retrieved the jar of tea she'd set out in the sun. She knew she was pushing the boundaries but didn't care. She made another bag of popcorn and filled glasses with ice.

Jamie was checking her phone again when she walked back into the living room. "What did you pick?" She set the iced teas on the coffee table and pointed to the glass on the right. "That's yours—extra sugar and lemon."

Jamie stared at the tray, an odd look on her face, as she held up the movie case.

"*French Kiss*."

"Huh?" Jamie's head snapped up.

"The movie." Carla took the DVD from her. "Back-to-back Meg Ryan. My lucky day." The afternoon sun was coming in the French doors right into Jamie's eyes. Carla set the bowl of popcorn on the coffee table and motioned Jamie to scoot over. "Or you could put on your sunglasses." Jamie didn't respond to the teasing like she usually did. Why wouldn't she talk about what was bothering her? She yawned as she slid over and helped herself to a handful of popcorn.

"How can you not like romantic comedies?" Carla asked, after the kiss-on-the-train scene, looking over at Jamie. Her eyes were closed and her lips were parted. Her hands lay palms up in her lap, a piece of popcorn between her thighs. "Jamie," Carla said, softly, and touched her arm. Jamie sighed but didn't move. Asleep. Her head fell to the side, and Carla knew it was a sore neck waiting to happen.

Putting her arm across Jamie's shoulder she pulled gently until Jamie curled up on the couch, her head in Carla's lap. What had made her so exhausted? Jamie's chest rose and fell in shallow, even breaths. She stroked her fingertips through Jamie's hair. Jamie mumbled something and draped her arm over Carla's thigh. Shock waves of desire shot through Carla's body, and that tingly feeling launched from her thigh and raced everywhere. Could she survive the rest of the movie with Jamie asleep on her lap?

Jamie closed her fingers around something soft. Her head was on a pillow and she smiled as she opened her eyes. That nap. She was on her side and a movie was on the TV.

"Did you have a good nap?"

Carla's voice. Carla's lap. Jamie bolted upright. Her knee hit the coffee table and the iced-tea glasses fell with a thud, sending ice cubes all over. She started to get up, but Carla stopped her with a hand on her shoulder.

"I'll get a towel."

"I'm so sorry, Carla." When did she fall asleep, and how did she end up on Carla's lap?

"Don't be silly. It's just ice cubes."

Jamie's mind was fuzzy from sleep and her body felt hot. What time was it?

"I guess you needed the sleep."

"I'm…"

Carla stopped wiping up the spilled tea and looked at her. "Won't you tell me what's bothering you?"

Jamie looked away from those eyes that so affected her with their kindness. "It's been a rough couple days."

"The meeting will be over by this time tomorrow and you'll be vindicated. You're almost out from under it." Carla's voice was so sure, so comforting.

"That's not it," Jamie said, in a voice that sounded as defeated as she felt.

"What then?" Carla sat down next to her.

Loneliness and fear collided, and unwanted tears filled her eyes. "My house," she said, in a whisper. "The IRS put a lien on my house for back taxes. I'll never be done with this mess."

Carla touched Jamie's back.

"And I finished going through the patient files yesterday." Jamie laughed bitterly and fought the urge to relax into Carla's hand. "I added it up. Just with what we could trace it's ninety-three thousand dollars for last year alone." Carla was silent and her hand stilled on Jamie's back. "You knew."

"Suspected."

"That bitch!" Jamie surged to her feet, anger searing through her. Saying the damage out loud made it painfully real. She stormed to the kitchen. Her business…her relationship…her house…and God knew what else…all in jeopardy because of Marjorie. Her breath caught in her chest when Carla rubbed in a slow circle between her shoulder blades. “I’m going to lose everything.”

“No, you’re not. I’ll mortgage my house if I have to,” Carla said, fiercely. “You will not lose your house, you will not go bankrupt, and your patients will not be left without their doctor.”

Jamie squeezed her eyes shut, her thoughts in turmoil, her awareness focused on the hand on her back, stealing the reassurance Carla offered. “You’re not going to mortgage your house. I created this mess—”

“No, you didn’t.”

The strength of Carla’s voice infiltrated her, collecting all the worry and anxiety, soothing the broken pieces of her heart.

“Jamie, look at me.”

The first thing Jamie saw was Carla’s eyes. Always Carla’s eyes—the kindness and understanding she was used to but something more. Jamie’s heart jumped into her throat. Carla’s eyes sparked with fierceness, then darkened with…Jamie groaned. She knew what Carla wanted. Carla’s waist slid into her hands and she was lost in the soft compliance beneath her fingers. She trembled, her eyes locked on Carla’s, as her body gave in to the desire in those eyes.

Carla cupped the back of Jamie’s head, and her breath came hot and fast against Jamie’s mouth. She moaned when Carla’s lips met hers. Desire shot through her and she opened to the kiss. Carla’s mouth took hers, gently at first, then not so gently. Boundaries dissolved as the kiss took on a life of its own, hot and alive and sparking with electricity. Passion ignited and they clung to each other as their moans became one.

With Carla’s lips commanding hers, with Carla’s tongue in charge, Jamie surrendered. She wrapped her arms around Carla’s waist, sucking their centers together. She fought to explore Carla’s mouth as hers was explored. Their mouths tasted of butter and salt and need. The kiss was everything she remembered and new sensations all mixed together.

Jamie’s heart pounded, pushing desire through channels that welcomed it. Carla’s hand slid down the side of her neck, her fingers rested on her bounding pulse, then moved lower to the curve of her breast. Carla moaned as she rubbed her thumb over Jamie’s nipple.

It hardened, and arousal tumbled to Jamie's center. Carla pinched her nipple. Pain pricked the cocoon of lust, and awareness burst through. She pushed against Carla's chest. "I can't," she said, in a strangled voice as Carla kissed her way down Jamie's neck.

"I can't." Jamie choked out the words again. Carla's mouth was so warm against her skin, and she trembled with the need to arch her head back, to give in to the touch that was igniting her. Breathing hard she ducked under Carla's arm and backed away until she hit the counter. They stared at each other over the expanse of Carla's kitchen and twenty years. Carla took a step toward Jamie. Her face was flushed, her erect nipples visible through the blouse, her eyes glazed. She took another step. Jamie made a whimpering sound. Carla stopped and blinked, then blinked again. The desire in her eyes dissolved.

"I'm sorry," Carla whispered, her chest heaving.

Jamie's legs were jelly as she bolted for the door.

❖

Carla paced in her living room, trembling with leftover desire. She turned off the movie and the room fell silent. Lust retreated and regret wrapped around her like a corset, squeezing the breath out of her. She'd taken what she shouldn't. She knew Jamie well enough to know honor and responsibility were the cornerstones of who she was. She'd kissed a woman she knew wasn't available. She had to fix this. She reached for her phone, startled when it rang. "Jamie?"

"Sorry to disappoint you, honey. I'm running a few minutes late for dinner."

"Oh, Mike, I did something awful," Carla said, as tears blurred her vision.

"What's wrong? You sound like you're crying."

Carla slumped to the couch, and the story tumbled out through ragged sobs and cold self-reproach. She'd lose Jamie forever, and not even Mike's comforting words could make her believe otherwise.

❖

Jamie stumbled into her house and headed straight for the liquor cabinet. A drink to calm down, wait for Sheryl, fix her favorite dinner, put her favorite CD on, and this would all go away. She laid it out like a treatment plan. She could fix this. She fumbled the top off the bottle of Wild Turkey, too ashamed to drink her father's Scotch. Pulling the fiery liquid into her mouth, she held it there to burn away the taste of Carla. Some dribbled down her chin and onto her shirt—Carla's shirt. Ripping it over her head she tossed it to the floor.

She paced the living room, conflicting thoughts chasing her from one end to the other, as she tried to corral her emotions. There was no way to make this go away. Yes, there was. Carla would have to go. She couldn't be trusted. She could fix this. Sheryl deserved better. She'd be a better partner. She'd never run again. She'd never eat pancakes again. Or popcorn. Or watch a romantic comedy. She'd go shopping any time Sheryl wanted. She ran through the list as if beads on a rosary.

Tears stung her eyes and she couldn't stop the trembling. Images and sensations bombarded her—Carla's eyes sparking with desire, soft lips, her body in Jamie's arms. Her stomach clenched and she put her hand over it as she tumbled to the couch. She checked her watch. Wait for Sheryl. Fix dinner. Beg forgiveness. This would all go away. It wasn't too late to save what mattered.

Jamie pulled out her phone. Call Sheryl. If she didn't answer at least she'd hear her voice. There was a message. How had she not heard the ring? She listened to the message, trembling at the coldness in Sheryl's voice. "I'm not coming home tonight. I can't believe how irresponsible you've been. You've jeopardized everything." She listened to it again and crumpled onto her side. Sheryl wasn't coming home. There'd be no fixing this.

She called her back, praying for Sheryl to answer. "Please…please come home. I need you. I'll make everything right. I'm so sorry. Please, Sheryl." She waited as if Sheryl's voice would fill the silence. "Come home…please." Holding her head in her hands, she sobbed.

CHAPTER TWENTY-EIGHT

Jamie stood next to Pete in the elevator as they rode to the fourth floor of the Santa Clara County District Attorney's office. Her hands trembled as she tugged at the cuffs of her navy blazer. Too little sleep the last few nights, too much coffee this morning. Her heart pounded and she forced herself to slow her breathing. She'd avoided Carla all morning. She'd fired her CPA for letting the IRS situation get out of control. Now she needed her mind clear and focused on the meeting. The briefcase in her hand was full of evidence of her innocence and Marjorie's guilt. She'd finally have her justice.

Jamie tapped her fingers against her leg as she waited for the door to open. By tomorrow everything would be back to normal. She'd go back to the office and thank Carla for everything she'd done and tell her it wasn't going to work out. Flowers were on their way to Sheryl's office, and she didn't care how she explained them. When this meeting was over she'd call her with the good news and then go home and fix a romantic dinner. She wasn't going to lose her business or her house or her relationship.

Stepping off the elevator they presented themselves to a woman behind a desk, who led them to the end of the corridor. Opening half of an imposing double oak door for them, she asked if they'd like anything to drink.

"Coffee, please," Pete said.

"I'm fine," Jamie said. Two steps into the office she stopped when she saw the woman rounding the desk to greet them. Anne Clayton was an impressive figure, tall and trim with short dark hair. Jamie remembered the piercing brown eyes that didn't miss anything.

She was high up in the DA's office and had been a patient. Jamie relaxed a little. It must be good news.

"Dr. Hammond, please come in. Pete, it's nice to see you again." Anne shook their hands and pointed to chairs in front of her desk.

"Jamie, please. How are you, Anne?"

"Overworked and underpaid," Anne said, her voice edged with sarcasm. "But my back is great. Have a seat and let's get started."

The assistant returned, with coffee. "No calls," Anne said, as she stirred cream into hers.

Jamie tried to relax into the chair, but Anne was focused on her in a way that made her nervous. She crossed her legs and touched the briefcase next to her.

"Dolores Baker will be joining us. She's officially in charge of the investigation. I wanted to meet with you first."

Anne's voice was commanding but not loud, and Jamie could imagine her dominating a courtroom. Maybe she'd be prosecuting Marjorie. She wanted her to pay for the destruction she'd wreaked on her life.

"I didn't know about this until two weeks ago. I primarily oversee cases involving violent crimes. If I had known I would have involved myself sooner." Anne paused to sip her coffee.

Jamie relaxed a little. If Anne had taken a personal interest in the case it must be good news. Tomorrow she'd have her life back.

"I want to go on record that I have no doubts about your honesty and integrity. It's typical at the beginning of an investigation of this nature to look at everyone involved. You've been cleared of any personal wrongdoing, and from this point on you'll be treated as the victim of a crime."

Jamie smiled and Pete patted her arm. This was the news she needed. Anne rested her forearms on the large desk covered with stacks of files and law books. "I also want to tell you right now you're not going to like some of what you'll hear today. Hell, I don't like it, but I assure you every fact has been checked and it's indisputable."

Jamie swallowed hard as she met the piercing brown eyes, unsure what to make of Anne's cryptic comment. Had Marjorie done something else she didn't know about? She looked at Pete but he seemed unconcerned.

There was a knock on the door, and a young woman with short auburn hair entered. She nodded at Anne before introducing herself and then took the third chair in front of Anne's desk.

Anne gestured to her. "Your show, Dolores."

Dolores set a brown folder on the desk, looking uncomfortable as she pulled papers from it. She cleared her throat. "I'm sorry this investigation took so long, Dr. Hammond." She looked at Anne before facing Jamie. "Cases of embezzlement are never simple, but this one…" She shook her head. "Marjorie Vicker led us on quite a merry chase. Most embezzlers are good at covering their tracks by weaving intricate stories or implicating the people they stole from. This is a nasty piece of work on all those counts."

"Lay it out for them, Dolores," Anne said.

Dolores cleared her throat again and adjusted herself in the chair. "When we first questioned Ms. Vicker she denied all the charges against her, insisting it was just a misunderstanding."

Lies. Marjorie's pathetic lies disgusted Jamie, but at least the truth was finally coming out. Anne's gaze was fixed on her again, and the scrutiny made her uneasy.

"When we presented her with records from the insurance companies and her own bank records, she changed her story and insisted you were involved in it. She told a convoluted story about how the money went into her accounts first and then into hidden accounts you had in offshore banks."

Jamie started to protest but Dolores held up her hand. Anne's gaze had softened, but there was sympathy in it that didn't make sense. A bad feeling crawled up her spine. There was more.

"It took us awhile to untangle that mess," Dolores said, shuffling the papers in her lap. "It does happen sometimes that a scenario like that is true. We've investigated thoroughly and found nothing suspicious in your personal finances to support her claim. When we confronted her, Ms. Vicker couldn't give us any documentation to support her claim."

Jamie resented that she'd been investigated, but other than stupidity and misplaced trust she wasn't guilty of anything. It was reassuring to have it confirmed.

"Ms. Vicker's last hurrah, so to speak, was a doozy." Dolores tapped her pen against her knee and looked at Anne. Something passed between them, and Jamie's breathing quickened as that bad feeling intensified. "At first we thought she was lying again. In part she was, but in part she wasn't."

"Short version," Anne said, her eyes on Jamie.

Dolores avoided looking at Jamie as she continued. "Ms. Vicker claimed her mother had been skimming money from the business with your father's blessing and she was just continuing—"

"What!" Jamie sat up on the edge of the chair. "That's ridiculous. How dare she—"

"Let her finish, Jamie." Anne's voice silenced the room.

Jamie's neck felt hot and her stomach dropped. Anne's gaze was still too soft, and Dolores wouldn't look at her. There was something more. She braced herself. What else had Marjorie done?

"When we pressed her to support her allegation, Ms. Vicker claimed she's your father's daughter and was entitled to take the money because you cheated her out of her rightful inheritance."

Jamie went rigid as she stared first at Dolores and then at Anne. She jumped to her feet and headed for the door. More lies. She wasn't going to listen to them insult her father. Anne stepped in front of her and put a restraining hand on her forearm. "I said you wouldn't like some of what you'd hear." Anne's voice was gentle but the grip on her arm was firm. "I can't tell you how sorry I am you had to find out this way, Jamie, but we need to get through this."

Shock, anger, and a horrible sinking feeling collected in Jamie's gut. She sat down hard and gripped the arms of the chair, her insides turning to jelly. Pete touched her arm and she turned on him. "You knew my father since before I was born. Is it true?" Her voice sounded strange to her ears through all the blood pounding in her head.

Pete looked pale. "I have no reason to believe it is."

Anne came around her desk, took the paper from Dolores, and handed it to Jamie. "This is a copy of her birth certificate. I want you to leave here knowing as much as we do, Jamie."

Jamie took the birth certificate, trembling as she searched for the line that said birth father. John James Hammond. She held it away as if it burned her. Anne's fingers brushed against hers as she took it, and Jamie wanted to grab her hand and hold tight as shock waves of disbelief hit her. She tried to sort out her thoughts as her life rearranged itself into a sickening new reality. Her mom. This would have killed her. She focused on Anne's voice as her world tilted and fell into the abyss.

"Ms. Vicker told us a long, involved story about how your father told her mother shortly before his death that he'd written a new will which included both of them," Dolores said. "She claims he left her mother the house he'd bought for her and set up trust funds for them."

"Is it true?" Jamie asked, to no one in particular. Her voice sounded wrong, like she was speaking from far away.

"Ms. Vicker can't provide us with a copy of the supposed will," Anne said. "She claims you destroyed it, then kept her on as your office manager to keep her quiet."

Jamie tried to speak, but no words came out as her throat closed around the cry of disbelief that threatened to break through. "If it's true, I never saw it, and I swear my father never told me about a new one. He pretended he wasn't dying right up to the end," she added, as those last months took on new meaning—Mary taking care of him, breaking down at his funeral. She looked at Anne's hands folded across her thigh, one hip hiked up on the corner of her desk. A gold watch hugged her wrist, a Rolex crown on the dial. *Maybe that's what I'll buy Sheryl as an anniversary present.*

Pete was shaking his head. "As far as I know, I handled all John's legal matters."

Anne stayed perched on the corner of her desk, and Jamie anchored herself to her strong presence. She felt very small as she fought for control. Not in a million years would she have thought her father capable of—The kiss. She swallowed hard against the bile rising in her throat. She needed to get out of here. She needed Sheryl. They'd get through this. It would be all right.

"We don't believe that part is true," Anne said. "She's desperate to avoid prison and trying to muddy the waters any way she can. The paternity issue can't be denied, but there's no evidence to support the rest of her claim."

"Are you going to prosecute?" Jamie hoped her voice wasn't shaking. She studied the wall of law books behind Anne's desk. All that certainty.

"The easy answer would be to say yes," Anne said. "We have enough evidence, and the dollars we're talking about in this case are substantial."

"Good," Jamie said, as anger chased away some of the shock. "She and her mother were like—" Tears filled her eyes and she lowered her head to hide them. As a little girl she'd thought her father had two wives—one at home and one at the office. He'd been furious when she asked if all daddies had two wives. She wiped tears off her cheeks and didn't pull away when Pete touched her arm. "How long?"

"How long what?" Anne asked.

"The…affair." Jamie choked on the word. Had her mother found out? She'd failed quickly in those last few months.

"Ms. Vicker claims they became involved shortly after her mother went to work for your father." Jamie hated the calm tone Anne used for such a despicable act. "I won't pull punches with you, Jamie. That part is probably true. Your father bought the house she's living in in 1965. The title is still in his name. Since it wasn't mentioned in the will that was probated, no one knew about it. Ms. Vicker continued to pay the property taxes so no red flags were raised. Technically the house is yours as your father's sole heir. Given when he bought it and what property values have become, it's a sizable asset."

"I don't want anything to do with it," Jamie said. How did these people know more about her life than she did?

"Perhaps, but that's one of the things I want you to think about. You have two problems that should be your primary concerns. The sale of that house might be enough to cover what you owe the IRS. Don't let anger tempt you to make a decision that's not in your best interest."

Jamie heard the logic, but profiting from what her father had done was condoning it. She'd save herself. She didn't need his help…lying, cheating bastard. The words rose up through layers of crumbling love and respect. He wasn't who she'd believed him to be.

"Your second problem is with the insurance companies and, I imagine, with your state board over insurance-fraud issues. My office will support your claim that you had no knowledge of what Ms. Vicker was doing. I want you to think about what's best for your business."

My father's business, Jamie wanted to say. Twenty years and she was still trying to make him proud.

Anne paused, and when Jamie met her gaze, her breath caught at the concern in her eyes. "Dolores, I'll meet with you later. Pete, if it's all right with you, I'd like to talk to Jamie alone."

"I'll wait for you downstairs." Pete patted her arm as he got up.

Jamie slumped back against the chair, trembling with anger and disbelief.

"I can't imagine what you're feeling." Anne's voice was soft. "If I can do anything to help, it would be my pleasure to return the kindness you showed me when I hurt my back."

Jamie cleared her throat, gathering herself. "Thank you, Anne. I don't know what to do with all this." She shook her head as if she could jostle the pieces into place.

"I hope you have good people who can help you through it."

Jamie nodded, too numb to think. She had Sheryl. They'd pull together.

"If you have any questions, call me." She handed Jamie a business card.

Jamie stood and picked up the briefcase, squeezing the handle. Useless evidence. Anne shook her hand, holding it longer than she needed to before walking Jamie out of her office and escorting her to the elevator. Nothing more was said as Anne reached in and pressed the button for the first floor.

CHAPTER TWENTY-NINE

Jamie looked out the window of Pete's Mercedes as he navigated the streets of downtown San Jose, regretting she'd let him pick her up. She wanted to be alone. She now had the why and wished she didn't. Her head throbbed and her gut was churning dangerously. It took her a few minutes to realize Pete was talking to her.

"Jamie, I had no idea. I knew your mother. She was a special woman. I would never have covered his actions. I'll look into the particulars on that house—"

"Can we talk about this another time?" Jamie's voice was oddly calm.

"Of course." Pete patted her arm in a grandfatherly way. She wanted to be mad at him, but her father had fooled everyone.

"I couldn't figure out why Marjorie would steal from me," she said, as if to herself, staring out the window at people going about their business, oblivious that their lives could be undone in an instant. "I thought if I knew why she did it I could make peace with it."

But there was no making peace with this. Marjorie hated her for something she knew nothing about. Her life was on the brink of ruin and she hadn't caused any of it. She folded her arms tight against her body, trying to keep herself from falling apart.

"You'll get through this, Jamie. You're strong like your—"

Jamie choked back the sob that tried to escape. She didn't want to be anything like him. Her mind slammed against itself. The kiss.

"Take me home." She couldn't go back to that office. His office. She couldn't face Carla.

Jamie bolted from the car as soon as it came to a stop in her driveway. She was blind with rage as she tore off her clothes and stepped into the shower. Water as hot as she could stand scalded her as she scrubbed her skin. What he'd done made her feel dirty. All those years she'd been around them and never suspected. Had anyone known? Colleagues? Patients? Oh, God. She pressed her forehead against the tile and laid her palms alongside as the water beat down on her back. Her thoughts ricocheted from disbelief to anger and back again. Her mom. Had she known? Suspected? Were her bouts of depression because of him? She collapsed to the floor of the shower, sobbing as her childhood crumbled around her, no longer the perfect, loving family.

Photo albums circled Jamie as she sat on the living-room floor, wrapped in the green terry-cloth bathrobe she'd pulled from the back of her closet, a long-ago Christmas present from her mom. She flipped pages, examining every picture for evidence of his betrayal, as if she needed more than his name on a birth certificate. Marjorie was older. Had Jamie been wanted? Or was she just an inconvenient accident? Her mother loved her, of that she was certain, but her father? Fear and confusion gathered in her stomach as questions chased each other, too many to grasp.

She dropped another tear-soaked tissue onto the floor. So many pictures of her and her mom in Carmel without him, and now it all made sense. He'd been with her, with them. All those nights he was supposedly at his office or at meetings was he with them, too? In the house he'd bought for them? What about all those weekend seminars? Had they gone with him—a vacation? Her stomach was an angry lump of pain, and a headache throbbed in her temples. She fought the urge to tear up every single picture of him. She didn't know how long she'd been there when the front door opened.

She stepped on one of the photo albums as she dashed to Sheryl and threw her arms around her. "God, I'm happy to see you." Jamie peppered Sheryl's cheeks with kisses and then kissed her possessively on the mouth. "I love you so much. Please don't be mad at me."

"Why are you home so early?" Sheryl pushed against her waist.

No, pull me closer. "I had a meeting with the DA this afternoon."

"Is it over?"

"Yes." She kissed her again, aching for Sheryl to kiss her back. Really kiss her. Like she was forgiven. Like they were okay.

"The tax problem, too?"

"Yes." She'd sell that house and use the money to save theirs.

"That's great."

Sheryl's smile thawed some of the panic that felt like frostbite in her heart. They'd be okay. "Sheryl—"

"What happened to the living room?"

Jamie clutched Sheryl's hand as she walked to the kitchen.

"Sheryl—"

"I have some good news about my promotion."

Jamie tugged on Sheryl's arm until she turned around. "My father had an affair with Mary. Marjorie is his daughter." She wanted Sheryl to fill in the gaps, to understand.

"What?"

"An affair. My father was cheating on my mom with Mary." Sheryl laughed, and Jamie backed up as if slapped.

"You're kidding. What does that have to do with her embezzling?"

"My father had an affair, Sheryl! That's what I found out at the fucking meeting."

"Don't yell at me. I see you're upset, but it's not that big a deal. My father had affairs all the time. It's just the way men are."

Jamie stared at her. She felt disoriented—like she didn't belong in her own life. She gripped the edge of the counter. "Your father had affairs and you don't think it was a big deal?" This was the first she'd heard about this.

"Jamie, your mom was sick a lot," Sheryl said, as if to a child. "Maybe your father thought it was a decent compromise. He stayed with her, right?"

"Compromise? Since when is cheating a compromise?"

"Isn't the important part that it's over?" Sheryl ran her fingers through Jamie's hair, straightening it, and kissed her on the cheek. She set a take-out bag on the counter. "There's enough for you if you want some."

How could Sheryl be talking about dinner when she'd just had the worst day of her life? If she went out and came back in again would she be in the right life—the one where Sheryl wrapped her arms around her and held her and said how horrible it was and how sorry she was. The life where they went to bed and curled up together, just the two of them, like nothing else mattered.

"The superintendent was at the seminar. And that bitch wasn't. He told me he respected how dedicated and hard-working I am. Said I'm the type of person he wants on his team. Isn't that great?"

Jamie covered the space in two strides, wrapped her arms around Sheryl, buried her face in her neck, gulped in her perfume. "I need to be close to you. Please." Tears rolled down her cheeks as Sheryl's arms came around her, and she kissed the side of her head.

"I have to go to a meeting."

Jamie's chest tightened and she gathered fistfuls of Sheryl's expensive suit. "Stay home with me. Please. I need you."

"I'll try to leave early, Jamie, but it's an important meeting. I'm back in the lead for the promotion. And I might know for sure before the Christmas break." Sheryl spun Jamie around and kissed her on the mouth. "Maybe we should plan that vacation for our anniversary. New York?"

Jamie frowned as Sheryl lifted containers out of the bag and pulled plates from the cabinet as if it were just another night. Who was this woman who was happy when she got what she wanted and distant when she didn't? Who didn't understand what had happened to her this afternoon? Who wouldn't stay home with her? She stepped back and let her arms fall to her sides as her world tilted for the second time today.

"Oh, and thanks for the flowers. Everyone teased me about having a secret boyfriend."

Loneliness hit hard and fast, and Jamie sucked in a breath. She wrapped her arms around herself. "Can you drop me at my office on your way? I left my car there." She couldn't stay here in an empty house. Not tonight. Maybe tomorrow things would look different.

"Sure. I need to leave in half an hour." Sheryl put a plate in the microwave.

Jamie tucked the white tank top into her jeans and pulled a black V-neck sweater over her head. Squeezing the pendant around her neck she whispered, “I hope you didn’t know, Mom.” Tears filled her eyes. Sheryl was hollering for her to hurry as she finger combed her hair.

Maybe she’d go up to the Castro. That’s where she and Penni had always headed to blow off steam. She felt reckless. She felt released from obligations she’d never wanted. She didn’t owe her father a goddamned fucking thing and felt like a fool for having been the loyal, responsible daughter all these years, while the other daughter got a free ride on her dime.

She rifled through her clothes until she found her old brown leather bomber jacket in the back of the closet. Yanking it off the hanger she stalked out. *Yeah, I can have some fun tonight.*

CHAPTER THIRTY

Sheryl kissed Jamie on the cheek. "I'm glad your problems are over."

Jamie nodded but didn't move. Wasn't there more to say? The country song ended and silence filled the Lexus.

"Sheryl—"

"Do you want me to wait while you get your keys?" Sheryl's finger tapped the steering wheel and she looked at Jamie. Was there love in her eyes?

Jamie got out. They'd get past this somehow but not tonight. Maybe she was right—the important thing was that it was over.

The last of the sunset was fading to the dull gray of twilight as Sheryl drove away. Loneliness welled up as Jamie faced the clinic. She zipped her jacket and tugged the collar up. She couldn't get warm. Inhaling the smell of the leather she detected traces of smoke from the many bars she'd been in back when it was her official "cruising babes" jacket. She gripped the doorknob for a long time, wishing her car keys weren't sitting in her desk drawer. How could she walk back in knowing what she knew? Finally, she took a deep breath and shoved the door open.

She walked slowly through the clinic, seeing it with new eyes. She'd had little say in any of the decisions about it. He and Mary had chosen the location, designed the layout, and Mary had decorated it. Now it made sense. He'd even had the nerve to let Marjorie work for him. His own separate little family.

Jamie's stomach clenched and her head spun as things she'd rarely admitted oozed into her awareness, let loose as if his betrayal had split her open. She'd never wanted this clinic. It was his dream. She'd agreed because she loved him and thought he needed her help. She spit out a bitter laugh. After his death she kept it going because she felt responsible for keeping his dream alive. A hot rush of rage filled her as the truth came tumbling out. He wasn't worthy of any of her sacrifices.

She stood in the reception area, hands in her jacket pockets, clenching and unclenching them. Her eyes wandered from the new furniture to the new watercolors to the fresh bouquet on the front counter. Carla. She'd decorated her clinic the way Mary—Jamie banished the memory of yesterday's kiss. She'd fire her tomorrow.

Walking into her office and turning on the light, she lost the struggle not to cry as anger and outrage gave way to overwhelming sadness. *Oh, Mom, what am I going to do?* Tears flowed faster and she ached for her mom's reassuring arms around her. Carla had eradicated every trace of him from this office. Gratitude mixed with regret, but she didn't have a choice. Carla had to go. Her phone rang, piercing the silence—Penni's ring. Support she could count on. She sat on the edge of the desk and answered.

"Why didn't you return my calls? How'd it go?"

"Not so good."

"I'm sorry, Jamie. Damn that woman. How could she get away with it?"

"She's not."

"Then why isn't it good news?"

Jamie glared at the couch. Had he and Mary done it on the old couch? Had she sat on the very spot where he'd fucked her? She was being crude and didn't care. What he'd done was crude, and if he were here she'd stand up to him and not back down this time. "My father was fucking Mary. Marjorie is his daughter." Jamie had never heard such a long silence from Penni.

"What? Did you say—"

Jamie said it again. The words lashed the inside of her mouth.

"How do you know? Travis, I'll be there in a minute."

"His name's on her birth certificate."

"Oh, my God, Jamie. Are you all right?"

Jamie closed her eyes and clutched the phone as if she could drink in the understanding in Penni's voice. "I don't know. I'm kind of ragged."

"Where are you?"

"My office."

"Is Sheryl with you?"

Jamie hesitated, pressing her palm against the desk. "She dropped me off."

"Dropped you off?" Jamie held the phone away from her ear as Penni spewed out a stream of incredulity. She didn't interrupt—she refused to defend Sheryl this time. "Why the hell isn't she taking care of you? No, don't tell me. Where's Carla?"

"Home, I imagine."

"Call her."

Carla was the last person she wanted to see. "I'm going up to the city like the old days."

"Jamie…that's not such a good idea. Stay where you are. I'll be right there. It's Jamie, honey. I need to go—"

"No." Jamie laughed as she fiddled with the zipper on her jacket, pulling it up and down. She should want to be with Penni, but there was something appealing about brooding in solitude. "Um, you're probably right." She laughed again. "I'll just go home. Sheryl said she'd be right back."

"I'll come over."

"No."

"You shouldn't be alone."

She choked back a sob. "I'll be okay." She picked at a small rip in her jeans. "Am I overreacting, Penni? I mean…" She shrugged. "Maybe it's not a big deal, right?"

"Who told you that? No, never mind. Listen to me, Jamie. There is no overreacting to something like this. It rewrites your whole life. If it were me I'd be spitting mad and in shock and crying my eyes out all over Lori's shoulder."

Why didn't she have a shoulder to cry on? Jamie tugged the zipper all the way up her throat. It felt good to be encased in the tight jacket.

"I'll be there in twenty—"

"No. I'll be okay." Jamie heard muffled voices, Penni's and Lori's, but couldn't make out what they were saying.

"I'll call you later and check on you. We love you. Call Carla. She phoned twice to ask if I'd heard from you."

Jamie ended the call. Fatigue glued her to the desk and she clutched the edge as her bravado faded. What was she thinking? She wasn't twenty-something anymore, and dashing off to San Francisco for a night of drinking didn't seem like that much fun all of a sudden. Besides, a hangover tomorrow with a full day of patients would be miserable. Like it or not, she had responsibilities. She'd go home and curl up with a movie to distract her until Sheryl got home.

She was halfway to the door when she stopped. There was one thing left that hadn't been eradicated from his office. "My office, goddamn it." She yanked open the door to the credenza behind her desk. Anger surged again as she grabbed the bottle of Glenlivet. How dare he leave her to clean up his mess? How dare he put her in the position of losing everything she'd worked for?

The bag of cookies and card she'd shoved in there this morning fell to the floor. She set the cookies on the desk and held the yellow envelope with her name in purple on her open palm, staring at it. Closing her hand around the card she crushed it until her hand cramped, and then she let it fall to the floor.

She started for the door, strangling the neck of the bottle. She'd pour his fucking Scotch down the drain. She'd wipe every trace of him from her life. From the clinic. Her clinic, goddamn it.

She stopped, letting a smirk curl her lip. Why not toast to dear old Dad first? Grabbing his picture she set it in front of her on the desk. She poured a healthy dose of the Scotch and held it up in a mock salute, staring at the ugly brown liquid as she swirled it in the heavy tumbler. His Scotch. His tumbler. She'd cherished the connection with him. Choking back a sob, she downed it in one angry swallow that burned down her throat. Then she slammed her fist into the photo, driving it into the desk as glass shattered. "You fucking coward!"

❖

Carla was steps from Jamie's office when she heard Jamie scream a curse and then the sound of breaking glass. She'd almost driven on by the clinic as she had several times since leaving the office with no word from Jamie. She'd left half a dozen messages, the last two begging Jamie to let her know she was all right. Seeing the light from Jamie's office, she'd done an illegal U-turn and run over the curb as she jerked her car into the parking lot.

"Jamie!" Ripping her sweater off her shoulders, Carla wrapped it around Jamie's right hand. The glazed look in Jamie's eyes scared her as much as the blood. She gripped Jamie's arm and dragged her to the break room, where she elbowed the faucet on and held Jamie's hand under the stream of water, looking for the source of the blood that was leaving a pink trail in the sink. She found several cuts on the outside. Wrapping a towel around her hand, she squeezed tight as she held it up by Jamie's head. "Sit," she ordered, backing Jamie toward a chair she kicked away from the table.

Jamie wrenched away and bolted from the room, Carla a step behind as she lurched into the bathroom and vomited. Carla laid her hand on Jamie's neck as she retched again. Her skin was cold and clammy. She cupped Jamie's elbow and helped her up. "Rinse." Carla handed Jamie a paper cup of water.

"Sit," Carla said, as she closed the toilet lid. She wrapped a fresh towel around Jamie's hand, and held it up.

"I'm sorry." Jamie's voice was raspy.

"Hush. Let's get you back to your office. I need to look at your hand more carefully and see if we need to take you to the ER. Stand up." Carla wrapped her arm around Jamie's waist as she helped her to her office. The leather jacket was soft and smelled of Jamie, and the tight jeans would have been sexy under different circumstances.

Carla settled Jamie on the couch, then pulled the blanket off the back and draped it over her shoulders. She was pale and trembling and wouldn't meet Carla's eyes. What had happened? She unwound the towel and inspected Jamie's hand, cradling it in hers, pressing gently around the cuts. They looked superficial, but the amount of blood scared her and this hand was special. "We're going to the ER."

Jamie rubbed her forehead, her breathing ragged. "Please…just a few minutes," she said, in a shaky voice, as she unzipped her jacket.

"Jamie—"

"Please."

When Jamie's eyes met hers she almost gasped. They were so pained, so…lost. What had hurt her so badly she'd hurt herself? "Tell me what happened."

"I got my why," Jamie said, in a whisper, her arm wrapped across her stomach. She looked like she might be sick again.

"It was personal, wasn't it? Marjorie had a grudge against you personally."

Jamie's eyes met hers, bruised, dark with a terrible hurt Carla wanted to take away.

"How did you know?"

"Never mind that now. Tell me the rest."

Jamie took a shuddering breath and the story poured out of her as tears rolled down her cheeks.

Carla listened, cradling Jamie's hand against her stomach because it was the only comfort she dared offer. Everything in Jamie's eyes said to take her in her arms and hold her. Every part of her wanted to do just that. But they were already in ambiguous territory from yesterday's kiss. She hoped the card had returned them to the safe confines of friendship.

"How awful for you to find out that way. You must feel so overwhelmed. Tell me how I can make it better."

Jamie looked up and her expression went from lost to startled before she straightened. "I'm all right."

"What's wrong with you?" Carla's voice exposed all her frustration and she tightened her grip on Jamie's hand. "You've just had your life ripped apart and you're sitting here bleeding, and you tell me you're all right? I want to help you through this."

"I don't need your help. I don't want—" Jamie got partway up and then leaned over, steadying herself on the coffee table.

Carla reached for her hand—the towel was coming loose. Jamie pulled away and she understood. "This is about yesterday, isn't it? And about your father."

Jamie's head snapped up, eyes filled with anger and hurt and confusion. "I can't—"

"It's all right, Jamie." Defeat landed hard on Carla's shoulders and tears filled her eyes. The card hadn't mattered. She heaved herself off the couch, wobbling as exhaustion hit her from too little sleep and too much worry. She was going to lose Jamie and there was nothing she could do. All the innocent people that man had hurt. She forced herself to keep breathing as her heart broke. "Come on. We're going to the ER. Call your partner and have her meet us at Good Sam. I'll leave as soon as she gets there."

Jamie shook her head slowly but didn't move.

"Never mind. What's her number? I'll call her."

"No."

"Oh, for heaven's sake. I know why you don't want me to take care of you but—"

"She's not home." Jamie's voice was barely audible.

"What do you mean she's not home? You mean she doesn't know either? What's wrong with you that you won't let anyone take care of you? Isn't that what you do for people all day long? How bad does it have to get before you—"

"She knows," Jamie blurted out.

"She…knows? Then why isn't she here holding…?" They both looked at Jamie's hand.

"I don't know," Jamie yelled. "I can take care of myself." She yanked her hand away from Carla and the towel unraveled.

"Obviously you can't." Carla grabbed Jamie's hand, wrapped it, and held it up between them.

"What are you doing here?" Jamie's voice was sharp with accusation.

"I came looking for you. I was worried sick when you didn't come back or return my calls."

"You came looking for me?" Jamie stared at her, her head tilted, a puzzled look on her face.

"That's what friends do for each other." Their eyes met. Was she imagining the instant of longing in them before Jamie looked away?

"You didn't need to do that."

"When I hurt my back, didn't you scold me for not calling you for help?" Carla didn't know whether to scream or cry. Why was she trying to comfort someone who didn't want her to?

"That's not the—"

"Why do you make it so hard? Everyone from Penni to your staff tries to help you, and you ignore all of us."

"I can take care of myself."

"Really?" Carla was so angry she could barely control herself. "You're working yourself to death. You barely let your accountant or attorney help with the embezzlement. I had to help you behind your back, for God's sake. And it wasn't even your fault."

Jamie looked like she'd been slapped. "But it's still my responsibility…" Jamie's brows pulled together, as if she was trying to figure something out.

"Responsibility isn't all there is to life, Jamie. Happiness matters, too. Your happiness, not your father's. Your dreams, not his."

Jamie's mouth opened but nothing came out. She'd never looked so broken. Without thinking, Carla gathered her into her arms.

"No," Jamie whispered, her body stiffening. "I can't."

"You can't what? Let me hold you because you're hurt and upset and I care about you?" She rubbed Jamie's back, trying to relax her.

"I need you," Jamie whispered.

"I need you, too." Carla met Jamie's eyes. They held fear and desire in a hopeless standoff.

With a strangled cry Jamie wrenched away from Carla and stood, steadying herself against the coffee table before stumbling to her desk and collapsing into her chair.

"What, Jamie? You think I'm going to kiss you again? I won't put you in an awkward position. I promised you that in the card." Tears filled Carla's eyes as she sat down in the chair across from Jamie. The woman she loved and she couldn't help her. "Hold your hand up."

Jamie bent over and picked something up from the floor. When she straightened, she was holding the crumpled yellow envelope.

"You didn't even read it. I tried so hard to get the wording just right." Shaking her head Carla pushed herself out of the chair as she brushed tears from her cheeks. "Come on. Let's get that hand looked at." She was nearly to the door when her phone rang. Pulling it from her pocket she stepped into the hallway as she answered it. "I'm sorry, Mike…Yes, I'm all right…I'm at Jamie's office…"

❖

Jamie was vaguely aware Carla was talking to Mike as she anchored the envelope with her right elbow and slid her left index finger under the flap. She pulled out the card and read it. Her stomach fluttered. Carla was taking the blame for the kiss, apologizing, promising it would never happen again, pleading for their friendship to continue. The memory of the kiss circled her and she let it. Her heart lifted. It might have been wrong, but everything about it had felt right.

The pieces of her life fell into place in a new arrangement. Carla came looking for her. It was Carla who'd helped her figure out what Marjorie had done, Carla who'd gotten the insurance companies to help, Carla who'd redecorated her office, Carla who'd encouraged her to play softball. Carla who'd known it was personal, and comforted her. She took a deep breath as if finding something beautiful that she'd lost. Her heart tripped over itself as feelings tucked away for twenty years demanded their freedom. She trembled as the truth broke through. She was in love with Carla.

"All right. I'll call you later. And Mike? Thanks."

"Is it true?" Jamie asked, as Carla walked back into the office. She looked exhausted and sad. Jamie's heart stuttered. She'd hurt her, and that was the last thing she wanted to do.

"Every word. I won't put you in an awkward position again and—"

"No. The part about you love me."

"How can you not know that?"

"Carla—"

"It's all right, Jamie. Like the card says, your friendship means everything to me. I can't lose you again. I'll leave the clinic if—"

"No. I don't want you to." Jamie's voice crackled with panic. She met Carla's gaze and fell into those eyes. Kindness. "I want you to stay." Jamie shook her head. That wasn't what she'd meant to say. There was more. Carla nodded, but the sadness still clouded her eyes. Jamie's heart broke and love seeped through the cracks, too strong to be denied. Why couldn't she say what she'd waited twenty years to say?

"I'm glad. Now let's get you to the ER."

Jamie crossed to Carla in rapid strides. Her hand was throbbing but so was her heart. She was breathing hard, desire consuming her with each step. Something in Carla's…everything…her voice with its soft cadence that invited disclosure…her soft curves that offered enclosure…her warm gaze that spoke of understanding…undid Jamie. She meant to hug her but at the last second…

She captured Carla's mouth in a searing kiss. Her feelings took free rein and she moaned as desire obliterated everything else. She tangled her uninjured hand in the soft hair and held Carla to her as she drove her tongue deeper into the warmth—stroking, probing, seeking, withdrawing to nip at Carla's lower lip, before pressing back into the warmth. She slid her hand down to Carla's breast. She wanted more. Carla's fingers wrapped around her arm, stopping her. Reality broke through.

"I'm sorry." Jamie backed up until she hit the desk, her breathing uneven as desire battled with responsibility. She knew what she felt, but acting on it was wrong. She cradled her injured hand against her stomach and tried to find the right answer.

"There's nothing to apologize for. Intense emotions sometimes get crossed. You've been through a lot today."

"I'm no better than him." Her mind spit out the words but her heart ached for Carla.

"You're nothing like him," Carla said, forcefully.

Jamie couldn't take her eyes from Carla, from the understanding that was always there.

"Please," Carla said, her voice softening as she moved toward Jamie. "Keep your father's behavior where it belongs. You'll never know the why, Jamie. Don't compare yourself to him. Don't turn judgment back on yourself because he's not here to hold accountable."

"What he did was wrong, Carla."

"I'm not excusing it, but I understand about feelings overruling responsibility."

"That night." That night that meant so much to her had come at a price for Carla.

Carla nodded.

"But you did the responsible thing by going home to Mike."

"I did the responsible thing by my parents' standards, society's standards. I wasn't brave enough to do what I knew in my heart was right for me. I spent twenty years being responsible to the wrong dream. Not a bad dream. Just not the dream I wanted." Carla's smile was heartbreaking. "It took me too long to realize that sometimes you have to step outside of being responsible to find what makes you happy."

"You and Mike."

Carla nodded again. "I don't know anyone who tries harder to do the right thing or to put other people first. But you're so hard on yourself. It breaks my heart to see you so bound to responsibility for everything but your own happiness. I don't like your father much. He gave the illusion of putting other people first, but he didn't. He was about taking and you're about giving. Let him go, Jamie. Don't let him drag you under. Live your own life."

Jamie absorbed what Carla was saying. Live your own life. Follow your dreams. Isn't that what her mom had told her so many times? And Penni—two women she loved and trusted? She'd never heard that advice from her father or from Sheryl. She took a deep breath as her life shifted into something that finally made sense. "Can we sit here for a few minutes? I think you're right about my hand, but I need to…be with you…for a bit. Please don't be mad at me." She was afraid to look at Carla. Afraid of what she'd see in those beautiful amber eyes.

"Like I said in the card, things are complicated between us—the surprise of meeting again, leftover feelings." Carla's voice was like a soothing caress. "Aren't we just trying to make that transition from lovers to friends? We'll get through it."

Jamie knew in her heart she wanted more than friendship, but she needed to do it right. She didn't want to be like her father, but she also couldn't be responsible to the wrong dreams any more. For tonight a friend was exactly what she needed. Jamie smiled as she stepped toward Carla. Cradling her hand, she rested her cheek against Carla's shoulder. As long as she had this shoulder to lean on she could make it through anything. "How do you always know the right thing to say?"

"Maybe because I know you." Carla wrapped her arms around Jamie. "Do you know what I thought about you that night in Atlanta?"

"That I was hot and sexy?" Carla laughed, and the sound fed the lonely places in Jamie.

"Besides that. I thought you were one of the kindest people I'd ever met." She smiled when Jamie looked at her. "Yep. Your mom would be proud of how you've lived your life."

Tears stung Jamie's eyes, and exhaustion was catching up to her. She kissed Carla on the cheek and stepped back. Now that she knew what she wanted she'd make it happen. "Will you go with me to the ER?"

"I'll go anywhere with you. After all, how much riskier can it get than a Melissa Etheridge concert and a lesbian bar?"

"You probably thought I knew how to show a girl a good time back then."

Carla wrapped Jamie's hand in hers. "I don't think a trip to the ER on a Monday night can top that night."

"I'm glad you came looking for me." Carla's arm came around her waist and she relaxed into the support that would get her through this.

❖

"I'm following you home," Carla said as they pulled into the clinic parking lot.

"Carla, I'm—"

"Exhausted. I'm following you."

The drive home was tense. What if Sheryl was there? What if she came out to greet Jamie? At least her hand was all right—some stitches but no damage to muscles or nerves. She collapsed against the steering wheel with relief when she saw the dark house. Another disaster was more than she could bear. She walked to Carla's car and squatted down by the opened window. "Good night."

"Is your partner home?"

"Yes." Jamie lied because it was easier than the truth.

"Well, tell her to take good care of you. I'll see you in the morning."

Jamie watched until her taillights disappeared around the corner. She missed her already. Tomorrow morning was a long time to wait to see the woman she loved.

Jamie made it into sweats before collapsing into bed. She tried to stay awake. She needed to talk to Sheryl. How was she going to explain that she was in love with someone else, that she wanted out of their relationship? Her eyes closed and she was asleep in seconds.

Jamie sat bolt upright and looked at the clock. 3:23. She knew. Maybe if she hadn't been wondering about her father's absences, working late all the time, meetings and seminars on too many weekends, maybe if she hadn't been chastising herself for missing the clues to his cheating, she would have continued to ignore the signs. Marching to the guest room she didn't know whether to laugh or cry.

Sheryl squeezed her eyes shut against the bright light. "What are you doing?"

"How long, Sheryl?"

"How long what? It's the middle of the night, Jamie." Sheryl sat up. "What happened to your hand?"

"The cheating. How long have I missed the clues?"

"What—"

"I guess I know why you think cheating isn't a big deal. Who is it? One of those women you go to brunch with? Someone who can help you get promoted?"

Sheryl blanched and then her face turned angry.

"Never mind." Jamie laughed. It didn't matter. This was the night to claim her freedom, from a father she no longer respected, from a partner she no longer loved. She walked out.

"It's a him and it doesn't mean anything."

Jamie turned around and stared at Sheryl. "You…with a guy? You cheated on me with a guy?"

"It didn't mean anything. I was upset, and you were all wrapped up in that business problem." Sheryl's voice was a furious screech. "He comforted me…it just happened, Jamie."

Jamie stared at the woman she thought she'd spend the rest of her life with. Her perfect hair was in a swirl at the top of her head. Lines around her eyes weren't covered by makeup. She hated that damn perfume.

“What are you doing?” Sheryl’s voice became frantic as she followed Jamie to the bedroom.

“Leaving.” Jamie dressed in the clothes she’d had on and tossed stuff into an overnight bag. “You should be thrilled. Now you can have all the space you want.”

“Jamie…don’t be childish. Relationships go through hard times.”

“I’m not in love with you any more.”

“No one’s in love after ten years.”

“Oh, yes they are, Sheryl.” Jamie opened a drawer and lifted out her mother’s jewelry box. Carla’s note had been in the bottom of it for twenty years. She wasn’t leaving without it. Tucking it in the inside pocket of her jacket, she grabbed her bags and marched out, a smile spreading up her cheeks. The worst day of her life had just become the best day of her life.

She meant to go to a hotel but found herself on Carla’s street. Parking in front she stared at the house. Melissa was singing a ballad, and she let the song take her back, swaying as she remembered dancing with Carla in her arms. If she knocked on the door, Carla would welcome her into her home, into her bed, into her life. There was nowhere she’d rather be. She started her car and circled the block for one more look before driving to the hotel. She’d waited twenty years. She could wait a little longer.

CHAPTER THIRTY-ONE

Phew. I forgot what a pain moving is." Penni plopped herself on the couch and took a long swig from the Corona. "But it got me out of an afternoon of housecleaning and entitles us to gorge on the classic post-move dinner of pizza and beer." They both swooped for the cardboard box on the coffee table, bumping elbows to grab the first piece.

Jamie settled into the overstuffed chair. She was exhausted but she was free, and that's all that mattered. It wasn't too late to find her dreams again. It wasn't too late for happiness. She closed her eyes, smiling as she chewed the ultimate comfort food. The week was ending a whole lot better than it had begun.

"I wish you'd just moved in with us."

"I'm a little old to be crashing on someone's couch." Jamie stuffed a big bite into her mouth, moaning as she chewed.

"You need more sex if pizza makes you moan like that."

"Ignoring you," Jamie mumbled around the mouthful of cheese and pepperoni.

"Hmm," Penni said, bouncing on the sagging couch. "I know you took this house on short notice but it could use some sprucing up—has that definite eighties look. And what's with all the boat pictures?"

"A retired merchant marine and lifelong bachelor—brother of one of my patients. They had to move him into a care facility and didn't want to sell right away, so I'm renting it."

"Ahh. So what's the wicked witch gonna do?"

"Don't know. I'm hoping she'll move out and sign off on the house if I make it worth her while."

"You shouldn't have to make anything worth her while." Penni's voice rose with anger. "I am so pissed that, on top of everything else, she was cheating on you. God, I want to—"

"Stop," Jamie said, picking up another piece of pizza. "She's not worth your time. She hasn't been worth my time either in too long, but I couldn't see it. I don't know why it took me so long to realize how self-absorbed she'd become and how unhappy I was." Jamie shook her head. How had she been so blind? "I thought if I just tried harder it would work."

"That's kind of what you did with your father, too—kept trying hard to earn his love. He was as self-absorbed as Sheryl. You know, I always thought it was odd that he never came to any of your games."

Jamie pressed the cold Corona against her hand. The stitches itched. "Guess I got some mixed-up ideas about love, huh?" Jamie picked at the label. "It's weird. I'll never forgive him, but what he did…I feel like I've been set free."

"It's about time." Penni patted Jamie's knee. "What's going to happen to Marjorie?"

"I don't know and I've decided I don't care. That's up to the DA. As soon as Pete gets that house transferred into my name, I'm going to throw her out on her ass. And I'm thinking about making some changes with my business. I don't want to be owned by it any more."

Penni sat on the arm of the chair and hugged Jamie, planting a sloppy kiss on her cheek. "I'm proud of you. You're starting to remind me of a feisty pitcher I once knew."

"I'm starting to feel like that person again. Ready to conquer the world, bag the babes…well, one at least."

"Is she thrilled you moved out?"

"I didn't tell her." Jamie held up her hand to stop Penni's protest. "I need a minute to catch my breath. It's been a hell of a week."

"Oh, for heaven's sake. You've been in love with her for twenty years. This is your chance for happiness. Grab it."

"I wish it were that simple. I still need to figure out how to tell her about Sheryl."

"Damn, I forgot about that. Don't suppose you could tell her you ended your relationship without naming names."

"I can't be dishonest with her. I feel guilty enough I haven't already told her. I'm scared. I hope she understands."

"She loves you. She'll understand. Time for pints and spoons," Penni said, jumping to her feet. "Race you to the freezer."

❖

Jamie tried both sides of the bed, looking for a spot that wasn't lumpy or caved in. Plucking her phone from atop the paperback on the nightstand she dialed and waited for the voice she needed to hear.

"I miss you." Carla had left for San Diego last night. "I hope it's okay to call."

"It's better than okay. I miss you, too."

"How was your day?" Jamie closed her eyes and drank in the voice that felt like home.

"A lot of fun. We went to a dog show this afternoon. I might want a friend to live with."

"Lucky dog." Jamie envied the pup that got to curl up on Carla's bed. Maybe she should tell her about Sheryl now, and then she'd have time to think about it before they saw each other.

"And the girls took me to dinner and a movie for my birthday."

"Wish I'd been there. I could get used to romantic comedies."

"You mean I've converted you?"

"Might take a few more but I'm coming around." *Tell her*. "Um… How's Lissa?" Jamie clenched her jaw. No, that would be chickening out. She needed to do it in person.

"Great. She teased me about going back to that bar."

"You didn't go, right?"

"It was tempting. And they're talking about going on an Olivia cruise this summer with the girls they've become friends with. They want me to come with them."

"That's my dream vacation."

"I can't think of anything more fun than being out and proud on a boatful of lesbians."

Jamie wanted to be on that boat with her. "Will you have dinner with me tomorrow night? I want to talk to you about something, and I have a late birthday present for you." Jamie planned to wear the dressy burgundy shirt she loved with a big white bow on her chest. Her heart skipped a beat. If Carla didn't forgive her for not telling her about Sheryl, how would she survive?

"My plane doesn't get in until ten. Monday night?"

"It's a date. I'm going to miss blueberry pancakes tomorrow."

"Me, too."

"Well, I'll let you get back to the girls."

"I'm headed to bed. Steph loaned me a new book from her stash. She's thoroughly enjoying my conversion. She's got me addicted to lesbian fiction."

Jamie fingered a well-worn paperback that was one of her favorites—the lesbian fiction equivalent of comfort food. "Not a bad addiction. Good night, Carla."

Jamie held the phone to her chest, her heart pounding with love. They'd settled into an easy friendship after Monday but she wanted so much more. Carla was already in her heart; now if she could just get her in her life. She crossed her fingers, praying she'd understand about Sheryl.

CHAPTER THIRTY-TWO

Carla lifted the pan of enchiladas from the microwave and set it on the table as Sara bounded into the break room and sat down next to Don. Her freezer was overflowing from all the cooking she'd done last week, her escape from emotions that were still trying to settle. It wasn't the new life she'd expected, but she was trying to make peace with it.

"Love the table and chairs," Sara said, "and all the dishes." She held up one of the new glasses, and Don poured iced tea into it.

Carla set a bowl of black beans in the microwave as the staff passed around the enchiladas and salad, conversation light and punctuated by frequent laughter. It was as if the office had let out a collective sigh of relief. Jamie had taken them all out to dinner last week to celebrate the end of the Marjorie incident, as everyone was calling it. Even Betty joined them. Leaving out the personal details, Jamie simply said it was over and the clinic would be fine.

Jamie seemed fine, too, much to her relief. At moments her brow furrowed, but then the moment would pass and she'd pull herself back with a smile. She seemed not only less stressed but softer, like she'd settled something within herself. Their friendship was on solid ground, a bittersweet blessing. The memory of those two precious kisses had pushed Carla far beyond convincing herself she'd ever be in love with anyone but Jamie. She'd called Vanessa and ended things.

She folded her arms as a burst of nervousness swept through her about dinner tonight with Jamie. It was a nice gesture, but she had to keep reminding herself it wasn't a date. Carla attributed the new openness from Jamie to their clearing the air, getting the old feelings out in the open so they could move on to really being friends. But at times she caught Jamie looking at her with an intensity that set her heart fluttering and confused her.

"Shall I go get Jamie?" Sara asked.

"No." Carla set the bowl on the table. "I'll get her."

"Your ten minutes are up." Jamie's eyes were closed and she looked sinfully relaxed on the couch, her feet propped on the coffee table.

"I was letting it thaw out." Jamie held up her hand. "Wanna warm it up for me?"

Carla's heart skipped a beat. Jamie had been teasing her all week in a way that seemed flirtatious, but she must be mistaken. "How's it feel?"

"Good." Jamie wiggled her fingers. She tossed the ice pack on the coffee table and got up.

The back door opened and a woman hollered for Jamie. Carla was almost to the door when someone plowed into her. "Ow," she said, holding her right temple and clutching the doorframe, trying to regain her balance.

Jamie grabbed Carla's waist and steadied her. "Are you all right?"

"I think so." Carla rubbed her temple. It hurt. The staff crowded into the hallway, a medley of worried faces.

"Jamie, what the hell's going on? You ignore my calls and—"

Carla stared. Sheryl? No, it couldn't be. She knew Jamie?

"What!" Sheryl stared at her and her expression raced from shock to anger. She whirled on Jamie, who looked just as shocked. "Do you know who this is?"

"Sheryl—" Jamie stepped in front of Carla.

"This is that woman with the lesbian daughter. What's she doing here?"

Carla stared from Sheryl to Jamie, her mouth open. "I work here." She stepped away from Jamie as she reached a shattering conclusion.

"Work here?" Sheryl's voice rose as she stepped around Jamie and got in Carla's face. "You're a liar. Jamie would never hire you after what you did to me."

"Sheryl, stop it!"

"You're just a loudmouth bitch who can't control her daughter."

"Sheryl!" Jamie held Sheryl's shoulders and backed her toward the desk.

Carla bolted out the back door of the clinic, afraid her legs would give out as the pieces fell into place with heartbreaking clarity. That high-handed, homophobic woman was Jamie's partner. How was that possible and why hadn't Jamie told her? Anger followed close on the heels of the shock.

It wasn't until she reached her car that she realized she didn't have her car keys. *I'll walk home before I'll go back in there.* She was halfway across the parking lot when a hand grasped her arm. Yanking free, she whirled around.

"Are you all right?" Sara asked, concern and understanding on her face.

"Yes. No. I need my car keys." Carla folded her arms. Her head hurt and she couldn't stop trembling.

"Carla—"

"Please, Sara?"

"I'll be right back."

Carla paced, trying to ignore the raised voices coming through the open window. She felt ambushed, unsure of everything she thought she knew about Jamie. Sheryl's identity explained some things but left too many unanswered questions. As soon as Sara rushed back with her keys, she was in her car and out of the parking lot, tears blurring her vision. Why had Jamie deceived her?

"You hired that bitch?" Sheryl's voice was venomous.

"Yes. No. She's not a bitch. Arrgh." Jamie ran her hands through her hair and tugged. "It's none of your business."

"How dare you hire the woman who cost me my promotion!" Sheryl glared at her with hard eyes.

Had she ever seen real warmth, real love in them? Jamie started for the door. She had to get to Carla.

"Don't walk away from me." Sheryl grabbed her arm, the red nails a stark contrast to Jamie's white shirt. "You cancelled my credit cards. Do you know how embarrassed I was yesterday at Macy's?"

Jamie stared at her. Credit cards? This was about credit cards? "They're my credit cards, and you're on your own." Sheryl's face drained of anger and filled with surprise. "You better look for a place to live. Maybe your…friend…will let you move in with him." Jamie wanted to laugh as surprise transformed to anger again. Did Sheryl's emotional spectrum even include love?

"Please, Jamie," Sheryl pleaded. "It's just a misunderstanding. We can work it out. You don't want to walk out on ten years, do you?"

"Yeah, I do."

"I admit I made a mistake, but please don't punish me." Sheryl's eyes filled with tears.

"I have to go." When Jamie got to the parking lot, Carla was pulling out. She bent over, hands on her thighs, and dropped her head. *Damn it, I should have told her.*

"Can I help?" Sara asked, coming up next to her.

"Is she all right?"

"Physically, yes. But she's pretty upset, Jamie. Go after her. Don and I will cover your patients."

Jamie sprinted to her office and took her car keys from the drawer, ignoring Sheryl's tears and pleas. She'd cared for the wrong woman for too long. Please, forgive me, she repeated, as she drove to Carla's.

Chapter Thirty-three

Jamie walked up the flagstone path, her heart pounding like a teenager on her first date. Would Carla understand? She rang the doorbell and waited, rolling up the sleeves on her shirt, arranging her hair with her fingers. Her breath caught when Carla appeared in the doorway. She was responsible for the bruised expression and the red, puffy eyes. "Can I come in?"

"Why aren't you at work?"

"You're more important to me than anything." Jamie searched Carla's face for the love she needed to see. Her stomach tightened at the guarded expression. She had to fix this. The rest of her life depended on it.

"Not important enough to tell me the truth?" The hurt made her voice sound flat.

"I'm so sorry, Carla. I need to explain. Can I please come in?" Carla didn't move or say anything, and Jamie was afraid any hope of a future with her would end right here. "I'm not losing you. Not again. Not over this." She walked past Carla. Melissa's voice was coming from the stereo and she hoped it was a good sign. She stood in the entry and reached for Carla's hands, but she crossed her arms.

Jamie stepped close enough that her breasts touched Carla's arms, close enough to smell the perfume she loved. "I messed up. I should have told you, but when you first told me the story I was too embarrassed. And then I just didn't know how. I was afraid you'd think less of me or, worse, you'd leave." Jamie held Carla's arms. "I love you."

"You let her say awful things to me." Carla backed up, pulling a Kleenex from her pocket and wiping her eyes.

"I'm sorry. I shouldn't have let it come to such an awful confrontation. I planned to tell you tonight at dinner. And I was going to tell you I moved out—"

"How could you be with someone like that?" Carla marched through the living room.

"Because I got lost, Carla." Jamie followed her as fear tensed her stomach. What if Carla wouldn't forgive her? "Ever since that night—"

"She's a bully…homophobic…egotistical…" Carla stopped at the open doors to the patio.

Jamie scooted in front of Carla and squeezed her shoulders. "I. Left. Her." Was Carla's gaze softening? "I moved out Monday night."

"You left her? Why?"

Jamie wiped tears off Carla's cheeks with her thumbs. "Because I'm in love with you. I fell in love with you that night—"

"But…you're not…you've changed, Jamie. I don't know what to think."

"Carla, I lost track of who I was. Until you came back into my life and made me remember that night—the carefree fun, the passion that neither of us expected…" Jamie searched for the words that would open the future she wanted by closing the past she didn't. Carla's eyes were softer but her arms were still crossed. Was it too late?

"I forgot about my dreams. I confused love with loyalty and responsibility and forgot about happiness. I was on autopilot, I guess." Jamie shook her head as the path to her unhappiness became clear. "It started with my father. I should never have agreed to the clinic. But I loved and respected him, and I couldn't disappoint him. After a while that became the way I handled everything. I stopped feeling my own unhappiness. So it was easy to do the same with Sheryl—let her dreams become more important than mine, take care of her without expecting her to support me." Carla's eyes showed some of the understanding Jamie desperately needed.

"I kept trying to please people who never cared about my dreams, never supported me or loved me for who I am, only for what I could give them. I can't live that way anymore. I fell in love with you that night—real and powerful and full of hope, and then it was gone before I could grab onto it. I want us to have the happy ending we both wanted. Every day for the rest of my life I want you," she whispered against Carla's lips. She held her breath as she waited for Carla to determine her future.

Carla closed her eyes, a smile tugging at her lips. "Say it again."

"I love you with all my heart."

"Promise you'll never break my heart or lie to me again." Carla opened her eyes, the smile tempered by a tentative look.

Jamie kissed away tears as she rubbed her palm over Carla's chest. "I'll take very good care of this heart." She caressed the inside of Carla's breast. "And what's over it."

Carla crossed her arms again. "Out and proud isn't just a phrase to me, Jamie. I've believed in it since watching you live it that night. Sheryl…giving Lissa and Steph a hard time—"

"I never should have stood by as if it wasn't my concern. Talk about a lack of backbone. I'm so sorry." Jamie would give anything never to have put that hurt in Carla's eyes.

"I won't hide who I am—not in public, not in your office."

"I don't want you to."

"You work too much."

"I'll work less."

"Vacations?"

"Absolutely. As many as you want."

"And…do you even wear tank tops any more?" Carla's voice was husky.

Jamie traced her hand down Carla's abdomen. The muscles tightened under her fingers. "I'll wear one every day."

"I want more nights like that." Carla's eyes sparked with desire and her lips parted.

"I was just getting warmed up." Jamie pulled Carla's blouse from the skirt and slid her hand up soft skin to her breast encased in the satiny bra. She moaned as she cupped it and rolled Carla's nipple between her fingers. "Anything else?"

"No…ahh…" Carla leaned into Jamie's hand. "Maybe one more thing…"

Jamie kissed from her ear to the base of her throat and sucked gently as she caressed Carla's other breast.

"Could you do something about the pressure between my legs?"

Jamie groaned as she backed Carla to the couch and fell on top of her as gently as possible. Her mind was fuzzy with need as she fastened her mouth to Carla's, and their tongues danced against each other. Carla's fingers tugged on her shirt as she worked her hand inside Carla's bra and massaged the soft flesh that filled her palm. Moans escaped, but she wasn't sure if they were hers or Carla's.

"Damn your buttons. Help me," Carla said, her voice as impatient as her fingers. "I never forgot how it felt to touch you," she whispered.

Jamie slid Carla's fingers aside as she worked her buttons open. Carla's hand slid inside, and her palm rubbed back and forth from one breast to the other, making both nipples painfully hard. "God," Jamie rasped, afraid she'd explode. Her clit clenched dangerously, and she shifted away from Carla's thigh. Not yet.

Jamie stroked Carla's knee, then under her skirt along her thigh. Her mouth found Carla's again, and she kissed her hard and deep, making up for all the lost years. She played her fingers over Carla's panties, teasing her until she groaned, then slipped inside, spreading the wetness. Her fingers were at Carla's opening when her mouth was suddenly empty.

"No…wait." Carla placed her palm against Jamie's cheek as she tried to sit up. "Jamie? Honey, look at me."

"What?" Jamie couldn't focus on Carla's words. The pressure in her center was climbing to critical levels again, and all she could think about was how badly she wanted Carla.

"I want to take a bath with you. I want our first time together to be—"

"Special." Jamie groaned as she lifted off Carla and tried to turn her lust down to a simmer. She didn't want their first time to be a heated groping on the couch, either. "Bedroom," she said, as she stood and extended her hand.

Carla giggled. "We look like a couple of oversexed teenagers making out in the backseat of their parents' car."

"How would you know about that? I thought you were a nice Southern girl?"

"Not so nice." Carla plastered Jamie to the wall and proved her point with a kiss so passionate Jamie's legs gave out. Carla's arm around her waist kept her up as they stumbled down the hallway, bumping against the wall as they kissed their way to the bedroom.

Jamie opened her eyes when Carla's lips left hers. "Wow." The space was so intimate it took Jamie's breath away.

"You like it?"

"It's beautiful." Jamie walked arm in arm with Carla to the canopy bed they'd looked at. A bedspread embroidered like a sunset in shades of peach, lavender, and pink lay over ivory sheets. Pillows were piled against the headboard, and Jamie rubbed her palm over one. "Guess we can't toss these on the floor like in that hotel." She wasn't teasing. The room and what was going to happen in it made her tremble.

Carla took Jamie's hand. "Nervous?"

Jamie nodded. Carla's accent was more pronounced, and it slowed her down as if she were back in the heat and heaviness of that long-ago trip to the South. She'd never been back to Atlanta, had never gone to another women's music festival. She felt disoriented as missing pieces of her past searched for their counterparts in this moment.

"Me, too," Carla said, squeezing her hand.

Jamie swallowed hard as she wrapped her arm around Carla's waist. "We're really going to do this, aren't we?" She knew she would remember this night as clearly as she had that night in Atlanta.

"Well, I guess we could wait another—"

"No. If we wait much longer something's going to explode." Jamie's body was consumed with a need she hadn't felt in twenty years.

Carla led Jamie to the bathroom. She lit white candles along the edge of the Jacuzzi tub as it filled and then sat on the edge, holding out her hand. Jamie was rooted in the doorway, hands in her pockets, staring at the tub, a sweet smile softening her face. "Come here, honey." Her heart was bursting with joy, and the tingly feeling was having its way with her. She felt young and vibrant—a woman free to love and be loved in the only way that had ever fulfilled her yearnings for passion.

Carla slipped off Jamie's shirt and bra with trembling fingers. Candlelight flickered across Jamie's face. Carla traced her finger around the edge of her areola and the flesh puckered. With a last look at Jamie's flushed face she took her breast into her mouth and circled her nipple with her tongue. She wrapped her arms around Jamie's waist, holding her up as she feasted on her breast, sucking on it, then tracing her tongue around her nipple, then sucking on it again.

Carla wanted to laugh and cry and sing as she released Jamie's breast. She hadn't had a woman's flesh in her mouth since that night, but the softness was etched in her memory. With Jamie's eyes locked on hers, dark and steamy, she stood and slid her blouse off her shoulders and then her bra. Her breasts felt mercifully free and painfully full. Her nipples ached for contact, and she stepped forward until they met Jamie's. She closed her eyes at the sensuality of the contact. Shivers went through. She had no more experience making love to a woman now than she had twenty years ago, but she'd made love to Jamie a hundred times in her mind. She reached for a clip to pull her hair back.

"Leave it loose." Jamie sifted her fingers through it, her eyes full of the love Carla had ached to see for so long.

Carla turned off the faucet, and they watched each other as the rest of their clothing was discarded in a pile at their feet. She held out her hand and they stepped into the tub together, moving into the positions they'd taken that night. "Tell me what you remember." She wrapped Jamie's arms across her stomach and leaned her head back on her shoulder.

They shared stories of that night and played much as they had—scooping soap bubbles over each other, washing each other. By unspoken consent they let passion swirl around them but not consume them. When the memories settled, Carla stood up and stepped out of the tub, then extended her hand to Jamie.

Water dripped from Jamie's body as she wrapped the towel around herself, and Carla wanted to lick each drop. She ran a brush through her hair, lifting it away from her shoulders. In the mirror she saw Jamie's eyes fastened on her, tears sliding down her cheeks.

"What's wrong?"

Jamie stepped into her arms. She was trembling. "I haven't been this happy since that night. I wish…" Jamie's voice broke.

"It's the same for me, but it's never too late to find our happy-ever-after."

Jamie kissed the angle of her neck, then trailed her tongue up to Carla's jaw and across to her mouth. The kiss was so heartbreakingly tender Carla's eyes filled with tears.

"Thank you for rescuing me," Jamie said, her lips against Carla's.

"Just returning the favor." Carla took Jamie's hand and led her to the bed. She was going to share it with the right woman. Sliding between the sheets they snuggled against each other, Jamie's cheek above her breast and her palm on Carla's stomach. They sighed at the same time.

"So what happens next, Ms. romantic-comedy expert?"

"Well, Ms. I-want-a-little-action-with-my-kissing," Carla said, stroking her fingers through Jamie's hair, "the lovers look longingly at each other and dissolve into a heated kiss as the music swells. Speaking of which."

"I'm not sure if I want to do this next part with anyone else in the room, but that first part sounds worth exploring." Jamie slid on top of Carla and fit their centers together as Carla spread her legs.

"That night I learned what blind need was, what I'd only read about in romance novels. Remind me," Carla said, exaggerating her Southern accent. Jamie's eyes darkened and her chest moved in quick, shallow, breaths as she rocked against Carla.

Carla cupped the back of Jamie's head and pulled her face down until their lips grazed each other. Sliding her tongue along Jamie's lips, teasing her, she let passion escalate the kiss to a prolonged caress of tongues.

"Move with me, my beautiful Southern girl," Jamie whispered, as she rocked her pelvis, matching her rhythm to Carla's.

Carla slid her heels up Jamie's calves, opening herself. Wetness coated her thighs, whether hers or Jamie's she didn't know. Jamie stopped rocking, her face tight and flushed. Carla held Jamie's butt and pushed herself up into the heat of Jamie's center, responding to the depth of need in Jamie's eyes. "Don't hold back. Let me see you come."

Jamie moaned as they ground against each other. Bracing herself on her elbows, Jamie lifted her center. "Inside. I want you inside me when I come. Hurry."

Carla found Jamie's opening and slid into her. Her heart opened in a flurry of desire at the rightness of being inside the woman she'd never stopped wanting. She needed this connection in her soul. Stroking deeply, she watched Jamie's face change with the first flicker of her orgasm. Her jaw tightened and then relaxed as Carla felt the warm flesh tighten around her fingers.

"Oh, God…yes…yes." Jamie arched her back as she came, crying out Carla's name. She rode Carla's fingers, driving them deeper. With one final thrust she collapsed onto Carla, trapping her fingers inside.

"Guess you had a little pent up—" An urgent mouth on hers, a demanding tongue, teeth that gently nibbled her lips, cut her off. Jamie straddled her thigh, leaving a trail of wetness. Carla groaned when familiar fingers stroked her clit. She lifted into the touch, her belly full with demanding need. She wrapped her arms around Jamie's back and found Jamie's mouth as fingers entered her, gentle but demanding.

Jamie traced a path with her tongue across Carla's cheek, then sucked on her ear lobe. "I want to take you in my mouth."

"Yes…please," Carla croaked. Jamie slid down her body, stopping to take a breast into her mouth and tease her nipple to a painful peak. She arched into Jamie's touch as anticipation of what Jamie would do sent desire, hot and demanding, through her body. Heat flared in her center as she waited for Jamie's mouth to give her release. She moaned when Jamie's tongue traced delicately around her clit and again as the teasing tongue refused to give her what she needed. She held the back of Jamie's head and pulled her mouth against her. She felt Jamie smile against her flesh, and then her hand covered Carla's breast and played with her nipple.

Tension built in Carla's belly and her muscles tightened around Jamie's fingers. Her heart was pounding against her ribs. She was so close. Jamie pressed her tongue flat against Carla's clit and stroked it hard and fast as she moved two fingers in and out. When Jamie stroked harder with her tongue, a deep rumbling started in Carla's chest and escaped her mouth as a long cry of pleasure. Carla's voice was thick with her Southern accent as she urged Jamie not to stop, demanded more pressure, a deeper thrust. She shoved herself onto Jamie's fingers and against her tongue. Carla rode out another orgasm, crying out Jamie's name over and over, as her body melted.

Jamie laid her head on Carla's thigh, but kept her fingers deep inside as their breathing quieted. "You had a little pent up, too." Jamie slid up and kissed Carla tenderly, spreading Carla's wetness across her lips.

"I don't know whether to laugh or cry, Jamie. My memories of that night were so accurate I swear part of me feels twenty-two again." Carla opened her eyes and laid her palm against the soft cheek. "But…all those lost years…" Her eyes filled. "I don't know how I lived without you, without this, all those years."

"Hey. I'm not going anywhere."

Carla sat up and pulled Jamie into a fierce hug. "I can't lose you again, not even for a minute." Carla was shaking with joy and need and an irrational fear of losing Jamie, as if the universe would continue to torment them.

"I'll move in with you tomorrow—"

"Don't say that if you don't mean it."

"Would this weekend be soon enough?"

Carla devoured Jamie's mouth with a possessive kiss. "If that's the best you can do." Carla laughed, releasing all the tension of the last couple months. This was her future and it was perfect. They fell onto the bed in a tangle of arms and legs, kissing and laughing, murmuring all the longed-for words of love and commitment.

Carla set two cups of coffee on the nightstand and slid onto the bed, careful not to wake Jamie. She was content to just watch her sleep, letting the sadness of that young woman who'd had to walk away release into the joy of knowing she'd have every morning of her life with Jamie. They'd made love deep into the night, healing their past and sealing their bond, leaving each other breathless and sated time and time again. This was the new life she wanted.

Finally Carla snuggled against Jamie. She stirred when Carla blew on her neck, squirmed when she traced her tongue around her ear. Flipping onto her back she smiled and sniffed the air between them. "You have coffee breath," she said, narrowing her eyes.

"And so will you in a minute." Carla tilted her head toward the nightstand. She couldn't stop staring at Jamie as her fantasy ending to that night played out before her. "Happy?"

"Indescribably," Jamie said. "A little sore, though."

"Guess running isn't the right kind of cross training, is it?"

Jamie kissed the top of Carla's head. "Do we have any orgasms left in us?" She gasped when Carla slid her hand under the sheet and stroked her clit. "Okay, you made your point."

"Can we call in sick today?" Carla snuggled into the crook of Jamie's arm.

Jamie groaned. "Damn. It feels like a weekend."

Carla sighed. "It's going to be a long, long, long day. Maybe we can come home for lunch."

"I like the sound of that. In fact…if my amazing office manager can arrange it, maybe we just won't go back after lunch."

"Consider it done." Carla rolled on top of Jamie. "We're going to have a great life."

Warm hands slid under Jamie's T-shirt and warm breath tickled her neck as Carla snuggled up against her back. "When did you do this?" Carla's bedroom was filled with dozens of flickering candles. A trail of rose petals in a rainbow of colors led from the door to the bed. Carla took her hand and led her to the bed. A single red rose lay on top of a pillow, a card tucked under it.

"When I sent you to the store. Open it."

Jamie looked from Carla to the card. She'd been redefining happiness by the minute all day as being with Carla and absorbing the love between them thawed the cold, empty spaces in her heart.

They'd spent the afternoon in bed, letting their bodies catch up on years of unfulfilled passion. They'd called Penni and Lori and basked in their congratulations. They'd had dinner on the couch watching another of Carla's favorite movies. They'd talked about changes for the clinic and about holiday plans like a long-partnered couple. Jamie felt her dreams coming back to her. She'd found the most important of them, the one that made her happier than she'd ever been. Her mother would heartily approve.

Jamie opened the card and stared at the two tickets nestled inside. She read the name of the performer and the date of the concert—Melissa Etheridge on New Year's Eve. She threw herself into Carla's arms, peppering her cheeks with soft kisses. "When did you get these?"

"Last summer. Mike won't mind if I take you instead." They tumbled onto the bed in each other's arms as the past merged with the present, waiting to become their future.

About the Author

Julie Blair has always believed that fiction is one of life's great pleasures. From the time she was old enough to hold a book, escaping into worlds where anything is possible and endings are usually happy has been a favorite pastime. Growing up a tomboy before it was fashionable, Julie attached herself to sports, especially softball, which culminated in her pitching in the Women's College World Series. Finally forced to grow up and get a real job, she landed in restaurant management for a decade before entering the rigors of chiropractic school. She has been a chiropractor for over two decades.

Julie has sat atop the ruins of Machu Picchu and stood five feet from mountain gorillas in Uganda, but her favorite place is curled up on her couch with her Labradors, Magic and Mandy, reading or writing. Living in the quiet of California's Santa Cruz Mountains, she enjoys gardening, hiking, red wine, strong coffee, smooth jazz, and warm fall afternoons.

Never Too Late is Julie's debut novel. She's hard at work trying to give voices to other characters with stories to tell—their struggles, their triumphs, their love affairs—mostly in self-defense, hoping they'll stop waking her up in the middle of the night with snippets of dialogue or ideas for scenes and settings.

Books Available from Bold Strokes Books

Courtship by Carsen Taite. Love and justice—a lethal mix or a perfect match? (978-1-62639-210-6)

Against Doctor's Orders by Radclyffe. Corporate financier Presley Worth wants to shut down Argyle Community Hospital, but Dr. Harper Rivers will fight her every step of the way, if she can also fight their growing attraction. (978-1-62639-211-3)

A Spark of Heavenly Fire by Kathleen Knowles. Kerry and Beth are building their life together, but unexpected circumstances could destroy their happiness. (978-1-62639-212-0)

Never Too Late by Julie Blair. When Dr. Jamie Hammond is forced to hire a new office manager, she's shocked to come face to face with Carla Grant and memories from her past. (978-1-62639-213-7)

Widow by Martha Miller. Judge Bertha Brannon must solve the murder of her lover, a policewoman she thought she'd grow old with. As more bodies pile up, the murderer starts coming for her. (978-1-62639-214-4)

Twisted Echoes by Sheri Lewis Wohl. What's a woman to do when she realizes the voices in her head are real? (978-1-62639-215-1)

Criminal Gold by Ann Aptaker. Through a dangerous night in New York in 1949, Cantor Gold, dapper dyke-about-town, smuggler of fine art, is forced by a crime lord to be his instrument of vengeance. (978-1-62639-216-8)

The Melody of Light by M.L. Rice. After surviving abuse and loss, will Riley Gordon be able to navigate her first year of college and accept true love and family? (978-1-62639-219-9)

Because of You by Julie Cannon. What would you do for the woman you were forced to leave behind? (978-1-62639-199-4)

The Job by Jove Belle. Sera always dreamed that she would one day reunite with Tor. She just didn't think it would involve terrorists, firearms, and hostages. (978-1-62639-200-7)

Making Time by C.J. Harte. Two women going in different directions meet after fifteen years and struggle to reconnect in spite of the past that separated them. (978-1-62639-201-4)

Once The Clouds Have Gone by KE Payne. Overwhelmed by the dark clouds of her past, Tag Grainger is lost until the intriguing and spirited Freddie Metcalfe unexpectedly forces her to reevaluate her life. (978-1-62639-202-1)

The Acquittal by Anne Laughlin. Chicago private investigator Josie Harper searches for the real killer of a woman whose lover has been acquitted of the crime. (978-1-62639-203-8)

An American Queer: The Amazon Trail by Lee Lynch. Lee Lynch's heartening and heart-rending history of gay life from the turbulence of the late 1900s to the triumphs of the early 2000s are recorded in this selection of her columns. (978-1-62639-204-5)

Stick McLaughlin: The Prohibition Years by CF Frizzell. Corruption in 1918 cost Stick her lover, her freedom, and her identity, but a very special flapper and the family bond of her own gang could help win them back—even if it means outwitting the Boston Mob. (978-1-62639-205-2)

Edge of Awareness by C.A. Popovich. When Maria, a woman in the middle of her third divorce, meets Dana, an out lesbian, awareness of her feelings brings up reservations about the teachings of her church. (978-1-62639-188-8)

Taken by Storm by Kim Baldwin. Lives depend on two women when a train derails high in the remote Alps, but an unforgiving mountain, avalanches, crevasses, and other perils stand between them and safety. (978-1-62639-189-5)

The Common Thread by Jaime Maddox. Dr. Nicole Coussart's life is falling apart, but fortunately, DEA Attorney Rae Rhodes is there to pick up the pieces and help Nic put them back together. (978-1-62639-190-1)

Jolt by Kris Bryant. Mystery writer Bethany Lange wasn't prepared for the twisting emotions that left her breathless the moment she laid eyes on folk singer sensation Ali Hart. (978-1-62639-191-8)

Searching For Forever by Emily Smith. Dr. Natalie Jenner's life has always been about saving others, until young paramedic Charlie Thompson comes along and shows her maybe she's the one who needs saving. (978-1-62639-186-4)

A Queer Sort of Justice: Prison Tales Across Time by Rebecca S. Buck. When liberty is only a memory, and all seems lost, what freedoms and hopes can be found within us? (978-1-62639-195-6E)

Blue Water Dreams by Dena Hankins. Lania Marchiol keeps her wary sailor's gaze trained on the horizon until Oly Rassmussen, a wickedly handsome trans man, sends her trusty compass spinning off course. (978-1-62639-192-5)

Rest Home Runaways by Clifford Henderson. Baby boomer Morgan Ronzio's troubled marriage is the least of her worries when she gets the call that her addled, eighty-six-year-old, half-blind dad has escaped the rest home. (978-1-62639-169-7)

Charm City by Mason Dixon. Raq Overstreet's loyalty to her drug kingpin boss is put to the test when she begins to fall for Bathsheba Morris, the undercover cop assigned to bring him down. (978-1-62639-198-7)

Let the Lover Be by Sheree Greer. Kiana Lewis, a functional alcoholic on the verge of destruction, finally faces the demons of her past while finding love and earning redemption in New Orleans. (978-1-62639-077-5)

Blindsided by Karis Walsh. Blindsided by love, guide dog trainer Lenae McIntyre and media personality Cara Bradley learn to trust what they see with their hearts. (978-1-62639-078-2)

About Face by VK Powell. Forensic artist Macy Sheridan and Detective Leigh Monroe work on a case that has troubled them both for years, but they're hampered by the past and their unlikely yet undeniable attraction. (978-1-62639-079-9)

Blackstone by Shea Godfrey. For Darry and Jessa, their chance at a life of freedom is stolen by the arrival of war and an ancient prophecy that just might destroy their love. (978-1-62639-080-5)

Out of This World by Maggie Morton. Iris decided to cross an ocean to get over her ex. But instead, she ends up traveling much farther, all the way to another world. Once there, only a mysterious, sexy, and magical woman can help her return home. (978-1-62639-083-6)

Kiss The Girl by Melissa Brayden. Sleeping with the enemy has never been so complicated. Brooklyn Campbell and Jessica Lennox face off in love and advertising in fast-paced New York City. (978-1-62639-071-3)

Taking Fire: A First Responders Novel by Radclyffe. Hunted by extremists and under siege by nature's most virulent weapons, Navy medic Max de Milles and Red Cross worker Rachel Winslow join forces to survive and discover something far more lasting. (978-1-62639-072-0)

First Tango in Paris by Shelley Thrasher. When French law student Eva Laroche meets American call girl Brigitte Green in 1970s Paris, they have no idea how their pasts and futures will intersect. (978-1-62639-073-7)

The War Within by Yolanda Wallace. Army nurse Meredith Moser went to Vietnam in 1967 looking to help those in need; she didn't expect to meet the love of her life along the way. (978-1-62639-074-4)

Escapades by MJ Williamz. Two women, afraid to love again, must overcome their fears to find the happiness that awaits them. (978-1-62639-182-6)

Desire at Dawn by Fiona Zedde. For Kylie, love had always come armed with sharp teeth and claws. But with the human, Olivia, she bares her vampire heart for the very first time, sharing passion, lust, and a tenderness she'd never dared dream of before. (978-1-62639-064-5)

Visions by Larkin Rose. Sometimes the mysteries of love reveal themselves when you least expect it. Other times they hide behind a black satin mask. Can Paige unveil her masked stranger this time? (978-1-62639-065-2)

All In by Nell Stark. Internet poker champion Annie Navarro loses everything when the Feds shut down online gambling, and she turns to experienced casino host Vesper Blake for advice—but can Nova convince Vesper to take a gamble on romance? (978-1-62639-066-9)

Vermilion Justice by Sheri Lewis Wohl. What's a vampire to do when Dracula is no longer just a character in a novel? (978-1-62639-067-6)

Switchblade by Carsen Taite. Lines were meant to be crossed. Third in the Luca Bennett Bounty Hunter Series. (978-1-62639-058-4)

Nightingale by Andrea Bramhall. Culture, faith, and duty conspire to tear two young lovers apart, yet fate seems to have different plans for them both. (978-1-62639-059-1)

No Boundaries by Donna K. Ford. A chance meeting and a nightmare from the past threaten more than Andi Massey's solitude as she and Gwen Palmer struggle to understand the complexity of love without boundaries. (978-1-62639-060-7)